OPERATION
LILA

OPERATION

ARBOR HOUSE NEW YORK

LILA

BY MARVIN H. ALBERT

Library of Congress Catalogue Card Number: 82-72067

ISBN: 0-87795-411-9

Manufactured in the United States of America

10   9   8   7   6   5   4   3   2   1

This book is printed on acid free paper. The paper in this book meets the guidelines for permanence and durability of the Committee on Production Guidelines for Book Longevity of the Council on Library Resources.

For Irmgard Klar

AUTHOR'S NOTE

In November 1942 Hitler violated his armistice agreement with France and moved to seize Toulon, the greatest naval base on the Mediterranean. The lure was the French fleet inside Toulon's harbor: eighty ships of war ranging from submarines to cruisers and battleships, which in German hands could determine the course of World War II.

What happened when Hitler's directive was carried out surprised both sides, and remains a subject of historical speculation and controversy.

The fate of the French fleet, the situation at Fort Revère, the exploit of the Toulon submarines—these are a matter of record, as are the ties joining them to the British offensive at El Alamein and America's Operation Torch.

All these events are history; the conversations attributed to the historical characters in this book are for the most part taken from what they actually said, which was often more incredible than any dialogue the author could have invented.

The story of British agent Jonas Ruyter and the woman named Nicole Courtel is conjecture: a fictional thread woven into the tapestry of these true events, as one possible explanation of the strange fate of "Operation Lila."

Portions of the secret directive which later became the basis for the operation which was code named "Lila":

Führer Headquarters
10 December 1940
12 copies

DIRECTIVE NO. 19
"Undertaking Attila"

In case those parts of the French Colonial Empire (North Africa) should show signs of revolt, preparations will be made for the rapid occupation of the still unoccupied territory of continental France. At the same time it will be necessary to lay hands on the French home fleet...

For military as well as political reasons, preparations for this operation will be camouflaged to avoid alarming the French.

Commanders-in-chief Navy and Air Force will consider, in conjunction with the occupying forces of the Army, how the French fleet can best be captured.

Preparations must be kept the closest secret.

signed: Adolf Hitler

ONE OCTOBER 8, 1942

IT WAS A bad night for it.

There was a low sea mist rolling in. If it got much thicker he wasn't going to be able to make visual contact with them. To make matters worse he was late for the rendezvous; and he still hadn't reached the place where they'd be looking for him. It wasn't much farther, but that final bit was going to take some doing.

Jonas Ruyter stood against a sea cliff with the weight of occupied France against his back and his boots ankle-deep in surf. This was one of the most rugged parts of Brittany's reach into the Atlantic Ocean: a stretch of the Quiberon peninsula named the Savage Coast. The surf hissed in and out of caves, undercutting the cliffs on either side of him, where centuries of pounding waves had gouged the solid rock. The Atlantic wasn't being that turbulent this night, thank God. But the night mist was solidifying while he hesitated.

Jonas squinted at the three-pointed semicircle of jagged rocks jutting out of the water two hundred yards from the shore. That was where they'd be looking for him, if they were still waiting, on the other side of those rocks.

He had expected to steal a small boat from the village of Carnac on the sheltered side of the peninsula. But German security around the bay had stiffened considerably since Jonas had last been there. Not only had he been unable to get near a boat undetected: getting out of Carnac had required him to hide from one enemy patrol for half an hour and then to dodge another just outside the village.

On foot, this was as close as he could get to his rendezvous point. Lacking a boat, there was only one way to cover the last stretch.

He didn't relish the prospect. He was a strong swimmer, and at this time of year the ocean was at least warmer than in mid-winter. But the night wind was cold and he'd be dripping when he climbed out onto those rocks, with no place to shelter and no way to get dry. Unless they picked him up immediately he'd soon become too numbed to swim back.

The coded orders he had received on his Morse radio—with Michael Sandoe's unmistakable touch on the telegrapher's key—had said "URGENT REPEAT URGENT." Michael would never use that loosely. He knew better than most that two of the three most dangerous aspects of any mission inside enemy territory were getting in without being spotted and getting out without being caught. The third of course being to remain inside for any length of time without being detected or betrayed—and winding up in a Gestapo or Milice cell getting one's flesh torn apart.

Jonas Ruyter had lasted inside Nazi-controlled northern France for a year and a half. Now they wanted him out. Urgent. Michael's message had been specific; he was to come out the hardest way. This way.

Safer and surer would have been working his way down to Spain and getting forwarded to England from there. But that could take too much time. This way, he'd reach England the night after receiving the message; or not at all, in which case they could immediately assign someone else to the mission.

Urgent.

Jonas took the signal flashlight from his jacket. It was protected against sea water inside the old standby, a pair of tautly stretched contraceptives. He stuck the flash under his belt, took off his jacket and tossed it aside. Then he pulled off his boots and threw them after the jacket. He wouldn't be coming back for them. He waded into the surf and began to swim.

He was in excellent shape for a man his age, the result of years of archeological digs under harsh conditions and the rigorous training by the SOE, Special Operations Executive. There was a strong tidal current running, and it kept pulling him off course. But he compensated by raising his head and shifting directions.

The swimming kept him warm enough. But the instant he climbed onto the semicircle of rocks the wind hit him and he began to shiver. With his clothing plastered to his skin the shivering grew as he clambered over the sharp-edged rock to the seaward side. Wiping burning salt from his eyes, Jonas peered into the misty darkness. The ocean waves were black under the mist. Nothing was moving through them.

His chilled fingers trembled when he got out the flashlight. Aiming it out to sea, he flashed the signal: four short, one long. Then he waited, watching.

There was no answering signal.

Jonas angled the flashlight off to the right and repeated his signal, then swung it to his left and repeated it again. Still no response.

Three possibilities. They could have come on time, given up on him, and gone back. Or they had been delayed by the German Raumbootes which patrolled the waters around this area of the French coastline. Or, his last hope, they were out there now, but unable to spot his signal through the mist.

Jonas backed into a niche in the rocks, which gave him some protection from the wind but none against the gnawing cold. He lowered himself to a sitting position, braced the flash on his raised knees, and signaled with it again.

If a Raumboote was out there and spotted his light, it would be the end of him. But there was nothing he could do to control that, so he put it out of his mind. Every five minutes for the next hour he repeated his signal.

By then every part of him was shaking uncontrollably, and he had to clench his teeth to keep them from chattering. His hands were so numbed that it required a determined effort of will to operate the flashlight. He kept drifting into sleep. He fought to hold his eyes open.

At his university Jonas had written a brilliant paper on primitive medical practices that anticipated the later findings of psychologists. Even before recorded history tribal shamans had begun noting the power of altered emotions to curb or cure a variety of physical ills, such as the ability of a small jolt of fear to cure hiccups. Strong anger could accomplish a great deal more.

Deliberately, he thought about Estelle, Karen and Bill: something he rarely allowed himself.

When, early in the war, the Luftwaffe had begun its devastating bombing raids on the heart of London, Jonas had moved his wife and children out, to a flat owned by Estelle's parents in Plymouth. But then the waves of bombers, intent on fulfilling Hitler's determination to break the British by terror, had shifted to other civilian targets less defended by the RAF.

On the continent the Luftwaffe, through sustained massive attacks on the port of Rotterdam, had proved its ability to practically obliterate an entire undefended city. Over England the Luftwaffe proved it again: smashing Coventry to rubble...and then Plymouth.

It had taken Jonas a long time to reach Plymouth after the blockbusters and fire bombs had accomplished their job. It had taken the diggers longer to get around to the house where his wife and children had lived. And still longer to extract their corpses.

They had gone down into the cellar when the bombers began to strike and had been trapped there when the building collapsed above them. They hadn't been killed by the blockbusters or the falling walls. They had died of suffocation, when fires started by incendiary bombs had swept the ruins and sucked the air out of their shelter.

Later, in Paris, Jonas had watched Nazi occupation troops cheering their bombers as they flew toward the channel. The troopers had sung a stirring war song popular in Germany at that period: "Bombs...! Oh Bombs...! Oh Bombs on England!"

Huddled in the rocks off the French coast, wracked by spasms of chill and flushed with fever, Jonas thought of his dead and fought the numbing cold with his hatred.

He had been out there almost four hours, and the mist had turned into solid fog, when he detected movement. The movement took shape and became a collapsible canoe sliding out of the fog toward him.

It was propelled by two hefty members of the Royal Navy's special COPP service, each using a double-bladed paddle. They vaulted out at the last instant, one standing waist deep in the surging waters, holding the canoe away from jagged edges of rock. The other searched for a moment before locating Jonas. He climbed to him swiftly.

"Sorry we're late, chum. Come *on*...let's go!"

Jonas forced the word through clenched teeth: "Can't..."

The other came close enough to register the condition of the hunched-down figure braced between the rocks. "Christ...Well, you don't look too heavy." He bent and got a firm grip on Jonas, and lifted him to his feet.

Jonas tried not to hang all his weight on the other man. "Thank God you saw my signal," he croaked.

"In this fog? Didn't see a thing. Just came in anyway, taking a chance you'd be here."

Jonas tried to grin but couldn't manage. "You must want me pretty badly."

"*Somebody* does. Me—I can think of some *women* I might want this much, but they'd have to be waiting in cozier spots than this one."

Jonas was half dragged down to the canoe. Fifteen minutes later, in the fog bank beyond the rocks where he had made his long vigil, Jonas was hauled from the canoe onto the casing of a waiting submarine. By the time it dived and turned back to England, he was wrapped in wool blankets in the commander's bunk gulping down hot tea laced with rum.

TWO OCTOBER 9—MORNING

THEY HAD KNOWN each other a long time, since well before the war. Michael Sandoe was an upperclassman at Cambridge when Jonas Ruyter arrived from Toronto on a scholarship.

If it had not been for the scholarship, Jonas would probably have gone to the University of Pennsylvania or some other American college strong on archeology. Though as a Canadian he was a subject of the British Empire, Jonas in fact hadn't a drop of pure English blood—if such a thing existed. His father's family had lived in England for several generations but was of Dutch origin. Jonas's mother, whom his father had met when the tool-design firm for which he'd worked sent him as its resident to Toronto, was French-Canadian, with the usual chip on her shoulder about British rule. She had made certain he grew up knowing French as well as English.

At Cambridge Michael Sandoe and Jonas Ruyter had only a nodding acquaintance. It was not until later, when they met again by chance, that they became close friends.

A year after graduation, Jonas joined an Anglo-French archeological team engaged in clearing the site of a Roman outpost discovered outside the old village of Chaumont-en-Vexin, some fifty miles from Paris. There was not much left from the Roman time except some foundation walls covered by earth and wild underbrush. Jonas became convinced that the rest had gone into building the church crowning the hill which rose out of the village center. After finding several blocks around the church exterior which bore mason marks that could have been ancient Roman, he returned the next day to explore the interior.

There was nobody else inside the church that day except an organist in the loft. He was an unusually good organist, and Jonas listened with pleasure as he examined the interior walls with a flashlight. Finally he climbed a narrow stone stairway to investigate the tower.

The stairway broke off at the organ loft, continuing into the tower on the other side of it. The young man at the organ stopped playing when Jonas appeared. Jonas started to compliment his artistry, but halted in midsentence when he realized it was Michael Sandoe. They stared at each other, and then Michael laughed.

"Caught, by God! Discovered indulging my secret vice."

Michael explained over dinner at the inn where he was staying in Chaumont-en-Vexin: "Mother played piano, rather well. In my callow youth I conceived a noble ambition to become a concert pianist. Unfortunately, by the time I'd met you at Cambridge, I'd discovered one small stumbling block. Lack of genius. It seems that a small talent is not quite enough. So...and alas."

He had joined his father's insurance firm and converted his artistic longing into a private hobby: organs. He'd been in Paris just over a year when they met again, establishing a French branch for the firm. He spent weekends exploring surrounding towns and trying out the older organs. The one in Chaumont-en-Vexin was over a hundred years old. Superbly fashioned, but he'd found it in deplorable condition. His offer to try to restore and tune it had been gratefully accepted, and this was the fifth weekend he'd been at it.

They were drawn to each other as they would never have been if their chance meeting had occurred at some party in London. Soon Jonas became a regular guest at the Sandoe country home in Surrey. It was Michael who introduced him to Estelle. He became best man at their wedding, and was named godfather to Karen, their firstborn.

Michael himself never married. He was one of those men with an exceptional talent for male loyalties, but for whom women remain forever a foreign country.

Estelle, expecting her second child, had remained in England when Jonas had gone off to France again. This time he'd been in charge of his own dig, in the hills north of Toulon, excavating remnants of a Celtic settlement which the Roman legions had demolished in the century before the birth of Christ. He had returned to England to be with Estelle for the birth of their son and had made shorter home visits later, but Jonas spent most of a year at his excavation.

During that year Michael had gone to the south of France to spend a week with Jonas. He had become one of the few who knew about Jonas's difficult personal situation. Certainly Estelle never had an inkling. It involved one of the young archeology students assisting Jonas in his work, a spectacularly good-looking girl from Toulon.

Only Michael ever realized how cruelly torn his friend had become, between love for his family and a passion from which he seemed utterly unable to extricate himself. No one else was aware of the trips Jonas made to see the girl after the dig had been completed. The war had put an end to that. But it hadn't ended the problem, not entirely. There had been deep guilt in his grief when Estelle and the children perished.

Michael wondered now, as he watched the murky dawn spread over London, if the problem continued to disturb his friend. If so, it was still there, in the same place.

Toulon.

Shortly after seven Michael's telephone rang. The caller was a Commander O'Donnell from the office of VACO—Vice-Admiral for Channel Operations—responsible for bringing Jonas back across. "Your man is in," the commander reported. "But not in the best of condition. Suffering from exposure, running a bad fever. We've had to transfer him to hospital."

He gave the address of the hospital, just outside Portsmouth.

Michael put down the phone and took a deep breath. After several moments he picked up the phone and made two calls. The first was to the War Cabinet's operations center, making an appointment with Colonel Shepherd for that afternoon. The second was to commandeer a car to take him to Portsmouth and back. Then he made himself a breakfast and washed, applying cold water to his swollen and burning eyes. He hadn't slept at all the night before.

At eight-thirty the car arrived. Michael climbed in and told the pretty Wren chauffeur his destination. She drove expertly, making swift work of getting the car through South London and on the road to Portsmouth.

It never ceased to irritate him, that he couldn't drive a car any longer.

He had joined the RAF early in the war, and had been shot down in a dogfight with a Folke-Wulfe over Dunkirk. He had survived and they managed to ferry him back across the channel in an old tugboat crammed with other evacuees. Besides losing much of his right arm his face had been badly burned; and his vision frequently blurred.

Later he found an outfit that could use him, even in his maimed condition: the Special Operations Executive, which gathered intelligence and generated sabotage inside enemy-held countries. Known as the Old Firm at its original headquarters near Sherlock Holmes's flat on Baker Street, the SOE's offices were now scattered in various parts of city and country. The Dorset Square offices to which Michael was assigned had previously belonged to the Bertram Mills Circus, so operations there came to be called the circus and its agents were often referred to as clowns.

Michael, knowing France well, was assigned to form his own group of "clowns" to be sent there, and to handle communications with them once they were in place. At the Wireless Training School at Thames Park he'd learned to operate a Morse key with his left hand; and his agents always recognized his distinctive sending technique. In turn Michael learned to recognize theirs, so well that no enemy telegrapher could fool him.

One of his group was Jonas, who had come to him after Estelle and the children had been killed.

Jonas knew France even better than Michael did. On his first prewar trip his Canadian brand of French had been embarrassing. But he had learned to correct that, to the point where no one in France would take him for a foreigner. Also, as an archeologist, Jonas had acquired friends among academics connected with the Musée de l'Homme in Paris, which became one of the earliest secret centers of resistance after the fall of France.

The SOE courses they'd put Jonas through had been a good deal more severe than anything in Michael's own training period. He had excelled in the physical-instruction classes devoted to unarmed killing. "Highly Motivated" was noted on his reports. His instructors, though younger and tougher, could seldom best him by completion of the course.

And yet—something always remained of the old Jonas: there was a warmth in him that not even grief and fury could extinguish. Women felt it more immediately than men—though it was certainly part of what had drawn Michael to him.

Estelle had once described it as kindness born of strength. Michael remembered a nurse in a ward where Jonas had recuperated from internal injuries sustained from an explosion during a sabotage course. She'd complained with an edge of anger that surely the government could find something more suitable for a man of Jonas's age to do for the war effort. And the Norwegian girl who'd gone through SOE training with Jonas before being parachuted back into her own occupied country: she had said he was the sort of man she hoped she'd be lucky enough to marry if she survived the war. She hadn't, though: she died only weeks later under Nazi interrogation.

By then Jonas had been dropped into France with his radio and had made his way to Paris. For some months he'd been SOE's radio contact with the Musée de l'Homme resistance group—until it had been destroyed by the German secret police. Jonas had managed to break out of the Gestapo-organized dragnet, killing two SS men in the process. He had reached Marie-Madeleine Fourçade, who led another Paris-based resistance group which was to prove more durable. Jonas was working for her when Michael's "urgent" signal had brought him out...

The Wren driver swung the car to a stop at the small military hospital outside Portsmouth. Michael told her to wait for him and went inside. After a brief talk with one of the doctors, he made his way to Jonas's room.

He found him propped up in bed looking more fit than one would have expected from the doctor's report. Jonas had the gift of unusual physical vitality. It was still there, in spite of a flushed face and drug-dulled eyes.

"They tell me your temperature reached spectacular heights."

Jonas nodded. "Edge of pneumonia. But it's coming down now." His voice was hoarse. "I'll be fine with a few days' rest."

"The medical staff here suggests something more like two weeks."

Jonas smiled. "They think I'm a middle-aged man with slowed recuperative powers. We both know better. *You* aren't looking too well, Michael."

Michael lowered himself into the chair next to Jonas's bed. "Just a bit tired. They're overworking us these days."

But it wasn't only his weariness which troubled Jonas. More than a year had gone by since he'd last seen him. He hadn't forgotten the missing arm; but his memory of that burned face had dimmed, and now it struck him forcefully again. A good plastic surgeon had done what he could to re-create the face, but the skin grafts had an unnatural shine and his dark glasses made the result a grotesque mask.

Jonas asked lightly, "How are you coming along with that Ravel piece?"

Michael gave a rueful laugh. "Not much time for that, these days." After the loss of his arm he had joked that he'd now have to confine his hobby to the Piano Concerto for Left Hand, which Ravel had composed for a friend who had lost his right one. "Besides, I've come to the conclusion that adapting one single piece for the organ doesn't quite add up to a full-time hobby. I'll have to find another, after the war. What do you think of stamp collecting?"

"We'll find something more exciting than that for you," Jonas said. And then, in the same light tone: "What is the urgent job you dragged me out of Paris for?"

Michael looked uncomfortable. "To be honest with you, I don't actually know much about it. I expect I will before the day is finished. I've a meeting scheduled in London with Shepherd and an American named Riley, from their OSS."

"What is that?"

"Office of Strategic Services. It's a new outfit the Americans are putting together, roughly along the lines of the SOE, I gather. I'm assuming the meeting will be to brief me on your mission. But as of this moment all I know is that it *is* urgent..." Michael paused, watching Jonas. "And...that it would be in Toulon."

There was a short silence. Michael said: "I have to be in a position to tell them whether you would be willing to go there."

After a moment, Jonas told him quietly: "Yes. Of course I'll go."

THREE

THE WREN DRIVER got Michael Sandoe back to London with half an hour to spare before his scheduled appointment at the War Cabinet's operations center. As she maneuvered the car through the city he regarded the bombed-out blocks on either side. He saw this every day. But he never grew accustomed to it. There were too many places he'd known all his life which were no longer there.

And too many people he had cared about who were no longer alive.

It had taken a long time to achieve the ability to retaliate: almost two years. Most of the RAF had been confined to purely defensive duties during that time. America's entry into the war eight months back and the arrival of growing numbers of flying fortresses to supplement the British Lancasters were beginning to change that.

Less than three months ago they had begun striking back in force against selected German cities: a thousand-plane smash at Cologne; another against Essen.

From Michael Sandoe's agents inside enemy territory reactions to those raids were still trickling in.

Apparently, Reichsmarshal Goering had been so sure of his powerful Luftwaffe that he announced that if a single bomb ever fell on Germany people would have his permission to call

25

him "Meyer." Some Germans were now repeating a bitter joke: "Where's Meyer?"

But most Germans were not in a joking mood. Their first reaction had been one of shock; the fatherland was not invulnerable. The second reaction became indignation. The Germans called the smashing of Cologne and Essen atrocities against civilization.

It was incredible to Michael Sandoe that they failed to grasp that it was a consequence of what they had done to cities they intended to conquer. But this cause-and-effect relationship seemed to escape the Germans. They considered the Allied raids the work of barbarians with no feeling for priceless architecture and human life. And nothing had changed their certainty that they were winning the war; nor their faith in their Führer's omnipotent genius.

In spite of those first air strikes against Nazi targets, Michael had to concede that they were still justified in their faith. Hitler's Germany was at this point master of almost the entire continent of Europe. To the east, where Hitler had broken his pact with Stalin and attacked Russia, his armies were driving deep into Soviet territory with no sign that anything would stop them. In North Africa the Nazi forces had chased the British army clear across Libya and backed it up inside Egypt, where Rommel was predicting he would soon score another grand victory and make his headquarters in Cairo.

The situation there, Michael had been informed, was so serious that Churchill in desperation had sent a new general to take over the last-gasp defense line at El Alamein. But the new general was killed when his plane was shot down by German fighters before reaching Egypt. Churchill sent a replacement: a little-known eccentric named Montgomery. But whether any new general was going to be able to prevent a final military disaster in North Africa, and a Nazi takeover of the entire Middle East, no one could yet hazard a prediction.

As for what part Jonas was now expected to play in the scenario, Michael expected the next hour or so would supply some kind of answer.

His car turned into Great George Street and came to a halt. Michael asked the Wren to be back for him within two hours, with enough gasoline in the car to get him back to Portsmouth that evening.

He knocked at an inconspicuous back door, showed his pass to a pair of Royal Marine sentries armed with Tommy guns, and descended a flight of solid oak stairs set in reinforced concrete. He identified himself again to a sergeant posted on a lower landing and went down steel steps that rang under his heels. At the bottom he entered an underground maze of bombproof corridors and chambers which had been constructed more than a hundred feet beneath Whitehall, lower than the bed of the Thames.

To the hundreds of clerical aides attached to the Imperial General Staff, the War Cabinet, and the Joint Planning Staffs, this maze was known with some affection as "The Hole."

Michael went through the waiting room and the main corridor, lit by shaded hanging lamps and throbbing with the sound of air pumps and fans operating in myriad ventilation conduits. The weather board on the wall outside the War Cabinet room read "Cloudy"—keeping those who worked, ate and often slept in The Hole in touch with the outside world. When the sign "Windy" was put up it meant that London was under an air raid; down here one couldn't hear or feel the bombs unless there was a direct hit above.

Going through a series of small corridors, Michael passed the map room, the prime minister's emergency office and bedroom, the telephone switchboard center and one of the kitchens. He turned into a labyrinthine complex assigned to the Joint Intelligence Staff.

Colonel Shepherd's office was empty, with a scribbled note pinned to the open door saying he'd be back in a few minutes. The room was small and claustrophobic. Armored electric cables and hot water and heating pipes crossed it under the ceiling. Michael had to lower his head to enter and reach one of the two mismatched chairs facing Shepherd's desk.

Above a folding camp bed behind the desk hung a large wall

map of France. Michael looked at the new marker pin stuck on this map.

Green tape marked the demarcation line that divided France into two zones according to the armistice Marshal Pétain had signed when he surrendered his country to Hitler. There was red shading for the Occupied Zone in the north and west, ruled by the German army which had taken over Paris as its headquarters. Blue shaded the Unoccupied Zone in the southeast, ruled by the aged Pétain from his makeshift capital in the health resort of Vichy, under the supervision of a German Armistice Commission.

The marker pin had been placed at the bottom of the Unoccupied Zone along the Mediterranean: Toulon.

Colonel Shepherd came in with a plump, balding man Michael hadn't met till now: Paul Riley, the man from the research and analysis branch of the OSS. Since the fledgling OSS was recruiting the same sort of men used by the SOE—anyone from journalists to college professors who had special knowledge of areas and languages of interest to the Allies—it was not surprising that there was nothing military about Riley's dress or bearing.

The American suppressed an involuntary reaction to Michael's face as they were introduced, took the chair next to him, and thereafter politely avoided looking at him directly. Michael was used to that. People didn't want to stare.

Colonel Shepherd rested a hip on the edge of his desk, looking down at them. For Shepherd, a frail man just turned seventy, the army rank was purely honorary: something to give him credibility among the military officers with whom he dealt. Long ago he had been a member of the Foreign Office. Before and during the First World War he had carried out undercover intelligence work in Turkey and the Middle East. Retired between the wars, he had attempted to relieve his boredom with gardening and journalism. He had been delighted when the government, finding itself on the brink of another war in 1938, had called him back into service. His duties had recently been increased to include liaison between SOE and OSS.

"Well," he asked Michael, "how is Ruyter? Ill enough to create a problem for us?"

"I don't think so, sir. Given about five days rest he should be all right."

Riley said, "I sure hope so. We need an experienced man for this one. He just better turn out to be as good as I've been told."

"He's experienced," Michael told him blandly. "If he weren't good at it he wouldn't have lasted long enough to get the experience."

The American reddened, then grinned. "Point. Received and understood."

Michael looked to Shepherd. "It would help to finally know the nature of the mission."

Shepherd turned to gesture at the map of France. "Part of the terms of the armistice signed between Pétain and Hitler was an agreement that the French fleet should be interned for the duration and take no further part in the war. Pétain guaranteed that none of his ships would join us; and his admirals have sworn an oath to uphold that guarantee. Hitler in turn swore to respect the neutrality of their fleet and make no effort to touch it. However, none of us, I'm sure, have any illusions about the worth of Adolf Hitler's word of honor."

Michael nodded. "I know the prime minister's been worried about the Nazis getting their hands on the French warships ever since France fell."

"President Roosevelt's had the same worry," Riley put in. "I was among the State Department's representatives in Vichy until we got into the war. We conveyed the president's worry to Marshal Pétain. The old man sent his personal promise that his fleet will never go to the Germans. But frankly, I'm one of those who doubt Pétain has either the ability or the will to oppose anything Hitler really wants to do. The marshal may have been the great French hero of the First World War, but that was long ago. Age has turned him into a gutless wonder with some crazy notions. He's gotten too damn old to..."

The American stopped himself, looking quickly at Shepherd. "No offense, Colonel. I know a lot of older people who..."

"So do I," Shepherd cut in drily, "being one of them myself. I hope I can distinguish between an old man who sometimes has a problem with his memory and one afflicted with senility. I trust I am still one of the former—and I fear Marshal Pétain is becoming one of the latter."

"He's not senile," Riley disagreed, "just weak. His vice-premier, Laval, is getting to be the real power in Vichy. He's persuaded Pétain that if the war becomes a standoff, France can act as neutral intermediary between Germany and America. Help negotiate the peace settlement and come out with its own prestige restored."

Michael looked at the OSS man with new respect.

Shepherd shrugged. "If Laval and Pétain believe in that, they're both senile." He shifted his attention back to Michael. "At any rate, we now have reason to believe that Hitler will soon violate his promise and attempt to seize the French fleet presently interned in Toulon." Shepherd nodded at Riley, who took it from there.

The State Department, Riley explained, still had a few contacts inside Nazi Germany. The Gestapo had done an efficient job of wiping out internal opposition. Those left included some former members of Germany's old labor movement. It also included a network of German Catholics whose members openly worked for the Nazis but secretly prayed for their defeat. This network was very small; but it reached all the way up into the OKW—Hitler's Armed Forces High Command.

"Their man there is an officer of the OKW's economic and armaments branch. Some time ago he managed to photograph a directive Hitler's staff tabbed with the code name Operation Attila. Another member of the Catholic network, a German metals importer, slipped the photostat to our embassy in Switzerland during a business trip."

Riley got out an envelope and unfolded a photostat. He handed it to Michael.

Michael read the photostat carefully. He studied Hitler's signature, then looked again at the date at the top: December 10, 1940.

"Isn't this a bit too old to still be valid?"

"That's what Vichy thinks," Riley told him. "We got copies of this to some members of the government there. Most say it's a forgery. A few admit it might be the genuine article, but figure it as an old plan Hitler has since dropped completely. We don't agree."

Shepherd gestured at the photostat. "Note the condition which would trigger this Attila plan: trouble in French North Africa. Well, we are about to give the Nazis that trouble. To begin with, America is stepping up its arms supply, tanks and planes to our Eighth Army in Egypt. When General Montgomery has enough he will launch a strong counterattack from El Alamein, to drive Rommel's forces back through Libya.

"Once that is under way, Rommel is also going to be hit from behind—and rather hard. You know the Americans have sent General Eisenhower here to organize a top-secret Allied operation. It now has a code name: Torch. Convoys are being prepared for it, both in Scotland and the United States. Their job will be to put American and British troops ashore at several points along the French North African coast—in Morocco and Algeria."

Riley leaned forward to rap his knuckles against the wood of Shepherd's desk, for luck. "There are fourteen French colonial divisions in those areas, so far taking orders from Vichy. We're hoping they'll cooperate and join us—and help us drive on into Tunisia. If that works out, Rommel will get caught in a vise, between Montgomery's push from the east and Eisenhower's from the west."

Shepherd told Michael sharply: "You understand, what you are learning here is *extremely* hush-hush."

"I understand," Michael assured him.

He also understood that the Torch landings would cause Hitler to instantly reactivate his Attila plan. Whatever new code name his staff decided to bestow on the move, the Nazi forces in the Occupied Zone of France would sweep south across the demarcation line and take over the Unoccupied Zone.

But this, Shepherd made clear, was not their concern at this meeting.

"We are concerned here only with the other aspect. The

certainty that they will seize Toulon. There are now some eighty French warships inside that naval base." Shepherd detailed the most important ones without referring to notes. "These include a battleship...two battle cruisers...three heavy cruisers...two regular cruisers...two light cruisers...an aircraft carrier... eighteen destroyers...fifteen torpedo boats...and eighteen submarines.

"If that fleet is taken," he concluded flatly, "and comes out manned by German crews, we'll have an absolute disaster in the Mediterranean."

Riley said, "I met with Eisenhower out at Telegraph Cottage last evening. Trying my best to explain why there's *no* chance of the French sailing that fleet out to join us, before the Germans grab Toulon."

He didn't have to explain it to Michael or Shepherd. They knew too much about each French admiral.

Most of the admirals considered themselves strictly bound by their oath of loyalty to their government. Which meant Vichy, and came down to Pétain and Laval. On top of which some were outright pro-Nazi—and violently anti-British. Their top officer, Admiral Darlan, now commander of all the Vichy armed forces, was an opportunist who still believed Hitler's side was the winning one.

"Churchill has also tried to explain the situation to General Eisenhower," Shepherd said. "He told him that in spite of detesting Darlan deeply, he would cheerfully crawl a mile on his hands and knees to him if that would persuade Darlan to bring the French fleet to us. But..."

Riley looked faintly disgusted. "Exactly. *But.*"

"So," Shepherd resumed, his attention on Michael, "what are the alternatives? The best of course would be if the Toulon fleet should come to join us. The worst would be for it to fall into German hands. We cannot expect the first and cannot allow the second."

He stood up, walked around his desk and settled into his own chair. "According to Jonas Ruyter's dossier, he knows Toulon well and has personal contacts among people there."

Michael nodded.

"Our German sources," Riley informed him, "are going to be trying to get further proof of the Nazi plan to grab Toulon's fleet, as they develop. Somebody has to find a way to get that proof into the hands of Admiral Marquis, the maritime prefect of Toulon, and the commander of its high seas fleet, Admiral de Laborde. So that when Hitler does make his move, they'll be prepared to prevent it.

"*Prepared*—that's the important word. No matter what proofs we give them, Marquis and de Laborde are too loyal to Petáin to sail the fleet out of Toulon while there's still time. Once Hitler breaks his treaty with Vichy by grabbing Toulon, it will be too late for it. There'll be only one thing the admirals can do at that point, to avoid the disgrace of letting the Germans have their fleet: scuttle it. Sink every French warship, right there in the harbor. But there's no way that can be done at the last moment—unless they've already made the necessary preparations to carry it out."

Shepherd put both hands flat on his desk. "*That* is the ultimate objective of Jonas Ruyter's mission. To establish contacts inside the Toulon naval base and to deliver final proof of Nazi intentions to Admirals Marquis and Laborde, and convince them of its authenticity. In the little time that will be left for the French navy to save itself from complete dishonor."

Michael asked, uneasily: "Has a date been set for the Allied landings in French North Africa?"

"Montgomery estimates he'll be ready for his counterattack against Rommel by the end of this month," Shepherd told him. "Eisenhower has scheduled Operation Torch for the eighth of November."

The grafted skin on either side of Michael's reconstructed nose became taut. He raised a hand slightly, looked at it, lowered it. "That's in less than a month," he said quietly. "Jonas needs at least a week before he's fit to be sent on this mission. We'll need time to get him into southern France undetected. More time for him to reach Toulon. Still more to make the contacts you want...That is shaving it a bit close, in my opinion."

"Much too close," Shepherd agreed. "That can't be helped."

"Look," Riley said, "we put two other men into Toulon, almost a month ago. Same mission. A French seaman with connections in the Resistance. And an SOE agent who knew members of an escape network your people set up in the area." The American leaned back in his chair and grimaced at the wall map. "They're both dead. Caught by the Vichy police. With the help of Gestapo agents working the Unoccupied Zone. We only learned about it three days ago."

"I see," Michael said, liking it even less than before. "So now you need somebody else to take their place, without any time at all to spare."

Riley spread both hands in a gesture of helpless agreement. "That's the situation."

"Both of the previous agents sent to Toulon," Shepherd told Michael, "were tortured before being executed. Fortunately, neither knew any of the secret matters we've disclosed to you here. If they had known, the Nazis would know it too, by now. All of it—our German sources, Montgomery's planned counteroffensive, Operation Torch. For the same obvious reason, you must not tell Jonas Ruyter any of these things."

"What *can* I tell him?"

"That he is to reestablish connections with people in Toulon who he feels can be trusted. Through them to attempt making contact with naval officers inside the base. And then to await further orders. Clear?"

"Quite clear. You want him to risk a messy death without being told what he's risking it for."

"I'm afraid so. If he can manage to avoid that unpleasant possibility, he will be contacted in due time. Which will have to be fairly soon, since the time left *is* short. At that point he'll be told what it's all about. And what he has to do about it. And *then*...he'll have to be ready to move very quickly. Because at that point it's bound to come down to a race against the clock."

"Another thing," the OSS man said. "The way the other two men sent into Toulon were caught, we've got to figure the Resistance groups in that area are being infiltrated by police informers and Nazi agents. Your friend better stay away from them. Form his own group—and keep it *small.*"

34

Shepherd opened the center drawer of his desk and drew out a thin folder. "An additional danger factor may be present there. An English fascist who has sold himself to the Gestapo. Unfortunately we have not been able to determine his real identity as yet. His trick is to pose as an RAF pilot shot down over France and look for people to help him evade capture. This traitor did considerable damage to Resistance networks around Lyons and Dijon, before he became too well known in the north. Now, we've been informed, the Gestapo has probably switched him to the south. Up to the same tricks."

Shepherd pushed the folder across his desk. "Here are descriptions of him and his mode of operation, obtained from survivors of networks he betrayed. Have Jonas Ruyter memorize them—and be extremely wary of anyone who remotely fits the description."

Michael took the folder with him when he left The Hole and stepped out into the clouded twilight of Great George Street.

The Wren was back, waiting beside the car for him. They got in and she drove him south to the hospital where Jonas was waiting.

FOUR OCTOBER 17—MORNING

IT WAS A few minutes before one o'clock in the morning when the Halifax bomber carrying Jonas Ruyter and Michael Sandoe began its sharp descent through dark clouds gathering over the Straits of Gibraltar.

The British fortress looming over this narrow western opening of the Mediterranean had been selected as the station from which Michael would maintain radio contact with Jonas—at least for the three weeks remaining until the execution of Operation Torch. Then, if the first phase of the Allied occupation of French North Africa succeeded, Michael was to be shifted to Algiers, where a new SFHG would be established to direct combined SOE-OSS missions for the Mediterranean area.

The landing at Gibraltar was observed through a powerful Zeiss telescope by Erich Mallebrein, stationed at a villa four miles away on the other side of Algeciras Bay, just inside Spanish territory.

Mallebrein was one of several assistants assigned to Lieutenant Karl Redl, who had been placed in charge of the Villa San Luis observation post by Abwehr, the Germany Army's intelligence service. Between them Redl and his assistants kept a round-the-clock watch on comings and goings at Gibraltar. Several times each day a list of everything they'd seen was encoded for radio transmission to the Abwehr station at Dax, in southwest France. From Dax the information was relayed to Germany—and, in certain circumstances, to other Axis stations around the Mediterranean.

Lieutenant Redl seldom added any speculation to what his staff observed. Such speculation was the job of specialists closer to Admiral Canaris, chief of the Abwehr. Redl and his men stuck to the facts which provided raw material for Canaris's specialists to chew on. Some of these facts were obviously of great significance; others were, taken individually, quite small.

The arrival of the Halifax bomber at Gibraltar, carrying passengers unknown, was one of the smaller facts. Erich Mallebrein automatically made a note of it in a logbook opened on the table beside the telescope.

It also became one final item added to the list of observations being encoded at that moment by Lieutenant Redl, for transmission by his chief radio operator, Sigfried Walendy. A more important item was included in this list: six heavily loaded cargo ships had anchored among the others already gathered in Gibraltar harbor. Still another: night-landing practice had been carried out at the Gibraltar beach by twelve vessels and several hundred Allied troops.

Lieutenant Redl refrained from adding the obvious: the enemy was building up for some sort of new operation. Abwehr headquarters had certainly drawn the same conclusion from previous lists, judging by its demand for more frequent transmissions from Redl's observation post.

Chief radioman Walendy had just completed this latest transmission when an RAF Halifax took off from Gibraltar. It was less than an hour since Jonas and Michael had landed from England. Observing the takeoff through his telescope, Erich Mallebrein had no clue that a man named Jonas Ruyter was the plane's only passenger. Noting only the facts which he could ascertain, Mallebrein jotted down the precise time of takeoff and the course the Halifax was on when it became lost to view in the clouds: northeast, in the general direction of southern France.

Normally, the next transmission by the Villa San Luis station was not scheduled until four hours later. But there was a special standing order covering any plane or ship which left Gibraltar. Mallebrein immediately passed this one on to the radioman. Walendy nodded, turned his set back on, and transmitted to Dax, which in turn relayed the information to several Axis airfields located in the direction taken by the Halifax.

Minutes later nine fast Italian and German fighter planes took off and spread out to hunt for it.

At this stage of the war, with the Axis holding a clear air superiority over the western Mediterranean, an impressive percentage of Allied planes was being shot down every week— their missions aborted, whatever their secret nature.

The ME-109's machine guns roared, shredding Jonas's parachute and splintering the trees immediately around it. Jonas was grateful for the accuracy of the plane's gunnery. The plane had dived for him just as his chute had got snagged in the upper branches of some oak trees. He had punched the harness buckle open and fallen free, hitting the ground awkwardly but up and charging through the underbrush an instant later. He was almost twenty yards away when the machine gun bursts chewed up chute and harness.

Jonas watched the Messerschmitt pull out of its dive, narrowly miss treetops on the next hill, and swiftly gain altitude. He tried to put more distance between himself and the point where he'd hit ground. But he couldn't see in the darkness under the trees and his ankles got snared in ground vines, spilling him face down in the dirt.

When he looked up again he saw the fighter wasn't coming back for another try. Which was sensible of its pilot. If it hadn't gotten him with that first barrage, there was nothing for him to do but pepper the woods at random: an extravagant expenditure of ammunition. There was better quarry in the air.

The Messerschmitt nosed over in a sharp banking turn and sped after the Halifax, which was vanishing into a mass of low clouds. Moments later the fighter, too, was swallowed by the clouds. Jonas listened to the whine of the ME-109 and the drone of the Halifax, waiting for the noise of the machine guns. It didn't come; and soon the sounds of the planes, pursued and pursuer, were lost in the distance.

The heavy cloud cover gave the Halifax at least a chance of making it back to Gibraltar. Jonas wished it luck. The odds were against it. There were just too many more Axis fighters between it and home, and too few Allied fighters to come out and ward them off. That was the reason Allied missions in this theater of war generally were delivered to destination by boat, rather than plane.

But boats took a lot of time. Too much for the kind of pressure on this mission. Jonas still didn't know the details of that pressure. Michael had only been allowed to tell him it existed: a very close deadline about which he would eventually be briefed if he survived the preliminaries.

Jonas stopped worrying about the Halifax's problems and concentrated on his own.

His first immediate problem was to get as far away from here as he could before daylight. The Messerschmitt would have radioed his position. That wasn't as dangerous down here as it would have been up in the Occupied Zone, where you had all the spread-out SS units to worry about. But the Vichy police in this unoccupied one-third of the country could be damned efficient; and too many of them agreed with the Germans that Allied agents were even more deadly enemies of France than Resistance fighters. Also, there was the Milice: a paramilitary organization of French fascists eager to prove its zeal to the Gestapo. At dawn they'd start closing in on the point where Jonas had landed.

The other part of the problem was to get out in the right direction. And finding one's directions in this area was not simple.

Jonas had been dropped northeast of Toulon, somewhere into the heart of the sparsely inhabited Maures Massif. In prehistoric times the Maures had been a mountain range rising above the Mediterranean coast. Time had worn the mountains down to a jumble of high, close-packed hills covered by low forest of sea pines and cork oaks. Lack of valleys made for a scarcity of farms or villages inside the Maures. Tight ravines twisted between hills which leaned into each other, with little to distinguish one hill from its neighbors. Cutting through the entire massif was one paved road and a dirt track; interior paths turned into goat trails.

All of this made the Maures fairly safe for a drop and a good place to hide, but also an easy place to get lost.

Jonas struck a match, which flared bright in the darkness, hurting his eyes as he checked his compass. That lined up north and south for him, and he didn't want to go north. The main railroad line skirted around the Maures up there, providing the fastest way to Toulon. But the nearest main-line station was the first place the enemy would check for an agent who'd been dropped in the area.

Jonas stubbed the match in the dirt. Going south would be slower but safer: a long hike to put his landing point far behind him, then the branch railroad from Bormes to Hyères, changing there to electric tramlines the rest of the way. But the compass couldn't give him the best route to get through the hills and forests; and taking the wrong routes could add days to getting out of the Maures.

The thing to do now was to climb: head for the highest hilltop and sort out precise directions at sunrise by locating landmarks along the coast. Untangling himself from the vines, Jonas got to his feet and unfastened the suitcase strapped to his chest.

It was a well-worn suitcase, purchased in London from one of the French refugees who'd provided his shoes, raincoat and hat, along with the other clothes he wore or carried. The suitcase contained, in addition to legitimate traveler's items, an SOE wireless transceiver inside a smaller leather case. Jonas placed his arms into the side straps and settled it across the back of his shoulders.

After some searching he found a steep upward slope and began his night climb.

At dawn Jonas climbed a wind-gnarled tree on the crest of the hill he had chosen. Hill and tree were still in dark shadow. But breaks between hills to the south revealed the early golden light spreading across the Mediterranean. Far off to the left Jonas could see the Gulf of St. Tropez. To his right the Giens peninsula reached out into the sea toward the island of Porquerolles.

Much closer, on the other side of a low hill south of his position, rose a long slope untouched by the sunrise. The monastery ruin of the Chartreuse de la Verne remained invisible in its surrounding forest. But Jonas knew it was there. He knew exactly where he was now.

Only a few miles east of the Chartreuse he had supervised his own dig at the pre-Roman Celtic village site—and had met Annick Courtel.

She had had her own special interest in that excavation. Though born in Toulon, her mother had come from Brittany, where Annick was a common name going back to the Celts. Jonas and Annick had talked about the probability of Celtic blood in her ancestry. They had talked about so many things.

In the other direction from the Chartreuse ruin would be the path that wound behind a hill to the west, leading to the village of Collobrières. Jonas remembered the first time he had taken that path with Annick, catching the bus from the village down to Bormes where they'd taken the local train into Toulon. He remembered the other times, later, when he'd gone to Toulon alone: seeking her, driven and thwarted by irreconcilable desires and realities, knowing he could not have both and could not have either without letting go of the other...

Harshly, Jonas wiped the memories from his mind and climbed down from the tree. Picking up the suitcase, he hung it on his back again and started down the southern slope of his hill. Now and then he stopped to listen. With the daylight the hunters alerted by the Messerschmitt would be moving in.

After an hour, pushing hard and beginning to sweat under the rising sun, he neared the dusty path that ran between the monastery and the village. Halting among the trees at its edge, he listened again and then moved forward half a step for a swift look up and down the path.

It was empty. But there were fresh tire tracks on the path.

Because of the fuel shortage in both French zones there was

little traffic and any vehicle still running was easily identified. Wealthy collaborators could afford the stiff black market gas prices and taxis. Government allotments went to its functionaries, including those charged with enforcing Vichy laws. No wealthy sightseer would have driven this path so early in the morning. It had to be one of the units searching for him, checking out the monastery.

Jonas crossed the path and entered the forest on the other side. He couldn't risk taking the bus from Collobrières, even if one still ran. The village was too near where he'd landed; no stranger could evade a rough interrogation by the watchful police and Milice.

Units hunting a parachutist would not have enough men to finecomb miles of dense forest. But they would block the few roads. It was unlikely that an Allied agent, without an intimate knowledge of the Maures, could find his way out without using one of the roads.

But Jonas knew the Massif, and now he had his bearings. Working his way through the forest, he calculated that he should reach Bormes before dusk. He proceeded warily, making little noise, listening for any unnatural sounds. But in spite of his concentration, another memory crept into his mind: a morning when Annick had turned off that path with him, into this same part of the forest.

With it came an image of something else: an exquisite little bronze ornament he'd found while excavating one of the ancient Celtic graves. He had hung it on a leather thong to form a pendant—and late that afternoon, under these trees, he had given it to Annick.

That had been strictly forbidden. All finds were supposed to be recorded and turned over to the museum. But so much of what had happened between him and Annick had been forbidden...

As he worked his way through the woods, Jonas kept remembering that bronze pendant, the last time he had seen it: it was nestled against the softness of her fair skin, between her naked breasts.

FIVE OCTOBER 17—EVENING

THE LIFE OF a hunted man in the Occupied Zone had taught Jonas how to break up a trip by using local transportation from town to town. Spot checks of passengers, whether conducted by Vichy or the Germans, were usually confined to long-haul trains, and to main stations where the volume of people coming and going justified the effort.

From the station at Bormes, a local branch of the southern railroad covered the forty kilometers to Toulon in approximately an hour. Jonas bought a ticket only as far as the next stop after Bormes: the little resort town of Hyères. The short ride passed without incident. But when he descended from the train there was a nasty surprise waiting.

A makeshift barricade had been set up on the station platform, with two uniformed cops and a plainclothes police inspector at the checkpoint through which passengers funneled. There were also two members of the Milice at the ends of the barricade, burly men in Nazi-style uniforms, wearing black ties, berets and armbands. They carried hostered pistols and weighted truncheons attached to the belt.

Another man, standing apart from the others, was observing the traffic. His leather trench coat identified him as one of "the mystery men," so called because their presence in the Unoccupied Zone was unofficially acknowledged by Vichy. Most were agents from either the SD or Gestapo branches of RSHA, the German secret police.

Whether this surprise inspection at Hyères was part of the search for Jonas, or something else, there was only one thing to do. Lining up obediently with four other debarking passengers at the checkpoint, he shifted the suitcase to his left hand and got out the wallet with his identity papers.

There was an elderly woman ahead of him. The inspector examined her papers and then one of the gendarmes went through her handbag. She was passed through. Jonas was next. He put the suitcase down, opened his wallet and handed it to the inspector. The man studied his face, then his papers.

His *carte d'identité* and driver's license named him as Jean-Jacques Blois, born in Orleans, now a resident of Narbonne. There was a card exempting him from military service because of essential government work. Another card, signed by both a deputy of the Vichy Interior Ministry and an official of the state railway system, identified him as an engineer employed in the inspection of train and tram lines—which served as cover to go anywhere he chose.

All of these were the work of experienced SOE forgers which meant they were very good indeed and based on the latest information available in London. But there was always a risk: the official stamps required to authenticate such papers were subject to frequent change in the north and the practice was beginning to be adopted in the south.

The police inspector found nothing wrong with his papers. He handed the wallet back. "Your suitcase, please."

Jonas crouched beside the suitcase and opened it. He watched one of the gendarmes paw through its contents. The radio was hidden in the woods half a mile from Bormes, along with an alternate set of identity papers for emergencies. Later, after he had reconnoitered the situation and found a safe method of transport, he would go back and bring it to Toulon.

Also hidden with the radio was the pistol issued to him by SOE. Jonas seldom carried a weapon during a mission. The danger was too great and the protection it provided was questionable. If you were found carrying a weapon they slammed you into a cell for prolonged interrogation no matter how good your papers. And against a group this size he couldn't shoot his way out; they'd down him before he could take out more than two of them. His other weapons—hands, elbows, feet—could kill as effectively as bullets, and silently. The unarmed combat course had taught him that; experience had confirmed it.

The inspection over, Jonas closed the suitcase and carried it through the checkpoint. There was a warning shout behind him. He turned back quickly.

The passenger who'd been behind him, a teenaged boy carrying a knapsack, was running across the tracks. The Milice thug at that end of the barrier jumped onto the tracks, drawing his gun and truncheon as he sprinted to cut off escape. The boy swung the knapsack with both hands to knock him out of the way. But the Milicien dodged the blow, doubled the boy over with a kick to the stomach, and clubbed him twice across the head as he went down.

The boy sprawled unconscious on the gravel with his scalp bleeding. The knapsack had come open when it fell, spilling out papers. Squatting, the inspector examined them. Then he looked up at the man in the leather coat watching from the edge of the platform. "Anti-Vichy leaflets."

The German nodded, satisfied. "It would seem," he said in slow, careful French, "that my information was correct."

"So it seems," the inspector agreed. He didn't look happy about it. While most French police were prepared to carry out Vichy instructions, and many relished dealing brutally with "agitators," few liked getting their orders from the Germans.

Jonas walked away with his suitcase. A block from the station was a tram stop. He waited almost ten minutes for the tram he wanted. It was dark when he reached the outskirts of Toulon, switching there to another tram which carried him inside the city and made its last stop at Place Albert Premier, in front of the main railroad station.

Inside the station, he noted the group of police hanging

around near the bar, passing time between train arrivals. After checking the train schedule, Jonas went out, crossed the Place to the Café de la Gare, and ate a hefty dinner seated at a table beside the window.

He was exhausted. The hot meal had helped, but not enough. He was dawdling over a second cup of coffee when the train from Lyons pulled in. Waiting until most of the arriving passengers had left the station, Jonas carried his suitcase two blocks to the four-star Grand Hotel. That was something else experience had taught him: the police were less suspicious of people who traveled first class and checked into the best hotel in town. Like people everywhere, they had an automatic respect for anyone with money.

Jonas got a room on the top floor, overlooking the Place de la Liberté. He switched off the lamps and opened the window shutters. The night was still early enough for couples to stroll among the palm trees in the Place. Over the roofs on the other side Jonas had a view of the double bay from which Toulon rose like an amphitheater. Off to the right he could make out part of the naval base and military harbor—even the superstructures and bows of some of the larger warships.

Behind his hotel, the bulk of Toulon rose to the base of the Mount Faron cliffs, which formed an enclosure hindering further expansion inland. Jonas reviewed the places within this compact city where the few people lived whom he could probably trust with his life. *Probably*...people changed, and the change could occur with startling abruptness in wartime. Making contact, even with these few, was always hazardous.

Jonas closed the shutters and drew the curtains. Tomorrow's problems would wait out the night. They were too dangerous to be handled with a weary body and mind.

He was sound asleep by the time a small group of men sat down over cups of tea in a place called "Werewolf" to finalize the fate of the Toulon fleet.

Hitler was fond of romantic code names, reflected in those given to the various Führer headquarters from which he ran his war. There was Spring-Storm in Austria, Rock-Nest in the mountains near Belgium and the Wolf's Lair in East Prussia. FHQ Werewolf had been built in a thickly wooded area of the Ukraine, close to Vinnitsa. Hitler had been there since mid-July, personally directing the offensive against Stalingrad and the Caucasus.

It was late that afternoon when Field Marshal Gerd von Rundstedt flew in to Werewolf. At sixty-six the Wehrmacht's most experienced senior officer, Rundstedt was now its commander-in-chief for western Europe. He had been summoned by Hitler for a conference on countermeasures to be taken in case an Allied offensive in the west, predicted by a growing number of reports from their spies, actually occurred. But hours after his arrival Rundstedt was still being kept waiting, while Hitler remained in the staff map room, shouting at the field generals commanding his Russian campaign.

Martin Bormann, Hitler's personal secretary and deputy for Nazi party affairs, came to explain the delay to Rundstedt. As Rundstedt knew, Hitler had confidently expected the conquest of Russia to be completed by the end of summer. The generals blamed their failure on unexpected stiffening of enemy resistance; and they were worried about pressing the offensive in the face of an early winter. Hitler kept insisting that these difficulties were excuses for their reluctance to turn aggressive— what he called their "dawdling."

"He is quite right, of course," Bormann stated, and looked to Rundstedt for a reaction.

The field marshal declined to give him any. Russia, thank God, was not his sector of the war.

Hitler had still not emerged from the staff map room when Heinrich Himmler, chief of the SS, arrived by plane. Bormann brought him to join Rundstedt in the waiting room of the wooden blockhouse which served as Hitler's Werewolf living quarters. Rundstedt had no love for either of these men. Looking at them together reminded him of a comparison made by some forgotten Wehrmacht officer. He had described Bormann, with his short heavy build, as a Machiavellian hog—and the slight, bespectacled Himmler as a cold-blooded, prissy stork.

Others had since claimed to have thought that up; but none

would have wanted the claim to reach the ears of either man. "The Hog and the Stork" had become, after Hitler, the two most powerful officials of the Third Reich. And, Rundstedt knew, they detested each other, a natural result of their power struggle.

It was an uneven contest. Bormann had few official powers; Himmler had many. As chief of the SS, Himmler controlled the criminal police and secret police, both inside Germany and in the conquered territories. Besides running the SD and Gestapo, he was overlord of the concentration camp system; of the program for mass extermination of Jews, gypsies and Slavs; of campaigns against the Catholic and Protestant churches. He also controlled the Waffen SS, the fighting arm of the SS, begun as a pack of party thugs and now a formidable battle force, still growing in troops and strength of armor. While it could not rival the Wehrmacht, the traditional German army, it had already achieved a spectacular reputation for valor in war.

With all this, Himmler should have had little to fear from Bormann in his desire to be the second most important man in Germany.

But Bormann was *next* to Hitler. Physically and emotionally. All the time. He never took a vacation, not even a single day off. Wherever Hitler went, Bormann went. He had constant private access to him and also had cultivated an intimacy with others closest to the Führer: his doctor, his masseur, his photographer. He kept tightening his hold with clever behind-the-scenes manipulations.

One example was the secretaries who took notes of all important conferences. They were hired by Bormann; and it was he who edited their final typed minutes. Frequently, Hitler didn't bother to read them, accepting Bormann's version in a verbal summary.

Then there was the matter of money. Bormann had solved Hitler's financial problems by pressuring German businessmen into donating a percentage of their profits as a voluntary sign of appreciation.

Through these and other tactics, Bormann had made himself Himmler's most potent rival. Hitler, Rundstedt was sure, was aware of the rivalry. He encouraged such antagonisms between the highest members of his circle. It was a way of insuring against their joining in any conspiracy against him, a possibility which always nagged at Hitler.

There was less than an hour to go before midnight when the Führer finally returned to his living quarters. A tired-looking General Jodl, chief of the Supreme Command Operations Staff, arrived first and announced that Hitler would join them after freshening up. Bormann conducted them into the dining room and ordered a secretary to prepare tea and sandwiches.

When Hitler entered the room and slumped into his chair at the table, Himmler and Bormann automatically took the seats of honor on either side of him. Rundstedt sat across from them, with Jodl beside him, holding a briefcase stuffed with papers.

Hitler was still fuming about Russia as the secretary poured tea: "These generals are all the same!" His voice was hoarse and there were dark pouches under his bloodshot eyes. "Timidity! Hesitation! They seem unable to grasp a simple truth: we have already *won* this war! The Russians are down to fighting like swamp rats trapped in their last ditch! All we need now is one all-out final effort against them, carried out with ruthless determination!"

He picked up his teacup, then put it down again because his hands had begun to tremble. He clenched them into fists on the table. "Ruthless determination," he repeated quietly.

General Jodl nodded emphatically. The General Staff had been purged of officers who argued with Hitler. Only the lackeys were left. It was Bormann who had warned them that "insufficient optimism" was ground for treason.

Bormann placed a soothing hand on Hitler's clenched fists. "Perhaps those who fail to understand should be required to reread the record of the miracles you have already accomplished in so short a period. That will teach them all they need to know. Your decisions have *always* proved correct."

Hitler sighed. "Not quite always, Martin. I believed we would be done with Russia by last month and now free to use all our weight for the final crushing of England."

Himmler was not about to let his rival monopolize the flattery.

"That was not an error on your part," he said in his prim, schoolmasterish voice. "It is the fault of those who fail to carry out your plans properly. That is a problem you have always had to cope with. Fortunately for the German people, when destiny chose you to change the course of history, it chose a man with the strength and sureness to shoulder the burden alone if need be, and to override the doubts of lesser men."

Field Marshal Rundstedt experienced a distinct queasiness. But Hitler swallowed it with a modest smile. "Speaking of lesser men, let us now have a summary of the latest reports from our so-called intelligence agents." He nodded to General Jodl.

Jodl moved his teacup to one side, took a folder from his briefcase, and read from the typed reports.

According to Canaris's Abwehr agents as well as the most recent air force intelligence photographs, the buildup of convoys in Gibraltar and the harbors of Great Britain was continuing. Reports on the mission of the convoys, however, were extremely contradictory.

Canaris's agents in England believed the convoys were intended for a strike at Norway, while the Gibraltar convoy would attempt a massive reinforcement of Malta, Britian's island fortress in the Mediterranean.

Grand Admiral Raeder's naval intelligence believed the convoys from England and Gibraltar would be combined for a single operational goal: major landings in the Mediterranean, on the coast of North Africa directly behind Rommel's forces.

From Vichy, Pierre Laval sent word that his agents had learned an Allied attack was planned against Dakar, on Africa's Atlantic coast. But General Juin, commander of Vichy's forces in Africa, thought the convoys were to supply British troops in Egypt.

Foreign Minister Ribbentrop's spies in Portugal reported that the target of the enemy convoys would be an invasion of the Channel coast of France. The German ambassador's spies in Switzerland said the target was Syria and Palestine; those of the ambassador to Turkey said Holland.

The German commander for the Mediterranean Theater, Field Marshal Kesselring, reported that Rome's Supermarina agents had definite information the Allies planned an invasion of Sicily and the Italian mainland...

"Which is highly improbable," Hitler said flatly, raising a hand to halt Jodl's recital. "We know exactly how many ships the English have available. Not enough, certainly, to support large-scale landings *anywhere*."

Rundstedt spoke carefully: "I have heard a report from one of Ribbentrop's spies in America of large convoys being prepared to cross the Atlantic and join the British ones for a major operation."

"That Ribbentrop spy," Hitler said scathingly, "happens to be the same one who reported a rumor that America is about to achieve a goal of building one new ship every twenty-four hours! Which is so impossible as to deserve no consideration at all. No, the Americans are far from ready at this stage to join the British in any appreciable numbers. And when they are, the British will find them as useless in battle as the Italians are to us. Americans are spoiled children. If it comes to genuine fighting, give them a slap on the ass and they'll want to run home crying to mama."

Bormann snickered. Himmler fashioned a stiff smile.

"I am inclined to agree with Canaris," Hitler resumed. "The enemy convoys probably have two different objectives. One could be a small-scale strike on the coast of northwest Europe. Which our troops will fling back as decisively as they did the similar attempt at Dieppe in August. The Gibraltar convoy is most likely intended for the supplying of Malta. In which case our navy and air force will destroy it as they have other such attempts in the past.

"However," he added, "we must be prepared for the *possibility* of some larger enemy operation in the west. In your case, Field Marshal Rundstedt, this means preparing to carry out my Attila directive, if the enemy operation should touch on France or French North Africa."

At a nod from Hitler, General Jodl extracted a second folder from his briefcase and placed it before Rundstedt. "You will note that Attila has been brought up to date and renamed

Anton. But the major objectives remain the same. First, the crossing of the demarcation line by our forces to occupy the southern zone of Vichy France. Then the seizure of the French fleet at Toulon."

"I'll need more troops," Rundstedt said.

"All of you keep asking for more troops!" Hitler snapped. "Kesselring...Rommel...you. The answer remains the same: *No*. My main effort must continue to be applied here, in Russia. You don't *need* more troops. The French forces will not resist you."

Bormann nodded. "No French commander will move without orders from Marshal Pétain. And Pétain has come to depend on Laval too much to make a decision without him or against his advice."

"Rest assured," Hitler told Rundstedt, "I will have Laval under a tight rein when and if the Anton operations become necessary." His tone became sardonic: "This time, field marshal, you will achieve glory without the loss of a single German soldier.

"However," he added, "the second stage, the taking of the fleet at Toulon, will have to be carried out delicately. Our intention there must be concealed and denied until the last moment—when it will be too late for the admirals to prevent it. You must wait until after you have completed the occupation of the rest of Vichy France. Then—using units which you will have secretly moved into positions around Toulon—a sudden lightning stroke! Completed before anyone in the base can recover from the surprise. I want those warships! Intact!"

Rundstedt had opened the Anton folder and was glancing through the updated directive, checking the new points. There were only a few; basically the entire operation remained feasible.

Hitler turned to Himmler: "You have my authorization to increase your Gestapo network in the Toulon area. Enough to insure that our preparations for the final strike do not become known."

"That will present no difficulty. The police there have been most cooperative, so far."

"Of course. The police are the only Frenchmen we can depend on. And why? Because we give them what any police officer or soldier wants." This was a favorite theme; every man at the table had heard variations of it before. "Say they have to shoot women and children to get a terrorist hiding behind them. In the past they had to worry: would they be blamed for doing so? With us they can go ahead and do their duty without hesitation or guilt. Because we who command also take full responsibility for any actions necessary to keep order."

Himmler cleared his throat. "If I may make a further suggestion?"

Hitler gestured for him to go on.

"General Hausser's Das Reich Division of the Waffen SS—after having performed remarkably well in Russia in spite of taking enormous losses, I'm sure everyone agrees—was returned home for reorganization into a full Panzer Korps incorporating other divisions and a substantial increase in tanks. Hausser is now ready to return to action. Wouldn't his new Panzer Korps be a perfect instrument for carrying out this lightning smash into the Toulon naval base?"

Rundstedt looked up angrily. "The Wehrmacht is quite capable of carrying out an operation of this nature without the assistance of your SS."

Bormann intervened: "But Field Marshal Rundstedt, you were just complaining to the Führer that you need more troops for it."

Himmler shot a suspicious look at his arch rival, his mind working swiftly. Why was Bormann supporting him in something certain to add to SS prestige? A hope that the SS might fail in it? No—with Vichy subservient, the operation's success was assured. It had to be because Bormann wanted to appear fair and unprejudiced, especially when he already knew the Führer's decision.

Everyone was aware of Hitler's fondness for General Paul Hausser. One of the few high-ranking Wehrmacht officers who had switched to the Waffen SS, Hausser was largely responsible for its superb training. And he had never been known to argue with a Hitler order.

If that was Bormann's reason, he was proved right. "An excellent choice," Hitler declared quietly. He looked to Rundstedt. "You will notify General Hausser to get his Korps in readiness for Toulon. I believe General Jodl's staff has prepared a rough of that operation; you and Hausser will work out the details, between you."

Rundstedt choked down his objections.

Jodl was getting out two new folders. He put one before Rundstedt and handed the other to Hitler. "I have taken the liberty," he said respectfully, "of suggesting a code name for the taking of Toulon. Subject, of course, to your approval, mein Führer."

Hitler read it aloud from the folder's cover: "Operation Lila." He considered it, then smiled. "A good name. It augurs well."

SIX OCTOBER 18—MORNING

JONAS AVOIDED THE Place de la Liberté. The big open square was a potential trap by day. To cross it was to risk being spotted out in the middle, where there was no chance to turn away quickly and vanish before the spotter was certain of his prey.

He walked to the left and turned into the palm-shaded Avenue Colbert. There was a cool wind from the sea. His hat brim was tugged low and the collar of his raincoat turned up. He registered approaching faces, tensed for recognition. His manner was casual, his eyes alert.

He was afraid here. That could never be entirely eliminated.

Once he had taken part in the rescue of a woman who had been captured by the French auxiliary of the Gestapo. She had been two days and nights in the infamous Rue Lauriston headquarters before they broke her out. Jonas remembered her vividly. It was not something that could be forgotten; not when moving like this through an enemy city.

But it wasn't a new kind of fear. With practice Jonas had learned how to use it to stay alert, without letting it reach the jittery stage.

As in the rest of France there were few automobiles, but more bicycles and horse-drawn vehicles. Reaching the main thoroughfare, Boulevard Strasbourg, he found it more crowded than in the past. Swarms of refugees from the Occupied Zone had jammed into all the towns along the south coast. Home-owners were doing a thriving business renting rooms to those who still had money. Rich or poor, they were easy to spot among the other pedestrians; anxiety had settled into permanent lines in their faces.

Dodging a clanging tram, Jonas crossed the wide street with-out sighting anyone he knew. One of the streets flanking the ornate opera house on the other side contained a café Annick's father frequented for cards and political argument with his friends. Keeping away from it, Jonas took the other. He turned into the alleylike Rue de l'Humilité, going in the direction of the red-light district.

Once he was in it he could relax. No one he'd known ever came there. Calling itself "Little Chicago," the district was a warren of gaudy bars, brothels and clip joints catering to the navy trade. Even this early in the day the whores were already lounging in doorways, shouting inducements from windows to packs of young sailors roaming the ancient, narrow streets. But Jonas knew he wouldn't find what he was looking for here. Officers seldom hung around Little Chicago: they patronized more discreet establishments.

First he had to find a safe house he could use for an extended period as his base of operations.

One of the three people in Toulon he was fairly sure he could trust was Serge Mandel, a young antiques dealer with a shop just off the open markets of the Cours Lafayette, on the other side of the red-light district. Serge, an amateur archeol-ogist, had often come to watch the work of Jonas's team in the Maures. Their friendship went deep enough so that, whatever Serge's present politics might be, he was unlikely to betray him to the police.

The crowds in the Cours Lafayette had a distinctly different appearance from those in Little Chicago or Boulevard Stras-bourg. Here housewives shopped, milling among the stands of vegetables and fruits, seafood and meat, under the tall plane trees. There was no way to cross the Cours quickly. Jonas ma-neuvered between the crowd of shoppers to reach the other side. Serge's shop was open; a woman in her thirties stood behind the counter.

Jonas asked the woman if she had a pair of opera glasses, not too expensive. She opened a case and showed him several, quoting prices. He selected a pair with an old leather case and shoulder strap. High-powered binoculars would have better suited his needs. But around a naval base they could attract suspicion.

Jonas asked the woman for a lower price. "Serge usually cuts it a bit when I buy from him. Perhaps, if he's around...?"

The woman's frown was on the edge of anger. "If you have bought here it hasn't been in some years."

"No," he conceded. "I used to visit Toulon more often in the past, but..."

She cut him short. "My brother was drafted in 1939. His army unit was captured in 1940, and the Germans still haven't released him."

"I'm sorry to hear that."

She sighed and shook her head. "Three postcards from Germany...that's all I've heard from him."

That left only two other people in Toulon he could trust. Jonas considered them as he left the shop and entered a café farther down the Cours. He bought a *pastis* and asked to use the phone at the end of the bar.

Joel Reynaud had still been curator of Toulon's Natural History Museum when Jonas had last seen him; but he was old and talked of retiring. Jonas dialed his apartment. There was no answer. Then he called the museum and asked for him.

The man who answered the phone sounded unnatural. "Who are you?"

"An old friend of Monsieur Reynaud."

There was a pause at the other end. Then: "In that case I am sorry to tell you Monsieur Reynaud was arrested several months ago for making unpatriotic statements...concerning our government." The man paused again, before adding nervously: "If you wish to know the camp where he is now interned, I would suggest you contact the police or..."

Jonas hung up the phone.

That left one.

He had not wanted to contact Annick, unless it became essential. The last he had heard from her, at the end of 1939, had been a short, stiffly formal note informing him that she was getting married. It had been a vicious struggle to stop himself from rushing back to prevent it. But at the same time he'd experienced a sense of relief. Her note meant the end of an emotional impasse that had become too cruel for both of them.

Three years had passed since then. Yet Annick remained the single person in Toulon about whom he had no doubts at all. No matter what lingering resentment she might still feel, in trouble he could depend on her. But he had never met her husband, a man named Vincent Viviani. He knew nothing about the man's political affiliations, his feelings about Vichy and the war—nor what Annick might have told her husband about him.

The other problem was personal. It was fear, mingled with reluctant hope, that seeing each other might renew their obsession. This time it was she who was married, perhaps with children of her own. He didn't want that kind of pain again, for either of them.

But there was no one else left. To carry out the mission without any native contact he could count on, at least in the initial stage, would heighten the risks of failure, detection, capture.

Jonas picked up the phone and dialed Annick's family home. She and her husband might be gone, but almost certainly her parents still lived there, as well as her kid sister—three people whose feelings about him might be a source of danger. But he had to start somewhere.

Jonas let the phone ring a long time before hanging up. He paid for his drink and the use of the phone, then went out to take a tram to the upper reaches of Toulon.

It was a long, two-floor house, old and solid, with thick stone walls plastered smooth and painted a dark orange which was fading in places. Through the opera glasses a sloping roof of curved tiles cut a wedge into his view of the city cascading down to the bay far below.

Jonas was concealed by deep shadows inside a stand of umbrella pines on a slope above the house. The hillside up here, below the base of the Mount Faron cliffs, were covered with wild pine woods. Like other dwellings in this area, Annick's family home was isolated from neighbors inside a walled estate surrounded by the woods. A narrow, twisting road that led to it ended there. The only other house in sight was a similar one inside the other end of the estate. That was where Annick's uncle lived with his wife and son, none of whom Jonas had met.

Annick's grandfather had been head of a very successful insurance firm, and though in the end he'd run it into the ground through unsound investments he had managed to leave his two sons the estate and enough money to pursue their careers. Annick's father ran a local newspaper, The *Toulon-Matin*.

Jonas frowned that he'd neglected a simple way to find out part of what he wanted to know. He should have bought a copy of the paper and checked its present political slant. But that could still be done, after he'd checked what he could learn here.

Focusing the opera glasses on the house at the far end of the estate, he studied it for some minutes without detecting any activity. Since he could only see part of it from this vantage point, that didn't necessarily mean no one was there. But even if someone was, elementary precautions should be enough once he entered the estate. At that level the two houses were screened off from each other by a grove of pines. Jonas returned his attention to the house directly beneath him. He had been in place more than fifteen minutes and nothing had changed. It was the rear of the house which he could see, with the shutters along its entire length closed. There was no car in the parking space and, although there was a cold wind, there was no smoke from the two chimneys at either end of the house. The padlock on the gate in the estate wall was locked.

Jonas put the glasses back in the case and moved out of the woods to the entrance road. He climbed the gate and dropped inside the estate.

There was a swing on a tree branch beyond one end of the house; seeing it reminded him of Annick's kid sister as she'd been during his first visit here, over four years ago. When pushed hard the swing went out above a steep slope—it was a dizzying drop to the bottom of the city. He remembered the way the girl had kept begging him to push her *harder,* and then screaming with terror and excitement when the swing reached its apex.

Her name was Nicole; she was sixteen when he met her: a bright, saucy, flirtatious creature, aware of her allure and even trying it out on him. But that had changed into sulky stiffness after she'd come into the house unexpectedly early one afternoon and discovered him in bed with Annick. He was never quite sure if the change signified disapproval or jealousy.

Just as he was never sure if it was Nichole who had told her mother, or if Madame Courtel had finally sensed the truth for herself: that Jonas was not simply the admired director of the dig her eldest daughter was taking part in, but a married man with whom Annick was having an affair. After that he had no longer been a welcome guest in this home.

Jonas made a wide circle, keeping to the fruit trees around the edge of the garden, until he could see the front of the house. There was a wide patio the length of the lower floor, and an iron-railed balcony along the upper story. Here, too, all the shutters were closed. Quickly he crossed the patio and tried the knob of the front door. It was locked; it never was when someone was home.

After a few generations a family's arrangements became set. The key to the cellar door was in the rock garden near the other end of the house. He entered the cellar, pried up a brick from the floor near the furnace and found the spare front-door key.

Inside the entry hall Jonas shut the door behind him and relocked it, then stood and listened. The house was silent. He began his exploration and in the living room came across the first piece of depressing news. There was a framed photograph of Marshal Pétain on the mantel above the fireplace.

Jonas scowled at it, then went into the study. Copies of *Toulon-*

Matin were stacked on a chair next to the desk, and several had been dumped on the floor. He picked up one. The front page had an outraged headline about recent Allied bombing raids on Occupied France. There was a photograph of Pierre Laval meeting with German Foreign Minister Ribbentrop to discuss the political and social improvements being introduced by the Vichy government. Another article quoted a speech by the pro-Nazi author, Céline, complaining that the government's deportation service was not sufficiently efficient in searching the orphanages of France for children with Jewish blood.

At the bottom of the front page, inside a thick black border, Annick's father was named as the paper's founder, with the date of his birth—and his death, less than a year ago.

Jonas remembered the man: much older than his wife and in frail health, with a bad heart. He turned to the next page and read the name of the new publisher-editor: Girard Courtel. The son of Annick's uncle. Replacing the paper exactly where he'd found it, Jonas went through the rooms of the ground floor.

Except for the books filling wall shelves in every room and hallway, the interior had the feel of a prosperous farmhouse. The furniture was heavy, old-fashioned, acquired over decades with an eye to durability and comfort. That was as he remembered it; but something was remiss. The disordered newspapers in the study, a pair of woman's shoes lying in a hallway outside an open closet, unwashed dishes left in the kitchen sink. Annick's mother was compulsively tidy about housekeeping.

Jonas climbed the stairway to the upper floor and entered Annick's bedroom. Her single bed had been replaced by a larger one, but the room didn't have the look of being used regularly. He opened the closets. The clothes, both male and female, included a dress Jonas remembered that Annick had worn one of the last times he'd seen her. She and her husband used this room when they visited; they didn't live here.

He was nervous about the time passing. From the bedroom, window-doors led to the upper balcony. Unlocking the doors, Jonas pushed a shutter open and looked out.

The balcony afforded a magnificent view of the entire Bay

of Toulon. But what interested Jonas more was the house at the other end of the estate. From the balcony he could make out its roof, and a pathway that cut through the screen of pines. No one was coming this way. He closed the shutters and doors and went back down to the study.

He found a phone book for the Toulon area, but no listing in it for Annick and her husband. He searched the desk drawers but there was no private address book nor anything else to tell him where they lived. He returned to the living room, and then went back upstairs, without finding what he was looking for. But he found out other things.

There were clothes belonging to Annick's mother in the master bedroom, but items were missing from the dresser and bureau. Apparently, she no longer lived here on a permanent basis.

But the sister, Nicole, definitely was using her own room. Her things were scattered about it, books dumped on the floor beside her unmade bed. There was a picture of a handsome young man in his late twenties on top of her bureau. Jonas stared at it, remembering him at once: a graduate student in archeology who had come down from Berlin to take part in the dig at the Celtic settlement in the Maures.

Dithelm Demenus, scion of a prominent Prussian family with a long and respected tradition of breeding dependable military officers for Germany's wars—smiling at him out of a photograph on which he'd written: "To my beloved Nicole..."

He picked up a copy of that day's *Toulon-Matin* on his way back to the hotel. There were a number of things he could try next, but not until that night.

He could keep phoning Nicole, disguising his voice and attempting to pry Annick's address out of her. Then there were the two remaining contacts he had to check out. One owned a café on the quay of the commerical port, which had been a favorite rendezvous for Jonas and Annick. The other was a woman who ran a beach club on the other side of the Mourillon promontory, also favored by young naval officers. He couldn't risk an approach to either in daylight.

He had lunch sent up to his hotel room and read through the newspaper while he ate. There was more of what he expected, pro-Vichy propaganda larded into almost every article, sprinkled with judicious bits of fawning on the Nazi conquerors. Nor was he surprised when he saw Nicole's name above one of the stories.

Annick's sister had always intended to go to work for the *Toulon-Matin*. She had written about a visit to Paris, with a special permission to cross the demarcation line from both Vichy and Nazi officials. She'd interviewed the German military commander of Occupied France, General von Stülpnagel, and he had spoken of the future financial rewards the French were bound to reap from their honored position in Europe's New Order. She reported how well mannered the German occupation troops were, how respectful and polite to all good-intentioned Parisians.

Jonas threw the paper aside and tried to stop remembering the laughing, shouting young girl in the swing.

SEVEN OCTOBER 18—EVENING

THE SUN WAS setting when Jonas made his reconnaissance stroll around the perimeters of the Toulon naval base.

The base was divided into two unequal parts: the main base of the West Maritime Arsenal and the much smaller Mourillon Arsenal to the east. They were separated by the Vieille Darse, the oldest of Toulon's harbors, now filled with pleasure boats and small fishing and commercial vessels. Jonas started with the West Arsenal where most of the French fleet, and all of its larger warships, were docked.

It was a long hike. The vast installations spread west from the center of the city, to the promontory of La Seyne. All of the installations, including the docks of the military harbors, were hidden behind high stone walls. The walls were topped by rusty barbed wire and by green metal tubs, each large enough to hold two armed sentries and a pair of swivel-mounted search-lights. At greater intervals there were the warning keep-out signs: "TERRAIN MILITAIRE—DEFENSE D'ENTRER."

There were only two entrances along their entire length: the Porte Principale and the Porte Castigneau. Both had tall gates of thick steel plates riveted together. Open or shut, a team of navy guards stood duty outside each gate, with a second guard unit stationed just inside.

The Porte Castigneau was open when Jonas reached it. He

paused to light a cigarette. It was an excuse to stop and take a look inside the gates. He had barely flicked out the match when a marine approached him, holding his submachine gun at waist level.

"Do you have business here, monsieur?"

Jonas looked puzzled. "No..." He indicated his cigarette by way of explanation.

"Then move on."

Jonas moved on. When he finished his tour of the West Arsenal walls, he boarded a trolley car that carried him around the Vieille Darse, getting off at its eastern end. None of the big ships of the fleet were in the Mourillon Arsenal. It served as a supplement to the main base; there were repair shops, a navy training school, a torpedo workshop, auxiliary submarine pens.

A long walk around the landside perimeter showed Jonas the same defenses as at the West Arsenal: high walls, armed guards, only two gates. Impossible for any unauthorized person to get into.

It was dark when he finally went to the old civilian harbor of the Vieille Darse, whose quays began outside the West Arsenal and continued around to the Mourillon Arsenal. The Cronstadt Quay was the most popular, with bars, restaurants and souvenir shops facing the water. Day and evening, its outdoor tables were crowded and animated.

Jutting out from the Cronstadt Quay, far out over the harbor waters beyond the yachts, fishing boats and commercial vessels, was a pier called the Petit Rang. Jonas walked out along its wide concrete promenade. There were strolling couples, people walking dogs, men fishing. All the benches were filled, some by young lovers, others by elderly people. By day there would be fewer lovers and many mothers with children and baby carriages.

Jonas walked out to the end. From that point he could see the bay side of the West Arsenal to his right and the Mourillon Arsenal to his left. The entrances to the West Arsenal's military harbor were visible in the night, along with the dark looming shapes of the warships. The bay side of the smaller Mourillon Arsenal was quite different: a long high wall dropped sheer into the water, with only a few narrow openings, including the entrance to the auxiliary submarine port. Jonas could not see inside.

He walked back along the Petit Rang to the Cronstadt Quay and moved among the crowded tables until he reached the Café Galleon.

Jonas prepared to light a cigarette as he neared the Galleon's windows, using his hands to shield his face. The interior was small and he saw the same owner he and Annick had become friendly with: André Prevot, a big, gregarious man talking to a couple of expensively dressed men in a booth.

Jonas turned and walked away. He would come back to tail Prevot when the café closed for the night. It would be too risky to reveal himself to the man until he knew something about his present affiliations. That left time now to look around the beach club on the far side of Mourillon. Turning off the quay, Jonas went through an open arcade to the nearly deserted Rue République, where he could get a trolley out to Mourillon.

While he waited at the tramline stop, a Citroën sedan passed him, slowing and then pulling over to the curb to park. The driver got out: a dark-haired young woman with a good figure, wearing a stylish skirt-suit with a fur jacket draped over her shoulders. He looked at her automatically; anyone inside France who could get gas to drive a car was a potential enemy. But he didn't recognize the danger soon enough: she was turned halfway from him as she locked the car.

Then she turned from the car and the light of a streetlamp revealed her face—and it was too late for him to turn away. She recognized him in the same instant. He walked toward her, smiling. His hands curved, poised to strike at her throat if she started to yell.

"Hello, Nicole."

"Jonas…" It was a whisper. She was staring at him, stunned. "What are you *doing* here…in France?"

"Looking for old friends." His voice was gentle, soothing.

She looked around quickly, badly frightened. But Jonas had already checked: there were no cops in sight.

"You must be crazy..." She was still whispering. "Or..." She didn't complete the alternative. Her tone suddenly firmed: "Listen, you can't stand out in the open like this. We've got to get you out of sight, before someone recognizes you and notifies the police."

Her fear for his safety was well done. He continued to smile at her. "You're right," he agreed. "Let's get in your car and drive someplace we can talk in privacy."

"I *can't* right now." She looked troubled; she was obviously thinking very fast. She glanced at her wristwatch and explained: "I have an appointment on the quay. An interview—with a man I can't afford to stand up."

He got ready to use his hands. But she surprised him, shoving her car keys into his hand. "You take my car. Go to the house. Nobody else is there. Do you remember where we keep the key in the cellar?"

Jonas nodded.

"Wait in the house," she told him tensely. "I'll come up by taxi, as soon as I can."

She spun away from him and hurried into the arcade. He didn't try to stop her. Waiting until he saw which way she turned on the quay, he strode after her. He reached the quay just as she entered the Café Galleon.

Jonas kept people between him and the windows as he drifted close enough to look in. Nicole was talking to André Prevot, who shook his head. She hurried past him to the phone in the back. She spoke urgently into the phone. Then she was listening, and speaking again.

When she hung up and turned from the phone, she was smiling.

Jonas faded back to get more people between them as Nicole emerged from the Galleon. He followed as she walked, more leisurely now, back to the arcade and through it toward the Rue République.

So much for the interview she absolutely had to keep on the

quay. Now the small, lingering doubt that had disturbed him was gone. He caught up with her as she reached the sidewalk. He put one arm around her waist to hold her while his other hand swiftly unlocked the car door.

She jumped in fright, twisting in his grip. Then she saw who it was. "You didn't..."

"No," he said, "I didn't." There was no one looking their way. He opened the door and shoved Nicole down into the car, leaning in after her so that his back cut her off from the view of anyone on the sidewalk. She opened her mouth to say something or scream, and he struck her squarely behind the ear.

Nicole slumped across the front seat. He pushed her over as he settled behind the steering wheel and shut the door, looking around quickly again. No one had seen. There was a low moan from Nicole. He struck her again, carefully and sharply, in exactly the same spot. Not hard enough to kill her, but it would keep her out for a long time: long enough.

Later, he knew, probably he *would* have to kill her. After he had forced some things he needed to know from her. All she could have told them over the phone was that there was an enemy spy in town. Maybe she'd given a description, when she'd told them he was on his way to the house. But it would be a description that would fit hundreds of other men. Right now he could still move around Toulon without being spotted; unless Nicole was available to point him out.

He started the car and drove through the city to the hills near the Mount Faron cliffs. Not to her house, but to a densely wooded area half a mile from it.

When she opened her eyes she saw the moon through the branches of pine above her. Then she saw Jonas outlined by the moonlight, sitting on the ground beside her. She tried to raise herself but gasped and fell back as the pain behind her ear exploded in her brain and ran down her shoulder paralyzing her arm. She lay absolutely still, her eyes squeezed shut, taking shallow breaths of air.

"Why?" she asked with her eyes still closed. "You hurt me..."

"You know why." There was a frightening lack of expression in his voice. "You told me to go to your house and wait, and then you called the police or some fascist friends and told them they could capture me there."

Nicole forced her eyes open. He was looking down at her but his face was a dark shadow. "I didn't..." she said weakly.

"What did you tell them?"

"You're wrong."

Jonas made an impatient sound. "You claimed to have somebody waiting on the quay for an interview. But there wasn't anybody. I saw you make the call."

She was afraid now. "I was supposed to have an interview there..." She had to take it slow, a few words at a time. "An official from the Interior Ministry. Down from Vichy for talks with the mayor. He wasn't there. I called the mayor's office. He was still with the mayor. Apologized for not being able to keep our appointment."

He shook his head. "I have to know exactly what you told the police. Did you give them my name?"

"If it was the police I called," Nichole said slowly, forcing each word, "they'll be surrounding the house by now. But they're not. Nobody is there."

Jonas was silent for some moments. Then he said, "Take off your jacket and blouse."

"What?"

Impatiently he moved closer and dragged her to a sitting position, ignoring her cry of pain. He stripped her jacket off. She was limp, unable either to help or to stop him. He ripped open the buttons of her blouse and tugged it from her arms. She lowered herself to the ground, moaning, and then was silent, closing her eyes. Jonas tore her blouse into shreds. She neither moved nor opened her eyes when he used the strips to bind her ankles together and tie her arms around the trunk of a tree. He used the last of the blouse to gag her, and then he left her.

It was almost two hours before he returned from reconnoitering the house and its surroundings. Nicole was asleep or relapsed into unconsciousness. She hardly stirred when he removed the gag and untied her.

He carried her to the car and drove her home.

A long hot bath, a large whiskey and four aspirins helped to dull the pain and drain off some of the stiffness. But she had to hold her head carefully getting out of the tub, not moving too abruptly. Drying herself and getting into her bathrobe was agony. She walked slowly into her bedroom. Jonas was still sitting in the chair by the windows waiting for her, nursing a whiskey.

Gently, one move at a time, Nicole lowered herself onto the bed.

"Don't fall asleep yet," Jonas said. "When will your mother be home?"

"Not until Christmas. She always had more friends in Paris. Since my father died she spends more time there than here."

"Where is Annick living?"

Nicole opened her eyes then, turning her head to watch his face. "Morocco."

He stared back at her. "I thought her husband was a doctor in Béziers."

"They moved when he was offered the position of medical supervisor at the French hospital in Rabat."

Morocco...it was a long way from Toulon. Much too far for Annick to be of any help.

Deliberately, Nicole told him the rest. "They have a baby, Jonas. A lovely boy. Not really a baby anymore, he'll be two years old soon."

There was nothing inscrutable about him now. Then she asked him, "Why did you think I would inform on you, Jonas?"

"You have Pétain's picture on the mantel downstairs. You work for a newspaper that's turned virulently pro-Vichy, pro-Nazi and anti-British. You write articles for it extolling the army that conquered and occupies your country." He paused, establishing eye contact with her. "So why didn't you betray me?"

"People visit me here sometimes. The Pétain picture fits with the paper I write for and what I write, which in turn gives me freedom to move about where I wish, with the use of my car and the cooperation of officials." Nicole hesitated. "A safe and convenient cover."

A cover...the word sounded odd coming from her; he still wasn't ready to accept it. "Are you telling me you're part of some underground resistance movement?"

"No...but sometimes I have to help someone who is."

Coldly, Jonas pointed a finger at the photograph of Dithelm Demenus smiling from the frame on Nicole's bureau. "Tell me about your German boyfriend."

"He is a young German," Mueller said. "That is all I know. It is all the boy caught with the leaflets at the Hyères railway station knew about him. Along with his code name—which is 'Falcon'—and the probability that the group of French terrorists run by this German traitor is hidden somewhere inside the Maures."

There was no anger in the way he used the word "traitor." Udo Mueller was uninterested in politics, national or international, except as they affected the performance of his work. He had been a policeman all his life; as a professional his attitude toward traitors depended entirely on whether they were useful or a hindrance. "If the boy had known more," he added, "he would have spilled it before he died."

"It's not much to go on," grumbled Reggie Stevens, who was a traitor of the useful variety. He lit a fresh cigarette off the end of the one he'd been smoking and dropped the butt into the ashtray on Mueller's desk without bothering to stub it out.

Mueller did it for him, his heavy seamed face expressionless. He had an allergy to tobacco smoke, and his sinuses were becoming irritated. But he kept the ashtray there for those smokers whom he wished to keep relaxed in his presence, and he did not tell Reggie to stop. Instead he heaved his short, thick-muscled figure out of his chair and opened his office window wide.

He stood there for several moments breathing the cold air,

looking down at the lot that was used for parking, and in the daytime by elderly *boule* players. On the other side of the lot was a side wall of the Toulon prison.

"We do have certain specifics which will be of help to you," Mueller said. "Though not about this German leading the Maures's group. Except that he is young, blond and handsome—a useless description for practical purposes."

He returned to the chair behind his desk. "The boy was supposed to deliver the leaflets to some person, male or female, who would be seated in front of a certain bistro reading the last pages of an old François Mauriac book, with a folded edition of the *Toulon-Matin* on the table. This person was not at the bistro when the police arrived. We may be sure they searched diligently, since there was one of my Gestapo associates with them. Probably the person had been watching the railway station and saw what happened there. We know, however, that he or she was to have taken the leaflets on to Toulon. Thus, my special interest. Berlin has become concerned about the situation in Toulon. This is why they sent me here."

"I know that," Reggie said impatiently. Reggie Stevens was tall, lean and elegant, an actor from Liverpool who had failed to make his mark in the London theater. But he had finally achieved some success as a singer in German cabarets in the last years before the war. His German was quite good. His French was less so—but that fitted the role he usually played these days.

He was a redhead with a luxuriant mustache when he arrived in Toulon. But since his cover was blown around Dijon and Lyons, and descriptions of him perhaps trickling this far south, Mueller had made him shave off the mustache and dye his hair black.

Mueller ignored Reggie's affectation of boredom. "We also know that the boy picked up the leaflets from the young German traitor outside St. Raphael, at the eastern end of the Maures Massif. So that gives you a place to start your search."

"So I slink around St. Raphael by night in my ragged RAF costume," Reggie drawled. "Whispering to any disloyal Frogs

75

I find that I need help in contacting a resistance gang run by somebody they call the Falcon—in the hope that he can get me to a functioning escape route. And once I have his hideout located I pass it back to you. Simple enough—and extremely dangerous, for me."

"You are a very good actor." Mueller's tone was sincere. "That is why you have always been able to perform this same part so successfully in the past. This time is not different—except for its objective. I want more than this Falcon's location. I want you to join his group. Let them know you are more excited by the idea of taking part in its activities than in escaping. You have my permission to kill some French cops if that is what it takes to be convincing. An enemy agent was just dropped into the Maures, perhaps with Toulon as his objective, perhaps with the help of this Falcon's group. In any case, I want you to stick with this German traitor until you learn who his contacts are here in Toulon."

"What about my new papers and cover story?"

"I will have your RAF papers and other British ID here by tomorrow afternoon. What name would you prefer to use this time?" Mueller felt it was always best to allow a man to choose a false name which had some special significance, thus making it easier for him to remember it.

Reggie thought about it. "What about using my actual first name, for a change? Last name...there's a role I used to dream of playing in the theater...make it Lear."

Mueller wrote "Reginald Lear" on an envelope containing photos taken of Reggie an hour ago. "As for your cover story, your plane was shot down during a bombing raid in the north, near Belfort. While trying to make your way through the south of France to Spain you were captured by the French police and imprisoned in Fort Revère, from which you have now escaped."

Reggie nodded. It was a solid cover, tailored to the situation existing down here. Most Allied airmen captured near France's southern coast were sent to Fort Revère, high in the hills above the Riviera, between Nice and Monaco. And there *had* been escapes there, so it could be done. "When do I start?"

"I want you to leave for St. Raphael immediately after I've gotten you your papers tomorrow." Mueller added generously: "Take tonight off. Enjoy yourself." He got a slip of paper from his pocket and handed it across the desk. "This is the address of Milice headquarters. They seized a number of young resistance suspects late this afternoon. The man in charge there is an officer of the French militia named Tontenoy. He has been given orders to allow you to observe the interrogation of these suspects and to conduct your own interrogation of any one of them, personally and in private."

Reggie's air of bored elegance had crumbled. His eyes were embarrassed, his face flushed. "What did you tell him about me?"

"Only that you are under my command and are to be given whatever you wish." That, Mueller knew, would probably be the prettiest girl among the suspects; although Reggie was not averse to an occasional boy.

The Englishman mumbled "Thank you," picked up the slip of paper and quickly left the office.

Alone, Mueller reflected upon how simple it was to manipulate people if you understood their secret selves. Every man had his motivation. Know the motivation and control the man.

With Reggie Stevens the push was spite and the pull was latent sadism. He still smoldered over England's failure to appreciate his talents. He had first been enticed into his present role by the present of a frightened daughter of a German lawyer who'd been arrested for anti-Nazi statements—to amuse himself with in a release of long-repressed brutality.

An easy man to control.

Udo Mueller's own motivation remained the same as when he'd been a Berlin policeman, before he'd joined the security branch of the SS: to carry out his job efficiently and build a professional record of which he could be proud.

He had been helped in this, at times, by the fact that others often assumed he was related to the dreaded Heinrich Mueller, "Gestapo Mueller." They were not related; but it was this assumption which had led Udo Mueller, a practical realist ambitious to rise in his chosen career, to switch from the SD to the Gestapo.

Actually, the division of authority between the two had always been blurred, and was becoming more so. The SD was the SS intelligence and counterintelligence branch. The Gestapo was the secret police. Both were part of RSHA, the Nazi state security service, which in turn was a part of the SS—so ultimately all of them had the same boss: Himmler. But though he'd done well enough in the SD, Udo Mueller had done much better with the Gestapo. In spite of denying any family connection with its chief, he had risen rapidly to his present position—as an Amt IV kriminal inspektor.

His assignment to Toulon could lead to the next step. Berlin was suddenly obsessed with Toulon. If he succeeded here he was almost certain to move up to a top position as a regierungsrat. And he did not intend to fail.

There was a knock at the door. It was his secretary, Karl, a Gestapo kriminal assistant whose assignment in Toulon was partly due, like Mueller's, to a sound knowledge of French.

"The dossiers you requested from Commissioner Vallat, sir." Karl placed the portfolio on Mueller's desk and gave the Nazi salute before marching out.

Henri Vallat was a deputy commissioner of the Police Judiciare. As a career police official, Vallat wished to continue to move steadily up to the highest government position open to a man of good family and education, making no misstep between the present situation and a respected retirement. Which meant, now, absolute loyalty to Vichy, unswerving devotion to Pétain and unflinching cooperation with Germany.

Mueller opened the portfolio and took out the dossiers of informers whom Deputy Commissioner Vallat had begun placing, at Mueller's request, as waiters, pimps and barmen in establishments patronized by navy men. Mueller read each dossier through. Most of the men were petty criminals with simple motives: payment for information, immunity from arrest.

Replacing the dossiers in the portfolio, he decided it was time to close up shop. He wanted a good dinner and a decent night's sleep. He had a long day ahead of him tomorrow, to be followed by dinner at the home of the publisher of that cooperative journal, the *Toulon-Matin*.

EIGHT OCTOBER 19

IT WAS A sunny morning without wind or clouds, the air already warmed by the sun. Nicole woke to the smell of fresh coffee. Her head still hurt and her neck was stiff, but it wasn't as terrible as the night before. She went out to the balcony and looked down. Jonas, who had spent the night in Annick's room, was on the patio outside the kitchen, having coffee and toast. He had prepared a breakfast setting for her.

Nicole looked quickly toward the other house at the far end of the grounds—and then remembered that had been the last thing they'd talked about before she fell asleep. Her uncle and aunt loved Pétain and were in full accord with the editorial slant their son had given the newspaper. If they wandered over and saw Jonas, the cover story was he was an old friend of Annick's husband; Nicole had met him while visiting them in Béziers. His name was Jean-Jacques Blois, he was recovering from a heart attack and had decided to spend part of his sick leave in the Toulon area. He had called on her last evening and she had invited him to stay the night.

She took two more aspirins before getting into her bathrobe and sandals.

Jonas put down his cup when she came out to the patio. "Feeling better?"

"No worse than if I was recovering from a hangover and falling down the stairs at the same time."

At least she had her humor back. He poured her coffee as she sat down. "I'm deeply sorry."

"You should be. You should have known me better."

He thought how different she was from her sister. Annick was a blonde, tall and slim. Nicole was dark and shorter, lushly curved. She had been a disturbing young girl; now she was a disturbing young woman. Jonas stared at the ripe swelling of her breasts, partly exposed by the opening of her robe.

"You were shouting in your sleep last night," Nicole told him. "It woke me at one point. Do you do that often?"

"I don't know. Sometimes I have nightmares. It's having to be afraid all the time. The same reason I hit you, without taking time to make sure about you."

She was eyeing him curiously. "You shouldn't be involved in spying, if it makes you do things like that. You really hurt me, Jonas. You could have killed me. I think you were ready to."

She waited for him to deny it. When he didn't, she said: "I hate fanatics of any kind."

"I'm not a fanatic. No more than Dithelm."

"What he's doing is more straightforward. It wouldn't cause him to lose faith in someone he cared for. He could never tolerate what the Nazis were doing to his country. He simply wants to help get rid of them."

"What I want is just as simple."

"What *do* you want, Jonas?"

"Retribution."

Nicole frowned. Jonas told her, briefly, about the Nazis killing his wife and children. He told it unemotionally, as though it were something that had happened in another life.

She regarded him thoughtfully. Whatever the loss had done to him, he had not changed in appearance or manner. She remembered how strongly she'd been attracted to him at sixteen. The four years since had wrought changes in her, but he appeared to be exactly as she'd first seen him: that same alert face and wiry build; that faint smile, which could mean any-

82

thing. There was a permanence to the man—not of solidity, but of resilience.

"You didn't want to tell me about that," she said finally. "You told me for a reason."

"Yes."

"To persuade me to help you."

"I need *someone.*"

Nicole poured more coffee. She could feel his eyes on her. She took a drink, put her cup down, and her eyes met his. "Do you want to stay here?"

"This house would make a good base for me."

"All right. The story we thought up last night will cover that. There's plenty of room after all, no reason I shouldn't invite you to stay here instead of paying for a hotel."

"I need more from you than a place to stay, Nicole. For one thing I could use help in checking on a couple of possible contacts in town." Jonas explained about André Prevot and about Olga Cavallo, the woman who owned the beach club out on Mourillon.

Nicole didn't know Olga Cavallo and had never been to her place. "I'm at the Galleon pretty often, and Prevot is always fun to talk with—but I haven't any idea of his politics, if he has any. I've never heard him take sides in any political argument. Maybe that's just being a sensible businessman. He gets all kinds of customers. Refugees from the north. Others who are eager to collaborate with the Nazis. And the majority who just don't want any more fighting and are content to let Pétain be a well-meaning father to us all."

Jonas decided to let Nicole see what she could find out about Olga, while he checked on Prevot. "I'll also need the use of your car, sometime in the next couple days. With you as chauffeur would probably be safest, considering the kind of credentials you have. I have to get some things I hid in the Maures."

"I can arrange free time to drive you there tomorrow," Nicole said. "I can also get you in touch with Dithelm's group there. He and his friends could be of use to you."

"No," he said sharply. "I don't want contact with *any* resistance group. The Gestapo has the police trying to slip informers into all of them. They've already destroyed some that way. You might warn him about that, when you see him. Does he come here?"

"Very rarely. Too dangerous."

"Don't tell him about me," Jonas warned Nicole. "And try to let me know in time, if he does come, so I can keep out of sight."

After she'd gone upstairs to get dressed, Jonas walked to the edge of the patio. It gave him a good view of the entire bay area—and its harbors: the Vieille Darse in the middle, between the military docks of the West Arsenal on one side and the Mourillon Arsenal on the other. The eastern promontory of Mourillon and the western La Seyne formed sheltering arms around the harbors, reaching out toward each other. The opening between the two was further protected, to the south, by the Mandrier peninsula curving across the seaward approach.

Jonas looked down at the ships of the Toulon war fleet in their docks. If he had to keep watch on what was going on down there, this was a good place to do it from. And he had found something better than the opera glasses: there was a pair of binoculars, with strong lenses, in the downstairs study.

Waiting for Nicole to come down, he wondered why he had shouted in his sleep. He had dreamed about Annick at one point. He'd awakened from the dream with an almost painful erection, something that hadn't happened to him for a long time. His old obsession with her, brought back by sleeping in her room again, in her bed...

It didn't alter the fact that the affair between them was over; and would have been even if she weren't now someone else's wife and a mother. He'd known after his wife and children had died that he could never live with Annick. Because it would have been their deaths which had freed him to do so.

He thought of how much simpler things were for Nicole and young Dithelm Demenus: all they had to do was survive the war. Nicole had told about it last night. They'd become lovers just before the war and become engaged after it began: when he was leaving, ostensibly to return to Germany and join the army, but actually into the Maures with his friends.

They had been able to be with each other occasionally since then, and only briefly. But it gave Dithelm something, knowing that she was always there for him.

Jonas heard Nicole coming back to the patio. He turned and looked at her, and found himself envying Dithelm very much.

André Prevot scanned the groups of men watching the *boule* players between the prison wall and the parked cars as he came around a corner of the building opposite the prison. Seeing no one looking in his direction, he entered the back of the building and climbed the rear stairway to the second floor. He knocked at a door which had no name or number on it. Mueller's secretary, Karl, admitted Prevot and put him in a tiny windowless room. He told him to wait and closed the door.

That way, Prevot didn't get to see Reggie Stevens when the Englishman emerged from Mueller's office. Carrying a bag which contained the RAF uniform and papers, Reggie went down the rear steps. When he was gone, Karl brought Prevot to Mueller.

Jonas was standing among a group near a *boule* game when Reggie came out of the building. As Reggie strode off, Jonas kept part of his attention on the *boule* game and the rest on the building across the way. There was nothing about the man to stir interest in Jonas. Reggie no longer looked like the description which Jonas had gotten from Michael Sandoe.

Inside Mueller's office Prevot sat uncomfortably under the kriminal inspektor's scrutiny. After a time Mueller said, "Commissioner Vallat informs me that you have been helpful to him at times."

Prevot shrugged modestly. "Well, naturally a businessman wishes to cooperate with the authorities."

And naturally a businessman didn't want his café shut down because he was dealing with the black market, which was the only way a businessman could operate with any profit these days. Naturally, also, a businessman didn't object to having some side income from the police which his father-in-law, who was his partner at the Galleon, couldn't check—and which enabled Prevot to keep a little apartment in town where he could enjoy an occasional girl friend.

"I am interested," Mueller told him, "in an enemy agent who may have entered Toulon in the past few days. Do you know anything that would help us in this matter?"

Prevot shook his head. "Haven't heard about any more enemy agents since the last one I tipped off the commissioner about."

"That was good work on your part, Prevot. It enabled us not only to capture the British agent, but also to seize a large number of terrorists in contact with him. Now...there is another terrorist gang, which is led by a young German..."

Prevot was shocked: "A German? With the Resistance?"

Mueller growled, "Do *not* interrupt when I speak. Listen to me. This German traitor is known by a code name. It is 'Falcon.' His gang operates from the Maures but has connections here in Toulon. Now, I want you to see what you can find out. About this German who is called Falcon, about his gang's Toulon contacts, about any new enemy agent in this city. I want this information...urgently."

Prevot squirmed uncomfortably. "Look. That enemy agent I tipped the commissioner about...that was a chance thing. I just happened to overhear something about him so I passed it on. That's how I operate. I stay neutral, and people talk to each other around me, and sometimes I hear something of interest. But if I start *asking* people things, they'll start wondering about me."

"As of now," Mueller told him blandly, "you are no longer neutral. You will let it be known, quietly, that you have no love for Vichy or Germany—and we'll see who comes to you because they feel the same."

"I can't do that! It'll hurt my business, drive away customers who..."

"It will hurt your business worse if I have your café shut down permanently. Which I can do in the next half hour if you prefer."

86

Prevot sagged. He knew when he was licked. "All right. I'll try..."

"Good. Don't worry, you will be compensated generously if you are successful. If not..." Mueller made a dismissal gesture with one thick-muscled hand. "You will bring me a report of your progress. Here. Every day, at this same time. Good luck."

Prevot didn't feel well at all when he went down the back steps. Passing on things he just happened to overhear was one thing; deliberately digging for information was different, and it made him feel like a rat. A scared rat.

As he left the building he looked again toward the groups of men around the *boule* games, but didn't spot anybody who seemed familiar or interested in him. He hurried around the corner and walked away quickly. There was only one place where he could shake this depressing feeling.

Not the Galleon Café and not his house. The little apartment his wife and father-in-law didn't know about was only a few blocks away. The girl friend he'd been keeping there lately was a Dutch refugee with no family or money and no place else to go. An hour with her was exactly what he needed at this moment.

It was a dingy street, cobbled and too narrow for sidewalks, in the oldest part of town. The apartment Prevot rented was on the third floor of one of the rows of tall, seedy buildings that kept sunlight from the street. He used his key to open the ground-floor door, stepping into the dim entry and turning to lock up from the inside.

Before he could get the key in the lock the door was shoved open so violently Prevot was knocked backward against the banister. A man stepped in and kicked the door behind him. Prevot regained his balance and started an angry tirade but then stopped himself. There was something familiar about the man, but Prevot had to reach far back in his memory for it and by the time he recognized who it was the man had one arm against Prevot's throat and another across the back of his neck.

Before Prevot could break free the arms locked together like a vise with his neck caught between them, yanking his body forward and tilting his chin up until all his bulging eyes could see was wrinkled ceiling. The arms exerted a sudden wrenching pressure and Prevot heard a noise that was his spine breaking loose from the base of his brain.

Jonas continued to hold Prevot until the body ceased its spasmodic quivering. Then he lowered the body to the floor of the dim entry and went out the way he'd come, closing the door behind him. Now he could move around Toulon without constant fear that there was a collaborator who knew him.

NINE OCTOBER 24

ERWIN ROMMEL PACED the gardens of an Austrian sana-
torium near the Semmering Pass, filling his lungs with the frosty
afternoon air. He had been in bad shape when he'd arrived
there, suffering from afflictions picked up during his long North
African campaign: chronic gastritis, a bad liver, swollen glands,
infected sinuses. But the weeks of medical care, rest and fresh
mountain air had restored his health. He was impatient to get
back into action.

At fifty-one Rommel was firm of body and at the height of
his mental powers. His success in driving the British Eighth
Army clear across Libya and backing it into Egypt had gotten
him promotion to field marshal and earned him a flattering
nickname from the enemy: "the Desert Fox." But his drive had
become stalled before stubborn British defense lines at El Alamein; he had turned his army over to General Stumme and
returned home for medical treatment. That had been a month
ago, and the stalemate at Alamein hadn't changed.

Of course, much of the blame for that situation could be
placed on a failure to maintain an adequate flow of reinforcements and supplies. It was true that the British navy and air
force had been scoring heavily against the Axis ships and planes
carrying the supplies. But the failure was still inexcusable, considering the relatively short supply line across the eastern Med-

iterranean from Italy and Crete. After all, the Allied supply routes to the British forces in Egypt were much longer: thousands of miles by ship, all the way around the bottom of Africa and up to the Suez Canal...

Rommel's thoughts were interrupted by his adjutant, hurrying out to announce that Martin Bormann was on the phone from Werewolf.

There was a lot of static in the line connected to the switchboard of the FHQ in the Ukraine. Bormann sounded upset—an invariable sign that Hitler was in a temper. "Something unexpected has happened at El Alamein," Bormann told Rommel. "The British attacked our lines late last night. It wasn't regarded as serious at first. But now it's turned into a full-scale offensive. General Stumme was caught completely unprepared. To make things worse we've just learned that he died of a heart attack shortly after the British assault began. The Führer wishes to speak to you. Please hold on."

Rommel felt an old excitement rising in him as he waited.

Hitler did not waste words when he came on the line: "Rommel, this news from Africa sounds bad. The situation seems somewhat obscure, but there are rumors some of our forces have actually begun a retreat! Are you well enough to return there and resume command?"

"I'm quite recovered," Rommel assured him. "I can leave at once."

"Good. There must be *no* retreat, Rommel! Not one inch! I want a counterattack, with every man and every weapon. You have to allow your troops no alternative but victory or death. Is that understood?"

"Fully, mein Führer."

Rommel was smiling when he put down the telephone. He ordered his adjutant to arrange for a plane to fly him via Crete to the battlefront, and went to his rooms to shower. Already his mind was grappling eagerly with tactics, troop dispositions, armor and logistics.

The British defense at Alamein had proved frustratingly impenetrable. But the British on the offensive provided an entirely new deal of the cards. When it came to slugging matches, Rommel was the proven master. He prayed that General Montgomery would still be on the offensive when he reached Africa the next day. That would finally give him a chance to complete a promise he'd made some months back to Hitler and Mussolini. Within a week, he calculated, he could have both Cairo and the Suez Canal in his hands.

The coast of the United States was no longer in sight that afternoon when the convoy finished forming up. The S.S. *Fargo* was one of the last ships to take its assigned position. The chief mate and the radio operator stood on the flying bridge, gazing in awe at the sheer numbers of the ships.

"I been forty years at sea," the chief said in his thick Dutch accent. "Never I see anything like this, Sparky."

All radio operators were called Sparks. The chief used the diminutive because this one was only eighteen: a skinny kid with thick glasses whom the army wouldn't take because of his bad eyes. The U.S. Merchant Marine, with new ships being built for it at an unbelievable rate, would take anything it could get. It had taken the chief, in spite of being past his retirement age and not having sailed in some years. He didn't want to sit out this war. He had no friends or relatives left alive after the bombing of Rotterdam.

His smile was fatherly as he watched the kid trying to learn how to balance against the roll of the ship in the choppy Atlantic waters. He began explaining why the *Fargo* had been assigned to a position at a rear corner of the convoy, instead of in the middle of it.

Back at their anchorage, in Gravesend Bay off Brooklyn, they'd seen the thousands of soldiers boarding other cargo vessels which had been converted into makeshift troop transports. But none of the troops had been sent to the *Fargo*. Except for the six big Sherman tanks chained down on the open decks, it was strictly an ammunition ship this trip. Its holds were filled with cannon shells, bombs, dynamite, rifle and machine gun ammo. A floating bomb...if it exploded at the rear end of the convoy at least it wouldn't take too many other ships with it.

"That's why they call this the coffin corner," the chief explained.

Sparks didn't like the sound of it but didn't say so; his teeth were clenched as he struggled against a growing queasiness.

"One good thing, though," the chief said, "we got no danger of getting drowned. If we get hit, Sparky, we blow sky high. You'll see God before you see water."

Far ahead of them, two other men stood on the bridge of the convoy command ship: Rear Admiral Hewitt and General Patton, the officers in charge of the armada. They watched the convoy execute a course change, turning to the southeast. The first rendezvous was scheduled for the mid-Atlantic, with the other convoy sailing from Norfolk, Virginia. Then the rendezvous with the convoys from Great Britain, off the Straits of Gibraltar. And then, in conjunction with the Gibraltar convoy, the first American-commanded operation against the Axis: Torch, the invasion of Morocco and Algeria.

If it worked, and if General Montgomery's offensive gathered steam, the Afrika Korps was going to get its nuts cracked between them.

Patton enjoyed the image.

The Mourillon promontory had a long camel-back hump in the middle, dividing it lengthwise. The Maritime Arsenal was on one side of the hump, facing in toward Toulon's ports. The beach club owned by Olga Cavallo, the Narval, was on the other side looking out toward the sea. It was a private club, strictly for members and their guests. Since Olga decided who could belong, membership was confined to those she liked; and she'd been known to cancel those whose behavior or opinions she didn't like.

Most of the members were junior navy officers. "I was always a navy tart," she was fond of explaining. "And as I get older and older I find I like my navy younger and younger."

The building was an aging but well-kept villa, nestled inside a large garden screened on three sides by flowering hedges, palms and stands of cactus. It was too cool that evening for the garden or the patio facing the beach. And since it was too early for the night crowd, which patronized the bar and clubroom, the late-shift waiter and barman hadn't arrived yet.

They had the place to themselves.

The Narval had a faded Edwardian elegance: worn leather and polished wood, gleaming brass and velvet plush, discreet lighting and groups of cozy sofas and overstuffed armchairs around low tables. Olga, tiny and fragile in one of the big chairs, had a faded elegance of her own. She was a spry relic from the past century, somewhere between seventy and eighty, exactly where she didn't care to tell.

"And don't try guessing, it's impolite. After all, there are no wrinkles on my heart." Olga took one of Jonas's hands, turning it over with skeletal fingers and studying his palm.

"See anything interesting?" he asked her.

She gave him a roguish grin. "Don't tell me you believe in such nonsense. It's only an excuse for holding hands." Olga looked at Nicole. "Since it turns out you are his friend, and continue to be in spite of the perilous state of the world at the moment, I owe you an apology for the other day. I almost threw you out of here."

Nicole laughed. "You were on the edge."

Using her newspaper contacts, Nicole had first checked into Olga's reputation around town. Olga's scathing comments about Vichy officials and decrees turned out to be an open secret. Only her wide knowledge of skeletons in the closets of most of the Toulon authorities kept them from closing up the Narval. It was rumored that she'd written down some of the juicier tidbits and given them to some unknown friend, to discourage anybody from having her killed.

Nicole had come to the Narval to get her own personal impressions for the *Toulon-Matin*. Olga had reacted to the newspaper's name like a cat catching sight of a vicious dog. She'd told Nicole, among other things, "I don't care to talk to the kind of cowards who lick Nazi boots that have just dirtied their carpet."

"You want to be a bit more careful of what you say to strangers," Jonas advised her now. "The Gestapo won't be stopped by any amount of dirt you have about city officials."

"At my time of life they can't hurt me much. I'd die on them before they could get very far with that kind of foolishness. So what can they do? Arrest me as a threat to Vichy? Execute me as a dangerous member of the Resistance? I would be thrilled to have one last bit of unexpected excitement before I die."

Olga patted Jonas's hand, her smile wistful. "You are another unexpected thrill for my final years, popping up like this. A genuine spy, involving me in your intrigues. I'm all aflutter."

They discussed how she could help. She agreed to see what she could learn of what was happening in the base. Olga would tell the officers who came to the bar that Jonas was her godson. She pointed a finger at Nicole. "And you are his mistress. He's just the right age to want one as young as you." Olga looked at Jonas, her gaze speculative. "Though I give fair warning, some of my navy boys will try to steal her from you."

After leaving the Narval, Nicole drove Jonas home and he went up to the radio hidden in the attic.

Even when there was nothing special to report, Jonas sent one transmission each evening at this time, to let Michael know he was still alive and at liberty, and to receive any new instructions. The previous two nights he had tapped out Michael's code signal and his own at intervals over a five-minute period without getting a response from Gibraltar.

Jonas unwound the aerial and strung it from one end of the attic to the other. He got out the hand-sized transmitter and the slightly smaller receiver unit, and connected them into the main unit. Each movement was quick and neat, without the need to think about them. Here in the attic there was no need for the battery pack. He put it aside and plugged the radio into a house-current socket, using the screw-in adaptor. Settling the headphones on his ears and flicking the on switch, Jonas began tapping the signal.

He got a reply on his second try, and recognized Michael's unmistakable telegrapher's touch. Acknowledging, Jonas got his pencil ready to take down the message. There was a short burst of numbers, and then Michael's sign-off. Removing the headphones and flicking off the set, Jonas took a small code book from the case. Each group of four numbers translated into one letter of the alphabet. The numbers were reshuffled each day according to a prearranged sequence, to prevent enemy code breakers from working out the pattern.

The message was a single word: "Soon."

Jonas rewound the aerial and put everything back in the case. He hid it behind insulation stuffing in the attic roof and went back downstairs.

There was a white-haired man he didn't know in the living room, having a drink with Nicole.

She appeared entirely at ease as she made the introductions. "This is my uncle, Lionel Courtel. Uncle Lionel, Jean-Jacques Blois."

The two men shook hands, sizing each other up. Nicole asked if she could get Jonas a drink. As she went to the kitchen her uncle asked him, "How are Annick and her husband? Seen them since they moved to North Africa?"

Jonas shook his head. "My work has always kept me from making long voyages. Or it did, before I was hospitalized."

"Oh yes...Nicole was telling me about your heart ailment. Bad luck, unusual for such a young man."

Jonas smiled. "It is a long time since anyone called me a young man."

"Ah, that is why you should always try to have much older friends. To me you are still a boy."

Nicole brought Jonas his drink. Her uncle asked him, "How is the political situation in your home area? Many malcontents there? We've had some nasty incidents here recently. Terrorist activity, and arrests of fools who spread their propaganda."

Jonas sipped his drink. "So I've heard. No, in Narbonne we've had nothing serious."

"Some people still don't understand, we *must* accommodate to reality or drown in fantasy. The reality is that the Germans have won the war. All that is left is some mopping up around the edges." Lionel Courtel lowered his voice. "Let us be honest, just between ourselves, collaboration with the Germans is the only sane course. And potentially a profitable one. Certainly we have much to learn from them. Don't you agree?"

Nicole thought she saw something flicker in Jonas's eyes. But it was gone in the same instant and his reply was casual: "I think most of France would agree with you at this point."

Her uncle nodded. "Yes, thank God these Resistants are a minority. Irresponsible children who think they are playing parts in American films...cowboys and gangsters. Only the damage they do is real, and those who die don't get up again to play in other films. It's those broadcasts General de Gaulle makes for the British, stirring them up. Did you hear what that man said the day before yesterday?"

"I don't listen to the BBC," Jonas told him.

"Sensible of you, considering your heart condition. I get so furious each time..." Lionel Courtel sighed. "That man is nothing but a traitor, to his government, to his country and to his oath as an officer. Look at the way he abandoned his post and fled to join the English. Quite an instructive contrast to our Marshal Pétain, who remained with us in difficult circumstances, to continue doing everything in his power to serve the welfare of France and her people. This de Gaulle—Pétain put it succinctly when he called him a viper we nourished in our bosom."

Jonas took another sip. They sat and smiled and made small talk until Nicole's uncle looked at his watch and stood up. "Time for me to get back to dinner."

Nicole and Jonas walked him to the patio and watched him go off along the path toward the other house. When he was out of sight Jonas said, "I think we got away with it."

Nicole took a breath of relief and turned to kiss him. As their bodies touched he put his arms around her and his fingers spread greedily to pull her closer, and then his mind put an abrupt brake on what his body wanted to do, warning him: *This is very wrong...*

She lay wide awake in her bed for a long time that night, thinking of him. He had *wanted* to kiss her; and more than kiss her. She had felt the intensity of his desire like a jolt of electric current between them, and then the way his body had flinched from hers as he controlled it.

Nicole remembered vividly that moment when she'd been sixteen and had discovered Jonas and Annick in her sister's bed: the shocked excitement as she watched what they were doing, before jealous anger took over.

She thought about Annick; and then about what had happened to Jonas's family. He was so damned *alone* now. And he wasn't the kind of man who was meant to be without a woman.

She reminded herself that at twenty she was exactly half his age. But that didn't alter what she felt now. It was so strange... She knew Jonas wanted her—even needed her. More than Dithelm did; but that wasn't strange. What was, was how much she wanted this man to need her. She thought about his hard, sensual mouth... about the lean strength in his hands... and felt her own hands move between her thighs. And stopped herself. It wasn't that kind of release she wanted; she wanted *him*.

Kriminal Inspektor Mueller put down his phone, scowling at it. The caller had been Deputy Commissioner Vallat, reporting that police radios had picked up another Morse broadcast from somewhere in the Toulon area. Less than an hour ago.

The French still hadn't been able to break the code the sender was using. Neither had the experts in Berlin, where Mueller had sent the previous messages. Mueller looked forward to the arrival of the two mobile radio direction-finder units he'd requested from Germany. Once those arrived they'd be able to locate the illegal transmitter, and capture the enemy agent using it.

Mueller also looked forward to receiving some word from

Reggie soon. The last message from the Englishman was that he might be on the verge of a possible contact with the Resistance gang run by the mysterious young German. After that message Reggie had vanished from St. Raphael.

That had been three days ago. Mueller was not too worried. Whatever else was wrong with the English traitor, he was not a coward and he was resourceful. His role of deception suited him by temperament and training, and he relished it. Reggie would find that young German Resistance leader, if anyone could.

TEN NOVEMBER 7

IN THE DARKNESS before dawn the shepherd followed a path leading to the monastery ruins in the heart of the Maures. He knew his way through this part of the forest too well to need a light. Reaching the northwest corner of the ruins, he went to a burned-out tree that had been blasted by lightning some years ago.

He had come here for the last eight nights, and there was never anything. He didn't know what was supposed to be there, only that he would be paid well if he found something. Neither did he know that he was only one of several men doing the same thing, in other parts of the Maures Massif.

This time was different: there was a crumpled little ball of paper hidden inside the tree trunk.

The shepherd put it inside his pocket without bothering to open it. It was too dark and he couldn't read anyway. The sun was up when he reached St. Raphael. The man he gave the paper to drove to Toulon and turned it over to Udo Mueller.

There were three words scrawled in French on the paper: "I love Natalie." Mueller needed no code book to translate what Reggie's message meant.

He had established contact with the Maures Resistance group led by the mysterious young German who called himself Falcon.

99

* * *

The Führer Headquarters in East Prussia, Wolf's Lair, had been established long before Werewolf and was much larger. Several acres of the Güorlitz Forest had been partially cleared to make room for the forty-two buildings scattered around its grounds. A railroad track cut through the middle of it, connecting to the main line at Rastenburg Station, eight kilometers to the east. On this day there was a train waiting on the stretch of track: The Führersonderzug, Hitler's mobile headquarters when he traveled through conquered Europe.

Hitler's house and bunker dominated the north section of Wolf's Lair, with a dining area, a teahouse and Bormann's quarters grouped near it. Other buildings inside the security fences included the quarters for the Wehrmacht staff command officers, barracks for SS and RSHA detachments, a post office and telephone and teleprinter exchange, facilities for Hitler's servants, doctor and barber and the situation conferences center. There were also houses which Himmler, Goering and Ribbentrop maintained for their frequent visits, an additional teahouse and dining area, a sauna and movie theater.

Hitler was to spend most of the last three years of the war at Wolf's Lair. But this stay was ending after less than a week. The Führersonderzug had arrived here with him on November 1 after a two-day trip from the Ukraine, and was to take him away in the afternoon. He was scheduled to make a speech in Munich on November 9 before old Nazi party members who had taken part in his first big grab for power there—the Beer Hall Putsch.

At this time of year nostalgia for the early days of his rise to power gripped Hitler, and gathering with the party faithful of the old days took precedence over military problems. He was impatient as he spent the morning of November 7 in the situation conferences building, discussing the two theaters of war in which Germany's forces were engaged.

The news from one of them, Africa, was bad. Despite repeated radio commands from Hitler for "iron determination," Rommel and his forces were in full retreat across Libya, with

Montgomery and his British army on their heels. Hitler was furious.

"I should never have sent Rommel back there again. He's a sick man...perhaps *worse* than sick..." Hitler glared at the tiny marker flags on the wall map of Egypt and Libya. "Frankly, I think the fellow's lost his nerve."

But the Führer was somewhat mollified by that morning's report from North Africa: Rommel had reached a strong defensive position at Fuka, where he intended to dig in solidly enough to check Montgomery's advance.

The news from Russia, on the other hand, was excellent, and Hitler smiled as he turned to the map showing the situation there. General Paulus had finally taken Stalingrad and was establishing control within the devastated city in spite of continued street fighting by Soviet guerrillas. That put Hitler into a cheerful mood when he left the conference to have lunch in Kasino I. He was expansive with the favorites invited to share his table.

"All Rommel has to do now is just hold on a bit longer. From Stalingrad, our final steps to the defeat of Soviet Russia are short and sure. Then we can shift our armies from there, and Rommel can have more than he needs to conquer Africa. England—I said it before—is a drowning man clutching at a straw. The straw is Russia, the last of which we are about to burn—and England's last hope will be gone."

After finishing lunch Hitler went off to the train which would carry him to Munich. He was accompanied by his two most prestigious old comrades: Propaganda Minister Goebbels and Reichsmarshal Goering, chief of Germany's air forces. Martin Bormann was forced to trail behind them. Compared to Goering and Goebbels, Bormann and Himmler were newcomers in the Nazi Party.

Jealously, Bormann eyed the two walking beside the Führer. Goering strutting in a resplendent uniform strained at the seams by his corpulence. Goebbels limping along on his crippled leg, wearing a drab uniform that hung on his little body as though he had shrunk while the material stretched. Bormann comforted himself with the thought that their moment in the Führer's favor would be brief.

Goering had been under a cloud for some time because his Luftwaffe had failed to wipe England out, as he'd assured everyone it could. Goebbels was in disfavor because his compulsive philandering hurt his wife, whom Hitler liked. His position included control of German movies and theater, enabling him to make and break stars: and a man so physically unattractive just could not resist the opportunities to get beautiful actresses into his bed.

Hitler's anger at the two had abated temporarily because of the nostalgia surrounding the anniversary of his Beer Hall Putsch. But that would be over in a few days, and everything could get back to normal.

When they reached the Führersonderzug, Hitler invited Goering and Goebbels to join him in his parlor car. Bormann boarded the next car with his secretarial crew. Generals Keitel and Jodl, the chief of staff and the Wehrmacht's operations chief, went to the command car with their aides. The train was long enough to carry accommodations for all of them, plus a security force and special troops who manned the antiaircraft batteries of the armored wagons at either end.

One of the two big engines sounded its whistle and the Führersonderzug started on a twenty-two-hour journey to Munich, carrying with it the entire German military high command. It was 3:05 P.M. when it left Wolf's Lair.

At 10:25 P.M. Michael Sandoe finished decoding Jonas Ruyter's latest signal. He had to restrain himself from rubbing his burning eyes. Tonight they felt as they had when he'd crash-landed his plane with his face on fire.

Waiting until his vision improved, he reread the message in clear. Jonas had found the officer he intended to use to establish communication with the Toulon naval base. But he would withhold making the contact with him until he got Michael's go-ahead signal. Which, Michael reflected as he locked away his code book, depended on when they got the next signal from the German source being used by Riley, Michael's OSS contact. And that, in turn, depended on one other factor, which Jonas still didn't know: the operation that would trigger his mission into high gear was about to occur.

Leaving the Gibraltar radio shack, Michael returned to a small room, high on the Rock, where Paul Riley stood at the opened window with a pair of field glasses. The OSS man lowered the glasses, holding them out to Michael with a tense grin. "There they go..."

Michael's night vision was terrible; and with his one hand it was difficult to focus the glasses properly. But finally he saw them: one ship after another, coming through the night-shrouded waters of the straits from the Atlantic.

An endless stream of them, spreading out on entering the Mediterranean and angling off in the direction of Algeria to carry out Operation Torch.

ELEVEN NOVEMBER 8

THE FÜHRERSONDERZUG STILL had more than eight hours to travel before reaching Munich when the passengers first learned about Torch, during a stop at a small Thuringia station. Hitler was having early morning tea with his doctor and photographer when Keitel and Jodl hurried into his parlor car to tell him the news.

In the hours before dawn Allied convoys had begun landing great numbers of troops, predominantly American, at three points on the coasts of Algeria and Morocco: Algiers, Oran, and Casablanca.

Hitler stared at the generals for a long moment. Then he shoved to his feet, knocking over a bowl of fruit which crashed to the floor. His doctor and photographer remained seated, their faces blank. Ignoring the debris, Hitler listened stonily while General Keitel nervously added a few shreds of good news. No Allied troops had disembarked in Tunisia, which stood between them and Rommel's rear—and the Vichy forces in Algeria and Morocco were reported attempting to throw back the invaders.

"By pure luck," Jodl said, "Admiral Darlan happens to be in Algiers visiting his son, who fell ill while stationed there. He has already assumed charge of defending the French territories against the enemy. I'm sure, since Darlan has always cooperated with us fully as military leader of France, that he will..."

"Darlan," Hitler growled, "can't be trusted any more than any French officer! They bend with the wind, that's all they're good at. When will you learn, we can depend on no one but ourselves."

He paced the parlor car, thinking furiously while the two generals stood rooted in apprehensive silence. He kicked a fallen orange and it rolled the length of the car and came to rest under a leather-padded armchair. Abruptly, he stopped pacing and whirled on Jodl and Keitel, snapping out his orders.

Every available plane was to immediately ferry German troops to Tunisia, seizing it before the Allies could get there.

Field Marshal Rundstedt was to execute Operation Anton within the next few days. "And tell him to make sure General Hausser's objective is well camouflaged, until Anton is completed and the SS Panzer Korps can take the Toulon fleet without interference."

The thought of Operation Lila brightened Hitler's mood. Now that he had recovered from the initial shock, he saw that the strategy for coping with the North Africa problem boiled down to two straightforward moves.

One: Finish mopping up the Russians and transfer enough troops, planes and tanks from that front to make Rommel unbeatable.

Two: Take the French fleet, man its ships with Axis crews and use them to cut off the Mediterranean supply routes to the English and American forces before they could squeeze Rommel's army between them. Without additional supplies or reinforcements, both enemy drives would falter and disintegrate.

Martin Bormann burst into the parlor car, ashen-faced. "I just heard about the enemy landings in..."

Hitler interrupted: "Martin, I want you to get in touch with Vichy at once, in my name. Two points. One: I demand Pétain's personal guarantee that the French intend to defend their African territories against our common enemy—and will *continue* that defense with every ounce of their strength. Two: I want Laval to come to meet me in Munich. He is to be there by tomorrow afternoon."

General Keitel looked startled. "Do you mean, mein Führer, that we are still going on to Munich for this party rally, while the enemy forces are mounting this major operation?"

"Of course. Some of the oldest and most faithful members of the party are waiting to hear me speak. The enemy is not going to prevent that, on top of everything else."

Keitel bowed unhappily, and headed back through the train toward the command car. Hitler told Bormann: "Another point—call Rome. I want the Duce to join me in Munich, so we can work out plans for Italian troops to cross their border with France and seize control of the French Riviera region simultaneously with our Anton operation. But don't tell him that, just get him to Munich and I'll explain it."

Bormann hurried off to make the calls. General Jodl had started in the opposite direction, following Keitel, but was called back by Hitler.

"Jodl, I don't want our forces to invade Unoccupied France until I have Laval firmly in hand. He'll arrive tomorrow, that's the ninth. Tell Rundstedt he is not to launch Anton before the tenth—and not later than the eleventh, three days from now."

Toulon's double bay was glassy black and a heavy cloud cover brought darkness before the sun set that evening. Jonas waited for Nicole in the Chantilly, a tea salon on tiny Place Puget in the center of the old town. The place always gave him a certain sense of security, a multiple means of escape in an emergency. Big windows afforded an unblocked view of the narrow streets converging on the Place, and a rear door provided a fast exit into a maze of crooked alleys and interconnected courtyards.

The salon's radio was blaring a rebroadcast of Marshal Pétain's indignant reaction to the Allied invasion of French North Africa: the American criminals had betrayed the long friendship between their two countries; France's loyal colonial forces would never surrender to the invaders.

Jonas had spent the day going from one bistro to another, listening to what people were saying about the surprise landings so he could later radio his own estimate of French reactions to

Michael in Gibraltar. The workers were jubilant, predicting the eventual defeat of Hitler now that the Americans had entered actively into the war. Businessmen and functionaries were skeptical whether anyone could beat the Nazis; they shared Pétain's indignation.

Nursing an orange drink and watching the approaches to the salon, Jonas listened to the news broadcast which followed the marshal's speech. It declared that all Frenchmen in North Africa were united in defending their territory against the Allies. Listeners were warned the Allies might attempt to use North Africa as a base for an assault on France itself. All loyal citizens were asked to be on the lookout for advance secret agents sent by the enemy, and to report anyone suspicious to the police immediately.

Jonas ordered tea for Nicole when he spotted her striding toward the Place along Rue Hoche. She'd been interviewing an assistant to the Vichy minister of education, who was in Toulon supervising changes in school courses to conform with new government edicts. "But all he could talk about were the landings," Nicole told Jonas when she joined him. "He was on the phone to Vichy when I got to his hotel suite. I have some news for you that hasn't been on the radio."

Nicole paused when the waitress brought her tea. She continued between sips: "First, Algiers has already surrendered to the Allies, though not Oran or Casablanca. Second, Vichy is scared to death the next Allied move will be an assault on southern France. Pétain has been on the phone to Germany, begging for permission to rearm the French Army, so it can help the Germans fend off any such assault. Hitler said he'd give it serious thought."

Jonas's smile betrayed a mean streak that surprised Nicole. "Hitler will give serious thought to everybody in Vichy being idiots. He'll never let France become a serious military force again."

After leaving the Chantilly Jonas headed for his hidden radio. Nicole went off to the Narval, where Jonas was to join her after he had finished transmitting to Gibraltar.

108

* * *

The two radio direction-finder units Mueller had requested from Germany were in different parts of Toulon when they picked up the enemy agent's transmission again. They had arrived in Toulon two days ago and had begun operating immediately. The enemy agent had sent four code messages since then, and with each transmission the two units had moved closer to each other—and closer to the location of the secret radio.

Each unit was disguised as a bakery van with French license plates. There were two men in each van: a driver and a radio technician hidden in the back with the direction-finder equipment. The slowly turning antenna on the roof of each van was concealed inside a fake ventilator. As the vans moved through the streets the technicians kept in constant radio communication with each other and gave route changes to the drivers. Between them, the two direction-finders had triangulated on the general location of the secret transmitter. If this evening's transmission lasted long enough, the vans would be able to pinpoint the exact location.

But the agent finished sending his coded signals before the vans could get closer. The vans stopped as soon as the transmission ended, less than a quarter of a mile apart with the enemy radio somewhere between them. One of the drivers, wearing overalls of a baker's assistant, got out to telephone his report to Kriminal Inspektor Mueller.

Their units were now close enough to pinpoint the enemy transmitter the next time it was used.

In ordinary times, the officers using their membership at the Narval changed regularly as navy vessels left Toulon and others came in to take their place. But none had left since they had all been interned inside the military harbor. Nicole found the usual crowd of men at the Narval when she arrived that evening. Some stood at the bar. Others shared tables with girl friends or were dancing to the phonograph. The rest were gambling in the game room.

All were relatively young junior officers. Officers of higher rank had homes or apartments around Toulon, with wives and children, and didn't hang out in places like the Narval. There were a couple of bars they dropped into from time to time; but Jonas and Nicole had realized early that it would be impossible to find what he needed there. The more senior officers, even those who might dislike Vichy policies, were bound by their responsibilities, and too aware that future promotion depended on solidly pro-Pétain admirals, to speak their minds.

Only the junior officers were rebellious enough to vent their feelings.

Olga greeted Nicole and led her to a corner table. "I see some of the boys are ready to descend on you," Olga warned. "Shall I shoo them away?"

Nicole laughed and shook her head. "No. They're always fun, and much too gallant to get obnoxious."

"Just call me if they get out of control."

As soon as Olga left three young officers came to join Nicole. They brought a bottle of wine and settled in with flattering attention.

They didn't know Nicole's last name, nor that she worked for *Toulon-Matin*. Since nobody she knew belonged to the Narval, the subterfuge was successful. Jonas, whom everyone knew as Jean-Jacques, was Olga's godson and had a passion for cards. Nicole came simply because she was his mistress. It worked well.

She often arrived before Jonas, or sat alone having a drink while he gambled in the game room. But she was never alone for long. By the time Jonas joined her, there was a cluster of officers around her, relaxed and talking freely. With her ability to draw them out, and Olga's help, Nicole and Jonas had learned a good deal about what went on inside the naval base.

They knew that Vice-Admiral Marquis, the maritime prefect of Toulon, lived at his headquarters in Fort Lamalgue, outside the Mourillon Arsenal. And that Admiral Laborde, commander-in-chief of the Toulon warfleet, made his permanent quarters aboard his flagship, *Strasbourg*, inside the base at the Milhaud docks. And that both admirals remained completely loyal to Pétain and Vichy.

110

Unexpectedly, the three young officers at Nicole's table raised their glasses: "To the Americans in North Africa!"

Nicole raised her own glass. Their reaction to the landings was hardly a surprise. Since Olga chose the members here, no officer at the Narval was the kind who would meekly accept France under a conqueror's heel.

But few were as vitriolic as the one Jonas had finally selected as his contact. A selection which Olga had approved and Nicole had confirmed after gently probing the man.

She glanced around the Narval, but he wasn't in sight. She asked the officers about him.

"He'll be here sooner or later," one of them said wryly. "To gloat. He won his bet."

"Yes," Nicole agreed, "he certainly did."

The evening was wet and cold, sobering Roger Martin as he made his way to the Narval. He had already stopped at three other bars, collecting his winnings and treating the losers to generous drinks.

At thirty, he was first lieutenant of the *Orion,* a submarine stuck in the Toulon base. A stocky, ruddy-faced man with considerable nervous energy, Lieutenant Martin had been boiling at his enforced inactivity. He hadn't chosen a navy career just to spend it in port.

He was a rare officer in the French Navy: an enlisted man who had worked up into officer rank. His widowed mother was a seamstress in Menton who had worked hard to raise him decently on little money. He had joined the navy to take the financial burden off her and regularly contributed a substantial part of his paycheck to her. He had volunteered for the submarine service for the extra-danger bonus. He also had a visceral need for action, challenge, risk. None of which was being satisfied since the armistice with Germany; his frustration caused him to drink heavily when off duty.

Today he could afford it and to treat everybody to drinks. For several months Martin had bet that American troops would join the British against the Nazis before the year was out. Now that they'd hit the beaches of North Africa, it was payoff time.

His fellow officers at the Narval groaned when he arrived. Lieutenant Martin grinned and spread his arms wide in triumph: "Repent, ye losers and prepare! I'll pay each of you a little visit before this night is out!" He started toward the rear, then spotted Nicole.

"Well, how do you like this morning's delightful news?"

"Delightful," Nicole agreed. The three officers sitting with her, none of whom had bet against Lieutenant Martin, raised their glasses again as a sublieutenant proposed another toast:

"Here's to thumbing our noses at the Nazis and sailing out to join the Americans."

"No hope of that," a junior engineering officer added gloomily.

They all knew that. Admiral Auphan, the Vichy minister of the navy, had insisted that the Toulon fleet would stay put; it would not join the war on either side. The Toulon admirals, Laborde and Marquis, made it clear they would abide by the order.

Nicole asked Martin in a mocking tone: "Does your commanding officer know about your bet?"

"Martin's one of the luckier ones," the sublieutenant told her. "The commander of *his* boat thinks Vichy is full of..."

"Shut up," Martin growled. "What Captain Lambert thinks is his own affair. Don't go spreading rumors."

"Nobody is going to say anything outside of here."

Lieutenant Martin's good cheer reasserted itself and he smiled down at Nicole. "Where is Jean-Jacques tonight?"

"He'll be along."

"He probably can't stand to watch the results of his folly, and I don't blame him. Are you prepared to meet your doom?"

Nicole and Jonas had bet against the American landing. Martin had wagered a bottle of champagne against an hour of dancing with Nicole.

"I tremble with fear," she told him, "but I hope to survive the ordeal."

"Perhaps...we will see." Martin dismissed the officers at the table with a wave of his hand. "You fellows can scatter. She is all mine now." He went to the cloakroom to hang up his coat. When he returned Nicole was standing, waiting for him.

The phonograph was playing a slow, romantic tune from an old American film. Lieutenant Martin held her close as they danced, but not too tightly, permitting her to pull back from him if she wished. He whispered in her ear, keeping his tone light: "I think I could fall in love with you very easily."

Her own tone matched his. "I'm too young for you."

"But not for Jean-Jacques? I do see a certain odd logic in that. But he...he's a fine fellow and I like him—*he* is too old for you."

"I know it but what can I do? I'm crazy about him."

I've got to stop saying that, she thought. *It is becoming too real.*

Neither of them saw Jonas come in.

He stood watching them, the way Nicole moved, the way Lieutenant Martin was looking at her. A pang of jealousy upset him, though it no longer came as a surprise. There was no denying it: Annick was less and less in his thoughts, even when he slept in her bed. She was fading into the past, like Estelle. It was Nicole he had dreamed of, two nights ago. He was increasingly conscious of her sleeping presence in the next room.

She was nothing like her sister. As different from Annick as both were from Estelle.

Jonas contemplated the power of nature to heal old wounds and bring forth new appearances. Or was it a lack of constancy in his own nature? He didn't really care. He had lived too long with death; Nicole represented youth and new life. He was intoxicated by her.

Nicole was executing a turn in the arms of the lieutenant when she saw Jonas...and the way he was looking at her...and her heart lurched.

Late that evening the German High Command was scattered around Munich. The Supreme Commander, Adolf Hitler, was at his favorite restaurant, the Osteria Bavaria, sharing a screened-off table with a group of Nazi Party Gauleiters who had been among his staunchest original supporters. General Keitel and his staff were at work with their maps and directives in the command car of the Führersonderzug, in the Munich station. Bormann and General Jodl were using the phones at the Führer's quarters on Arcisstrasse to communicate with Berlin, Rome, Vichy and the German Armistice Commission at Wiesbaden— while military adjutants stood by to rush the most vital messages to Hitler.

One by one, the messages came through: Germany's special envoy to Vichy, Krug von Nidda, telephoned that in spite of the swift surrender of Algiers to the Allies, Marshal Pétain swore that the rest of French North Africa would continue to fight. As for any Allied threat against France itself, Pétain wished a personal note conveyed to Hitler: "I once more suggest you consider the advisability of France taking part in the protection of her own soil. I beg you to regard this as a sincere intention to enable the French to cooperate with you in defending the safety of Europe."

From Pierre Laval's *chef de cabinet*, Fernand de Brinon, came assurance that in response to Hitler's "request" Laval was on his way to Munich by limousine and would arrive the following afternoon.

The message from Rome was that Mussolini was ill but was sending Count Ciano to meet Hitler in his place. That would do; the Duce was certain to be enchanted by the prospect of Italy taking over part of southern France.

Grand Admiral Raeder, chief of Germany's naval forces, sent confirmation of the part he was to play in deceiving the French Navy into believing Toulon was not included in Hitler's take-over plans.

The most important messages of all were from the commander-in-chief (west), Field Marshal Rundstedt:

His First Army, commanded by General Glaskowitz, was taking up positions between the Loire and the demarcation line, preparatory to carrying out the first stage of Operation Anton.

Luftwaffe squadrons were already fueled and standing by to fly south and seize all military and civil airfields in the Unoccupied Zone. They would then make sure all French planes were grounded indefinitely, to prevent any observation of preparations for Operation Lila.

General Hausser had moved his SS Panzer Korps to temporary encampments outside Le Mans, southwest of Paris, where he would wait until the rest of France was occupied before starting his own move south toward Toulon.

Everything would be ready for Germany's forces to invade southern France by the night of November 10. Rundstedt would await the Führer's final order before setting the exact time of the invasion.

Jonas was certain the African landings meant that his mission was now about to break. But as he drove back to the house with Nicole he decided against another transmission. He had nothing urgent for Gibraltar, so it could wait until tomorrow morning.

"How about a late snack?" Nicole suggested when they entered the house.

"A small one. I'm not too hungry."

The inside of the house was cold. Nicole started a fire and Jonas went out to the storage shed to get more logs. When he carried them into the living room the kindling was blazing in the fireplace. Nicole sat on the carpet in front of it with her back against the sofa, staring into the flames. She did not look up when Jonas entered.

He set the logs down, then placed three of the driest on the fire. The fireplace had been built back in the days when they still knew how to make them properly. Little of the heat went up the chimney and the air inside the room was already turning warm. Jonas went into the entry hall to hang up his coat and jacket. When he returned, Nicole had taken off her jacket and tossed it on the sofa; she was still frowning into the fire.

Jonas added another log and turned as he straightened, looking down at her. The firelight made subtle changes in the structure of her face and gleamed on the silk of her blouse where it clung to the tips of her breasts.

"*I* can make that snack for us," he said.

She shook her head. "I'm not really hungry, either." Her voice was low.

"A drink?"

She smiled a little. "Nor thirsty."

He sat down beside her. The heat was intense against his face. The smell of burning wood was tinged with her scent.

"I think," she said slowly, "that it is time we stopped this nonsense."

"Which particular nonsense?"

"Don't joke right now," she told him fiercely. "You know what I'm talking about." She waited. When he didn't speak she started to get up to leave. She saw his face change and his hands caught her wrists. His grip was strong, not hurting her but when she tried to wriggle free he pulled her back down to him.

She struggled to get away from him, testing his strength and the strength of his desire for her, needing him to want her very much. He rolled her against the sofa, trapping her and holding her down until she lay limp and panting under him. Then he raised up, looming over her, looking down into her eyes. After a moment he made a sound that might have been a growl or merely a release of intolerable pressure, and let go of her wrists and began to unbutton her blouse.

He had been lusting for her and holding it back and now his reserve broke all the way. Her body was supple and strong and marvelously responsive. He made a feast of her and the sounds she made goaded him on and on.

When it happened it took her by surprise. Suddenly she felt herself back on that swing again, with Jonas pushing her high, screaming with fear and delight. But this time she stayed up so incredibly long her throat ached from shouting, and when she finally returned to earth, she was shuddering with startled pleasure and gasping air into her heaving lungs.

They lay quiet in each other's arms.

"My God..." he whispered.

"Oh yes..."

She pushed herself up on one elbow, looking down at him, her disheveled hair falling across his face. Her chuckle had a wicked edge. "Well... there is something to be said for age and experience."

His laugh was resonant with pleasure. He slapped her lightly across her buttocks. "Don't be impertinent."

She snuggled closer, her lips moving softly on his. He stroked her hair, the curve of her hip. But with possessive tenderness came other emotions.

"What about Dithelm?"

"You're the one making love to me."

"And when he is?"

Her answer was slow in coming. "I think it will be a long time before Dithelm and I can be together again... and only a short time I'll have with you."

"That is not sure."

"I know, nothing is. There is no decision that can be made now, Jonas. Or that needs to be. Perhaps later, when we see which of us are left when this war is over..."

"If any of us are." Jonas laughed softly. "You have a practical approach to problems."

"Is that how you see me?" Her voice was dreamy. "Practical?"

He didn't really care, if he was honest with himself, if she was being practical or impractical. All that mattered now was that he was the one who had her in his arms. He was prepared to take what joy he could, when he could.

His hands cupped her breasts and her nipples hardened under his palms. They explored each other for a time, lazily; they were so new to each other, with so much to discover. She bent and tasted his navel with the tip of her tongue. Her hand slid between his thighs, caressing. He started to tell her she'd have to learn to be more patient with him, that it would take longer before he was ready for her again.

But she surprised him... and then he surprised himself.

117

It was a few minutes after ten that night when the teleprinter at the headquarters of Field Marshal Rundstedt clattered with the order he had been waiting for:

Supreme Commander to Rundstedt

Number 974

TOP SECRET

Commence Operation Anton 11 November 0500 hours.
By order of the Führer

TWELVE NOVEMBER 9—MORNING

THE MAN STOOD in the same high tangle of pine trees from which Jonas had first reconnoitered Nicole Courtel's house. The early morning light had not yet penetrated the woods. Dark shadows of tree trunks and foliage crossed his figure, providing excellent camouflage while he inspected the house inside the walled estate below.

He was tall and thin, a man of forty with a hard, hawklike face and clever eyes. He wore a brown felt hat with a wide brim and gloves of supple leather which allowed his fingers complete freedom of movement. His trench coat was also of good leather, neatly tailored but loose fitting to conceal the bulge of the regulation pistol holstered on his left hip. His name was Andreas Keller.

The shutters of the house were still closed, and no smoke rose from the two chimneys. It was quite early, so that was not abnormal. There was a Citroën sedan in the parking space behind the house; no other vehicle was visible to Keller, in any direction. He looked toward the other house, at the far end of the estate. Smoke was now rising from one of its chimneys. That was the first sign of activity Keller had observed, inside the estate or in the surrounding area. He checked again, inspected the grove of trees separating the two houses, the woods outside the walls, the road that twisted up the hill to the locked gate.

As he looked again at the house directly beneath him the shutters of an upstairs window were flung open. Keller automatically drew back half a step. He made out a figure inside the upstairs window. It was gone before he could decide if it had been a man or a woman.

Some minutes later the downstairs shutters were opened, and soon smoke rose from the chimney at one end of the house. Keller remained in position, watching.

Jonas and Nicole shared a hearty breakfast seated close together so their arms and knees could continue to touch. They were sated from a night which hadn't included much sleep for either of them. Jonas drank a third cup of strong coffee before going out to make his radio contact with Gibraltar.

It was now some time since he had kept the radio up in the attic. Three days, he had learned in Paris, was the maximum safe period in any location before the Nazi mobile direction-finders closed in. He didn't know if there were units in the Toulon area yet, but it was a routine that had kept him alive so far and he stuck to it.

For the past three days Jonas had used an apartment in the old section of Toulon which belonged to a friend of Nicole's; he had gone to stay with an ailing father and left her the key. After his transmission the previous evening he'd taken the radio to a new location before going to the Narval.

Jonas scanned the woods when he emerged from the house, and again after unlocking the gate and stepping outside the estate wall. But he could detect no sign of anyone up there.

The radio was hidden in another part of the woods, half a mile from the house. Jonas started along the edge of the road in that direction.

Andreas Keller stepped out from behind the tree which had concealed him. One last time he looked down at the house and scanned the area around the estate. Then he set off in the same direction as Jonas, but staying inside the edge of the woods. When Jonas suddenly stopped and turned, Keller froze against the trunk of an umbrella pine. Jonas looked back along the

120

road and up into the woods again, then began climbing a path that led through the trees above the road.

Keller reached the path shortly after Jonas had disappeared, and climbed up after him, moving swiftly to catch up. After a minute Keller stopped and listened. In the silence of the woods, with the ground between the trees thickly covered by fallen branches and dead twigs, it was impossible to walk without making any noise at all. Keller heard Jonas moving away from the path, through the underbrush off to the right. Turning off the path, Keller went after him.

The second time he stopped to listen he couldn't hear anything. Keller stood still, waiting. After some seconds there was a dim sound off to his left: the snapping of a dry twig. Peering through the gloom of the woods in that direction, Keller made out a faint trail. He followed it, and after about twenty yards found himself on a knoll above a weed-choked ravine. Keller listened again, but there was no sound.

And then there was, directly behind him. Keller whirled but not quickly enough. Something struck him violently across the back of his head and he went down and out.

The man's hat had fallen into the ravine. He had wispy yellow hair and a wide bald spot on the crown of his head. Jonas crouched by his sprawling figure. The pockets of his trench coat were empty. He opened the coat, took the gun from the holster on the man's belt and went through the other pockets. There was a wallet with both French and German money. Jonas extracted a Nazi identity card.

Both the front and back bore the swastika-and-eagle stamp of the SS. The man's name was listed as Keller, Andreas. There was his photograph, birthdate and the serial number of his membership in RSHA—the Reich Central Security Office. The signatures of Himmler and his group leader endorsed his present rank: Keller was an over-inspector in section IV, subsection 3a. That was RSHA's counterintelligence.

When Keller came to Jonas was sitting on the ground beside him, holding his pistol.

"You're alive to answer questions," Jonas told him in a conversational tone. "First, naturally, is how you found out about me. But I'm also curious about why you came alone."

Keller said, "I came alone because two men you know instructed me to. One you know only by name, Paul Riley, an American." Keller's French was good and he spoke in a quick monotone, his eyes narrowed against the pain in the back of his neck. "The other is an Englishman who said to tell you the Ravel piece wouldn't be so good on an organ, anyway. I assume that is a private joke no one but the two of you would know about."

"Christ..."

"May I sit up?"

Jonas nodded but didn't put down the pistol.

Getting himself to the sitting position must have hurt but Keller was stoic about it. "Paul Riley and Michael Sandoe are being transferred to Algiers this afternoon. They weren't sure of hearing from you before they leave, so I have your instructions."

"I take it that means I'm about to go to work."

"Yes. It will take some time to fill you in on the necessary background. That is better done in person than by code transmissions."

"Is your RSHA card genuine?"

"Yes."

Jonas stood up and gestured with the pistol. "To your right there's a way into the ravine. You go first. Sorry, but I have to confirm."

"Naturally." Keller took time getting to his feet, and more getting his balance. Then he walked steadily to the point Jonas indicated and preceded him into the ravine. At the bottom he saw the low cave entrance concealed by a spur of rock.

Jonas moved sidewise to the cave and pointed to a spot ten feet away. "Sit there."

Keller lowered himself to the ground with his back to Jonas, so he would not be able to see the pistol pointed at him. He sat cross-legged with his hands under his thighs. Jonas pulled the wireless case from the cave and unwrapped the rubber coat which protected it against damp. He put the pistol down next to his knee, got the set ready and plugged in the power pack.

Opening his code book and notebook, Jonas got his pencil ready and began telegraphing his signal to Gibraltar. On the fifth try he received Michael's acknowledgment signal. Consulting the code book, Jonas tapped out the query about Keller, keeping it short.

Michael's answer was shorter and was immediately followed by his sign-off.

Keller remained motionless, gazing off in the other direction, while Jonas decoded Michael's message. Two words: "Trust him."

"All right," Jonas said, "we can both relax now."

Keller rose to his feet and turned to face him, touching the back of his neck delicately with his long, thin fingers. "What did you hit me with?"

"Forearm."

"Effective and painful." While Jonas put everything back in the radio case and rewrapped it in the coat, Keller went off to retrieve his hat. He smoothed his wispy hair before putting his hat back on. He sat down on the spur of rock, suddenly feeling his weariness. Jonas stuffed his wireless case back inside the low cave and handed over the pistol.

Keller stuck it into his belt holster and began briefing Jonas on Operation Anton. He confined himself at that point to its first phase. Jonas listened attentively, not interrupting, adjusting his thinking to this new information.

The basic information about Anton, Keller explained, had been passed on to him some time ago by a member of a small, secret anti-Nazi Catholic network inside the German Army's Operations Staff: A Beamtem officer in the administration office. Since this department, responsible for troop rations and payroll, worked with field units at every level, it had to be kept up to date on all army movements. Two days ago, Keller's man in administration had tipped him that Operation Anton was imminent and had been assigned to the First Army.

Keller's own RSHA assignment was to search for security

leaks in areas under Field Marshal Rundstedt's command, which gave him considerable freedom of movement. He'd immediately begun concentrating on the headquarters of the First Army's commander, General Blaskowitz. Rundstedt's order setting the date and hour for Anton had reached Blaskowitz at 10:30 the previous night, and Keller had gotten it minutes later from an air force liaison officer attached to the First Army HQ. Since Rundstedt's areas of authority—and thus Keller's—included Vichy France, he'd needed no excuse to start south at once. His RSHA rank had enabled him to make the all-night drive without being delayed by police and military roadblocks.

"You made good time," Jonas said.

"By driving *very* fast, although my night vision is not the best. I'm exhausted, and your knocking me out doesn't help."

"Take aspirin and a nap. What am I supposed to do about this information you've given me?"

"There is more." Keller filled him in on Operation Lila. "The date for Lila has not been set as yet, except that it is to be carried out shortly after the rest of southern France has been occupied by German and Italian troops. It is to prevent Lila from succeeding that you have been sent here. Hitler *must not* get his hands on the Toulon battle fleet."

Jonas was looking at Keller with a faint smile that held a mixture of skepticism and eager malice. "How do I stop him?"

"Your people want you to pass a warning about Operations Anton and Lila to one of the admirals in the Toulon naval base: Marquis or Laborde. Preferably the latter, since Laborde is the commander of the high-seas fleet. As soon as possible, before the phase of Anton is launched."

"That gives me less than two days. Do you have proof to go with this warning?"

"Unfortunately, no. Not yet, and I'm unlikely to get any real proof on time."

Jonas scowled at Keller. "Then neither Laborde nor Marquis will believe my warning. Certainly they won't act on it. Not without Pétain's permission, which they'll never get."

"As your people see it," Keller told him, "there are three

possibilities for preventing the fleet from being taken over by the Axis. First, they could try to destroy the fleet by bombing or via a commando operation."

"There are too many ships and men in the Toulon base for commando teams of any size to pull it off, even if they could get inside."

"True. As for bombing, the Axis has too many fighter aircraft protecting this area, in addition to the Toulon antiaircraft batteries. At present all of your Allied aircraft are needed in North Africa, and to lose any of them in a vain attempt on Toulon would be folly. Which brings us to the second option: that the French sail their fleet out of Toulon and join the Allies at Algiers."

"That they'll never do," Jonas said flatly. "Because they won't believe my warning, not until after it comes true, and then it will be too late."

Keller nodded. "Part of the Anton operation will be to bottle up the fleet inside the harbor, in preparation for Operation Lila. Which leaves the final option: the French scuttle their ships inside the harbor."

Jonas was staring at him, narrow-eyed, suppressing incredulity, weighing the possibility. "That's my mission? To get them to sink their entire fleet, themselves?"

"Every ship. But scuttling that many, some among the largest in the world, cannot be done on the spur of the moment. When Operation Lila strikes it will be swiftly. At that point it will be too late, *unless* the French have prepared for the scuttling in advance.

"Now, we are agreed that the Toulon admirals will not believe your warning about Operation Anton until after it has begun. But when it does, on the exact date and hour you warned them it would, they will have to consider the *possibility* that the second part of your warning may also be true: Operation Lila. We are hoping that will induce them to begin the necessary preparations for the scuttling."

"Preparing and carrying it out are two different things," Jonas said. "I'd have to give them *proof*."

"I will be trying my best to get that for you. Together with the precise time set for Lila, when that is decided. In fact, *this* is the crux of your mission. Your people will also convey the first warning to the admirals by radio. The delivery of your Anton warning to them, before it begins, is simply to establish your credentials, as it were. So that when they get your next warning, delivered in the same way, they will have reason to regard it very seriously indeed."

Keller paused to emphasize the point: "It is your second warning, coupled with evidence documenting the Operation Lila order, which will be crucial. If we can get that to the Toulon admirals, before Lila is executed, we hope they will do the only thing left for them to do, in order to save the French Navy from the total dishonor of letting Hitler take their fleet away from them."

"There are an unpleasant number of ifs to that hope."

"Yes, but it is all we have."

THIRTEEN

THERE WAS AN hour left before sunset when Nicole drove away from the house to meet Dithelm. She had spent the last half hour at the typewriter in the study, helping Jonas rephrase his warning note until each point was succinctly covered. He had walked her out to the car, and when she kissed him he held her tightly before letting her go. The look on his face had been a struggle between his sense of fairness and the fear of losing her.

"Don't worry," she told him, "I'll be back. Meet you at the Narval. And good luck."

Jonas just stood there and watched as she drove off, heading east along the coast toward Le Lavandou, the beach resort just below the southern edge of the Maures Massif.

Forty minutes later she and Dithelm were sitting close together on a bench that faced the beach, holding hands as they watched the sun dip into the sea. Nicole felt odd about it, and thought she should feel more guilty than she did. But she was too honest with herself to falsify her emotions. She was still young enough to relish finding herself desired by two such interesting and different men. At this stage there was no moral imperative to choose between them; it would only hurt one or the other, and herself. The war did create situations in which certain decisions were better postponed—and if it was wicked to enjoy the prolonging of this one, so be it.

They were both dangerous men: working with danger and feeding on it, and pulling her to the edge of it with them, and she wondered if that was one source of the intense excitement they stirred in her. She couldn't be sure, she didn't know that much about herself yet. She was still exploring herself; being in love with two men was a newly discovered world, utterly unexpected.

If her kiss, when she met Dithelm, lacked her former passion, he had been too tense to notice: nervous about being out in the open like this, after so long concealed in the Maures forests. He was thin and haggard, older looking than his twenty-six years.

"You look undernourished," she told him. "Have you been eating enough?"

Dithelm smiled. "Not high cuisine, but enough. It is lack of sleep mostly. Having to worry for the others, as well as myself. Having to shift our hiding place regularly, because of Milice search patrols." Dithelm squeezed her hand and kissed her cheek. "Don't worry. I'm all right."

There was a large poster on a billboard near their bench. It showed a badly wounded French soldier moving on crutches through a bombed-out village, with a frightened woman holding her baby in the ruins of a house, while an arrogant British officer grinned down at them from the sky. The headline proclaimed: "It is the English who did this to us!" Above the poster was a Vichy government notice: "The Prefecture of Police warns that anyone defacing these official posters will be considered to have committed an act of sabotage against the Authorities and will receive the most severe punishment."

Yet, someone had painted across the poster: "If we let the Germans shit on us, the Allies have to clean up the mess!"

"Is it you who painted that little message?" Nicole asked Dithelm.

"Some of the youngest boys in my group. I can only warn them to be aware of how dangerous it is and to be careful. But they are not running any greater risk than all of us have to. And will continue to, until the Nazis are swept from my fatherland as well as the rest of Europe."

"Your fatherland—you can still think of it as that, in spite of everything going on there?"

"It *is* my fatherland…my country. I love it deeply. If I did not, I wouldn't hate what the Nazis have made of it."

Nicole told him, then, that the German army would begin an invasion of southern France in less than two days—though she didn't tell him about the second phase, Operation Lila.

His excitement was intense: "I hope you added that to the rest of the information in the briefcase?"

She nodded. "It's there." She told him some of the details. He didn't ask how she had learned about it. That was her major usefulness to Dithelm's group: her ability to use her position on *Toulon-Matin,* and her acquaintance with Vichy officials, to obtain secret information, or news the rest of the country wouldn't learn until much later. Though his group had begun to carry out occasional acts of sabotage against establishments owned by collaborator businessmen, its most important function was distributing anti-Vichy leaflets and a four-page underground newspaper called *Vérité Sud.* These were turned out on a hand press Dithelm had "liberated" from a profascist printing plant in Toulon and transported into the Maures.

Nicole's briefcase contained items she'd written for his leaflets and paper, drawn from the latest inside information. These included a rundown on the equipment being stripped from French factories for transport to Germany and a secret Vichy-Berlin agreement to ship a major portion of France's farm produce to Germany, which was going to mean a hungry winter for the French.

"I haven't been able to find out who informed to the Gestapo about your last shipment of leaflets to Toulon," Nicole told Dithelm. "Have you learned anything more?"

"No. But it had to be one of my Toulon contacts who betrayed us. That was another reason for changing our hiding place. And I've cut off communication with all of them. This leaves you as my only contact there. I'm going to need your help with something else before long. The next two issues of *Vérité Sud* will use up most of the paper I have left. We'll need more."

Nicole said, "*Toulon-Matin* has plenty of it."

He smiled at her, but it was an automatic smile, his mind occupied, calculating. "Exactly my thought. Check the warehouse they store it in for me: how well it is guarded, police movements in the area, difficulties of breaking in and getting away..."

Dithelm fell silent, working out something else. He was changing, Nicole decided: becoming more used to his new role as a quasi-military leader. If he survived long enough, she thought, he was going to become very good at it.

"If the Nazis occupy the south it will alter everything down here. Including the nature of our Resistance. We will need better arms, and more of them, along with a great deal more ammunition. Make some careful inquiries for me, try to find out where the Toulon Milice have their armory. I'll need the same information as with the paper warehouse: nature of the building, guards, entry and escape routes."

Nicole kept her voice steady. "If you escalate your activities into real warfare they'll retaliate in kind, Dithelm...and not only against you. Against everyone suspected of Resistance sympathies."

"That is inevitable anyway, once Hitler's troops take over this area. We have to prepare for the change. Get that information for me, Nicole. Based on that, I'll decide which to strike for first: the arms or the paper."

Nicole's mouth had gone dry. "Be very careful, Dithelm. I told you about that Gestapo agent recruiting informers..."

"There will be more Gestapo before long, and more informers. I want to get in my first strike before they are too many." He was silent for a moment, thinking again. "I'm almost certain now, I'll want to go for the arms first. With the best men I've got. I'll slip them into Toulon a few at a time. We'll need to use your house, Nicole...as a safe place to rendezvous before the raid, and to hide in afterwards, before returning to the Maures."

Nicole nodded. She would have to warn Jonas when the time came.

"Some very good new men have joined me recently," Dithelm told her. "Even an English pilot! Reginald Lear, and he calls

130

himself *Reggie*, can you imagine?" he laughed. "Only an Englishman could choose such a ridiculous nickname. He was captured after his plane crashed and put into Fort Revère. But he escaped and was trying to get to Spain through this area when he found us. Now he's not so eager to get to Spain. I think he finds our kind of war more romantic."

Nicole was frowning, remembering something Jonas told her: "There's an English traitor who may be operating for the Gestapo somewhere here in the south, posing as an RAF pilot."

"Do you have any information on what he looks like?"

"Reddish hair, bushy mustache..."

Dithelm smiled. "Reggie's nothing like that. And he has already proved himself. He shot a member of the Milice patrol that came so close to the last hideout we had to leave; and he helped us get away from the rest. A good man. He'll definitely be one of those I bring with me, when we come to Toulon."

The sun was gone. They sat together and watched the darkness spread across the sea.

"I wished to reach a definite city on the River Volga, in the very heart of Soviet Russia," Hitler told the faithful Party stalwarts packed into Munich's Loewenbräukeller. "That city happens to bear the name of Stalin himself...I wished to *take* that city...And now, I can tell you that we *have* taken it! Stalingrad is captured! It is ours!"

The uniformed Gauleiters inside the beer hall stamped their boots and pounded their steins on the tables as they roared their approval. They went on stamping and pounding and their cheers became a chant, repeated over and over:

"God protect our Führer! Germany has unlimited faith in you!"

Pierre Laval, chain-smoking as he paced miserably outside, could hear their howling. He shuddered as he continued his nervous pacing, a smallish, pudgy figure who never looked well dressed no matter how expensive his clothing, his invariable white necktie askew and his dark, vaguely oriental eyes drooping with fatigue and anxiety. The mob in the streets around him took up the chanting from inside, though they didn't know exactly what it was for. That didn't matter to them, they were cheering for their magical leader.

I am trapped among howling maniacs, Laval thought. An SS lieutenant walked silently beside him. The French premier could not bear to look at him: a huge young fellow with the features of a Neanderthal brute and hands that could rip a man's arms from their sockets. Assigned to "guide and protect" him, Bormann had said. More likely to keep him from running away.

Laval had arrived in the afternoon, weary from the long drive. He was more than weary now, and no wiser about why Hitler had sent for him. Except that the German leader was furious at the failure of French troops in Africa to throw the Allies back into the sea—furious at the swift fall of Algiers—furious at reports that the rest of French North Africa was likely to collapse soon—furious.

Laval had tried to reassure him that Pétain would continue to refuse his permission for any French surrender, anywhere. He'd reminded Hitler that he, Laval, had personally said over the French radio that he hoped for a German victory over the English.

"Ah yes," Hitler answered, "but now that the Americans have joined the English your hopes may be changeable."

"You can trust," Laval swore, "in my continuing faith in Germany."

"How can anyone trust a man so tricky his name is the same spelled backward or forward?"

Laval forced a titter at the joke, though he had grown sick of all its variations long ago as a child.

Hitler did not laugh. His eyes bulged with a fixity that sent shivers along Laval's spine. Country people in his part of France said when you shivered like that someone was walking on your grave.

Laval was terrified of Hitler, and of his own uncertainty about what was really on the man's mind. It was this terror which had impelled him to sew a cyanide capsule into his lapel before coming to Munich.

A feisty, tough-minded man used to handling trouble, Laval felt capable of facing a simple, swift execution, if fate brought him to that. But Hitler's executions were sometimes neither simple nor swiftly over with.

Inside the beer hall the maniacs were screaming again. The Roman Colosseum must have sounded like that, Laval thought, when Nero ordered a batch of captives to be thrown in among wild pigs and hunger-maddened lions. He fingered the poison capsule in his lapel and prayed he would not have to use it; prayed that if he did have to he would be able to use it quickly enough.

Lighting another of the cigarettes which had yellowed his teeth and stained his fingers brown, Laval continued to walk back and forth through the shouting mob, not looking at the SS lieutenant marching in silence beside him.

What *was* it Hitler had brought him here for?

Jonas was playing poker when Lieutenant Roger Martin came into the Narval. He was a bit tipsy again, after visits to other bars to collect his winnings from losers he'd missed the night before. Taking off his coat as he came through the game room, he stopped by the table as Jonas lost a hand and paid the winner.

"How are the cards treating you?"

"Not too well tonight."

"Chess is harder on the nerves but easier on the pocketbook."

"You're on." Jonas took what was left of his money and went to get a chessboard and pieces while Lieutenant Martin took his coat into the cloakroom.

Jonas glanced toward the Narval's entrance but Nicole was still not there. He took an empty table and when Martin returned from the cloakroom they set up the pieces. There were officers playing chess at two other tables but they were amateurs. Lieutenant Martin, drunk or sober, was not. He took two pieces, hid them under the table, then raised his closed fists. Jonas tapped his left fist, got the white piece and opened with a classic pawn-to-king-four.

The game didn't stay classic long. The lieutenant let Jonas

take control of the center squares and started an unorthodox but effective attack on white's castled king. Jonas got his defense solidified, and while Martin took time to ponder his next move he went to the bathroom to wash his hands. Jonas then stepped into the cloakroom, took an envelope from his pocket and stuck it into an inside pocket of Lieutenant Martin's coat. Then he went back to the game.

People went in and out through the cloakroom while their chess battle continued over the next hour and a half. There was no way Martin could decide who had left him the envelope, even if he found it before leaving the Narval. Jonas had won the first game and was losing the second when he saw Nicole come in. He conceded defeat and got up to join her.

"How was Dithelm?" he asked, with more tension than he'd intended.

Nicole eyed him mockingly. "Do you want to fight or dance?"

He relaxed, smiling. "Neither. I want to take you home to bed."

"In that case..." She waved to Roger, kissed Olga good night, took Jonas by the hand and went out to the car with him.

Roger Martin was definitely drunk when he left the Narval with just enough time left to get back to the base by the regulation hour. A taxi delivered him to the Castigneau Gate, and after showing his ID to the sentries he made his way carefully through the dark labyrinth of the West Arsenal to the bachelor officers' quarters near the depot between the submarine docks and the Milhaud piers. Climbing a flight of stairs to his room, the lieutenant stripped off his clothes and fell into bed without discovering the envelope Jonas had planted in his coat.

FOURTEEN NOVEMBER 10

CAPTAIN LAMBERT LOOKED troubled when he stepped from the submarine *Casabianca* onto the military quay and walked back toward his own sub, the *Orion*. Beyond it, along the Milhaud piers, the superstructures of some of the greatest ships of the French fleet rose higher than any building in the base: the flagship *Strasbourg*, the *Colbert*, the *Algérie*, the *Marseillaise* and five others. Off to the left the rest of the big ones loomed against the early morning sky, at their moorings inside the Missiessy Basin, out along the Quay Noël and around the Vauban drydocks. They'd all been stuck there in the same positions for so long Lambert felt it was like walking through a neighborhood one knew too well, where the surrounding buildings were no longer noticed because they never changed.

He noticed today because of the unusual activity already beginning around them.

The possible motives of the conqueror for all this activity was what Lambert had been trying to figure out with Captain L'Herminier, commander of the *Casabianca*. Late yesterday the Axis Armistice Commission had unexpectedly ordered all vessels of the fleet refitted for sea.

In response to this order both the *Orion* and the *Casabianca* were scheduled to be towed across to the Mourillon Arsenal for repairs. These included replacement of their hatches and periscopes, previously removed to insure they could not submerge or even operate on the surface in rough waters. Why the sudden change? Suspicion about one motive which could explain Germany's unexpected eagerness to get the fleet ready for use nagged at Captain Lambert as he climbed back aboard his own submarine.

His first lieutenant, Roger Martin, was waiting for him on the bridge of the *Orion*, his face dark with worry. That was most unusual: Martin was a serious, reliable officer, but liked to play at being lighthearted no matter what difficulties cropped up. When Lambert reached him, Martin handed over a creased envelope.

"I just found this inside my coat, captain. I opened it, because I thought it might be some kind of joke. Now I'm not so sure of that."

The envelope was addressed to Admiral de Laborde. Lambert asked his first officer: "Who gave you this?"

"I havé no idea, captain. Someone could have stuck it in my coat while I was ashore yesterday, but I had eight hours liberty and I was in too many places to even hazard a guess. It might even have happened here inside the base. I never lock the door of my room." It wasn't entirely a truthful answer. The truth was that he didn't know who had put the envelope in his coat; but he was fairly certain it had been done while he was at the Narval. He'd searched his pockets for a cigar on the way there; and after leaving the Narval he'd come directly back to the base. He was quite sure nobody could have slipped into his room without waking him, and he'd discovered the envelope before going out for breakfast. Martin said: "I think you should read what's inside it, sir."

Captain Lambert took out the sheet of paper and unfolded it:

"In violation of the armistice agreement he signed with Marshal Pétain, Hitler has ordered his forces to cross the demarcation line and occupy all of southern France. This German invasion will begin at five o'clock on the morning of November 11. At the same time Italian forces will invade from the southeast. Assurances will be given that Toulon and the French fleet in its harbor will remain inviolate. However, once the Axis has the rest of southern France, Germany plans to take both Toulon and the fleet. The date for this second move has not yet been determined. When it is, I will send another warning, using the same channel, together with evidence to prove it.

"But the only real chance to save the French fleet is to sail it out of Toulon. Now, before the Axis makes such a move impossible."

The message, like the name on the envelope, had been typed. But Jonas had signed it with a pen, so his next warning would be easily identifiable as coming from the same source; and he had signed it with his own first name.

Lambert looked up. "This name 'Jonas' means nothing to you?"

Lieutenant Martin shook his head. "I don't know anyone by that name."

The captain refolded the message and put it back in the envelope. "I think you had better come with me."

Admiral Jean de Laborde was known as "Count Jean" in higher navy circles because of his imperious manner toward subordinates, occasionally even toward equals. He was on the phone from his flagship headquarters to Admiral Auphan, the minister of the navy in Vichy, and his tone was coolly disdainful. "There is no need for you to tell me every single detail of every communication between Vichy and Algiers and Munich. *Can* you simply get to the point?"

"We are in a rapidly changing situation," Auphan replied angrily. "Unless you fully understand all the ramifications, how can..."

"I do understand," Laborde interrupted sharply. "Fully."

And he did. Admiral Darlan, whom Marshal Pétain had appointed chief of all Vichy armed forces, had gone to Algiers to see his ailing son just before the surprise Allied landings and was now virtually a prisoner of the Americans in the Hotel Saint-Georges. Early that morning Darlan had radioed Vichy asking permission to arrange an armistice that would end all further fighting between French forces and the Americans in North Africa.

Pétain had telephoned Munich to ask Laval's advice. Laval had warned that if the marshal authorized Darlan to make such an armistice he, Laval, would immediately resign from the French government—and Hitler would consider it an injury for which all of France would suffer. Pétain had then made an open radio broadcast ordering that the fight against the Allied invasion of North Africa must continue.

In response, Darlan had sent another message, in a code known only to the highest officers of the French Navy, warning that the Axis was preparing to occupy the Vichy zone of southern France. Hitler's ultimate objective, Darlan added, was the seizure of the Toulon fleet. Pétain had tried to consult Laval by phone about this second message, but for some reason could no longer get him in Munich.

"But obviously," the naval minister said, "the Americans pressured Darlan into sending such a message, to sow confusion among us and discord between us and Germany."

"Obviously," Admiral Laborde agreed coldly. He had no love for Admiral Darlan, who had twice been responsible for his being passed over for promotion to the highest post in the navy. First, Darlan had been made chief of the navy, instead of Laborde. Later, when Darlan had been promoted to commander of all armed forces, he had seen to it that Laborde had been passed over again, in spite of being the logical choice by virtue of experience.

Laborde didn't blame Marshal Pétain for this. The marshal was inexperienced in politics, while Darlan was a master at it, difficult to outmaneuver when he was after something. And what he was after, Laborde had long suspected, was ultimately to become head of France. For Laborde the navy was everything; for Darlan it was a stepping stone, and Laborde loathed him for that.

"The important thing now," Auphan told him over the phone, "is not to let Darlan's moment of panic tempt us into thinking of moving the fleet out of Toulon. It *must* stay where it is."

"If *that* is the point of your call," Laborde replied furiously, "I don't need to be instructed on elementary..."

Navy Minister Auphan cut him short: "Marshal Pétain himself wishes to speak with you about this, admiral. Please hold on..."

Laborde automatically came to his feet, straightened his back and squared his shoulders as he waited for the chief of state to come on the line. Marshal Pétain was France's most respected military leader, a man for whom duty was always the first consideration. He was also the head of the government of France. No military organization could function without unquestioning obedience to authority. For Laborde the marshal was the personification of that authority, and his allegiance to him remained absolute.

Marshal Pétain came on the line: "Admiral, I regret that circumstances make it necessary for me to demand of you at this moment." His voice was firm and dignified as ever. Though some who hadn't met the marshal thought of him as a frail old man, Laborde knew better: Pétain remained stronger of body and spirit than most men twenty years his junior. "I must ask for your oath," Pétain went on, "that you will make *no* move, now or in the future, without a direct order from me. Please do not be offended. I have asked this of every high officer of our armed forces."

"I am not offended, marshal. It is your right to ask this. You have my word of honor, as a loyal officer."

"Good, good...I know I can depend on you, admiral. Please give my fondest regards to your lovely wife."

After hanging up, Laborde sat down slowly and stared across his mahogany desk at the map on the wall of his admiralty headquarters. With bitter envy he thought of the sort of maps British admirals, and now American admirals, would have in the command cabins aboard their flagships: maps of the battle formations of their fleets, sailing the oceans on which they were engaged in combat. Admiral Laborde's map was of the Toulon Bay, and the position of each ship of his fleet inside it, frozen to the docks.

He was more disturbed by Darlan's messages than he'd cared

to reveal to Auphan. Darlan always did what he thought was best for Darlan. He was the ultimate opportunist; and his dislike of England and belief in German victory was even greater than Laborde's. Admiral Laborde did not believe Darlan could have been forced against his will to send those messages favoring the Allies. If Darlan was prepared to switch sides, then he now considered it possible that the Allies might win the war.

That was a possibility Laborde could not bear to contemplate.

He hated the English. He had to hate them, and to hope Germany would beat them. Admiral Laborde was a lucid man who understood clearly that Hitler's Germany could not be defeated, nor even withstood. France had been sensible enough to accept this fact, early enough to save itself from a bloodbath. As Pétain had said at the time of surrender, too many Frenchmen had died in the first world war to permit it to happen again—and this time in a war already lost anyway.

But the British stubbornly and illogically had refused to accept the obvious and had gone on fighting. And were still fighting. Their navy was still engaged in active battles, a *fighting* navy.

If, in the end, Hitler did not crush England...if the English had chosen the right course...it would mean that France had chosen the wrong course. If de Gaulle and the few other disloyal officers who had followed him to England had acted correctly, then Laborde and the overwhelming majority of French officers who remained loyal to the Vichy government were acting incorrectly—even with what many would regard as cowardly impotence. That could not be true; it could not be allowed to become true. It would be a shameful humiliation which Laborde could not face.

He reassured himself. Germany *would* win, of course. France, having acted in a practical manner, would become a strong and respected part in Hitler's united Europe.

But, now that the Americans had vigorously entered the war, that became a little less certain.

And Admiral Laborde now hated America almost as intensely as he did England...

140

Shouting from the corridor outside broke into Laborde's thoughts. He looked up sharply as his chief adjutant, Captain Pacome, appeared. "What the hell is that?"

"Admiral, it's Captain Lambert of the submarine *Orion,* with one of his officers. I explained that you are far too occupied at the moment to see them, but Lambert insists."

There was a shout from Lambert: "I won't go away! I have to see the admiral, immediately!"

Laborde gestured and his adjutant called to Lambert. He entered with a young officer whom he introduced as Lieutenant Martin, his first officer. "I'm sorry, admiral, but Martin has found a message in his coat that I think you should have a look at."

"I must tell you," Laborde snapped, "your behavior is most unseemly and will not be forgotten. All right, give it to me." He took the envelope from Captain Lambert and read the message inside. Again, almost exactly the same as the warning from Darlan. Sheer Allied propaganda. He glared at Martin. "What does that mean, you *found* this. Who gave it to you?"

The lieutenant's reply was the same he'd given Captain Lambert: he had no idea who'd slipped the note in his coat; it could have been done anywhere, inside the base where his room was never locked, or outside at any of the many places he'd visited yesterday during his liberty period.

Laborde regarded him in stony silence for several seconds. "Lieutenant, I want the truth. Are you in contact with subversive elements?"

Lieutenant Martin held himself at rigid attention. "No, admiral, I am not. I give you my *word.* I don't know who that message came from."

Captain Lambert spoke up for him: "Lieutenant Martin is an excellent officer, admiral, utterly dependable and loyal to the French Navy. I vouch for him."

"In that case I will hold you personally responsible for his actions." Laborde crumpled the warning and threw it at his wastebasket. It bounced off the edge and rolled across the floor. "That garbage is either a prankster's hoax or an enemy trick.

One or the other. But I accept your explanation, for the moment. Dismissed!"

As Lambert and Martin left, Laborde's adjutant picked up the crumpled note to drop it into the wastebasket. But Laborde growled: "Give it to me. And get me the navy minister on the phone."

When he was connected with Admiral Auphan in Vichy, Laborde read him the message and explained the circumstances surrounding it.

"I'll have navy intelligence make a careful check on Lieutenant Martin," Auphan told him, "and keep an eye on his movements from now on."

"Good. That's why I didn't have him confined to quarters. He just may lead us to whoever gave him that provocative message."

That afternoon the *Orion* and the *Casabianca* were towed from the West Arsenal, across the Toulon inner roads to the auxiliary submarine facilities in the Mourillon Arsenal. Four other subs were already docked there beginning the repairs needed to make them seaworthy: the *Venus, Marsoulin, Iris* and *Glorieux.* As the *Orion* neared its new moorings, Captain Lambert spoke quietly to his first lieutenant.

"By tomorrow morning we'll know if that warning is a hoax. If it's not...tell me the truth, in confidence, would you be able to make contact with whoever sent it?"

Martin answered just as quietly: "I think I know a way to do it, captain."

"I rather thought so. Be ready to try it, just in case."

That night Hitler finally told Laval of his intention to occupy the remainder of France—except for Toulon. He explained some of his reasons and asked Laval how he thought France would react to the move.

Laval experienced a brief dizziness of relief. He was not going to have to die, after all, if he conducted himself with delicacy. "France will do what Marshal Pétain tells it to," he said with a restored assurance. "I myself will phone the marshal to explain that he must give in to your wishes, in the best interests of our country and its citizens. In any case," Laval added, "whatever the marshal decides, I think you should go ahead with it, if you feel it has now become necessary."

"I do." Hitler smiled at Laval for the first time since the French premier had arrived in Munich. "I was sure I could depend on you, Laval. But we will wait a little longer before you place that call to Pétain. Until tomorrow morning, just before dawn. I will have one of my adjutants wake you, with coffee, in plenty of time."

The coffee would undoubtedly be welcome, but Laval knew he would not have to be wakened. He didn't expect any sleep that night.

FIFTEEN NOVEMBER 11

AT 5 A.M. IN Vichy, Marshal Pétain's valet entered the sumptuous bedroom of the chief of state. He switched on a lamp and approached the bed carrying a silver tray on which rested a cup of coffee.

The old man struggled to wake up, the few wisps of his white hair askew around his shiny bald head. He braced himself against the brocade-padded headboard. "What is it?" he whispered groggily.

His valet knelt beside the bed with the tray. "I am sorry, marshal. The German ambassador is here, with a letter for you from Hitler. He says it is imperative that you read it at once. Shall I fetch your robe, sir?"

Pétain took the tray and set it on his legs as the last mists of sleep fled from his brain. "No. I'll get dressed. Tell Abetz to wait."

"But he..."

"Tell him to wait," the marshal repeated firmly.

"Yes, sir."

Less than ten minutes later Marshal Pétain entered his waiting room wearing his dress uniform with its seven stars on each sleeve and a single military decoration on his breast, the ribbon of the Médaille Militaire. His step was steady, his figure erect, his eyes alert. It was still dark outside and every lamp in the room blazed, their lights shining on his face. It was a remarkable face for a man in his mid-eighties: firmly-fleshed, with a healthy color and no wrinkles.

The German ambassador to France, Otto Abetz, rose to his feet holding an envelope bearing Hitler's official seal. Pétain's chief military aide, who had arrived with him, was already standing at attention. With a slight bow, Abetz handed the letter to Pétain, who took it without a word.

In it Hitler cited the threat to both their countries posed by the Anglo-American landings on the other side of the Mediterranean. Because of this it had now become necessary for German forces to occupy southern France and its coastline, in order to protect it against Allied aggression. Hitler assured Pétain that this move, which would begin before dawn this morning, would in no way affect the status of the Vichy government. The military occupation forces would continue to accord full respect to Pétain's authority over civil matters in his portion of France.

The marshal fixed Abetz with a cold stare. "As French chief of state I protest this invasion of Unoccupied France! It is a naked violation of Hitler's sworn word, and of the armistice treaty which bears his signature!"

"Please understand the Führer's motives," the German ambassador told him blandly. "French military forces are not equal to defending your country against an Anglo-American attack. Some of your highest officers have already proved themselves unreliable. Admiral Darlan and General Giraud are examples. Under these circumstances Germany is forced to undertake the protection of French soil. That is the purpose of our move, to which the Führer hopes you will give your cooperation and consent."

"My consent? According to this note your forces have already *begun* this invasion!"

"They have begun to move," Abetz agreed, "but they will not reach the demarcation line until dawn. By then the Führer hopes you will have..."

He was interrupted by the ringing of the phone. Pétain's aide answered it and then held out the phone to the marshal. "It is Laval, calling from Munich."

Pétain seized the phone, and without waiting for Laval to speak told him harshly: "I wish you to convey immediately my formal protest to Hitler, personally. You will tell him..."

"Please!" Laval's cry sounded on the edge of hysteria. "There is no time left for this nonsense, marshal. We both know our French forces cannot possibly defend themselves against the Allies—or against the might of Germany. You have to act quickly, now, to save France. I have spoken with Hitler and I can assure you he has made this decision solely to protect our country from the enemy. Not a shot must be fired to prevent this. If there is *any* attempt by our forces to stop the Germans, France will be destroyed! We'll wind up as another ruined Poland!"

Pétain's aide watched an expression come over the marshal's face that was often there when Laval lectured him: an uneasiness which gradually changed to a kind of puzzled fear. When Pétain put down the phone he was finally showing his age, and a deep weariness. "Very well," he told Abetz in a voice which had lost its strength, "I do understand the circumstances which have forced Hitler to take this measure. I cannot but submit to his decision. But I *must* make an official and public protest."

"Do so," the German ambassador conceded quickly. "But first I beg you to take the steps necessary to prevent bloodshed between our two countries."

Within minutes Marshal Pétain's order was being transmitted from Vichy to all French military and police units south of the demarcation line: they were to surrender themselves to the invaders; there was to be no attempt to oppose them. A short time later the marshal repeated his orders in a radio broadcast to the French people. Any resistance, he warned, would be fatal for France.

There was no resistance. In obedience to Pétain, French forces and military installations surrendered themselves as soon as the invaders appeared. Advance motorized units of the German First Army swept south unopposed, so swiftly that by late the following day all of southern France would be in their hands. But designated German air force formations were even swifter. By the afternoon of Operation Anton's first day, the Luftwaffe was in control of every French airfield, including those around Toulon.

Vice-Admiral Marquis, Toulon's maritime prefect, left his headquarters at Fort Lamargue and was driven down the hill below to the Mourillon Arsenal. From there he was taken by launch across the Toulon inner roads, past the commercial port and the Vieille Darse, to the flagship *Strasbourg* docked at the West Arsenal. The *Strasbourg*'s captain had him piped aboard and conducted to Admiral Laborde. As soon as they were alone, the two admirals settled down to discuss what to do about the rapid approach of the Wehrmacht's forces.

They had reached no acceptable answer when a phone call came through from Navy Minister Auphan. Laborde took the call after gesturing for Marquis to listen on the phone extension.

"I've been in communication with Grand Admiral Erich Raeder," Auphan reported from Vichy. "I put the question to him: Will Germany guarantee to keep its hands off the French navy? His reply was a counterquestion: Will you and Marquis guarantee to defend your harbor and fleet against the Allies if they should attack there?"

"It's our duty," Laborde reminded him, "to defend our fleet and our territory against an attack by *anyone*."

"I don't need a lecture on duty, Laborde, I need a straight answer. Raeder wants your guarantee worded as he's put it, and he wants it in writing, from both of you. If we give him that, along with a repetition of your promise that the fleet will remain where it is, Raeder will see to it that the Wehrmacht will not enter Toulon nor attempt to seize the fleet."

"What does the marshal want me to do?"

"He feels we must give an affirmative reply."

"That's all you had to tell me. Raeder will get his guarantee. In writing."

Marquis waited until Laborde put down the phone. Then he hung up the extension and growled, "Sure, we have no choice.

148

But that doesn't stop my thinking about that warning you got through Lieutenant Martin. The first part has certainly turned out to be true, down to the exact day and hour. Makes you wonder about the second part, no matter what the Germans guarantee."

"We have to assume it is still part of an English trick," Laborde said. "It's an *old* trick. You happen to learn a man's wife is unfaithful to him. You tell him this—and add a lie: that his mistress is about to leave him. When the first part proves true, he'll be inclined to believe the second part, the lie. *We* have to be on guard against being so easily hookwinked."

Marquis shrugged. "Anyway, we have to obey the marshal's orders. So, as I said, no choice."

After Marquis left the flagship, Laborde received another call from Vichy; this one was from Marshal Pétain. Laborde rose to his feet as he took the call.

"You have my utmost sympathy, marshal," Laborde told him sincerely. "This day is a difficult one for you."

"A difficult day for *France*," Pétain corrected him. "What I have to suffer means little in comparison. I have simply had to carry out my duty, that is all. The moral concessions I've been required to make are repugnant to me, but I gladly take that shame on myself to save France from terrible reprisals. I'm sure you understand: we have no hope of resisting Hitler's demands. We must give in, and save what we can."

"I do understand, sir. I'm sure all of France does."

"Some will not. But my conscience belongs to God and my honor to none but myself. *I* know I have done what is best for my country." With an abrupt shift in tone, Pétain asked, "Have you heard anything further from Darlan?"

"Not since yesterday, marshal."

"You may. I called to warn you. Darlan has finally revealed himself as worse than a scoundrel. He has now become a *rebel*—against military discipline and against the government of his country. He has ignored my orders and concluded a treaty to join our North African forces with the Americans, against the Axis!"

"My God..." Laborde was stunned by the enormity of what

149

Darlan had done. Opportunism was one thing, but this was outright *treason*—there was no other word for it. The worst thing of which a military officer could be accused; worse even than cowardice.

"I am preparing a formal declaration," Pétain continued, "stripping Darlan of French citizenship. So if there are any further communications from him you must regard them as coming from a man without a country. His action has endangered all of France. Hitler is furious with us, understandably. To save France from his wrath I am forced to make further moral concessions to him. This is a sacrifice I make for my country. Any dishonor, I take on myself."

"There is no dishonor for you, marshal," Laborde told him with emotion that would have surprised those who considred him a cold man. "Quite the opposite, sir. This is *duty,* as you and I understand it."

Less than ten minutes after the call from Pétain, Admiral Laborde's chief communications officer brought him a message just received by wireless from Darlan in Algiers. "It was sent in our private code, admiral." As decoded in the *Strasbourg*'s communications center it read:

"Darlan to Laborde—The German violation of the armistice agreement releases French officers from any further obligation to honor it. In occupying the Vichy zone of France the Germans have also in effect made Marshal Pétain their prisoner. I remind you of the standing military rule that troops must not accept orders from a superior officer who is a captive of the enemy. As his legal successor it is now up to me to act in his place for the good of France. I have an agreement with the American Generals Eisenhower and Clark, for whom Vichy no longer exists as a government. We are going to join them and fight the Germans.

"Marshal Pétain, forced by his captors to say things with which his heart does not agree, will of course publicly condemn me for my actions. It is a game which must be repulsive to our former chief, whose conscience is entirely clear. Acting in accord with what I know to be his true inner wish, I ask the high seas fleet to leave Toulon now, while a few hours yet remain, and sail out to join me and the Americans.

"Long Live Marshal Pétain!"

Laborde's smile was sardonic as he lowered the message. "A masterpiece of double-talk," he told his communications officer.

"Will there be any reply, admiral?"

"Yes." Laborde wrote swiftly on a sheet of paper and gave it to him. The communications officer couldn't suppress a grin at the brief, unequivocal answer:

"Laborde to Darlan: *Merde!*"

The message was encoded and sent. Admiral Laborde kept the French fleet, the fourth most powerful in the world, where Pétain had ordered it to remain, inside the Toulon Naval Base. By that evening the last chance to slip out was gone.

In the clear cold twilight seaplanes of Germany's Luftflotte began appearing over Toulon. They came from the east: the naval air base at Hyères, which had been taken over by the Germans several hours ago. They came in pairs, flying low over the bay, checking to insure that none of the ships of the French fleet were attempting to move from their docks.

From the terrace of Nicole's house, she and Jonas watched the first pair turn back to the east as a second pair flew in to take over the low-level patrol. "There's something going on around the entrance to the bay," Jonas said. Groups of work-boats were moving back and forth between the tip of the Mourillon cape and the Mandrier peninsula, but she couldn't make out what they were doing. She went inside to get the binoculars.

They hung in a closet of the study, next to her father's old hunting shotgun, the only weapon of her father's she hadn't given away. Nicole didn't like guns; but the shotgun was a beautiful piece of craftsmanship, with silver trim on its stock, and even as a child she'd loved it as an art object. Back on the patio, she focused through the binoculars on the bay entrance. After a time she passed them to Jonas.

The workboats were laying down a heavy boom, from Mourillon's grand jetty to the St. Mandrier jetty, blocking the only way out of the Toulon bays.

Captain Lambert observed the workboats from the Mourillon Arsenal. Lambert knew what the boats were doing. They were French, but supervised by German and Italian delegates of the Armistice Commission. The blocking of the bay entrance had been ordered by Admiral Laborde, obeying the latest terms of the new agreement between Vichy and Berlin.

Lieutenant Martin stood on the *Orion*'s deck with the engineer officer, Sublieutenant Parizet, checking the conning tower hatch which had been replaced by an arsenal work crew. When Lambert climbed aboard, Martin nodded toward the bay entrance: "That makes *three* barriers between us and the sea." The other two had been put in place before the heavy boom now being laid: an antisubmarine net stretching from the grand jetty to Mandrier's vieille jetty and a light boom across the exit from the Mourillon Arsenal's harbor.

"I've just been discussing them with the commanders of the other subs," Captain Lambert said. "We're going to get their construction details from the work crews laying them down. When we have that, we'll think about how to deal with each barrier. No chance of the rest of the fleet getting through them, of course, but subs just might be able to."

"Are we going to try?" Parizet asked. The engineer officer had been one of the virulently anti-British ones in the past. But like most of the crews and officers in Toulon, the invasion of Occupied France begun that morning had switched his anger to the Germans. All he wanted now was a chance to get out and fight them.

Captain Lambert damped his ardor. "Not without orders from Admiral Laborde. But if and when that comes, I want the *Orion* ready to go, on a moment's notice. The other submarine commanders I just talked to feel the same. None of us intend to submit tamely to becoming prisoners, if it comes to that, and if we can help it."

He sent Parizet below for a final check of the new engine silencer valves. When they were alone, he told Lieutenant Martin: "The order confining everyone to base stands until the admiral is sure the new agreement holds. In a few days we'll know. If the German troops honor their promise not to enter Toulon, limited shore leaves will be permitted again. I'll see to it you're among the first to get an evening ashore. Use it well."

"I'll try, captain," Martin said. "There's no way I can *force* contact with whoever gave me that note. But I'll do what I can to make it easy for him, if he wants contact."

At his desk in the building across from the rear of the Toulon prison, Udo Mueller unwrapped a stick of chewing gum as he contemplated a typewritten paper before him. It was the latest message from Reggie, decoded by Mueller's secretary.

Reggie was still with the Falcon Resistance group in the Maures. He confirmed that the group had broken communications with its Toulon contact named in his previous message. Apparently Falcon now had only a single contact left in Toulon. It was a woman, and might be Falcon's mistress. Other than that Reggie had been able to learn nothing about her: no name, address or occupation. He was sure no one else in the group knew who she was, except Falcon himself. But Reggie expected to meet her soon. In the next week or so he was to accompany Falcon and others to Toulon to carry out two armed robberies. They were to use the unknown woman's place as their hideout. At that point Reggie would finally be able to give Mueller the last item he wanted before he closed down the Falcon group.

Mueller stuck the gum between his teeth and neatly folded the wrapper, tucking it into his breast pocket. He chewed while he considered giving in to his impatience. He knew where the Falcon group was and had Milice units standing by on the edge of the Maures to move in and capture it when he gave the word. But only the group's leader knew the female contact in Toulon. Under torture, Falcon would almost certainly tell who she was. Ninety-nine out of a hundred broke sooner or later under intensive interrogation. But Falcon might just prove to be that one in a hundred who could not be broken, who died before they told everything.

If that happened, the female contact would remain unknown;

153

perhaps she possessed information about other undercover activities in Toulon. Berlin had made it plain that what was going on in Toulon was of extreme importance at this time. It was best, Mueller decided, to wait; only a bit longer and Reggie would meet the woman. Then Mueller could take her along with the rest of them.

In the meantime, there was the Toulon contact captured as a result of Reggie's previous message. Mueller heaved himself to his feet and started down to the basement to see how his new assistants were making out with the man. The Milice had failed to get much out of him; but now that he'd been transferred here, the results might prove more useful.

Mueller had taken over the entire building two days ago, on instructions from Berlin. Now, since the seizure of southern France, he understood why. New instructions had arrived that afternoon, together with four additional Gestapo assistants assigned to him. He had also been given a direct connection with a pro-Nazi intelligence officer inside the naval base, along with wider-ranging powers.

At this point Toulon was to become the last area of France to remain unoccupied. No Axis troops would enter it. But there was no longer any reason for even the pretense of concealing the Gestapo presence in the city.

Mueller heard the screams before he reached the basement. As he stepped inside, he decided to have sound-absorbent padding fastened to the basement door. The first room had been turned into a makeshift office. Several other rooms had been made into cells, and the screaming came from one of them.

The oldest of the new Gestapo assistants was typing up his interrogation notes when Mueller entered. He jumped to attention. Mueller noticed that the man's hands still bore stains of dried blood.

"Anything new out of the prisoner?"

"No, Herr Inspektor, only repetitions of information he already gave the Milice. He admits to being a contact for his Falcon group of terrorists, but still maintains he is no longer in connection with them and doesn't even know where they are now. He still claims he had never met any enemy agents and that he doesn't know anyone else who was in contact with Falcon."

"One of Falcon's other contacts here is a woman," Mueller told him. "Perhaps Falcon's mistress, a girl friend or wife. See if he knows anything about *her*."

"Immediately, sir."

Mueller did not go back into the cells with the man. It was not that he was squeamish about the inflicting of pain. But he wasn't like Reggie: it was not a source of pleasure for him. Interrogations were messy affairs. It was impossible to be in the same room for any length of time without getting sprinkled with some of that mess.

Settling into a chair beside the desk, Mueller folded his hands on his stomach and gazed blankly at a wall, chewing his gum. The screaming dwindled to incoherent groans and then mounted to high-pitched screams again. Mueller occupied his mind with other matters.

He thought about the enemy agent operating the radio transmitter in Toulon. An extremely experienced agent, obviously; each time, he changed the radio's location before the direction-finders could pinpoint it.

Mueller thought about Lieutenant Roger Martin of the French submarine *Orion*.

An informant in the French Naval Ministry had informed the Gestapo in Vichy about the warning message Admiral Laborde had received through Lieutenant Martin. It had been passed on to Mueller, who had discussed it with his man inside the base. The lieutenant's quarters had been searched without turning up anything of interest; and would be searched again, at regular intervals. If he were preparing to leave the base, Mueller would be informed so he could have him followed.

With luck, Lieutenant Martin might lead to whoever had given him that message. With even more luck, it might turn out to be the enemy radio operator, or else the female contact in Toulon for the Maures group. Unlikely, but the thought gave Mueller a pleasurable feeling of order. He liked investigations that could be tied up neatly in the end.

His gum had lost its flavor. Mueller unfolded the wrapper

from his breast pocket, put the used wad in it and dropped it into the wastebasket. He took out a fresh stick of gum, unwrapped it and put the wrapper in his pocket as he began chewing again.

The screaming stopped abruptly, as though cut off by a scissors. Minutes later the assistant and a younger Gestapo interrogator returned.

"The prisoner has died," the older one reported. "His heart gave out, quite suddenly. Unfortunate but unavoidable."

The younger one had blood on his shirt and tears in his eyes. "I'm *sorry,* Herr Inspektor. I was very careful, but it happened without warning. I tried..."

Mueller cut him short. "Did he reveal anything about the woman contact?"

The older man shook his head. "Nothing, sir. There was no time."

Mueller got up and left the basement. His decision was confirmed. A little more patience was required—only until the young German who ran the Maures group led Reggie to the woman in Toulon.

SIXTEEN NOVEMBER 13

THE FLAME OF the candle flickered in the damp drafts of the burial vault. Jonas shivered as he finished sending his message to Algiers. This was the third day he had used the Courtel family tomb in the Central Cemetery. His report this morning was as gloomy as the crypt's interior. With all navy personnel still confined to the base, he was unable to reestablish contact with Roger Martin. The Narval had been empty the previous two nights, and would be so this evening, according to Nicole's information.

Michael's reply from Algeirs was equally frustrating. Jonas rejoined Nicole, standing watch outside the tomb. "Keller hasn't been heard from for three days."

"That doesn't necessarily mean he's been caught. Perhaps he's just too busy trying to get what we need, someplace where he can't use his radio."

"That's what everybody's hoping."

Nicole helped Jonas transfer the SOE radio behind the cushion of the Citroën's rear seat. A strong mistral was blowing shreds of cloud across a sunny sky as she drove out of the cemetery. Two blocks away they were stopped by a Milice roadblock.

It was not entirely unexpected. Since the Axis control of the rest of the south coast, the number of Milice and police raids, searches and patrols in Toulon had grown. It increased the risks involved in moving the radio, without lessening the necessity. That was the reason Jonas needed Nicole, for extra protection.

The roadblock consisted of a small truck parked across an intersection and four uniformed Milice stormtroopers carrying submachine guns. When Nicole stopped the car three of them converged on it, ordering her and Jonas out. Two demanded their papers while the third began searching the car, beginning with the trunk. Everything now depended on the thoroughness of the search. Time became the vital factor.

The Miliciens were not impolite. Anyone who could use a car these days might be someone with important connections, *if* they hadn't stolen the car. The one examining Jonas's papers looked from his photo to his face and asked what he was doing in Toulon. Jonas began his standard answer, slowly and carefully, when the one with Nicole suddenly registered her family name: "The people who own the paper you work for have the same name."

Nicole gave the man her most charming smile. "My father started *Toulon-Matin* and my cousin runs it now but I am part owner."

The third Milicien had finished with the trunk and was starting on the passenger section of the Citroën; he opened the glove compartment, then looked under the front seat. The one with Jonas asked Nicole, "And this gentleman?"

"Is a guest of my family," she told him.

The man beside her signaled to the one examining the interior of the car. "Forget it, these are good people."

He gave Nicole and Jonas a smart salute as they got back into the car, and waved them on around the truck.

There was cold fog in the streets of Le Mans. Himmler left the Dauphin Hotel, where he'd taken over an entire floor for his brief visit, and strolled arm in arm with SS General Paul Hausser toward the Place Thiers. Two officers of Himmler's personal bodyguard preceded them, and another pair followed.

"I came on impulse," Himmler told Hausser, "merely to wish you Godspeed and good fortune in the carrying out of Operation Lila."

"I'm very pleased you've come to see us off," Hausser said. "The troops will be honored."

Operation Anton was almost completed. Axis forces now occupied every military installation in the south of France—except Toulon—and all French troops had given up their arms and were confined to barracks. Most important for Hausser, all French planes had been grounded, so there was no aerial danger of spotting his moves; and all French radio stations had been seized. By tomorrow night everything would be ready to begin his move south toward Toulon.

"This will be the first trial of our new SS Panzer Korps," Himmler said. "Many Wehrmacht officers, jealous of our growing reputation in battle, would love to see it fail."

"It will not fail," Hausser assured him. "This I swear to you."

Himmler smiled. "You have taken enough Russian cities to be a better judge of that than anyone else I know."

"And Toulon is not defended by Russians," Hausser added, "with a Stalin ordering them to fight to the death."

"No, these are Frenchmen, with a Pétain who will order them not to fight back."

"So I've been assured."

"So I *promise*." Himmler squeezed Hausser's arm with deep affection. An American officer had described Hausser before the war as "the ugliest man I ever saw wearing a uniform." Himmler thought him beautiful.

It was true that General Hausser had never possessed standard good looks. His nose was too long, too pointy, his expression too nervously rigid. A year ago he'd been severely wounded in the face and hands during a Russian artillery barrage. It had left a large, lumpy scar on the right side of his face, and most of the vision in the right eye had been lost. But Himmler, who loved animals, looked upon General Hausser as the most superb breed of all: a fighting animal, whose honorable wounds were badges testifying to his courage, toughness and reliability.

Three members of an SS tank crew, coming toward them out of the mists, recognized their general immediately and greeted him with grinning salutes. But when they realized the mousy little man with him was the Reichsführer of the SS, its supreme authority under Hitler, they lost their easygoing attitude and stiffened to frozen attention, eyes straight forward.

Hausser gave a crooked smile as he passed them with Himmler. "You see how much more respect they show you than they do me?" he joked. "Behind my back they even call me papa! Do you think that is a proper way to regard their commander?"

Himmler said with all seriousness: "You *are* their father. You created the fighting arm of the SS, you taught them war, you lead them in battle. Those who were not with you in the Bordino and Yelna campaigns know your reputation from those who were. Their fondness for you is the greatest tribute a fighting man can offer to his leader."

Hausser, who knew this, nodded and smiled his crooked smile.

At the Place Thiers they entered the Restaurant Mirabeau, where another pair of Himmler's SS bodyguards were holding two of the best tables. Himmler and General Hausser took the one nearest the big window, where they could see the ancient Eglise de la Couture outlined darkly in the shifting fog. Two bodyguards settled at the other table, while a second pair stationed themselves outside the restaurant entrance; a third took up a position across the square.

Himmler watched Hausser kiss the silver SS death's-head insignia on his cap before setting it on the table. The gesture pleased him. A man with a deep feeling for ritual himself, Himmler appreciated it in members of the SS, which he considered a reincarnation of a mystic order of knighthood.

"What will you have to drink, general?" he asked. Hausser ordered a large whiskey. Himmler said he would have tea. "One of my men will already have the cook here preparing a plain vegetarian lunch for me," he told Hausser. "But you may have whatever you wish."

160

"I will eat what you eat, Reichsführer." Hausser would have preferred a thick, rare steak, but he knew Himmler's faith in health foods. It did not detract from the general's respect for him. Great men were entitled to strong, even eccentric, beliefs. And so many of Himmler's had proven their value.

Many of the traditional Wehrmacht generals—and Hausser had been one of them before joining the Nazi Party and building the Waffen SS into a powerful instrument of war—made fun of Himmler's conception of the SS as a concentration of the best Germanic bloodlines of the "Race Soul." They ridiculed the oath of fanaticism each candidate took before receiving his emblematic SS dagger: "I believe in God and Germany which God created. I believe in the Führer whom God has sent to us. I swear obedience unto death to those Adolf Hitler has appointed my superiors, so help me God."

Hausser had seen the results in Russia. The almost suicidal assaults of the SS shock troops were a kind of fanaticism he admired, and shared.

He was less enchanted by some of Himmler's other pet theories: his hatred of marriage as a "devilish ruse of the Catholic Church"; his order that all unmarried women over thirty must enter special brothels to be impregnated by SS soldiers, or be arrested as enemies of Germany if they refused. But a great visionary's small flaws did not diminish his greatness.

"Are you certain you have everything you need to take Toulon?" Himmler asked. "Troops, weapons, tanks, trucks?"

"More than enough. It will be the work of a single hour, no more. But I can use some sailors of the German Navy. My troops are not familiar with harbors and naval installations. If I could have about a thousand experienced seamen to guide us through the base once we break inside, and to assist in taking control of the ships..."

"You shall have them," Himmler promised. A waiter brought his tea and the general's whiskey. "Before we drink," Himmler told Hausser, "please share a minute of silence with me. Try to *feel* what happens."

Himmler placed his hands on the table and closed his eyes.

Hausser waited out the minute, and when Himmler's eyes opened they were shining with confidence. "Did you feel it—the Race Soul merging with ours?"

This time General Hausser's smile was embarrassed. "I don't understand much about such advanced ideas, I'm afraid. I never had time to learn anything other than fighting. I'm just a plain soldier, Reichsführer, with a plain soldier's wounds and a plain soldier's brain."

Himmler patted Hausser's scarred hand. "Never mind, so were the Knights of the Round Table. The Toulon fleet is your Holy Grail, general. Go get it for me."

SEVENTEEN NOVEMBER 14

JONAS WOKE WITH the fullness of Nicole's breasts in his hands. An arm was around his waist, her fingertips splayed against the small of his back.

Her room was still dark, but dawn light showed in the cracks of the shutters. Carefully, he extricated himself from Nicole and slid off the bed. She rolled on her stomach, not waking.

It had turned unseasonably warm during the night and when they'd finally fallen asleep they hadn't bothered with covers. Their naked bodies generated enough heat. Jonas stood gazing down at the darkness of her figure sprawled on the shadowed bed. Sunlight penetrating a chink in the shutters laid a thin golden-white line across her ripe buttocks. He remembered the satiny smoothness of her skin there, and he had to restrain himself from getting back into bed with her. It was extraordinary; after the prolonged love-making of the night he was ready to take her again. She had awakened in him a relentless virility.

She had also awakened in him a new fear of death.

It was unlike the fear he had learned to live with, before Nicole. That had become something he could accept and control, centered on the probability of pain before the release of oblivion. Now death meant loss: losing her, losing the joy of her. Having her had reopened a compartment within him which was only concerned with living. That part of him secretly hoped

Andreas Keller would not be heard from again, which would abort his mission. Then there would be nothing but to go on hiding, with her; waiting out the war, with her; instead of having to make the moves which would invite death.

Quietly, Jonas gathered his clothes and left Nicole's room. He washed and dressed quickly before going downstairs. He got her car keys from the kitchen and drove up into the woods to radio Michael in Algiers.

Keller had been heard from. After decoding the message from Michael, Jonas sat under the trees working out what he would have to do if Nicole learned that cancellation of shore leaves would not be lifted today. The compartment in him that wanted to concentrate on continuing to live was locked. He had to contact Lieutenant Martin by that night.

The wind was rising, a heated wind blowing from the south. The sunlight was gone when Jonas drove back to the house. Smears of brownish cloud obscured the sky, containing as much dust as moisture. Jonas tasted sand on the wind, carried all the way across the Mediterranean, from a dust storm somewhere in North Africa.

Nicole was finishing a bath when he returned. He stood in the bathroom doorway, watching drops of water run down her body as she got out of the tub and reached for her towel. She looked at his expression and laughed softly. Dropping the towel she came into his arms, dripping wet.

By sunset the wind died. The low cloud cover, spreading from the hills behind Toulon to the horizon where black sea met night sky, showed neither stars nor moon. The air was still and heavy, as though held inside a dark fist. It was too warm and muggy to wear his uniform greatcoat. Lieutenant Martin carried it over his arm when he stepped off the *Orion* and walked toward the end of the Mourillon Arsenal's submarine pens. He was acutely conscious of the note tucked deep inside his inner pocket.

Dust, floating down from the clouds, mixed with the salt tang of the sea and the accustomed smells of the navy waterfront: tar and rust, paint and oil, marine vegetation and timber pilings rotting in the stagnant waters under the docks—all abnormally strong in the close, motionless air. It was a thoroughly disagreeable night, irritating nerves already over-tense.

The Axis had abided by the terms of its new agreement with Vichy. Though the rest of southern France was under occupation, Toulon remained an inviolate free zone. The only Wehrmacht troops around were small groups on short leave passes from garrisons outside the city. None carried arms except for the military police patrols, making sure the rest behaved themselves, reflecting well on German discipline and friendly intentions. Under these circumstances Admiral Laborde had restored limited shore leaves.

The time and numbers were severely restricted. Laborde didn't want to risk incidents between French sailors and Wehrmacht troops. Commanders were instructed to keep this in mind when selecting the men for shore leave. Vessels with small crews, such as submarines, were permitted only one pass at a time. Captain Lambert had given the first four-hour pass to Roger Martin.

The lieutenant left the Mourillon Arsenal by the main gate. He showed his pass to the guards inside the gate, and again to the guard detachment stationed outside. A single taxicab stood by. Its availability light switched on when Lieutenant Martin came out. He hesitated. From here it was less than a fifteen-minute walk across to the Narval on the other side of the Mourillon promontory. Martin covered his hesitation by getting out one of his cigars and taking his time to light it. A dark automobile was parked at the curb across the street, with two shadowy figures in the front seat. They'd been smoking, but had flicked their cigarettes out when he emerged from the Arsenal. If it hadn't been for that he wouldn't have noticed them in the parked car.

He got into the taxicab and told the driver to take him to Place Raspail, in the heart of the old section of the city.

The Gestapo driver in the parked car waited until the cab

was a block away before following it. Though the nondescript man in the front seat beside him was French, it was he who was in charge of this job. Deputy Commissioner Vallat had recommended him to Kriminal Inspektor Mueller as an accomplished tail. His name was Jean Desitter and being inconspicuous was part of his normal profession as a pickpocket. For Desitter this job was relatively easy: the man being tailed had no experience at the game and his cabdriver was also in the Gestapo's employ.

There were a lot of bars and restaurants around the Place Raspail, facing the big covered market in the middle, serving its customers, vendors and suppliers. Though most of the market stalls were closed by now there was still plenty of activity: cleaners sweeping and hosing away the day's garbage, products being hauled in for the next day from horse-drawn wagons. Lieutenant Martin got out of the taxi and strolled into the market.

When the tail car arrived the cab driver pointed to the market entrance. Desitter had a twinge of anxiety. If the lieutenant suspected he was being followed, the covered market had three other exits from which he could slip away quickly.

Ordering the Gestapo man to circle the market, Desitter hurried inside. Lieutenant Martin was strolling back in his direction, carrying a purchase, a large box of cigars. The pickpocket turned away to interest himself in crates of noisy chickens being stacked between two of the stalls. Martin went past behind him, going out the same way he'd come in.

Desitter relaxed and slowly counted to ten before going out the same way. The lieutenant was nowhere in sight. The cabdriver pointed to the largest café facing that side of the market, the Grand-Paris. Instructing the driver to tell the Gestapo man to park and wait, Desitter hurried over to the front window of the café.

The interior was a large square room with fourteen tables and a long bar overhung by frosted-globe lamps. There were only a few customers at the tables. Lieutenant Martin was alone at the bar.

Desitter recalled having been in the place in the past, but couldn't remember one important point. Moving swiftly, he entered a narrow alley which plunged into the block alongside the café, reached the deep end and turned into another that ran behind it. He was more relaxed now. The Grand-Paris had no back door, nor any window providing a way out to either alley.

Satisfied, the pickpocket returned to the front of the Grand-Paris and went in. The lieutenant was engaged in a casual conversation with the bartender. Desitter took a place at the bar close enough to hear the bartender complain about some bet he'd lost to Martin. Breaking off, the bartender asked Desitter what he'd like and went to make the *pastis* he ordered. Lieutenant Martin glanced incuriously at the newcomer and then returned to his drink.

The instructions from Mueller were to try to spot any clandestine contact the lieutenant might make inside the city. If nothing more likely turned up elsewhere, Desitter decided, he'd give Mueller a list of possibles. Starting with the bartender and the owner of the *tabac* in the market.

A pair of Wehrmacht soldiers came in as Desitter got his *pastis:* a sergeant and a corporal, their uniforms neat, their expressions tentatively friendly. They eyed Lieutenant Martin's uniform. Mindful of their orders that failure to make a good impression would result in severe punishment, the sergeant asked politely if they could buy him a drink.

Martin finished off the one he had. "Sure. Why not?" Relieved, they took their place beside him and ordered white wine for themselves. Martin asked for another whiskey. The soldiers raised their glasses in a toast: "To peace between our nations." The lieutenant was willing to drink to that.

Desitter nursed his *pastis* and watched him in the mirror behind the bar. Lieutenant Martin did not appear discomfited by the presence of the Wehrmacht. If he intended to make any clandestine contact tonight it was not here, or not yet.

The soldiers were telling Martin they hoped he was not angry that it had become necessary for the Wehrmacht to extend the

167

occupation to Southern France. "It's for your own protection, after all," the corporal said. "If the Anglo-Americans attack here, it's quite obvious you'd be unable to defend yourselves without our help."

"Quite obvious," Martin agreed, and finished off his drink. What was obvious to him was that if the Werhmacht high command did intend to grab the Toulon fleet, its troops were not yet in on it. He opened his box of cigars and offered them. But neither soldier smoked. "At least let me buy the next round," Martin insisted. They were pleased to accept the offer.

Martin ordered refills and put a large bill on the bar next to his cigar box. "Excuse me, I've got to pee." The soldiers grinned as he walked off toward the rear of the café.

Desitter turned his back to the bar and watched. There was a door marked "Toilet" at the end of a short corridor. He saw the lieutenant go in and shut the door behind him.

Martin locked the door from inside. Lacking any window, the toilet was provided with ventilation by a plasterboard set at an off-angle across a square opening in the ceiling. Closing the toilet seat, he stood on it and reached up, pushed the board up and away. Tossing his coat through the opening, he reached up with both hands, got a grip, and hauled himself up. It was a tight squeeze, but he got through. He picked his coat off the floor and rose to his feet.

He was inside a second-floor storage room. Dim light from its single barred window lay across stacks of canned goods. The door had an old-fashioned lock which required a key to open it from the outside, but only a twist of the small knob to unlock the inside. Martin twisted and stepped onto a staircase landing. He went up the stairs swiftly. At the top there was a ladder to the roof trapdoor. He opened the slide lock and climbed out.

Crossing a series of roofs, he found what he wanted near the other side of the block: a fire-escape ladder leading down to an alley. Four blocks from the Raspail Market he hailed another cab and ordered the driver to take him to the Narval.

Inside the Grand-Paris Desitter let almost five minutes go by before he got worried. Crossing the interior of the café, he knocked at the toilet door. "Hey, give somebody else a turn!"

There was no response. Without bothering to try again, he turned and ran outside.

The Gestapo man, waiting behind the wheel of his car, looked up as he rushed over. "What's happened?"

"He's given us the slip!"

"Given *you* the slip, you mean," the Gestapo man said scathingly. "You were responsible. All right, I'll take over now. Go get your driver."

Desitter hurried off, badly frightened. The Gestapo man got a paper out of the glove compartment. It was a short list Mueller had given him, of places Lieutenant Martin was believed to frequent in Toulon. The Grand-Paris was there, along with six other places. He was checking their locations against a city map when Desitter returned with the cabdriver.

The Gestapo man sent the cabbie to check out two of the places on the list and assigned two others to Desitter. He took on the remaining two himself, starting with the Narval.

Nicole was seated in a cane chair in the Narval's front garden, her patience beginning to wear thin, when she spotted the cab approaching along the beach road. She remained absolutely still, hidden in dark shadow between two heavy palms, watching the taxi slow to a halt and then recognizing the figure of Roger Martin as he climbed out of the taxi. She took a deep breath. Otherwise she didn't move or make a sound, not even when Martin went past without seeing her and entered the Narval; nor even after the taxi pulled away. She stayed in place, watching the road.

Inside, Olga greeted Lieutenant Martin with a kiss on both cheeks. "I'm certainly glad to see you again. Glad to see any of you. This place had been like a morgue the past few nights. Not that it's that much livelier tonight."

He saw what she meant when he accompanied her into the front room. The phonograph was playing but only two couples were dancing. A third girl, seated with a signals officer from the battle cruiser *Dunkerque,* made up the rest of the available women. As for men, in addition to the one at the table and the two dancing, there were four at the bar: all navy, no civilians.

"First drink's on the house," Olga told him. "The usual?"

Martin nodded abstractedly. "I have to hang up my coat first," he said, loud enough to carry. While Olga went to the bar he walked back into the game room. Another four officers were playing cards.

"Join the game?" one of the players asked as he passed.

"Maybe later." Martin entered the cloakroom and hung his coat on a peg. There were no others; the night was too warm. He patted the coat and returned to the bar.

Olga had his drink ready. "To better times," she said quietly, raising her glass. Martin clinked glasses with her and drank down most of his. Olga put down her own barely tasted drink and strolled off, toward the rear of the Narval.

Martin wondered if it was *her*. It had occurred to him before: that Olga might have left that message in his coat, or at least was connected with whoever had done it. He doubted that it was any of his fellow officers. It had to be a civilian; and if it wasn't Olga he hoped like hell whoever it was showed up soon. The men he had evaded would be trying to locate him, and he had to assume they'd get to him soon. With an effort, he restrained himself from turning his head to gaze after Olga.

In the cloakroom she went straight to his coat and reached into the inside pocket. Finding the folded piece of paper, Olga went up the back stairway to her living quarters and gave it to Jonas.

"I have to talk to you right away," Martin had written on the paper, "even if you don't have what you promised yet."

Lieutenant Martin was having another whiskey when Olga rejoined him at the bar. She smiled at him and picked up her drink, taking another sip. As she lowered the glass her eyes met his directly. He wondered where she'd learned to talk like that, without moving her lips. Her voice was so soft nobody else could have heard it.

"The garden out back," she told him, and sipped again at her drink as she watched him stroll to the rear of the Narval.

170

Mindful that the men hunting him might enter the Narval at any moment, the lieutenant picked up his coat before going out the back door into the garden. The sudden darkness blinded him. After taking a few steps along a gravel walk he stopped and waited. His eyes were adjusting to the silhouettes of trees on either side when a voice a few yards to his right said, "Over here."

The voice didn't come as a complete surprise. Olga's godson—if that's what he really was—had been one of the possibilities Martin had considered. He found him standing against a high hedge, barely visible in its shadow. Neither man could make out the expression of the other's face. "We'll have to talk fast," Martin said. "I was followed tonight. I managed to lose them, but a lot of people know this is one of my hangouts."

"What's happening inside the base?" Jonas asked.

"First, I want to know who you really are and who you represent. Are you from de Gaulle and his Free French group in London?"

Jonas had already decided to give the lieutenant his full trust. If Martin had come to betray him the place would be surrounded by now. Jonas had been watching from a rear upstairs window and Nicole was out front. Martin had come alone. There came a time in any mission where you had to put your life in another's hands; as he had with Nicole, as he was now with Lieutenant Martin.

"I'm not French," Jonas told him. "I'm Canadian, and I'm here as part of a joint British-American intelligence mission."

Martin was delighted. "That is good news—especially about the Americans." Like most Frenchmen, Martin still distrusted the British. "Maybe I can win some more money betting the Americans will land *here* soon?"

"I don't know anything about plans at that level. All I know is my own job, and not too much about that so far. Has your admiral ordered the fleet to prepare scuttling charges in case the Axis tries to take the ships?"

"No." Martin ignored Jonas's soft curse and countered: "Have you gotten the proof they do intend to?"

"Not yet. Trying to get hold of something conclusive enough to move a Vichy man like Laborde isn't easy."

"Then we're still in trouble." Martin told Jonas about the new orders from the Axis Armistice Commission to refit the French fleet for sea duty. "Now to me that sounds very much like they want our ships ready so that they can take them over and use them immediately. My commander and some others think the same. But the admiral doesn't seem to see it that way."

Jonas took an envelope from his pocket and gave it to Martin. "This may change his mind."

"What is it?"

"Sometime tomorrow inspectors from the Axis Commission are going to begin checking every ship of your fleet. With a new order that no ship will be allowed more fuel than absolutely necessary for exercising its engines inside the harbor. Anything more than that will be pumped out and taken away."

Lieutenant Martin whistled. "That adds up to two orders seeming to contradict each other. Get the fleet ready to sail, but don't allow any ship enough fuel to get far out of the harbor."

"It makes sense from Hitler's point of view. He wants your fleet operational, but he doesn't want it able to run away before he can take it over."

Martin nodded. "That's how I see it." He gestured with the envelope Jonas had given him. "This *should* at least make Laborde take it as a serious possibility. But even if he does...even if it makes him order scuttle charges prepared...he'll never give the actual order to use them, no matter what happens. Not without Pétain's agreement. There is no chance at all he'll scuttle the fleet—unless you can bring us *proof*. Unequivocal proof, that can't be explained away."

"When I get that, you'll get it."

"That brings up another problem I came to tell you about. Laborde allowed limited shore leaves today, but there's no way to be sure how long that'll continue. My guess is this new information you've given me will make him cancel them again, indefinitely. I won't be allowed off base."

"How will I get in touch with you?"

"My sub, the *Orion*, has been shifted to the Mourillon Arsenal, on the other side of the hill here. You know the two gates there?"

"Yes."

"We're docked nearest the main gate. If you do get that proof, on time, come there and ask for me. I'll have briefed the guards stationed outside the gate. They'll fetch me. Use the same name you signed to that first warning: *Jonas*."

In front of the Narval the Gestapo man brought his car to a halt and climbed out. Nicole didn't move until he'd gone past her and entered the building. Then she left her hiding place and walked around the side of the building to warn Jonas and Lieutenant Martin.

Inside the Narval the man showed his Gestapo card and asked for Lieutenant Roger Martin. When Olga said Martin wasn't there he pushed past her to see for himself. She followed him, insisting again, at the top of her lungs, that Lieutenant Martin hadn't been in that night. The officers in the place backed her up. Unable to determine if they were lying, the Gestapo man explored every room on both floors before going back to his car for a flashlight. He prowled the grounds around the building, but couldn't find any trace of Martin there, either. Finally, he drove away to check another of the lieutenant's habitual hangouts.

By then Lieutenant Martin was on his way back to the base.

The SS Panzer Korps had left Le Mans after sunset. Shortly before midnight it began rolling across the now meaningless demarcation line, manned now by Wehrmacht guards supplied by the First Army. Three vehicles pulled off the road and stopped while the rest continued to flow across the line: an armored half-track headquarters vehicle, a dispatch motorcycle with its sidecar mounting an MG-34 machine gun and one of the new Tiger tanks, a huge fifty-six-ton monster painted Panzer gray.

General Hausser stood in the open turret hatch of the Tiger, its great cannon projecting below his waist like a gigantic steel penis, watching the interminable lines of the vehicles roaring past. The BMW R12 and R75 motorcycles. The hundreds of tanks: the Tigers and the old PZ II-Fs, IIIs and IVs. The three-ton half-track support vehicles, the ammunition carriers, the combat engineer equipment carriers. The tractors towing self-propelled cannons and the Famo eighteen-ton half-tracks of the Tank Recovery Company, pulling trailers for carrying off damaged tanks. The four-wheeled and eight-wheeled armored radio cars. And the great variety of personnel carriers: four-wheel and eight-wheel armored cars, one-ton half-tracks, Opel Blitz trucks and Ford G917T three-tonners. All carried a capacity load of troops and there were more riding atop each of the tanks, armed with MP-40 submachine guns, stick grenades, Kar 98K rifles with spigot grenade launchers.

Some of the troopers' faces were more familiar to General Hausser than others: those who had served under him in Russia. There were not many of those left. The Das Reich SS Division he had commanded there had earned its reputation at a cost of seventy percent casualties.

Those who had survived deserved this rare chance at an easy victory, Hausser reflected as he watched their faces stream past on the roaring vehicles. And it wouldn't hurt the newcomers who'd been recruited to bring his new SS Korps up to full strength. A brief taste, to whet the appetite, before they all got back to real fighting.

General Hausser climbed down from the massive Tiger and signaled as he boarded the half-track flying his command pennant. The dispatch motorcycle led the way back into the speeding line, followed by the command vehicle and the tank. The SS Panzer Korps rolled south through the night, down roads from which French police had been removed, past military camps where French troops were confined to barracks, under skies across which no French planes were permitted to fly.

The endless columns of tanks, trucks, motorcycles and armored cars would continue to roll south only by night, spending the days in areas cordoned off by the Wehrmacht, until they reached the final staging area for Operation Lila: an isolated encampment already prepared by the First Army near the town of Brignoles, in the hills north of Toulon.

EIGHTEEN NOVEMBER 15

ACCORDING TO ITS fuel gauges the *Orion* had very little left in its tanks: a bit less, in fact, than the maximum permitted by the new regulation of the Axis Armistice Commission. The two inspectors—one Italian, the other German—didn't let it go at that. Though both were strictly desk navy, and neither had ever served on submarines, they had detailed manuals with instructions detailing the checking procedures. A hose was run from the *Orion* to a fuel truck on the dock, so the inspectors could double-check.

One of the inspectors remained below with the *Orion*'s engineering officer. Lieutenant Martin accompanied the other to the truck. When the fuel line was attached Martin waved to Captain Lambert up on his bridge; the captain signaled down to the sub's engine room. The *Orion* began pumping fuel to the truck.

The pumping continued until the last drop came through the line. The inspector with Lieutenant Martin checked the fuel gauge of the truck's trailer tank. It tallied exactly with the amount indicated by the sub's gauges.

The inspector signaled and the fuel was pumped back into the *Orion*. That much was needed to run the engine with the tail clutch disengaged from time to time, so that the dynamo would keep the batteries charged.

When the fuel line was disconnected and rolled up, Lieutenant Martin watched the two Axis inspectors move along the dock with the truck to the next submarine. The *Orion* was the second sub they'd checked out. They'd begun with the *Casabianca*, the largest of the six subs in the Mourillon Arsenal; its captain, as senior officer, was now serving as commander of the Arsenal's Reserve Submarine Group. That left the other four still to be inspected: the *Venus, Marsoulin, Iris* and *Glorieux*. The inspectors would find that those, too, had only the minimal amount of fuel permitted. After Martin had returned with the warning from Jonas, they had worked all night, tampering with their fuel gauges and rigging a blockage in the fuel line between the tanks and the check taps.

What the gauges registered and what could be pumped out was only the fuel in the line, not in the blocked-off tanks, which were nearly full.

Captain Lambert came down from the *Orion*'s bridge, jumping from the deck onto the quay beside his first lieutenant.

"Our little trick is working," Martin whispered.

The captain crossed his fingers and walked to the bay end of the submarine quay, where the light boom which formed the first barrier was stretched across the narrow entrance. He raised his binoculars to see what was happening on the other side of the inner roads, in the vast main base of the West Arsenal.

Part of his view was hidden by the long Petit Rang pier which jutted out from the fishing and yachting port of the Vieille Darse. But beyond Lambert could see the Milhaud docks and some of the Vauban dry docks. Tankers had anchored close to both and were pumping "excess" fuel out of the big warships there.

There would have been no point in the rest of the fleet trying to trick the commission inspectors. The two main barriers which had been placed between the end of Mourillon and Mandrier sealed the only exit from the bay. German planes flew day and night patrols over the harbors; they carried bombs and mines, and with any movement of the fleet would radio for bigger bombers from the Luftflotte station near Hyères, less than four minutes flying time away.

Only a sub would have any chance at all of getting out of this trap, *if* Admiral Laborde ever gave permission for them to make a try for it. Even with a submarine, it would be an odds-against try.

Captain Lambert shifted the focus of his binoculars to the Petit Rang. Activity on its promenade was as on any normal morning: strolling couples, men fishing, mothers pushing baby carriages and watching their older children play. The civilian population of Toulon seemed unaware that anything unusual was going on in the naval base.

He paid no special attention to a man and woman at the end of the Petit Rang, standing beside their bicycles.

Jonas and Nicole had taken two family bikes from the shed; the gas shortage had suddenly become acute. With the occupation of the south, Axis military vehicles were soaking up all available supplies. That meant fewer buses, with less frequent runs on all routes. And for a while even established collaborators, such as the family which owned *Toulon-Martin,* were going to find it difficult to get enough to run their cars. The little left in Nicole's car had to be hoarded for trips that were absolutely essential—and short.

After walking their bikes out to the end of the Petit Rang, Jonas and Nicole had an even better view than Captain Lambert of the anchored tankers taking fuel from the warships.

Nicole said, "At least now they know your second warning was also true."

Jonas nodded. But what interested him more lay in the other direction. Once more he scrutinized the Mourillon Arsenal's seawall, and its few narrow openings. The nearest was the entrance to the small auxiliary submarine base where Roger Martin was now stationed. From where Jonas stood he couldn't see any of the subs inside.

He did see the tiny figure of a naval officer standing on one side of the blocked entrance, looking in his direction through binoculars. But Jonas had no way of knowing it was Martin's commander.

"Let's go," he told Nicole. They walked their bikes back along the pier promenade to have a look at the situation at the Mourillon Arsenal's main gate, the one nearest the sub pens.

Captain Lambert lowered his binoculars and strolled back to the submarine quay. The commission inspectors had just finished with the *Venus* and were moving on to check out the *Marsoulin*. The trick *was* working.

As agreed at the conference presided over by the *Casabianca's* skipper last night, all six subs in the Mourillon base would wait until the inspectors had completed their work and left, before removing the blockages from their fuel tanks and repairing gauges.

Aboard the flagship *Strasbourg*, Admiral Laborde also waited until the last of the Axis inspectors had departed. Then he summoned his general staff officer, Rear Admiral Dornon, and Vice-Admiral Marquis. A brief conference found them in agreement. They issued two sets of orders.

First, all shore leaves were again canceled, and all navy personnel were henceforth confined to base. Second, the commander of every vessel in the fleet was to assign special demolition crews to prepare scuttling charges. The explosives were to be attached close to the keel, rigged to blow holes in the bottom large enough to sink each vessel swiftly. On the bigger ships the scuttle charges were to be double-placed, on either side of the keel, so they could only be raised and restored by expending more time and manpower than an attacking enemy—unspecified—could spare over the next few years.

Preparing the scuttling charges took the rest of that day. While the work went on, Admiral Laborde sat at his command desk painstakingly composing a message explaining his action to Vichy.

Germany, Laborde pointed out, had repeatedly warned that the Allies might attack Toulon at any time. It was the duty of a naval officer to prevent his ships from falling into the hands of an enemy. The Toulon fleet no longer had enough fuel to sail out and defend itself. Therefore, the only way left to pre-

180

vent the fleet falling to an attacking enemy would be to scuttle it, if the attack seemed likely to succeed.

Laborde added, sincerely, that he remained loyal to the personal oath he had given Marshal Pétain. He emphasized that he had only made the *preparations* for scuttling, a reasonable precaution under the circumstances. He would never actually execute such a terrible action without first consulting Pétain.

It was an hour past sunset, when the last of the scuttling charges had been wired in place, that Admiral Laborde sent the message notifying Vichy.

"Laborde deliberately waited until every ship was ready to be blown up *before* advising us! It is inexcusable!" Pierre Laval paced back and forth across the green carpet, the smoke of his cigarette swirling in the lights of the crystal chandeliers. He hated to talk or think sitting down. He was better on his feet, as he'd proved so often back in his days as a brilliant lawyer pacing a courtroom in pretended fury to sway judges and jury. But this was not a court: it was a luxurious conference room in the Hotel du Parc, now the chief government building of Vichy. And Laval's fury was genuine.

He had been presiding over a lovely party at his château in Châteldon, ten miles from Vichy, when Navy Minister Auphan had phoned with the news and invited him to meet with himself and Pétain. He had walked out on his party immediately. Laval had first notified Germany of what Laborde had done—and then had to wait almost half an hour for the Germans to phone him back with their first reactions.

Laval was still surprised that they hadn't insisted immediately on having Laborde replaced as chief of the Toulon fleet. In fact, their failure to insist on it confused and frightened him.

"It is entirely within Admiral Laborde's scope of authority," Auphan now reminded him, "to carry out such preparations. He does require higher authority before actually executing an order to scuttle, but that he is well aware of." The navy minister looked for support to Marshal Pétain.

Pétain nodded solemnly. "I don't understand your anger,"

he told Laval. "Considering that the fleet can no longer sail out to fight against an Allied assault, Admiral Laborde felt..."

Laval interrupted despairingly: "But Hitler will think it is directed against *him!* Can't you see that?"

"It is directed," Auphan put in quietly, "against *anyone* who might attempt to seize our fleet."

Laval turned on him. "The Germans I've spoken to feel themselves insulted by this act. They are afraid that when Hitler learns of it he'll consider it a lack of trust in his word."

Auphan stared at him. "Do I understand you correctly? Do you mean that you have already told the Germans about this, even before coming here to discuss it with the marshal?"

"Of course I did."

Auphan continued to stare at Laval. The premier of France, second only to Pétain, having to ask representatives of another country what to say, what to think... He was unable to conceal his disgust.

Laval glared at him. "You seem still unable to grasp the realities, my dear admiral. Our future, the future of France, depends on retaining the good will of Hitler."

"Is that what we have—his good will?"

"If we did not," Laval informed Auphan coldly, "this entire country would by now be nothing but smoldering ashes!"

Marshal Pétain raised both hands and slapped them down on the table to bring this angry exchange to a halt. "This argument is pointless," he declared imperiously. "And that will be enough of it. Premier Laval," he told Auphan, "is quite right in saying we must take care not to offend Germany at this point when we are so weak. And Admiral Auphan," he told Laval, "is right in saying that Laborde did not exceed his authority...and will not."

"But to even *imagine* sinking the whole fleet!" Laval blurted. "Let alone to actually prepare the means for doing so! The man is insane!"

The marshal shook his head. "No. Admiral Laborde is quite aware of the enormity of such an act. He is, I assure you, fervently praying to God that it will never become necessary. I had just finished speaking with him by phone before you arrived. Laborde has once more given me his word of honor that he will make no such move on his own. If a situation does arise which he feels might require the order to scuttle, he would first inform me of the reasons. And he will accept whatever I decide as final."

Laval's tension subsided. "If that ever does come up, I will depend on you to let me know about it before coming to any decision. So I have time to inform Hitler."

Pétain nodded. "I am fully aware of the need for that."

Admiral Auphan was aghast. "I had hoped," he told Pétain shakily, "that tonight you would decide it best to instruct Laborde to give the order if and when he finds the fleet in danger of seizure—by any foreign power."

"I cannot do that. Certainly not ahead of time, before I am informed of what is happening."

"At that point there may not be time for discussion, marshal. It could come down to an immediate decision, on the spot, if our fleet is to be kept out of enemy hands."

"I have to consider the fate of all France, admiral. Which means I must hold Admiral Laborde to his pledge to let the decision rest with me."

Auphan suddenly felt much older than the marshal, though at forty-seven he was almost thirty-eight years younger. "If that actually means that such a decision depends on Adolf Hitler," he said unhappily, "then he is the real government of France. In that case, I would feel it necessary to resign my post as navy minister."

"Good!" Laval growled.

Pétain shot him an admonishing look, and then turned to Admiral Auphan with a kind but firm expression. "Admiral, we must deal with reality if we are to save France. The reality is that we must do nothing to anger Germany."

Auphan's heart constricted. "I'm afraid that is a kind of reality I am no longer able to cope with, marshal."

Pétain sighed. "In that case, Admiral Auphan, I must, with the greatest sadness, accept your resignation."

NINETEEN NOVEMBER 18—MORNING

AT SIX A.M. IT finally came.

For three days Andreas Keller had vanished again. No message, no response to repeated urgent signals from Algiers. But when he suddenly came on the air this morning his code message was a long one.

While Michael Sandoe copied down the blocks of numbers in Algiers, Paul Riley sat beside him decoding as fast as he could. When the message ended they divided what was left and got it done in ten minutes.

The OSS man made a sighing noise. "I hear the drum roll, partner. He's got it."

"No," Michael corrected him, "he's going to *try* for it."

"At least he knows *where* now."

Sandoe nodded, and began tapping out a reply. Most of it was a prepared message, already encoded, and it took time.

The OSS and SOE brass had come up with a new concept for handling what they were waiting for, if Keller succeeded in getting hold of it: a way to double its chances of reaching the Toulon admirals. The idea was for Keller to try for *two* copies of whatever proof of enemy intentions he could find. One for Jonas to try smuggling into the Toulon base through his contact there. The other destined for a British Lysander which would attempt a fly-in pickup, then try to slip through enemy interceptors and parachute it into the base attached to a floating flare. Keller was to radio again if and when he got what they needed. An exact time for him to rendezvous with the plane would then be set.

Michael finished this message with the location chosen for the plane to land for the pickup. There was a silence of over fifteen minutes before Keller's reply came through. He would do his best to accomplish what was asked of him. Because of the logistics problems he had a request concerning Jonas.

In response, Michael transmitted a single word: "Agreed."

Keller signed off and Michael and Riley sat back and looked at each other. The American's excitement was too much to contain. "We're into the homestretch, Mike."

There were now three hours to wait before the scheduled radio contact with Jonas. They spent part of it composing and encoding new instructions for him, based on Keller's needs, working to get it as succinct as possible.

At one point Riley scowled and ran a blunt finger over one part of Michael's version. "That's telling him too much, before he has to know. Suppose he gets caught? The idea's supposed to be for a whole new ballgame, with your friend no longer our only pinch hitter. So if he can't pull it off we've got the other option, and vice-versa. If he knows this part too early, and blabs it under torture, he blows our other option."

Michael suddenly hated the man. Why did the Irish, even when born and brought up in America, have to use that liltingly sad tone when they laid out the bad news for you?

But he knew his reaction was unreasonable. Jonas wasn't Riley's dearest friend, so he could speak of the worst thing that could happen to him without flinching. Riley was also right. Michael struck out the explanation, leaving in only the bare instructions. Once more, Jonas would have to operate for a while without knowing what it was all about.

Riley nodded approvingly. "He'll get the explanations from Keller," he said gently, "if they both live to reach each other."

Jonas used Nicole's attic for that morning's radio contact with Algiers. It was now a long time since he'd transmitted from her house. The last place he'd used had been on the eastern out-skirts of Toulon near Cape Brun, so this would be safe again for a few days.

After Michael's sign-off, Jonas decoded his message. He was frowning as he reached the end. It instructed him to transfer immediately to the town of Draguignan and check into its best hotel, the Bertin, where Andreas Keller would contact him either by phone or in person. Keller might get to him either by that evening or within a few days. Jonas was to stay put and wait.

It puzzled him. Draguignan was some fifty miles away from the naval base, deep among the foothills of the Pre-Alps to the northwest. An odd place for the rendezvous. Jonas considered radioing again for an explanation, but decided against it. If Michael wanted to give an explanation, he would have included it in his message.

He began packing the assorted elements of his radio equipment into the leather carrying case. Whatever was up, he'd have to continue radio contact with Algiers from the Draguignan area.

But carrying an SOE transceiver was going to make his trip that much more dangerous. The risk would grow once he was outside Toulon, moving through areas now under the Occupation authorities. The number of identity checks and searches had increased tenfold: with patrols and checkpoints manned by military police units of the Wehrmacht as well as the Milice and Vichy police.

Jonas considered the alternate means of transport. Nicole's car didn't have enough gas to get him to Draguignan. Trains were subject to boarding by inspection patrols at each station. There were even surprise checks of trams and buses now, as they entered or left the city.

He decided, finally, to use a bicycle, at least for getting out of Toulon. Once he was well away from the city he could hide the bike in a stretch of woods, hike to a village and take local buses the rest of the way. It was going to be a slow way, but a reasonably safe one.

He put his pistol and spare ammunition inside the radio case.

Under these circumstances they didn't add to the risk he ran carrying the radio. He hesitated over his alternate set of identity papers and finally left them where they were, behind the attic insulation. He was going into an area he didn't know and a situation he did not understand. Better to have another identity waiting for him in a separate place, just in case.

He took the radio case downstairs, arranged a shirt over it before shutting it, then put it into his suitcase with the rest of his clothes. Then he carried the suitcase down to the main floor.

Nicole wasn't there, and there was no way he could get in touch with her. She'd gone off to meet with Dithelm in Lavandou again, to give him the information she'd got for him: the warehouse where the *Toulon-Matin* kept its paper supply and a wooden blockhouse where the city's Milice stored weapons and ammunition.

To conserve gas she had taken the train from Toulon to Hyères, the nearest railroad stop to Lavandou, and would go the rest of the way by bus. With bus services drastically curtailed, she probably wouldn't get home until evening. Jonas couldn't wait that long. His instructions were to reach Draguignan as soon as possible; even starting immediately it was going to take him the rest of the day.

He wrote her a short note: "Have to go off for a time. Will contact you later. Take care of yourself." He wanted to add an expression of his love, but didn't. One of the fascist members of her family might come by; he was supposed to be a friend of her brother-in-law.

Going back upstairs, he had a look through several of the upper windows. Smoke was rising from the chimneys of the other house, but nobody was in sight, either outside or coming along the path. The road to the estate was clear. Jonas went downstairs, got the bike from the shed and strapped his suitcase behind the seat.

He went east and uphill after leaving the house, angling around the base of Mount Faron, pedaling through paths in the woods, getting off and walking the bike where the way became too rough or steep. He checked what was on the other side of each hillcrest before crossing it. Within an hour he was outside Toulon's city limits.

Several miles farther on Jonas took a country lane which climbed a long slope covered with farmed terraces. The shortest route to where he wanted to go was straight down the other side of the slope. Nearing the top, Jonas swung off the bike and walked the rest of the way, stopping when he could see just over the crest. The downslope was cut at the bottom by a road. Some hundred yards to the left it intersected with another. A police roadblock was square in the middle of the intersection.

They might have no interest in a man riding a bicycle. Then again they might, considering there was no other traffic and they were probably bored. Jonas backed away from the hillcrest, turned and rode the rest of the way back down, angling off to the right. It cost him almost an extra hour to make a big circle around the cops. Once he was well beyond the roadblock he resumed going north and east, sticking to country lanes and wooded paths to avoid running into another roadblock.

Once again he wondered: Why Draguignan?

Brignoles, an old hilltown of some five thousand inhabitants, was situated twenty-seven miles west of Draguignan and thirty miles north of Toulon. A couple of miles from Brignoles, in a short, deep-cut valley with worked-out quarries burrowed into its arid slopes, the SS Panzer Korps was encamped, waiting.

Above the main section of the camp but well within its extended barbed-wire perimeter, a farmhouse stood on a hillcrest where the bare, rocky slope gave way to the rich earth. The farmer and his family had been removed so that General Hausser could use it as his operational headquarters. He had no idea where they'd been removed to: that was not his concern. Keeping his fighting men and machines in readiness during these final days of working out the last tactical details for Operation Lila was concern enough for any one man.

Especially when they kept throwing last minute surprises at him. Like the fact that the eight hundred German sailors who were supposed to guide his SS units through the maze of the Toulon naval base had not shown up, and thus could not be keyed into the final plans. Like finding out that the entire French fleet had now been wired up with scuttling charges, which shortened the time he would have to seize the ships after his lead tanks crashed through the gates of the base.

General Hausser had communicated to Himmler that the failure of the sailors to arrive was the result of deliberate stalling on the part of traditional military officers: part of their continuing jealousy toward the increased prestige of the Waffen SS. He had also given his opinion about the best ways to deal with the altered situation at the French base caused by Admiral Laborde's stiffened attitude. His feelings about this second matter had been given both to Himmler and to Field Marshal Rundstedt, who as commander in chief had the ultimate authority over this sector and operation.

Hausser was not overly perturbed about either of these two problems. They did not present major difficulties, merely annoying minor ones which had to be taken into consideration and compensated for. He spent most of that morning in the main room of the farmhouse, which had been turned into the situation conference room, making minute penciled notes on the detail maps of the Toulon naval base.

Shortly before noon Hausser stepped outside the building to rest his eyes. Standing in the cold sunlight, he took in the surrounding ranges of low mountains. Some of the slopes held little but rocks and scrub, others were thick with pines and oak trees; but all were covered with dull red dust from the bauxite quarries for which the Brignoles region was famous. These days, the general knew, most of that bauxite went to Germany for the manufacture of aluminum. As the Führer had long ago predicted it would, all of Europe now had its place in serving the needs and purposes of the Third Reich.

Seven miles to the south the Loube Mountain rose almost three thousand feet into the sky, between General Hausser and his objective. But he could see Toulon and its harbors clearly, in his mind's eye, imprinted there by constant study of the maps.

He lowered his gaze to scrutinize the activities of his SS Panzer Korps, which filled the valley below him.

The Wehrmacht's administration office, he had to admit, had done a good job in short order. They had the encampment prepared, the barracks, guardhouses, tents and sheds all set up, by the time the Korps had arrived. They'd even erected camouflage nets, though that was not really necessary since no French planes, not even civilian ones, were permitted to fly over this area.

More necessary were the Wehrmacht troops on guard around the exterior of the barbed-wire perimeters, making sure none of the local French population came near the place. The people of Brignoles could not help but be aware, of course, that there was a military camp close by. But they had no idea of its true nature, assuming it was just another of the Wehrmacht encampments scattered around the south of France, part of the normal occupation forces.

General Hausser smiled at what he saw and heard in the valley encampment below. Almost directly beneath him, the men of Major Fick's I SS Langemark Regiment were working on their machines and arms, or being put through double-time drills carrying full field equipment, or engaging in target competitions and unarmed combat practice. It was the same with Major Tychsen's II SS Langemark and Captain Steinbeck's Das Reich Panzer Division, and all the rest of the massed assemblage of armor and troops inside the valley. No tank, soldier or submachine gun was being allowed to lose one iota of battle readiness.

The sound of a car approaching the farmhouse headquarters reached Hausser. He saw two men, one in a naval officer's uniform, the other dressed in the civilian style favored by the Gestapo, climbing out of a military Mercedes-Benz 230. The car had been stopped between the officers' guard post and a barracks erected for the SS escort detachment; the two men were showing their papers to a pair of SS sentries.

Hausser knew the one in uniform: Commandant Hugo Schuldt, the Kriegsmarine intelligence officer assigned as liaison to Operation Lila. He was the one who had flown off to Berlin with the general's complaints.

General Hausser's chief of staff, Colonel Ostendorff, hurried from the farmhouse to meet Schuldt and the other man; he was accompanied by his aide, Lieutenant Rentrop. They brought the two arrivals over to Hausser.

Commandant Schuldt introduced the man with him. "General, this is Over-Inspektor Keller, from RSHA, currently attached to Field Marshal von Rundstedt's command. His car developed engine trouble outside Brignoles and had to be towed to a garage for repair, so I gave him a lift. Seems he's here to check your security, to make sure it is sound."

"Good. The more security the better." Hausser liked Keller immediately. Only the best men had eyes like that: men with that rare combination of professional skill and absolute faith in the cause for which they fought. You could depend on men like this to throw themselves against the muzzle of a machine gun if necessary, because they believed in what they were doing it for. It was a shame the man was a policeman; he would have made an excellent combat officer.

General Hausser gestured to Ostendorff's aide. "Rentrop will take you to the chief of our security force, Lieutenant Telcamp. He can introduce you around and show you whatever you want to see."

"Thank you, general." Keller walked off with Lieutenant Rentrop.

Hausser went inside the farmhouse to his makeshift conference room, followed by his chief of staff and Commandant Schuldt. As they grouped around the long, white-painted plywood table, the naval intelligence officer unbuckled the pigskin briefcase he had brought back from Berlin.

"You'll be pleased with this, general. The most recent maps of the Toulon navy base. With the present position of every single vessel inside it marked, up to the minute."

As Schuldt spread the maps out on the table, Colonel Ostendorff demanded: "And what about those nonexistent eight hundred navy sailors? Do you have them in that briefcase?"

The navy man almost blushed. "That was an unfortunate mixup, I'm afraid. Grand Admiral Raeder is extremely upset about it. I can assure you they will arrive within the next few days."

"Just as long," Ostendorff said sarcastically, "as those few days don't stretch. They won't be too much use to us if they arrive after we're already inside that base."

Commandant Schuldt cleared his throat and looked to Hausser. "That is one of the things I have to talk to you about, general. The date set for your attack."

General Hausser settled himself on one of the tall stools. "Fine, we'll talk about that. But first let's talk about the other little problems posed by Admiral Laborde placing those scuttling charges on his ships. Laborde himself being the main problem."

"General, Berlin feels—and both Grand Admiral Raeder and Field Marshal von Rundstedt agree—that to attempt to force the dismissal of Laborde would only stir up French suspicion concerning our intentions. In the French navy, and in Vichy. Marshal Pétain has absolute faith in Laborde's personal and professional loyalty to him. Men who know both of them well feel that faith is justified."

"I didn't ask to get Admiral Laborde fired," Hausser snapped. "What I did ask for was an informed assessment of his character and motivations. Along with sufficient time to allow his suspicions to be lulled before we go in there."

The navy officer nodded. "About that first point, general. Laborde has given his word of honor never to issue a scuttle order without Pétain's agreement. According to our best sources—in the French navy, in Vichy, inside the base itself and even aboard his flagship—Laborde will hold to his word."

Hausser relaxed, smiling. "Good. In that case I can overcome the problem."

His chief of staff glanced at him uneasily. "Suppose Pétain *gives* Laborde the permission to scuttle when we hit the base? That old bastard just might do that."

Hausser shook his head. "There will be no way he can, not

quickly enough to interfere with our operation as I have re-formulated it." He looked to Schuldt. "But much depends on one new requirement. I want the French navy guards stationed outside the gates of both the West Arsenal and the Mourillon Arsenal removed, and replaced by Wehrmacht guards. Can you accomplish that for me?"

The naval intelligence officer considered briefly. "I'm sure it can be handled. There are certain French navy intelligence men who can be persuaded to warn Laborde of a danger that armed terrorists and a group of enemy commandos may be planning to attack the base in force. At the same time we can warn Vichy of the same danger. Laval will see to it the French guards are removed, with our own taking their places as being more competent to ward off such an attack."

"It would be best if this could be done fairly soon, to give Admiral Laborde time to get used to the new Wehrmacht guard units outside his base, and to become assured they have no unfriendly intentions."

"I understand, general."

Hausser gestured at the maps of the Toulon base spread out on the table. "As I have reworked the execution of Operation Lila, the amount of time it will take us to reach those ships, from the moment we break through the gates, is now squeezed down to a bit more than half an hour. Consider what happens in that half hour..."

Gazing fixedly at the maps, Hausser seemed to be addressing himself: "First, we strike before dawn. With the French guards removed from outside the gates, no alarm will be given at our approach. When we smash through the gates it will still be night, most of the base asleep. I think we can grab Vice-Admiral Marquis in that fort of his before he knows anything at all has begun. Admiral Laborde will be awakened once we are inside the base, but no one at first will be able to tell him what has happened.

"By the time they sort it out, every one of our assault units will be on their way to the ships assigned to them. Laborde will phone Vichy. But it will use up more of the little time he'll have left to get through. And still more to wake the old marshal."

Commandant Schuldt was grinning. "And more time for Pé-

194

tain to grasp what the call is about. Plus more for him to decide whether to grant Laborde permission to scuttle. Our intelligence sources in Vichy are almost certain Pétain will call for Laval's advice before he can nerve himself to actually order the sinking of the entire fleet. In that case you are right, general. There will be no problem. Laval will advise against it."

Hausser shrugged. "I won't count on that, and it won't last long enough for Laval's advice to matter. By then my troops will be aboard the ships, in force. Before the French scuttling crews can be wakened, reach their posts to detonate the charges and receive an order to do so, the fleet will be ours."

Colonel Ostendorff had a suggestion: "We *could* cut all telephone lines between the Toulon base and Vichy. So Laborde couldn't get through to Pétain."

"Not advisable," Commandant Schuldt put in quickly. "Under that circumstance, if Laborde found himself *unable* to reach his chief of state, the admiral might take the decision on himself."

"I agree," Hausser said. "Better to allow him the phone call. We'll accomplish our objective while the French use up the little time they have left. Even should Pétain give permission, Laborde would then have to communicate the order to all his commanders. By then those commanders will be in our hands, together with their ships and crews."

"Well thought out, general," Schuldt said. "Neat, precise, taking everything into consideration."

Hausser fixed himself with a cold stare. "You forget yourself, commandant. I am not a student and you are not a teacher grading my answers to an examination."

The navy officer flinched. Unable to meet Hausser's eyes he stared instead at the silver death's-head on Hausser's hat. "Forgive me, general. I assure you it was intended only as an expression of my deep admiration for you. My enthusiasm got the better of me, but..."

Hausser halted the apology: "Enough. Now—what have you brought back concerning my demand for an extension of the attack date?"

"Everybody agrees, general. Some time has to be allowed for

Admiral Laborde to simmer down and begin feeling his suspicions were unfounded after all. So that when you strike it will catch him by surprise." Schuldt hesitated slightly. "But the Führer himself would not like this delay to extend longer than ten days."

"Excellent. I had been planning for eight days. We'll split the difference. You can inform Berlin I will attack the base before 5 A.M. on November 27. A bit less than nine days from this moment."

TWENTY

LIEUTENANT TELCAMP, THE officer in charge of the SS Panzer Korps' security, introduced Andreas Keller to the SS guards at the main gate in the barbed-wire perimeter, and then to the Wehrmacht unit in their own guardhouse outside the gate. He explained Keller's function, and that the RSHA man might later wish to question each of them separately.

As Telcamp led Keller back inside he said, "Well, that's about all of it. You've met each of my men, seen our security arrangements. I think you will admit our setup here is one of strength."

"A security fence is only as strong as its weakest link," Keller said. "The same applies to human security arrangements. I'll want to interview each of the clerical staff individually, as well as every member of the security details." He tapped the briefcase under his arm. "I have dossiers on some of them, but not all."

Lieutenant Telcamp had stiffened. He didn't like this Keller. But then, he had never met a Gestapo or SD type who was likable. Pompous, humorless men, every one of them, with an overinflated sense of self-importance and an insufferable confidence in their ability to frighten people. Well, they could not frighten the Waffens SS.

"There are no weak links in our setup," he said sharply, "human or otherwise. Each man, each guard..."

197

"There is an old saying," Keller cut in calmly. "Who guards the guards?"

Telcamp was close to losing his temper. "There are no weaklings or traitors in the Waffen SS."

"You would be surprised. I've caught a few of them myself. The variety of reasons behind their treachery always astounds me. Money, sex, religious convictions..."

"How long do you expect to hang around, Keller?"

"Some days, probably. Until my job here is completed."

Telcamp's smile was sardonic. "If you stretch your job too many days there won't be much point in it. We'll have already left here and taken Toulon."

Keller stopped and turned on him sharply. "Lieutenant, you are talking too much. Do not speak about your objective and do not tell me when it will take place."

Telcamp winced, realizing he *had* been caught in an error. "I...I don't know the date as yet, anyway."

Keller knew that. He said, "Just don't offer me any information unless I ask a specific question."

"I assumed you knew..."

"I do. That does not alter what I have said. Guarding one's tongue is a habit one must keep in practice, lieutenant."

Telcamp nodded, genuinely upset with himself. "I have to attend to my other duties now. If you need any further assistance, Sergeant Hauptmann will help you."

Keller watched Lieutenant Telcamp stride off, eager to get away from this RSHA man who made him feel so uncomfortable. Turning in the opposite direction, Keller walked to the barracks headquarters of the security and escort details. He asked for Sergeant Hauptmann, Telcamp's chief aide.

The sergeant almost saluted when he emerged to face Keller. The RSHA man was not exactly an officer, but respect was due him: Lieutenant Telcamp had said he was to be accommodated in any way he wished. "What can I do for you?"

"I'd like to get my car. It's being repaired in Brignoles, but it was only a broken fan belt, so I imagine it's ready by now. And I left my suitcase in it."

"No problem, I'll drive you to Brignoles."

Keller started to follow him and then stopped, putting a hand on his arm. "Wait, first I should get rid of some of the papers I'm carrying. Classified information will be better off in the safe until I need it."

"Certainly." Sergeant Hauptmann led Keller toward the barn at one end of the farmhouse. The barn door had been boarded up, but there was a single door in the side wall. An SS guard stood on duty in front of it. But since he knew the sergeant, and Telcamp had informed him Keller had free run of the camp, he passed them inside without question.

The interior had been scrupulously cleaned and was now divided by a maze of high unpainted plywood partitions. Keller and Sergeant Hauptmann went past the radio room, the telephone switchboard and teleprinter exchange, and entered the office of the stenographic pool.

There were file cabinets, three desks and the latest model photocopying machine, fresh from Berlin. Three uniformed stenographers were at work with their typewriters making a rapid fire clatter. In a curtained-off corner of the office stood a large heavy safe. It was there, Lieutenant Telcamp had explained, that all classified and secret documents were kept.

Only three men had the combination to the safe: Telcamp, his sergeant and General Hausser's chief of staff, Colonel Ostendorff. The curtain was to insure that none of the stenographers could watch when the safe was unlocked.

Keller stepped behind the curtain with Sergeant Hauptmann, acting as though he had every right, and it didn't occur to the sergeant to stop him. While Keller opened his briefcase Hauptmann knelt and worked the combination lock, then swung open the heavy door. Keller gave him a thick envelope from his briefcase. Hauptmann put it in the safe, swung the door shut and spun the dial to lock it.

As Keller followed the sergeant out of the office, and away from the barn to the car pool, he silently repeated the safe's combination until he was certain he would not forget it.

The car was hidden in the trees beside the road. Two of the four Miliciens were behind it, pissing against a tree. The third

199

rested behind the steering wheel, smoking a cigarette. The fourth was in front of the car in the shadow of a gnarled oak, leaning against its trunk and gazing sleepily at the vineyards sloping up from the other side of the road. He was bored; nothing remotely exciting had occurred that day.

Then he saw Jonas appear over the top of the opposite slope, riding his bicycle down toward the road.

The Milicien straightened away from the tree, but staying in its shadow so the bike rider wouldn't spot him. He rapped his knuckles against the car's front fender. "Hey, look up there."

The two who'd been relieving themselves came up alongside him, buttoning their flies. They regarded the distant Jonas riding down a path that would reach the road two hundred yards to their left.

"So what?" one of them said. "Just a local on his way home after a day in the fields."

The other said, "If he's from around here I don't know him. And I know almost all the locals."

The one who had spotted Jonas opened his belt holster and fondled the grip of his revolver. "Let's have a talk with him."

"What for?"

"Why not? Have some fun, throw a scare into him." The Milicien, his hand ready on his revolver, stepped out of the shade into the road. He shouted and raised an arm high in a beckoning gesture.

Jonas was halfway down the slope when he saw him—and the Milice uniform. His heart accelerated and a familiar bitter taste rose in his throat. If there was only one...

Two others stepped out onto the road beside the first man. Jonas fashioned a wide smile and lifted a hand from the handlebar, raising it and waving to them, as though in response to a friendly greeting. One of the men drew a revolver and fired it into the air. The report of the shot echoed sharply over the countryside. The only other sounds, the twittering of birds, abruptly ended.

Jonas nodded vigorously, made a placating motion with his raised hand and then pointed down to the road, indicating he'd

200

turn and ride toward them when he got down there. But he couldn't do that, not with the radio inside the suitcase strapped behind his seat. Without that he might have risked being questioned by the Milice. But they had a clear view of him all the way down, so there was no possibility of dumping it before reaching the road. He prayed they'd stay put where they were, expecting him to ride over to them when he reached the road.

But they didn't. They began walking along the road in his direction, two of them unslinging weapons from their shoulders. One appeared to be a hunting rifle, the other a submachine gun. A car slid into view out of the trees and turned onto the road by the three walkers. The driver made four. The other three climbed into the car.

Jonas cursed and pedaled as hard as he could down the rest of the slope. He was going very fast when the bike reached the road and flashed straight across it, speeding into the dense woods on the other side. There was an angry blast from the car horn behind him, and a squeal of spinning tires as the engine abruptly revved up in pursuit. Jonas kept going, deeper into the woods, crashing the bike through bushes and twisting around jutting rocks.

A goat trail materialized, winding down a steep incline between the trees. He went down it at a reckless speed, almost spilling over at every sharp bend. From above came the noise of the car screeching to a halt, of doors slamming open. The trail ended against a pile of boulders. Jonas stopped and jumped off, looking back up the way he'd come. He couldn't see his pursuers yet, so they couldn't see him. Yanking open the straps of the suitcase, he pulled out the radio case and climbed over the boulders with it, dropping down the other side where the goat trail resumed.

There was a burst of fire from the submachine gun above, bullets smashing off the boulders and thunking into the tree trunks near Jonas. But it was blind firing. They were coming down but they still couldn't see exactly where he was. One of them yelled for him to come back or they'd kill him. Jonas left the trail and cut sharply to his left, still going downhill, crashing

201

through tangles of brush, hearing them crashing down after him.

They were too many for him to handle, even with the pistol inside his radio case. If the car up on the road had a two-way radio, the driver would now be calling for reinforcements. Three were still too many for him to fight. They had at least one submachine gun, and at least one rifle that could drop him at a distance too great for his handgun to be of any use.

Jonas didn't have to think about what the situation called for; he'd been in others like it in the past. The only solution was to lose his pursuers as fast as he could. Trying to find some hiding place where he could hole up was no good. With reinforcements almost certainly coming within the next hour or so, they'd surround the area, seal him in and then take their time fine-combing it until they found him. He had to be far outside the area before the reinforcements arrived.

He stopped, panting and listening. They were crashing through the woods behind him, but still a long way back. He plunged ahead, still angling to the left, making a good deal of noise.

A submachine gun blasted at him, not from behind him but from somewhere above. There was a burning sensation across his left thigh and the radio case was torn from his hand. There was another burst from the submachine gun, but this one only ripped branches high above him and off to his right. Blind firing again from the high ground while the other two came down behind him. They weren't stupid, and they were probably used to hunting.

There was blood on his thigh but not enough to worry about now. The bullet had torn flesh but hadn't gone so deeply that it would slow him down. Jonas ripped open the case. The radio was destroyed, unrepairable. The pistol had survived. He shoved it in his belt, got out the spare ammunition clip and the code book and stuck them in his pocket. Then he started back along the same route, going toward the pursuers coming after him. This time he made no noise.

When he came to the dense spread of creeping juniper bushes he'd passed going in the other direction, Jonas went to ground

202

and snaked out of sight under them. He lay motionless, stilling his breathing.

He stopped breathing entirely when he heard them approach. Squinting ahead under the tangled juniper cover, he saw the bottoms of their boots. Two men, as he'd thought. And another somewhere up above with the submachine gun, but moving off in the original direction Jonas had followed. Holding his breath, he waited until they moved on past his cover.

He drew soft, shallow breaths. He gave it another thirty seconds, and then crawled out and moved in the opposite direction. After a hundred yards he began to climb, as quietly as he could manage.

The fourth Milicien was still behind the wheel of the car, speaking into the two-way radio. Jonas stopped in the bushes twenty feet away, watching. He didn't want to make any noise that would bring up the other three; not until it would be too late for them. He watched the driver hang up his speaker-phone and climb out of the car. Jonas backed deeper into the bushes, and then began silently shifting to his right.

The Milice driver walked into the edge of the woods and peered down. From the road he couldn't hear anything down there now. "What's happening?" he called. "Have you got him?"

"Not yet!" one of the men below called back. "What about those reinforcements?"

"I've got everybody on their way! Milice, police, Gestapo!" The driver took a deep breath and shouted louder, intending Jonas to hear: "That guy better give himself up right now! If he waits till the Gestapo gets here, he'll wish he'd never been born!"

Jonas chopped him across the back of the skull with his pistol butt. The man let out a quiet groan as he collapsed to the ground. He landed on his hands and knees, his head wobbling back and forth. Jonas rammed the heel of his shoe against the Milicien's temple, kicking him over on his back. The man sprawled out unconscious, breath rasping through his open mouth. Jonas bent and took the revolver from the man's holster and stuck it in his belt with his own pistol.

Getting into the Milice car, he switched on the ignition. It no longer mattered if they heard below. They couldn't get up here before he was gone. They'd be stranded, with no radio and with no telephone for miles, and nothing to do but wait until the reinforcements arrived. By then he'd be far away.

Putting the car in gear, Jonas drove onto the road. By the time he shifted to high gear he had the accelerator jammed to the floorboards, racing off toward the south coast.

Kriminal Inspektor Udo Mueller stood in the police station in the town of Collobrières, glaring at the three Miliciens who had lost the enemy agent. The fourth of their sorry group was lying in a doctor's office with his head bandaged, drugged with painkillers. Mueller wished the man was dead. The four incompetents each gave a different description of the man they'd lost—and they'd let him get away in their car. How could one operate properly with such men?

Mueller transferred his glare to the gendarme inspector seated stolidly behind his desk. But the French detective seemed unimpressed with Mueller's rage, continuing to devote his attention to carefully packing tobacco into his pipe. "Don't worry," he said blandly, "we'll catch him, sooner or later."

The Frenchman's lack of concern changed Mueller's mood. He studied the man thoughtfully. Many of these local police, he had come to realize, were secretly in sympathy with the Resistance and the enemy. Mueller made a mental note to have this one investigated, thoroughly.

He walked over to the bullet smashed radio on a table against the wall, examining it again. It was undoubtedly a typical SOE job, which meant the escaped man was undoubtedly an agent of the SOE...

The desk phone rang. The gendarme inspector picked it up, identified himself, listened. After a time he said, "Thank you. Stay by it, don't let anyone touch anything until we get there."

He hung up the phone and turned to Mueller. "A patrol unit of the mobile police have found the car. It was hidden in the woods, down near Bormes-les-Mimosas, close to the south coast."

Mueller walked quickly to a wall map of the area. "From that

204

point he could easily have walked farther south and caught a train west. By now he could be in Toulon...or on his way to Marseilles."

"Or in the other direction," the gendarme inspector said as he rose to his feet and put on his uniform jacket. "East along the coast to St. Raphael or Cannes."

Mueller shook his head. "No. It is *my* area that is his objective. I can feel it...I'm sure of it."

It was dusk when Jonas got off the bus at Les Arcs, miles to the north. There was a mixed group of police and Milice at the bus station, conducting an identity check and body search of arriving and departing passengers. Jonas submitted to both patiently. There was nothing about his papers to arouse suspicion. He had thrown away both weapons after abandoning the Milice car. The code book he had burned. He was simply a law-abiding French citizen named Blois, going about his normal business.

He passed inspection on time to board the only evening bus still running farther north, to Draguignan. As the bus pulled out of Les Arcs and carried him up through the hills with the Pre-Alps rising behind them, Jonas thought about the lost radio. Without it he was cut off from Michael in Algiers.

Except for the contact with Keller, if and when it came, from now on he was entirely on his own.

TWENTY-ONE NOVEMBER 19

"THE ASSAULT FORCES for the initial stage of the attack—
the closing of the jaws around the Toulon naval base—will be
divided into the three basic combat groups I have indicated,
drawn from the Das Reich Division, the Langemark Regiments
and the Adolf Hitler Divsion. These combat groups will assemble at the points marked on your maps, at 0300 hours on the
morning of X-Day, which has now been set for November 27."

General Hausser stood before a large wall map of Toulon,
on which the present position of every ship of the French fleet
had been marked. With his pointer he indicated the three points
outside Toulon where his attack forces were to be assembled
by three o'clock on the morning of Operation Lila. The senior
officer of each combat group, seated at the big table of the
farmhouse conference room, marked the assembly points on
his own copy of the map. Hausser's chief of staff, Colonel Ostendorff, stood at the back of the room with the naval intelligence liaison officer, Commandant Schuldt. Two SS
stenographers perched on stools to one side of the wall map,
swiftly recording on their shorthand pads.

"At 0400 hours," General Hausser continued, "each combat
group will move from its designated point to carry out its own
tasks. Combat Group One, under the leadership of Major Fick,
has the Mourillon installations as its objectives. Approaching

from the east, along this route, it will knock out the radio station and take the Fort Lamalgue headquarters of Vice-Admiral Marquis, cutting off communications between it and the rest of the naval base. Simultaneously, most of the forces of Combat Group One will seize the Mourillon Arsenal and its auxiliary submarine base.

"Combat Group Two will move south from its assembly point and take possession of the fort on top of Mount Faron, cutting its radio and telephone communications to the base below.

"Combat Group Three is the largest because its task is the greatest. Striking from the west it will seize the Saint Mandrier peninsula and its coastal batteries. With its tank formations operating as spearheads, it will smash through the Castigneau Gate into the West Arsenal. Having gained surprise entry, the units designated will move swiftly to board the ships of the French fleet and take their crews prisoner before they can assemble to detonate scuttling charges.

"Lieutenant Krag will be in charge of the units assigned to seize the vessels at the Milhaud piers. You will note that I have circled the position of Admiral Laborde's flagship, the *Strasbourg*, in red. The admiral and his aides are to be taken prisoner as quickly as possible and not allowed to contact the rest of the fleet.

"Lieutenant Kohler will lead the units assigned to board the ships along the Noël..."

General Hausser continued until he had outlined all the basic moves of Operation Lila. Then he went back to the beginning, three o'clock on the morning of November 27, and began dealing with the details.

It was late afternoon when he brought the briefing conference to an end. "Tomorrow morning," he told the officers, "each of you will receive a set of typed orders covering your own area of responsibility. Study them well. We will meet here again tomorrow afternoon, to deal with any questions you may have concerning them."

When the officers had left and the stenographers had hurried off to type up their notes, Hausser strolled back to his

208

living quarters with his chief of staff. "I want those sets of typed orders tonight, Ostendorff. So I can make any corrections before I go to bed."

"I'll see to it, general," the colonel said. "You'll have the first versions by dinnertime."

The abbey was secluded in a tangle of empty hills a mile and a half from the encampment of the SS Panzer Korps.

There wasn't much left of it. Built in the fourteenth century and abandoned in the nineteenth, most of its buildings had collapsed when extensive bauxite quarrying undermined their foundations. What remained was part of a roofless church and sacristy, plus two walls of a monks' dormitory. They perched precariously above the edge of the quarry, which had been abandoned like the abbey when its bauxite petered out twenty years ago.

Andreas Keller stood with his radio case inside the church looking up into the highest part of its ruin: a remnant of a bell tower, with stone steps still projecting from the interior wall. Carrying the case, he mounted the steps, testing each before trusting his full weight to it. The steps were solid but treacherous, with a deep mixture of bauxite dust and bird droppings. When he came back here at night he would have to bring a flashlight.

At the top of the tower he looked out and down. A dirt road ran past the bottom of the quarry, winding through the hills toward newer quarries. Even from this high vantage point Keller couldn't see his car inside the quarry; and he had made sure it was hidden from the road. At sunset it would be invisible, even if someone were to drive along the road after nightfall.

It would be best, Keller decided, to leave his car where it was and walk back to General Hausser's camp. When he left there late that night, his explanation that he wanted to check the exterior of the security fence would be more plausible if he went out on foot. If anyone should ask.

Keller looked up at the cloudless sky. There would be no rain tonight. He slid the radio into a hole in the wall, concealed it by shoving in some of the thick mixture coating the top step and climbed back down the tower interior.

A large wrought-iron cross had been set up in the nave of the church by the citizens of Brignoles, perhaps in apology for what their quarrying had done to the abbey. Keller went down on his knees in front of the cross and prayed before leaving the church to return to the SS Panzer Korps.

At ten o'clock that night Colonel Ostendorff entered the converted barn carrying the final version of the Operation Lila plans, each typed page approved and initialed by General Hausser. There were different sets of orders for each of the officers who were to lead the separate prongs of the attack, each in its own folder. But in addition each folder contained two identical documents.

One was an introductory page, bearing General Hausser's signature and outlining the basic aims of the operation. The other was a copy of the original directive for the seizure of the Toulon fleet, signed by Adolf Hitler.

Going through the maze of partitions, Colonel Ostendorff entered the stenographic services office. One stenographer was still at work there, typing up a long report on the final battle plan which was to be sent to Himmler, Field Marshal Rundstedt and Hitler.

"Is that going to be ready soon?" Ostendorff demanded.

"I'll need about another hour, colonel. I thought you would want it tomorrow morning..."

"I want it tonight, corporal."

"Yes, colonel."

Ostendorff went behind the curtain, opened the combination lock, put the folders inside the safe and relocked it. The SS stenographer was pounding at his typewriter when Hausser's chief of staff strode out.

Andreas Keller, standing against the shadowed wall of the security detail barracks, watched Colonel Ostendorff leave the barn. Keller waited until he went into the main part of the farmhouse, waited five more minutes and then walked briskly toward the barn carrying his briefcase. Appearing deep in thought, he nodded brusquely at the guard and went in without a word being exchanged between the two of them.

One of the stenographers was still at work. "Corporal, you will vacate this office for about five minutes. I need complete privacy to make copies of some of my documents, to be sent to SS Reichsführer Himmler."

The magic name and title did the trick. The stenographer immediately pushed back his chair and rose to his feet, almost standing at attention. "Yes, sir."

"Don't go far. Remain just outside this door until I am finished." Keller didn't want him going for a walk and being seen by a curious security man.

The stenographer stepped outside the doorway. "May I smoke, sir?"

"No." Keller shut the door and locked it from inside. He went to the man's desk and swiftly read what he'd been typing. It was interesting, but without a signature useless for Keller's purposes. He went behind the curtain, worked the safe combination and found the folders Colonel Ostendorff had just placed there.

Leafing through the folders he found what he'd anticipated: one set of orders would be sufficient. Especially with the two documents appended to it. Keller read the beginning of the one signed by Hausser:

KORPS BATTLE ORDER NR. 1: 19.11.1942:

1—The High Command has issued orders to seize the land fortifications and naval forces of Toulon in a lightning stroke to prevent the French fleet from leaving the harbor or sinking itself.

2—The officers and crews on the ships and on land are to have their weapons taken from them and to be made prisoners.

3—The assault forces will be divided into three combat groups...

Keller didn't have to read more. Together with the Hitler directive and one set of detailed orders giving date, time, objective and tactics, it was all the proof Admiral Laborde would need—if he could be persuaded the whole thing wasn't a forgery. He carried one folder across the office to the new photocopy machine and turned it on. One by one he began feeding the pages from the folder into the machine.

Four minutes later he had what Algiers had asked of him: two copies of every page.

Keller put the copies into two manila envelopes which he slipped inside his briefcase. The original folder he put back in the safe. Relocking the safe door, he crossed the office and let the stenographer back in. "You may return to your work now, corporal."

"Thank you, sir." The stenographer walked to his desk as Keller left the office with his briefcase.

Lieutenant Telcamp entered the security detail barracks and made his way to his living quarters at the far end. He had decided to turn in early, for a change. His room was small, with a window facing the barn end of the farmhouse. Telcamp reached out to turn on the light when something he saw through the window stopped him.

The RSHA man, Andreas Keller, had just come out of the converted barn and was striding away carrying a briefcase.

Though it was his profession to be suspicious, Lieutenant Telcamp warned himself not to let his dislike of the man spook him into any foolish thoughts. Keller's job here gave him leave to go wherever he wished, whenever he wished. Telcamp did not turn on his light. Instead he walked to the window and watched in the darkened room until Keller had gone out of sight. Then he opened the window quietly and leaned out.

Keller was heading for the main gate. There he spoke briefly to the SS guard detail, and then walked out.

Lieutenant Telcamp drew back from the window and stood in the dark for a few moments. He didn't want to do anything to earn himself a black mark on his RSHA dossier. But he could make some discreet inquiries without Keller's knowledge.

Leaving the barracks, he walked to the barn. Keller, the guard said, had gone in and out without saying anything. The lieutenant went inside and questioned everybody at work until he got to the corporal in the stenographer's office.

"What did he do here?" Telcamp asked him, keeping his tone casual.

"He wanted to copy some of his documents in privacy, lieutenant. Had me wait outside with the door closed."

"For how long?"

"Oh...eight or nine minutes, I'd say."

Telcamp went behind the curtain in the corner. The safe was shut and locked. He stood there looking at it, frowning. Then he left the barn and went to the SS guard detail at the main gate. He asked them, still keeping it casual, where the RSHA man had gone.

"No idea, lieutenant. For a walk, I guess. We didn't think it was our place to ask him."

"Quite right. What did he say to you?"

"Just about it being a nice night, with all that moonlight and no clouds."

"Which direction did he go in?"

One of the guards indicated the dirt road that ran past, coming from the town of Brignoles and going off into the hills where the quarries were. "That way," he said, pointing toward the hills.

There was nothing in that direction within easy walking distance except the quarries. The guard was probably right; Keller had merely gone for a moonlight stroll and would be strolling back before long. But...

Lieutenant Telcamp walked out to the dirt road and began strolling in the same direction that Keller had taken.

Keller turned into the bottom of the quarry and went to the man-made, square-cut cavern where he'd left the car. When he stepped inside the cavern the moonlight was cut off abruptly

213

and he had to feel his way around the car to the door. He left the briefcase in the car, got the flashlight and went back out into the moonlight.

The slope rising around the side of the quarry from the dirt road was an easy climb. He didn't have to turn on the flashlight until he was inside the remains of the church. Mounting the tower, he tugged the radio out of its hole and opened it. He looped the end of the aerial around the top step and unraveled the rest of its length as he carried the case down to the nave. Settling himself on the broken bricks of the flooring, Keller set up the transmitter and receiver and plugged in the power pack.

His notebook and pencil were tucked into the code book, with the brief message he had to send already encoded on the first page. Keller shifted the angle of the flashlight until it illuminated the page clearly. Settling the headset on his ears, he gripped the sending key delicately with his thumb and two fingers and began transmitting his call sign to Algiers.

Lieutenant Telcamp lengthened his stride along the dirt road, beginning to feel very foolish. He was getting too far from the Korps encampment and there was still no sign of Keller ahead of him. In all likelihood the man had strolled off the road some distance back, taking one of the side paths, and was by now far behind, returning from his stroll. The lieutenant hoped the guards at the gate didn't mention that he'd gone out after him.

He slowed his pace and halted, looking at the abandoned quarry beside the road, then up at the dark abbey ruin above it. The time had come for him to turn back. He could satisfy his curiosity, once he returned, by simply asking the man from RSHA what he'd been doing in the stenography office. Keller's answer would probably be caustic. On the other hand the RSHA agent was here to check on the soundness of the Korps security, and could not in justice fault the officer in charge for being too watchful.

Telcamp turned to go back, and stopped himself in midturn. He'd glimpsed a tiny flicker of light up there in the darkness of the abbey church. But when he held still, squinting at the point where he'd seen the light, it was no longer there.

Keeping his eyes fixed on the same point, he took a slow half step backwards. Still no light up there. He swayed slightly to his left and saw it again. It might only be the moon reflecting off a broken piece of metal, or...

The light shifted a bit.

Lieutenant Telcamp left the road and climbed the slope around the side of the quarry.

It took over three minutes of repeating his call sign before the Algiers recognition signal sounded in Keller's earphones. He transmitted his short message. When decoded in Algiers, it would read simply: "I have it."

Keller waited for the reply, pencil poised over his notebook. After several minutes the number sequences began coming through from Algiers. He copied them down swiftly. When the message ended he removed the headset from his ears, hung it around his neck and began decoding.

The first part of the message gave him the time for his rendezvous with the British plane in the mountains north of Draguignan: 11 P.M. the following night. The second part asked for the date and time set for the execution of Operation Lila.

Keller was about to begin encoding his answer when Lieutenant Telcamp said behind him: "What are you doing here, Keller?"

Without turning his head, Keller said, "I would advise you, lieutenant, to return where you belong and not inquire about matters which you are not permitted to know about." As he spoke he switched off the radio and put the headset back in the case. His movements were as casual as his voice. He closed the code book around his notebook and was about to slip it into his pocket when Telcamp warned harshly:

"Don't. I want to have a look at that."

Keller rose and turned with the book in his hand, appearing unconcerned about the Luger automatic pistol Telcamp had aimed at him. "If you look at what is in this book, lieutenant, nothing anyone can do will save your career. It contains secret messages between myself and the personal staff of SS Reichsführer Himmler."

He saw a flicker of fear in the SS lieutenant's eyes at the magic name. But Telcamp was too stubborn to give way to it. "We have excellent radio facilities at the camp," he said, "which you could have used at any time if your purpose is indeed legitimate. At the moment I must doubt it."

"I have explained these messages are secret. If I used your radio facilities that secrecy would be violated, and Reichsführer Himmler would be displeased. As he will be displeased by your present actions." But Keller knew the bluff wasn't going to work, even as he spoke.

"Nevertheless," Telcamp said stubbornly, "I must insist you give me that book." He made a threatening gesture with the Luger, and he was not bluffing.

Keller shrugged. "I don't care. It's your funeral..." He stepped forward holding out the code book.

Telcamp reached for it with his free hand. Keller let the book fall to the floor and grabbed with both hands for the Luger.

The SS lieutenant's reflexes were a shade too fast. Keller got his hands on the weapon but Telcamp fired before he could twist it aside.

There was a hammer blow to Keller's stomach, hurling him backward off his feet. But he clung to the Luger as he fell, and Telcamp was forced to fall with him to prevent it from being torn from his grasp. Keller's back slammed against the hard brick floor of the church and the SS lieutenant sprawled across him. Shifting his grip to Telcamp's gun hand and wrist, Keller raked the man's knuckles viciously across the jagged bricks. Telcamp's fingers sprang open and the Luger skittered away to the base of the wrought-iron cross.

Telcamp rolled off Keller and scrambled after it. Keller caught at his ankle but Telcamp kicked loose and reached the fallen Luger. Dragging his own pistol from its holster Keller shoved up on his left elbow and shot the lieutenant in the back, driving him face down across the floor.

But Telcamp had the Luger. Making a fast roll he came up in a sitting position. The muzzle of the Luger came up with him, but Keller fired first.

Telcamp's forehead disintegrated as the bullet punched through it into his brain. His head jerked back and cracked against the base of the cross. Keller watched his torso slump to one side, settling lifeless on the brick flooring.

Sticking the pistol back in his holster, Keller sat up and ripped open his blood-soaked shirt. The hole was an inch from his navel. The pain was not intolerable, but his stomach and intestines burned and there was a numbing pressure near the small of his back where the bullet had lodged.

He slid over to the code book and notebook, tore them into a small pile, got out a match and set fire to it. While it burned he forced himself to his feet. He felt dizzy from the blood draining out of him, but steadied himself angrily, knowing he hadn't lost that much yet. Pressing a hand to the wound to stanch the flow, Keller yanked down the aerial, carried it and the radio case outside the church and dropped them into the quarry.

Dragging Telcamp's body out cost him more blood and much of his remaining strength. Keller shoved him over, dropped the Luger into the quarry after him and returned inside to scan the church flooring with his flashlight. The blood, his own and Telcamp's, was soaking into the dirt and broken bricks. By tomorrow it would be unnoticeable. The books were now smoldering ashes. He crushed the ashes to powder under his heel and looked blearily at the cross. His lips moved silently before he walked out of the church, pressing both hands against his wound.

He made it down into the quarry and through the maze of diggings to the rear wall. The radio and the SS lieutenant lay between it and piles of rubble. Climbing the rocks, Keller kicked at them until he started a slide which covered both.

If he was lucky they would never be found among the hundreds of quarries. If he was unlucky, they'd be found—the next day or eventually. It was in the hands of God.

Returning to the car he got two shirts from his suitcase, wadded one against his abdomen and tied the other around his waist to hold the wadding tightly in place. Then he slid into the driver's seat and drove the car out of the quarry, turning away from Brignoles and the SS camp when he reached the dirt road.

It was impossible to drive fast. The road was narrow and kept twisting sharply as it went around the slopes of one hill after another. It took him more than an hour to reach the paved road that led to Draguignan.

Once on it he tried to go faster, but soon had to slow down again. His vision was beginning to blur, and he felt increasingly dizzy. What worried him more was the steady draining away of strength. Finally he stopped the car and got a flask of brandy from the glove compartment.

He drank until life coursed through him again. It was a false life, but if it got him there that was all that mattered. Starting up the car again, Keller found he was able to drive faster. But after a time the blurring of vision returned, and the dizziness.

Keller was five miles from Draguignan when he lost consciousness. The car swerved off the road and crashed head on into a tree.

In Algiers, Michael Sandoe closed down his transmitter, giving up after two hours of trying to raise a response from Andreas Keller.

"He's never done that before," Paul Riley said morosely. "No sign-off. No answer to our last question."

"The airwaves sometimes play odd tricks on us. Or, he may have been in a situation where it was necessary to cut off abruptly to preserve his security."

"Or—he got caught. Only one thing's sure: Keller knows the date for Operation Lila, and we still don't."

Michael took off his dark glasses and went to a basin of water on a corner table in his radio shack. He soaked a washcloth and pressed it lightly to his burning eyes. What disturbed him equally was the failure of Jonas to make radio contact at the scheduled hour that night. That left them with no way of being certain he had made it to Draguignan.

The plan was for Keller to deliver one copy to Jonas there

and then take the other copy into the mountains to the north where the plane was to land briefly and pick it up. Unless they heard from Jonas or Keller they couldn't tell if any part of that plan was still operative.

"I'll try to raise both of them again tomorrow." Michael gestured at the two camp beds against one wall of the shack. "We'll have to sleep here with the receiver kept open, and take turns listening in case they try to get through to us at an unscheduled time."

"Sure, but we've also got to decide what we do if neither of them makes contact again. In which case we'll have to consider the probability they've both been caught. Do we still send that plane in for its rendezvous, regardless?"

"I'm afraid we'll have to, won't we. Even if its chance of making the pickup becomes very slim."

Riley nodded sourly. "Yep...on account of, slim or fat, it'll be the only chance left."

TWENTY-TWO NOVEMBER 20

THE POLICE CAME for Jonas while he was having his breakfast in the tearoom of the Hotel Bertin.

It was more than thirty-one hours since he'd arrived in Draguignan and there was still no word from Keller. Cut off from Michael, there was no way to find out if he should continue to stay put or get out. He swirled the dregs of coffee in his cup, momentarily lost in thought as he scowled down at it, calculating how much longer he could risk waiting. When he looked up he saw the room clerk pointing him out to two gendarmes.

It was both too late and too soon for him to run. He didn't want them having a clear shot at him. When they got close he could at least make a try at disarming them before attempting to get away. Jonas put down his cup and watched them advance across the room. One was tall and the other stocky, and both looked competent.

"Monsieur Blois?" the tall one demanded when they reached his table.

"Yes?"

The stocky one held out a hand. "Your papers."

Jonas rose to his feet as he got out his identity papers. When the stocky gendarme took them he was close enough for Jonas to make a grab for the gun in his belt holster. But he didn't,

221

holding himself in check. Neither gendarme had drawn his weapon, and they hadn't brought out handcuffs to pinion his arms behind him, which was the first thing French cops did, before asking questions, when they'd been sent to arrest a man.

"Do you know a German named Andreas Keller?" the tall one asked.

Jonas said carefully, still poised to move if he had to, "I don't think so..."

"If he is one of those who work for the Germans," the stocky gendarme said with a tinge of disgust, "he wouldn't want to advertise it." He handed the identity papers back to Jonas, looking at him with open dislike. "Come with us."

Still no guns or handcuffs. Jonas walked out of the hotel with them. They got into a waiting police car, rode along the Boulevard Foch to the outskirts of the city, swung around the botanic gardens and came to a stop at the back entrance of the city's hospital. The two cops took Jonas up to a second-floor corridor and turned him over to a plainclothes inspector from the Draguignan gendarmerie.

The inspector dismissed the two cops. As they went off he asked Jonas nervously: "I hope they were not rough with you?"

"Not at all." Jonas had to work at not relaxing too much.

"Good. I'm afraid some of my men occasionally find it hard to understand that a policeman must have no political feelings if he is to carry out his duties properly." The inspector gestured at a closed door. "The German secret police agent you work for has been in an automobile accident, after having been severely wounded by a member of the Resistance he tried to capture."

He paused for a second, obviously hoping Jonas would volunteer some information. Not knowing what Keller had told them, Jonas remained silent.

"He is in poor condition, I'm sorry to tell you. Remarkable that he manages to keep regaining consciousness. He won't let us notify the Occupation authorities about what's happened to him. For certain security reasons, I realize that. But he also refuses to be operated on until he has spoken to you in private." The inspector, his fear of Keller's RSHA authority stronger than his professional curiosity, gestured for Jonas to go in alone.

Keller's head was swathed in bandages. His face was sunken and bloodless, his eyes shut. A nurse was checking intravenous tubes dripping fluids into the veins of both arms and another draining his abdomen.

"Leave us alone," Jonas told her.

Keller's eyes snapped open at the sound of his voice. Jonas looked at his eyes and marveled at his self-control. When the nurse had gone Jonas leaned over and told Keller, "You'd better let them operate on you." He had to lean closer to hear Keller's answer.

"Too late. Much too late. They didn't find me until after dawn. Better for me to die quickly now, anyway. The SS may be here in a matter of hours."

"What happened?"

"No time for that..." Life was fading from Keller's eyes. He fought to hold on a little longer. "I told them you work for me as an undercover agent. I showed them my RSHA card and warned them not to look at my secret papers. Is my suitcase still on the table?"

Jonas looked around and saw the suitcase on a table under the window. "Yes, it's there."

"Take my briefcase from it and get out of here. And don't come back." Briefly, pausing occasionally to regain control, Keller explained what was in the briefcase: the one copy for Jonas to get into the naval base, the other that was to be picked up by plane that night, in the mountains between Draguignan and the Verdon Canyon. "You will have to deliver it to the pilot for me...There is a map in the briefcase...I marked the location of the rendezvous..."

Jonas got the briefcase out of the suitcase. When he returned to the bedside Keller's eyes had closed. "There is nothing I can do for you?"

Without opening his eyes, Keller whispered, "Yes...Make sure at least one of those copies reaches Admiral Laborde...So I will not have died in vain..."

Jonas watched Keller's face relax, becoming younger as he let go. Death would not be long in coming.

Jonas took the briefcase and went out to the corridor. He told the waiting inspector: "Get him a priest."

The man stared at him, startled. "A priest...?" He'd heard that most of the Nazis were violently against the church.

"Quickly," Jonas snapped.

The inspector hastened to obey, striding along the corridor and instructing a nurse to phone the Draguignan cathedral. The man's anxiety to ingratiate himself with anyone connected to the Nazis was obvious.

As the nurse made the call Jonas used a crisp, businesslike tone on the man: "I have to take these secret papers to his superiors, fast. I'll need a car, with a full fuel tank."

"I can obtain that for you. With a police driver to..."

"No driver. I want no one accompanying me. I'll bring it back myself. Tonight."

The inspector didn't like it. But he liked less what might happen to him if he delayed secret German police business. "Of course. I understand. Come..."

Ten minutes later Jonas drove southwest out of Draguignan. The city was out of sight behind him when the road forked into two national routes. One dipped farther to the south. Jonas took the other, the Route Nationale 557, which swung up in a northwesterly direction. As he sped along it the road kept veering farther north, angling toward one end of the Verdon Canyon.

Getting back down to Toulon, after he delivered the first copy to the British pilot, was going to be harder and slower.

Even if the SS men didn't show up first, Keller's death would end his prohibition against notifying the Nazi Occupation authorities. In a few hours, at the most, Gestapo and Wehrmacht military police would be on their way to Draguignan. Soon after that they'd begin looking for "Jean-Jacques Blois" and the car he was driving.

Calculating on the safe side, he had about two hours. Then he'd have to find a place to hide the car, where it wouldn't be found for a couple of days. Long enough to reach Toulon via local buses. But he'd have to get rid of his present ID as well; and he would need something to get through the inevitable checkpoints.

Jonas considered the time involved if he phoned Nicole and asked her to bring him his other set of identity papers. It would be safest, and perhaps quickest in the long run. But that was for later. First he had the rendezvous to keep, for Keller, with that British plane.

Jonas continued north into the Provence highlands, driving faster, with the snow-topped peaks of the Alps rising ahead of him in the distance.

Giant bubbles gurgled to the surface of the small mountain lake as the car sank to its dark bottom. The dirt road which had brought Jonas this far into the complex, lonely tangle of low mountains continued on beyond the lake. But he wasn't likely to find a better place to get rid of the car.

He stuck a flashlight into a pocket of his jacket. The two copies of the Lila orders were tightly folded and wedged into the other. Removing Keller's map and compass from the brief-case, Jonas checked them against the surrounding stone peaks rising above him: some sharply outlined against the late after-noon sky, others blending into the snows of higher mountains which seemed quite close but were actually miles to the north. When he had his directions sorted out he put his identity papers in the briefcase, filled it with stones and flipped it into the water. As it followed the car to the bottom Jonas began his climb into a cold, silent chaos of twisted gorges, weathered slopes and haphazard patches of forest.

The dirt road wound its way in the same direction. Jonas took a narrow trail that rose above it. The trail climbed a cliff, with a slope of withered scrub below and a sheer wall above. His lungs were laboring in the high, thin air when he reached the top. He paused to check Keller's map and compass again, then tucked them into his breast pocket and continued east along a broken ridge between convoluted slopes.

The lake into which he'd sunk the car was four miles behind

when he heard vehicles approaching along the dirt road below. He hunched down among the ridge rocks and waited.

A battered Renault sedan appeared from the direction of the lake, followed by an open truck. Both carried Miliciens armed with rifles and submachine guns. Jonas counted fourteen men in all. He watched the vehicles grind over deep ruts clawed by plunging runoffs of recent rains. It became lost to view around a massive shoulder of granite. Standing up, Jonas moved on along the ridge, going in the same general direction.

The Miliciens had to be a man-hunting party, probably going in to scour the region for Resistance hideouts. Jonas hoped they intended to pull out of the area before dark, and that there were no other groups involved in the same search. An hour later he was disabused of both hopes.

Below him the dirt road came to an end below a pile of boulders between a cliff and a slope of beech and pine forest. The Renault and the truck had parked near the trees. Three tents were being set up. The Milice were here for a protracted hunt.

When the men finished erecting the tents, twelve of them started off to the east, up the forest slope. Jonas, standing under a high spur of rock, watched one of the pair who remained get a walkie-talkie out of the truck and begin speaking into it. A Milicien among the dozen climbing the slope carried another walkie-talkie, but wasn't using it at that moment. The one below was looking in a different direction, to the north, as he used his own.

Jonas squinted in the same direction. He couldn't spot any other group there, but he had to figure now that there was one. Getting out the map again, he checked the rendezvous point. It was roughly between the direction taken by the Miliciens climbing the slope and the probable location of the other group.

Moving out from under the rock spur, Jonas took a circling route to avoid the climbers and hiked on toward the rendezvous. The hunters would almost certainly quit at nightfall and camp until morning before returning to their search. A lot depended on how close the other group's camp was to the rendezvous point. And the rest depended on luck.

* * *

There was less than an hour left to sunset when he neared the rendezvous. Ahead of him a waterfall thundered down into the high valley he was traversing, dropping out of one end of a higher gorge. After consulting the route marked on the map, Jonas began to climb the rocks to one side of the falling water, sprinkled by icy drops flung from it. He reached the gap from which it issued and entered a tight, dim gorge, finding a ledge running along one of its walls.

A few feet below him a mountain stream rushed through the bottom of the gorge, pounding around heaps of fallen rock. It was joined by water seeping out of the cliff on Jonas's side, fed by underground springs higher up. He made his way cautiously along the wet, slippery ledge. Cold winds slapped off the cliffs on either side, buffeting him as they whirled on through the corridor of rock. But after some minutes he turned into a narrower side corridor, and was cut off from the winds. Climbing again, he reached a stretch of rock-strewn plateau.

Ten minutes later he was at the place chosen for the rendezvous, and he did not like what he saw.

He was at the top of a sheer cliff which curved around in a rough circle. It formed a natural enclosure, a great vertical-sided bowl about fifty feet deep and approximately five hundred yards across. It might once have been a volcanic crater, or a mountain lake which had drained away through an underground cave system.

Whatever had caused it, the ages since had changed its nature. Most of the bottom was relatively flat, carpeted with bright green moss around shallow pools spreading from water oozing down ice-colored gashes in the dark circle of cliff. There were scattered scrub bushes down there but no large trees, and fallen rocks were confined to the cliff base.

It was, Jonas acknowledged, a good place for a small, light plane like a Lysander, which needed only 300 yards to land and 250 yards for takeoff: a level surface with few obstructions, shielded on all sides from the tricky mountain winds above the bowl. In addition, a light signal flashed up to the plane from the bottom wouldn't be seen by anyone in the region unless he was standing as close as Jonas was now.

But it was a bad place for a man on foot, with the Milice combing the area. He could see only one way into or out of it. About twenty yards to his left a dry stream bed ended at the top of the bowl. During mountain rains water would funnel through and run to the bottom. Centuries of that had cut into the solid rock of the cliff there, creating a narrow, gradually sloping passage reaching all the way down.

Jonas climbed down through this passage, while there was still enough daylight. Reaching the bottom he walked swiftly, following the base of the curving wall. Dusk was closing in and shadowed the inside of the bowl. He had to use the flashlight to check the last hundred yards of cliff base. But when he reached the point from which he'd started, his worst fear was confirmed: there was only the one narrow way up or down.

He climbed back up the waterfall passage and settled down to wait above the big bowl. With the Milice around he didn't want to spend more time than absolutely necessary inside that trap.

As dusk closed around him Jonas resisted a strong temptation to slip away as soon as it was dark. If he wasn't down there to flash the signal at 11 P.M., the plane would circle a few times then fly away. It would avoid the possibility of getting caught inside the bowl. But in the end Jonas rejected it, for selfish reasons. If the pilot could manage to drop one of Keller's copies into the Toulon base, it would reduce the pressure on Jonas to get his own copy in there. In that case, should the danger of the attempt prove too formidable, he'd be able to back off. And stay alive.

But he wished he knew where that other Milice group had set up its camp. His chances of getting away depended on the distance from the bowl, when the plane came in for the pickup.

At eleven that night there were few clouds and plenty of moonlight. But Jonas heard the drone of the plane for five minutes before he saw it. The pilot was swinging back and forth over the region, trying to locate the landing place. Standing in the bottom of the bowl, holding the flashlight ready, Jonas cursed softly and viciously. If he could hear the plane so could the Milice, and under the bright moon they could see where it was circling.

Finally, the high-winged little plane appeared, skimming over the bowl, bounced around by the powerful mountain winds. Where Jonas stood there was hardly any wind at all. He aimed the flashlight up at the plane and began blinking the signal: three short, one long. The plane droned on beyond the cliff circle and he lost sight of it.

He waited in the center of the bowl, unsure if the pilot had seen the signal. After a minute the sound of the plane grew stronger again. Jonas aimed the flashlight at the point it was coming from and began signaling again as soon as the Lysander reappeared. It was flying much lower this time, barely missing the cliff top. Jonas kept flashing the signal, watching it begin a slowing turn as it vanished over the opposite cliff.

Twenty seconds later it came back, flying very slow and dipping into the bowl. Jonas sprinted away from the center to get out of its path. Its landing lights came on as soon as it dropped below the top of the cliff, nosing down sharply. The Lysander leveled off at the last second, touched down too hard and bounced into the air, then touched down again and rolled swiftly past Jonas with its wheel spats cutting through tangles of low brush, its propeller spin slowing. Jonas ran after it.

The plane stopped less than a hundred feet short of a pile of fallen rocks at the base of the cliff, swung around in the opposite direction and came to a stop positioned for its takeoff run. The pilot climbed out and dropped to the ground carrying a bulky package in both arms. Most of its bulk, Jonas saw when he reached him, was the parachute pack. Attached to it was a steel canister rigged with a wraparound float and waterproof flares.

The pilot set it down and extended a hand to Jonas. "Henry White, at your service." He was young, not more than twenty, about the same build as Jonas, with a cheerful freckled face.

He grinned up at the cliff tops. "Now if I can only slip past the air defenses over Toulon as easily as I got in here..."

"There's no time for a chat, you've got to get out of here fast." Jonas gave him one of the Operation Lila copies and nervously scanned the surrounding cliffs while Lieutenant White dropped it into the canister and screwed the lid back on tightly.

"Hand it up to me..." The pilot climbed the Lysander's short fuselage ladder and swung into the cockpit. He reached down and took the canister and chute from Jonas, pulling it inside with him before raising an arm in farewell. "Good luck to you."

"You too. Get going." Jonas stepped back as the engine roared, the propeller spin accelerating to a blur. The plane lurched forward, gathering speed as it raced over the makeshift runway, lifting off when it was halfway across the bottom of the bowl. The nose came up and the propeller screamed, taking the Lysander into a steep climb to clear the cliff on the other side.

The plane was almost out when submachine gun and rifle fire blasted at it from the cliff top directly ahead. Its angle of climb increased abruptly, and for a moment Jonas thought the plane was going to make it. Then the right wing dipped sharply and the Lysander went into a too-tight turn, its engine conking out as it circled back into the bowl. The Milice on the cliff kept firing into the little plane as it fell, rolling over on its back.

Jonas stood frozen, watching it come down. Either the pilot was working hard at the controls or the Lysander's natural stability in a glide had taken over. The rollover continued and the plane was right side up and leveling off when it landed. The wheels kept hitting the ground as it bounded past Jonas.

He screamed silently at the pilot to apply the brakes. But there seemed to be no brakes. The only thing slowing the plane as it rushed toward the base of the cliff was the scrub brush pulling at its wheels and the lowest blade of its stilled propeller. Then one wing tip dipped and got tangled in a patch of bushes. The Lysander spun around, its other wing smashing apart against the rock pile at the foot of the cliff, and it jolted to a stop.

When Jonas reached the plane the pilot was still inside the

cockpit, making no effort to get out. Climbing the ladder, he saw why. Only one shot had touched the pilot, but it had been an unlucky hit: the side of his forehead had been torn away.

Jonas pulled himself into the cockpit with the dead man, located the canister and unscrewed the top. Taking out the Operation Lila copy, he jumped back down to the ground.

There were the faint sounds of voices carrying from the other side of the bowl. Lights appeared at the top of the only way down—or up. Jonas watched the lights begin to move down. He counted four of them; not all the descending Miliciens might be carrying lights. Two more lights appeared at the top of the cliff.

Some were staying up there, to make certain no one got out of the bowl even if he managed to get around the Milice coming down after him.

But the descending lights were not at the bottom yet. The Milice were making their approach slowly and warily. They had no way of knowing how many armed men might be waiting down there: from the plane, or a Resistance group the plane might have come in to supply.

Eventually, however, they would learn there was only one man, and sooner or later they'd take him. If they took him the way he was, it was all over for him—and for the Toulon fleet as well. They'd turn him over to the Gestapo as a spy; and by the time his interrogation ended he'd be grateful for death.

There was only one way that might save him from that. Jonas looked again across the bowl at the lights slowly moving down. There might be just enough time.

Climbing back up to the cockpit, Jonas dragged the dead pilot out and let his body fall to the ground. Dropping down beside it, he went through his pockets until he found the pilot's identity papers. The pilot's photograph looked nothing like Jonas. Taking the papers with him, he climbed the rocks above the smashed plane.

Reaching the base of the cliff behind the rocks, Jonas ran a hand over the weather-torn surface until he found a narrow crevice. He stuffed the pilot's ID deep inside it, together with both copies of the Lila orders. But not Keller's map and compass. These remained in his pocket as he climbed back down to the dead pilot and looked again across the bottom of the night-shrouded bowl.

The lights of the Miliciens were spreading out as they approached. But they were still far away, and coming slowly, with long stops to check out possible ambush points.

Swiftly, Jonas began stripping off his clothing.

He stayed closer to the ground until they began converging toward the Lysander from their stalking positions. Then, when they were close enough but still hadn't seen him, Jonas called out, in English: "I surrender to you! I'm a British officer of the Royal Air Force and I demand the rights of every uniformed prisoner of war as agreed to by all civilized nations!"

The flashlights went out at the first sound of his voice; the shadowy figures dropped low, expecting an ambush.

"I'm not armed and I'm giving myself up to you!" Jonas called. He repeated the litany about his rights as a prisoner of war.

There were whispers. He saw shadows dart off to either side to make sure he really was alone and it wasn't a trap. One of the Miliciens called out in passable English: "Show yourself to us!"

Jonas took a deep breath and stood up slowly, stepping away from the bushes which had hidden him, his arms raised high above his head.

A single flashlight snapped on, reflecting off the buttons of the RAF uniform he wore. He squinted into the light and recited: "I'm not trying to escape or resist. International law recognizes my rights as..."

A shadowed figure clubbed him in the head with his rifle stock. Jonas dodged the main impact of the blow but it caught him across the ear and spun him to the ground. Other flashlights snapped on, converging on him. Another found the dead pilot sprawled near him.

"Who is this?" someone growled in French.

232

Jonas looked up stupidly at the speaker. "I don't understand French, I'm afraid... But in striking me you're violating..."

"Who is this dead one?" demanded the man who spoke English.

"All I know is he was an intelligence agent I was sent to pick up and deliver to Gibraltar. I was taking him out when you fired on my plane and killed him." Jonas put a hand to his ear. There was no blood but it hurt like hell.

Someone snarled, "Dirty Englishman!" A boot shot out and kicked Jonas in the stomach. He doubled up on the ground, gagging.

The Miliciens laughed and hands reached down and dragged him to his feet. A fist slammed into his mouth and he tasted blood. Another struck the back of his neck and he fell forward but was caught and held and struck again. He tried to repeat his rights as a uniformed prisoner of war but there was too much blood in his mouth and his gashed lips were swelling as they kept hitting him. They were French Nazis who had caught themselves a British officer and nothing was going to stop them from celebrating. The only uncertainty was whether they'd keep at it until they'd beaten him to death.

He dropped back to the ground as soon as he could manage it. A boot heel rammed into his side. Another grazed his neck. Jonas curled into a fetal ball with his ankles crossed to protect his testicles and his arms wrapped around his head to shield his face and ears. They went on stomping him.

TWENTY-THREE NOVEMBER 21

HE CAME TO in a jail cell, stretched out on a hard, narrow bunk. The first light of morning showed outside the barred window. The previous time he'd regained consciousness it had still been dark, when they'd brought him in here, to the gendarmerie in Bargemon.

There was one thing he no longer had to worry about: the dead pilot's blood on the uniform he was wearing. They might have wondered about that, since he hadn't been wounded. But it had been too dark up in the mountains for anyone to notice that before they'd started beating him. And now there was enough of his own blood staining the uniform.

Two men were arguing in French. Jonas turned his aching head and peered at them through eyes swollen almost shut. One was the uniformed leader of the Milice group that had captured him. The other was a swarthy, tough-looking man in a dark, pin-striped suit.

"This *is* France," the swarthy man was saying angrily. "And he is a *French* prisoner."

"I still say we should turn him over to the Germans."

"Don't make yourself trouble, Girard. At the moment you are covered with glory, so be satisfied with that. You have captured a British pilot. And I have phoned Deputy Commissioner Luyten, who is on his way here to deal with him according to the civil and military laws of France. Such as they are these days. Putting our political differences aside for the moment, I am sure you don't want people to begin doubting your patriotism as a Frenchman."

The Milicien frowned. Whoever the swarthy man was, he was someone of authority. Jonas pushed himself up on the bunk. "Sir," he croaked, "do you speak English?"

The man stepped close to the bunk, studying him critically. "Yes. I am Joel Brunet, mayor of Bargemon." He looked more like a successful farmer than a politician. But in this region he was probably both. He brought out a pack of cigarettes. "Do you wish to smoke?"

"I'd prefer some water."

"Get him water," Mayor Brunet told the Milicien.

But the Milice leader stayed where he was, his face sullen.

The mayor shouted through the cell door: "Roger! Bring a glass of water in here!"

A moment later a uniformed gendarme handed Jonas a glass. He finished every drop.

As Mayor Brunet gestured for the gendarme to leave, Jonas spoke in a clearer voice. "Mayor, I am Flight Lieutenant Henry White, an officer of the Royal Air Force." As though he had understood nothing they'd been saying in French, he repeated the formula which hadn't worked in the mountains: "I have surrendered, and under international law I have a right to be treated with the respect due any officer who has become a prisoner of war."

"Where are your military papers?" Mayor Brunet demanded. "None were found when you were searched."

Jonas looked surprised and glanced down at his uniform jacket. It was now badly torn, as well as bloodstained. "I don't know. It must have fallen from my pocket while I was scrambling out of my plane. Or perhaps when your men were beating me up."

"They are not *my* men," the mayor said with distaste.

The Milicien growled, "We didn't beat him up. He tried to resist and we had to subdue him." He was beginning to look worried.

Pretending not to understand anything, Jonas said to the mayor: "Nevertheless, I am wearing my uniform and insignia. Under military law..."

He was interrupted by the arrival of Deputy Commissioner Luyten, ranking law officer for the department in which Bargemon was located. Luyten had brought two plainclothes detectives with him, both chosen for their excellent command of English. Jonas was removed to a room with a table and chairs, and for the next couple of hours the detectives questioned him, alternating between sympathy and threats, with frequent consultations between them and the deputy commissioner.

Jonas quietly stuck to his story: He didn't know anything about the dead intelligence agent, except that he'd been ordered to fly in, pick him up and fly him out. Other than that Jonas insisted on sticking to the rules of war for captured soldiers. As he repeated several times, international law required him to give nothing but his name and rank in the Royal Air Force. And that was all he intended to give.

Finally Deputy Commissioner Luyten went to another room to phone Vichy army authorities. Jonas was taken back to his cell and locked in. It was evening before he was informed that military police would come for him the next morning. He was not told where they intended to take him.

It was a few minutes after nine o'clock that night when her phone began ringing. Nicole ran into the downstairs study and snatched it up. But it wasn't Jonas. It was Dithelm, calling from Lavandou.

"We'll come three nights from now," he told her. "Make sure your place is secure that night."

He didn't ask if it was all right to use her house as the staging base for his raid; that was taken for granted.

"I'll do what I can," Nicole said, "but you'll have to be careful. Remember, my uncle and aunt sometimes drop in without warning. And my cousin could be coming home from work at any time that night."

"You don't have to warn me about being careful. I'll arrive with only one of my men, so we can check it out and make certain it's safe before the others come in. I've become so careful lately I'm not sure if it is caution or fear. Reggie was joking about that yesterday—you remember I told you about him?"

"I remember."

"He'll be the one with me when I come. You'll like him."

After she hung up Nicole's thoughts returned to Jonas. His note had said he would contact her, but he hadn't. She tried to quell her anxiety as she returned to the kitchen to finish her dinner. But she couldn't stop thinking about where he might be, and how long she'd have to wait before he returned. Not all of her concern was his safety, Nicole recognized. Part of it was simply that she missed him. She'd become so accustomed to his presence she no longer felt complete alone.

Realistically, she told herself, Jonas was probably in no greater danger than when he was here with her. The previous night had been a sharp reminder of that. Her cousin had dropped by unexpectedly for a drink after finishing his work at the paper; and he'd brought that horrible Gestapo official with him.

The man had been polite enough, and respectful about her work as a newspaperwoman, commenting favorably on several of her articles. The political opinions he'd expressed had been far less fanatic than those of her own cousin.

But there was something beside his profession in Udo Mueller's matter-of-fact, watchful manner that made her skin crawl. It had taken her a long time to get to sleep after he had left.

She hoped he never came back.

TWENTY-FOUR

JONAS AWOKE TO the tolling of the Bargemon church bell across the square from his cell, summoning people to Sunday morning mass. Fifteen minutes later, while he was finishing the coffee and roll a gendarme had brought him, a Vichy officer of the Armistice Commission arrived. He was accompanied by a pair of husky military police, one French, the other Italian. They manacled his wrists behind his back and marched him out of the gendarmerie.

He was not told where he was being taken, and since Jonas wasn't supposed to speak French he couldn't ask. He was shoved into a military police car and driven south.

Udo Mueller's car circled the Place d'Armes. He told the driver to stop after turning into the Rue Anatole France, across from the West Arsenal's Porte Principale. Mueller climbed out and stood chewing a stick of gum, observing a squad of Wehrmacht troops marching up to take over the guard post outside the gate of the naval base. The French navy guards came to attention as one of their own officers emerged from inside the gate. The French officer and the officer in charge of the Wehrmacht squad saluted each other, two military men doing their duty: carrying out the new regulation of the Armistice Commission.

The French guards turned and marched inside the gate. The two officers again saluted each other and the French one followed his men inside the naval base. The heavy gates clanged shut and were locked from inside. The Wehrmacht troops took up their positions outside.

Mueller scrutinized a small crowd of civilians who had gathered to watch the changeover. They looked peaceful enough. Police were spread around the area to make certain they stayed that way. Mueller spotted a dark-haired girl he recognized standing apart from the rest of the crowd, the journalist-cousin of *Toulin-Martin*'s editor.

Nicole Courtel's presence didn't surprise him. The newspaper would have been notified of this change in the guard system, and she would have come to observe it as part of her professional duties. The girl certainly couldn't have any more idea than he did about the reason for the change.

It offended Mueller that he hadn't been informed of the reason. After all, Toulon was his city. He was the one responsible for maintaining safety and order. But all they'd told him was that the change would take place, and that he should make sure no ugly incidents were permitted to mar the occasion. This he had done by placing sufficient Vichy police near each of the gates to the two arsenals, with a Gestapo observer at each in communication with his car. Everything had gone smoothly. As he had just observed here, so it had been at the other three gates: the Wehrmacht squads had taken over the outside guard posts from the French without incident.

As the civilian crowd near the Porte Principale began to disperse, Nicole Courtel turned from the gate to walk away. She halted when she saw Mueller and nodded politely. Mueller nodded back, but made no move to join or beckon her. The girl nodded again, and walked off toward the Quay Cronstadt.

Mueller gazed after her for a few moments. She was quite pretty, with a lovely figure. And she had been quite civil to him when her cousin had invited him to her home for a drink. He had the impression she had found him fascinating; certainly she had listened to him with genuine interest. But Mueller had a wife and four children in Germany, and he was not a man given to philandering. Besides, he had other matters on his mind at the moment.

Getting back into the car, he ordered the driver to take him on a slow tour of the city. As the car cruised one street after another Mueller scrutinized passing buildings and passing faces. This *was* his city, his responsibility and therefore in a way his emotional property. And somewhere in it were hidden enemies whose identities and objectives he didn't know. Any of the people he observed might be one of them; any of the buildings might harbor others.

But that would soon change. The message received this morning from Reggie had given the two Toulon objectives of the Maures Resistance gang: a Milice arms depot and a paper warehouse. Mueller had already arranged for police traps to be set at both places.

It would be time, finally, for the capture of that entire gang. Reggie's message had also said he would meet the Resistance female contact the same night, well before the attacks.

Once he had *her* in his hands, Mueller was quite sure, he was going to learn a great deal more about the rest of his enemies inside his city.

The army police car negotiated a bumpy dirt road which hairpinned its way between wild ravines and massive slabs of naked rock. Jonas knew the region fairly well from the past. About a couple miles farther south would be the Haut Corniche, the highest road overlooking the Mediterranean coast between Nice and Monte Carlo. He leaned forward beside the Vichy military cop to ease the pressure on his manacled arms, and carefully studied the nearly treeless ridges and slopes. He wanted to know this immediate area in detail.

The road reached a high barbed-wire fence and followed its outside perimeter, past towers with spotlights and machine guns. The car was halted at the main gate by Italian army guards. The Vichy Commission officer in the front seat showed his papers and special pass and the car was allowed inside.

Half a mile farther it was stopped again at the gate of an inner ring of barbed-wire fence, this time by French gendarmes. Passed through the second gate, the car headed over a series of rises, between scattered groups of well-built modern barracks and army vehicle shelters. Jonas noted sentry posts and patrols. He registered features a man might later use for night cover.

To his right there were glimpses of the sea between jumbled hills which grew greener as they dropped to the shore far below.

He was inside Fort de la Revère, an army complex spreading across acres of the high ridges and rugged hollows of the Maritime Alps, a mile north of Eze Pass. Much of the terrain was devoted to interlocking steel and concrete pillboxes and underground bunkers, built between the two world wars by military-industrial experts convinced that such stationary fortification systems would provide the nation with an impregnable defense against planes and tanks. As with the Maginot Line, it had surrendered without a shot after the enemy went over and around it.

But the heart of Revère remained the older original fort, planted solidly across a long humped ridge. Jonas scanned its high, thick stone walls as the car parked outside it. The fort was at the dead center of the newer fortifications. Its walls were surrounded by a deep moat, relatively dry these days except during rains. Within the walls most of Fort Revère had been turned into a prison for Allied airmen captured in the southeastern areas of France. According to the reports Jonas had heard, there were several hundred in there now.

He studied everything in sight as he was taken across the moat via a steel-and-timber drawbridge which provided the only entrance.

The new SS security officers had been sent to General Hausser's command outside Brignoles, to replace Lieutenant Telcamp and investigate what had happened to him and Keller. This time the senior one was a captain. It was late evening when he and his lieutenant returned to the SS Panzer Korps encampment and reported their findings to Hausser's chief of staff, Colonel Ostendorff.

"First of all," the captain said, "there is *no* indication that security here at the camp has been breached in any way."

"I didn't think it had. Still, it is good to have it confirmed." Seated behind his desk in the farmhouse, Ostendorff regarded the security officers through singularly unemotional eyes, eyes which seemed to grow smaller with each passing year, as his once-handsome face degenerated into fleshy softness. "Since you fail to mention it, I assume you have still not found Lieutenant Telcamp."

"Not yet, colonel," the security captain admitted. "But the search for him is being intensified."

The lieutenant added: "We have all the Milice and French police in the Draguignan area taking part in the hunt, as well as Wehrmacht military police."

"You have stopped looking elsewhere?" Ostendorff demanded.

"Your men already looked around this area," the captain pointed out, "and failed to find a trace of Telcamp. Since he asked for Andreas Keller the night he vanished, and went out after him, we are going on the presumption that Keller had a lead to certain elements—potential saboteurs, perhaps—and that Telcamp joined him in following it up. And as Keller was found dying close to Draguignan we are concentrating the hunt for Telcamp there. The most likely explanation is that the two of them were waylaid, perhaps by the gang they were investigating, but it could have been some other terrorists. We have to presume that while Keller managed to get away, though severely wounded, Lieutenant Telcamp was killed outright, and his body buried somewhere in that region."

"You make a lot of presumptions," Ostendorff growled. "Do you consider presumptions an adequate substitute for information, captain?"

"No, colonel, but we have little else to go on, unfortunately, since Keller died before he could give anyone the information we seek."

"Most unsatisfactory. What about that French informer working for Keller? The man Keller spoke to in the hospital before he died?"

The lieutenant supplied the name: "Jean-Jacques Blois. We haven't been able to locate him as yet."

"Nor the car he drove off in," the captain added. "But the search continues, for Blois and the body of Lieutenant Telcamp, as well as for leads to who killed Telcamp and Keller. We have sent out Jean-Jacques Blois's name to all the police and all newspapers in southern France. I'm quite sure, colonel, that we'll turn up something on him before long."

TWENTY-FIVE NOVEMBER 23

THE EDITOR AND publisher of *Toulon-Matin,* Girard Courtel, was a sturdy, handsome man in his late thirties, and normally he had a look of cool self-assurance. This morning, however, he looked as worried as Nicole felt. They sat in his newspaper office, with the door shut, looking at each other nervously across the German request lying on his desk.

It was a form letter asking all newspapers to print an item urging any readers who had any information about a man named Jean-Jacques Blois to contact the nearest police station. There was a promise of a reward for information which proved useful, but nothing about Blois's background nor why the Germans were seeking him.

"He didn't say anything at all about his political views while he was staying at your house?" Girard Courtel asked her, re-framing what he'd asked earlier. "Nothing to make you think he might be associated with the Resistance, for example?"

Nicole studied her cousin as she carefully worked out her answer. "No, I told you, nothing like that came up. But now, I think we have to assume he was up to something wrong. Or the Germans would not be after him, would they? I have to admit, now that I think back on his stay, he didn't act quite normally. Whenever politics came up he became rather wary. I think your father's impressions of Blois will confirm mine on that."

She appeared to hesitate, and then added in a troubled tone: "I don't think it would be wise to spread it around that we know this man, Girard. Safer to let sleeping dogs lie."

Girard nodded slowly. "That is my feeling, too. *If* this Blois is some kind of secret political agitator, or worse, any association with him, however innocent, could get us all in trouble." He tapped the request on his desk. "We'll print this item, of course. We have to. But that is all we do. No mention, to anyone, of knowing anything about him."

"I'm grateful to you, Girard. After all, it was my house he stayed in, not yours."

His smile was an unhappy one. "My motives are not entirely altruistic, as I'm sure you know. These days, if the Germans become suspicious about any member of a family, the rest of the family invariably suffers from it too. That's just the way it is, and we must be realistic about it. But...that leaves us with one possible source of trouble: if he is caught, and tells about staying with you, and meeting my father..."

Nicole was ready for that: "Then we all swear that he used a different name when he was here. That we had no idea of his real name. He said he was a friend of my sister's husband, and we believed him. He gave us a false name and we believed that, too. And it turns out both were lies."

Her cousin liked it. "No way they can check with Annick and her husband. Morocco's cut off from us now. I'll fill my father and mother in on what we've decided, so they'll be prepared if it ever comes up." His hands trembled as he lit a cigarette. "But let's pray it never does."

"It almost certainly won't. If the man has disappeared, they'll probably never find him."

Nicole was trembling too when she left his office. Her legs were so shaky it was difficult to walk normally and she collapsed in a chair when she was back inside her own office.

Where the hell *was* Jonas?

Jonas watched the rain hiss outside his cell. It had begun raining yesterday afternoon after they'd locked him away; it

246

had let up sometime in the night and begun again when daylight began filtering thinly through the clouds which had slid down from the higher Alps toward the seacoast.

The cell was in one of the old stone buildings built out from the inner face of the fort wall. It was partly underground, and its high window was only a foot or so above the level of the ground outside. There were no bars on the window; it was too small for a man to force more than his head through. There was also no glass in the window, and raindrops kept splattering into the cell, adding wet discomfort to the biting cold.

Jonas could see out the window by standing on a slab of wood which served as his bed, and which, together with a tin bucket for a toilet, was the only furniture in the cell. The window faced a small courtyard. All he could see through it was the base of several stone walls, and the rain beating at the walls and ground.

The ground was uneven, solid rock, and none of the rain was absorbed into it. The water formed pools and streams which, when they rose high enough, finally reached runoff drains.

Jonas stepped down from the plank bed and backed into the driest corner of his cell. He tried jogging in place to stir his circulation and get some warmth. But that renewed the pain in his bruised face and body. Finally he just paced the cell, swinging his arms.

And waited.

They had put him in solitary until they could deal with two different lists of bureaucratic arrangements which had to be completed before they could intern him as a prisoner of war, and do the necessary paperwork. Until they did that, Jonas could do nothing about the vital hours steadily leaking away.

This was Monday morning and time would run out on any chance to thwart Operation Lila before dawn on Friday. Less than four days. And the situation at Fort Revère continued to delay the first step needed, which was to be moved from this cell to the prison section holding the Allied airmen.

Since the Axis powers had taken over southern France twelve days ago, Fort Revère had been placed under the control of the Italian Occupation authorities. There were already rumors the Germans were not satisfied with the results and might soon put the Gestapo in charge. But at the time Jonas was sent there, though the fort's administration was still nominally managed by French military officers, it operated under the supervision of the Italian army.

The French army units stationed there remained, but had surrendered most of their weapons and carried out their duties without them, in compliance with the orders of the Vichy government. Troops from Italy manned the machine-gun towers, sentry posts and patrols. The armed guards in charge of the prisoners were now gendarmes selected for their loyalty to Marshal Pétain. And, officially, Fort Revère was now under the joint leadership of two army officers, one French, the other Italian.

Neither, Jonas had learned, cared to deal with minor matters on a Sunday. So when he was brought in they had him tucked away to await Monday morning.

Now Monday was here, and still he waited.

Shortly before lunchtime he was taken from the cell to an office where he was asked all the routine questions and gave prepared answers. Then he was put back in the cell. An hour after lunch two Italian military police finally took him out again, and turned him over to a pair of armed gendarmes.

The rain was dwindling to a drizzle as the cloud cover began to break open, showing bits of sky. The prisoner barracks and the high wire-mesh fence around them had a dark wet shine. Jonas took in the four watchtowers at the corners of the fence, and the two atop the main wall overlooking the entire prison enclosure. There was a steady dripping of rainwater off the conical iron roofs protecting the tower guards with their machine guns and searchlights.

The gendarmes took Jonas past the guard detail at the only opening in the fence and marched him across the enclosure. None of the prisoners were outside in this weather. Jonas saw faces watching from barracks windows as he passed. The gendarmes left him outside an officers' barracks and went off to

248

give the senior officer an official paper transferring Jonas into the prison.

Jonas opened the door and stepped inside. Air force officers crowded a few long wooden tables in what served as a combination kitchen, dining area and recreation room. Some of the men were playing cards and checkers while others were drinking tea or coffee. A few were American but most were British. Some gave Jonas a friendly welcome; others eyed him warily.

A friendly one pointed to a doorway. "You bunk in there with Briggs, Nelson and Rossman."

Jonas didn't have any time for settling in. "I have to speak to whoever's in charge of your escape committee, right now."

One of the wary ones said, "You're out of luck then. We don't have anything like that."

Jonas knew better. "Every prison camp has an escape committee."

"No point in it here. Solid rock, didn't you notice?"

Three British airmen came in from the drizzle, asking to borrow some sugar. One was a lieutenant, the other two noncoms. Each gave Jonas a brief, expressionless glance. They left with their half cup of sugar, without a word to him.

Among the officers who remained, even those who had been friendly before now had guarded looks. What had happened was obvious. Jonas moved against a wall and stayed there, not trying to renew conversation.

There was no flooring of any kind covering the naked rock of the uneven ground inside the building. Water from the rains seeped in under the walls. It collected at the lowest point, where a steel-mesh grille the size of a man's spread hand covered a drain hole. Jonas watched the water gurgle away into the hole while he waited.

A huge RAF corporal came in and beckoned Jonas. "Senior officer's ready to welcome you to our little community."

Jonas went outside with him. The drizzle was ending and bigger patches of blue showed between drifting clouds. The corporal studied his battered face. "Had some trouble, looks like."

"Milice trouble."

"Looks like they used you for football practice."

They reached the smallest building in the prison compound. The corporal motioned for Jonas to enter and took up a position outside the door.

There were two men seated inside, waiting for him in a room with three chairs, a table, two camp beds and a homemade bureau and desk. One was an RAF major, the other an American Air Force captain. They smiled at him, but without real warmth. Neither offered to shake his hand as the RAF officer gestured for him to take the remaining chair.

"I am Squadron Leader Reece," the major told him. "This is Captain Blumencranz, senior officer for the Americans among us. First, let's dispose of the formalities..." He glanced down at the transfer paper on the table before him. "...Flight Lieutenant Henry White. What sort of plane were you flying when you were shot down?"

"You sent three men who know White to look me over, so you know I'm not him. Lieutenant White was shot down in a Lysander, trying to fly out secret papers I'd given him. He's dead. My name's Jonas Ruyter. I'm SOE, on an intelligence mission for London." Jonas looked to Captain Blumencranz. "And for the American OSS, as well."

The captain made a face, as though he was impressed. "Now that's interesting."

Jonas ignored the American's lack of sincerity. "You have to help me get away from here. And fast, or it'll be too late for the job I was sent to do."

Major Reece had written the name "Jonas Ruyter" in a notebook on his table. He looked up. "Perhaps if you could tell us about this job of your..."

"I can't do that. I can tell you how important it is. It could help us win the war faster. Or lose it, if your escape committee doesn't help me."

"I'm afraid there is no hope of escape from Fort Revère, what with the..."

Jonas interrupted him, keeping his tone patient: "This place has a reputation for escapes. I know of at least a dozen who got out of here over the past two years and made it back to London." He gave two names he remembered. "And I know of one who escaped quite recently. Reginald Lear, likes to be called Reggie. He's joined a Resistance group I have a connection to."

Reece's expression was bland, his voice gentle: "I know the name of every man who has been imprisoned here. There has never been a Reginald or Reggie Lear."

It took Jonas several seconds. When he spoke his voice was quiet, steady: "That means he's a Gestapo plant. I don't know why the Nazis have held off seizing the group he's with. Maybe waiting until he can also give them the woman who is my connection to the group. A young woman I care about, very much. Another reason I have to get out of here, before she's..."

"A very touching story," the American officer said drily.

Jonas didn't get angry. Both men were acting as they were supposed to do. The burden was on him to come up with something that would make them believe.

He started by pointing to his face. "Does this look like they put me in here as a spy?"

"I wouldn't be surprised to learn you are a very brave man," Major Reece told him. "Willing to absorb a certain amount of physical punishment to make your role more convincing for us gullible folk."

The American smiled coolly: "And willing to risk waking up in here one fine morning to find your throat slit."

"All right..." Jonas addressed the RAF officer: "Let's try naming people I know, who might have friends among your men."

Major Reece poised his pencil over the notebook. "That makes sense. Go on." He wrote down each name as Jonas gave it.

Jonas named the pilot who'd flown him and Michael to Gibraltar. He named a pilot who had twice dropped him into northern France. He named two women in Paris who ran an escape route for slipping Allied airmen out of France to Spain. He named Michael Sandoe.

Reece sat up a bit straighter. "I know Michael, going back to well before the war. My family and his have country homes near each other."

"Michael is my oldest and best friend."

The RAF major relaxed a bit. "In that case...but of course, I imagine the enemy might have a dossier on Michael, with all sorts of personal information about him...But, did you ever attend any of those house parties his family used to have in the country?"

"In Surrey. Yes, a number of them."

"I went to many, odd I never met you there."

"Name some people you did meet at their house."

Reece did so. Most Jonas didn't remember having met; some he remembered but didn't know much about; for a few he was able to come up with personal details that checked with what Reece knew.

Allowing himself to relax a bit more, Reece went on: "There was one girl I almost fell in love with, but she married some engineer from..." He stopped himself. "Good Lord..." Reece turned back to the first page of his notebook. "The man she married was named Ruyter. Estelle..."

Jonas supplied her maiden name: "Atkinson. Yes. Michael was our best man."

Reece tossed his pencil aside and leaned back in his chair, grinning. "You lucky dog. I won't even ask if she's as lovely as ever. Must be. With those cheekbones and..."

"She's dead," Jonas told him. "In a bombing raid. With our two children."

The RAF major's face sagged. He took a deep breath, let it out slow. "I'm dreadfully sorry."

"I don't need sympathy, major. I need help to get out of here."

Reece sighed. "And in a hurry. You explained that. But I'm afraid it presents a problem. Or several." He gestured toward the American. "Captain Blumencranz is in charge of our escape committee. Perhaps you should explain the situation, captain."

"It's like this," Blumencranz told Jonas. "Everything's changed around here since the Axis took over. Escapes used to be pulled with the help of sympathetic guards. Or ones we could bribe with dough smuggled in by a priest who comes once a week to hear confessions. Now those guards are gone. In their place we've got a real nasty bunch of gendarmes. Plus the Italian MPs, some of whom might help for bribes, but we haven't had enough time to find out which, and how many—and how much."

Major Reece was nodding: "We've had to scrap all the ways out used in the past and come up with new possibilities. None of them have been fully worked out as yet."

"And the first ones we do work out…" the American said, "…well hell, Ruyter, none of us want to stay in here. There's one rumor the SS and Gestapo might take over this fort before long. Another that all of us officers are due to be shipped off to a camp in Germany for safer keeping. Everybody wants out before either of those things happens. And some have been here a long time. You just got here."

There was no other way. Jonas told them about the Toulon fleet and Operation Lila. And the time squeeze.

They heard him out. Major Reece turned to the captain: "What about Route 6?"

"I've been thinking the same thing." But Blumencranz did not look pleased with his thoughts.

"Tell me about it," Jonas said.

"We've given every new way out we're testing a route number. There're six, and this one's last on the list because it's the one we like least. But it's also the only one you could try right now. Because it's the one that might work without outside cooperation. Only we don't know everything about Route 6. Nothing about the other end of it. Two of my best boys tried to get far enough through for a look. We had to pull them back on a line, semiconscious."

"Part of that route," Major Reece explained to Jonas, "goes through a sewage pipe. The air in that stretch is foul. Fermenting filth giving off poisonous gases. On top of which what is beyond that might turn out to be a dead end. An outlet too small to get through, or blocked up with wire mesh or metal bars."

"We've got some tools to deal with that," Blumencranz said.

"Smuggled in under the robes of our helpful priest. Whether they'll be good enough to break you out, I don't know. Depends what you find when and if you make it that far. If you want to be our guinea pig."

Jonas nodded. "If I make it you'll know others can."

"Unless we figure you got out, when actually you're passed out at the other end from the sewer gas. Then we won't know till the others try it a couple days later and find your body."

"Got any other possibility for me?"

"No."

"Then lay it out for me. The part you know, what you suspect about the rest. And everything you've got on the terrain and good and bad routes outside the fort, if I get through."

Luftwaffe General Sperrle adjusted the monocle which distracted from the odd shape of his face: the upper half normal, but spreading down from the nose like the bottom of a squash. Picking up SS General Hausser's pointer, he moved it across a large map of the seacoast around Toulon.

"The extra planes you asked for," he told Hausser, "will arrive tomorrow morning here at the airbase outside Hyères. They will join the others already operating from there."

Hausser, flanked by Colonel Ostendorff and Commandant Schuldt, the Kriegsmarine liaison officer, said: "That will give them almost three days to prepare. It should be enough."

"They will be ready." Sperrle swung the pointer along the coast to Toulon. "On the morning of the twenty-seventh some will supplement the present patrols over the harbor, to bomb and depth-charge any vessels attempting to pull away from their docks." He shifted the pointer to the area outside the narrow exit from the bay of Toulon. "The rest will begin seeding the waters here with mines, should any vessel trying to escape manage to get that far."

Commandant Schuldt spoke up uncomfortably. "The navy inspectors of the Armistice Commission have assured us no vessel of the French fleet has enough fuel, in any case, to get more than a few miles out of Toulon."

254

Hausser turned to him. "I am sick of navy assurances. I was promised eight hundred sailors and only eighty have arrived."

"General, I phoned Hamburg earlier today. The rest are on their way and will arrive..."

"I don't care any longer when they arrive. I can do without them. My own officers are studying detailed layouts of the Toulon base so they can direct themselves in there. The failure of the navy to cooperate as promised is obviously an example of old-fashioned officers deliberately causing problems because they hate the rise of the Waffen SS. Himmler will see to it that those responsible will suffer for it."

Hausser turned back to General Sperrle: "I want those extra planes to begin mining the sea outside the bay at precisely 0430 hours. At that point my forces will have broken into the base and will be swarming to board the fleet. But they will concentrate first on the big ships, which may give some smaller vessels a chance to pull away from their docks. Your planes will drive them back. If necessary, sink one to make the others give up the attempt as useless. Not a single one must get away from us."

"You may count on that."

"I shall, Sperrle. Himmler himself has assured me that you understand fully how important it is to the Führer that Operation Lila be a complete success."

TWENTY-SIX

AT 1 A.M., SECONDS after a searchlight beam from a wall tower swung across the prison compound buildings, the three men went out the window and dropped to the ground. Keeping low, they crossed the open space to the next barracks. Captain Blumencranz led the way with Jonas behind him and a stocky flight sergeant named Higgins bringing up the rear. They moved slowly, trying to avoid splashing through the deep puddles of water.

They dropped flat against the base of the other barracks, a split second before another searchlight swept the open space they had just crossed. Then the captain rose crouched and went around the corner. Jonas and Higgins followed closely as he led the way across another open space to the next barracks. They all flattened on the wet ground again and waited, shivering in the cold.

Jonas turned to look at the sky. It had rained again briefly during the night and then stopped again. Dark, heavy clouds pushed by air currents merged and parted, displayed bright stars and then veiled them. Jonas wanted more rain. It would increase the messy difficulties of Route Six. But if he made it out of the fort, and the guards discovered his escape before he could get far enough away, the rain would make it hard for the dogs to follow his scent. Even the strong scent he'd be leaving along his trail after traversing the sewer. But not a drop fell now.

A six-man sentry patrol came in sight, precisely on schedule: a circuit of the inside of the prison compound once every hour. They sloshed through the puddles between the buildings; there was no indication that the prisoners were not asleep behind the closed shutters of the barracks. The patrol marched past the three figures blending into the base of the barracks wall. When they were gone Blumencranz led Jonas and Higgins away from the officers' buildings, into the enlisted men's section of the prison.

They approached the cookhouse, its shutters locked from inside, the door closed with a heavy padlock. Nobody was allowed inside at night. Higgins went to work on the padlock with a piece of bent wire. Blumencranz and Jonas put their backs to him and watched the sweep of the nearest searchlight.

"Down!" Blumencranz whispered, and the three dropped to the ground.

The searchlight's beam reached the cookhouse, trailed slowly across above them and moved on. Higgins bounced up and had the lock open when the other two got to their feet. Jonas followed Blumencranz inside and Higgins swung in and shut the door. Blumencranz snapped on a flashlight.

The uneven rock of the floor shone wetly from rainwater seepage. But most of the water had already flowed off through the drainhold over which many of the prison buildings had been erected. Blumencranz sat in front of the drain's steel mesh cover, balancing the flashlight on his crossed ankles. Higgins and Jonas knelt across the drain from him.

Fort Revère had not been built originally to contain a prison camp. So all of its drainage-system conduits had been made large, to provide the fastest possible runoff during mountain rainstorms. When the prison had been set up inside the fort, the drains under that section had been made much smaller to cut off escape attempts through them. This had been done by inserting a pipe the thickness of a man's thigh inside each drain-off shaft, and filling in the excess space between the smaller pipe and the larger with stones and concrete.

The former guards had known about this and had made unannounced inspections to make sure the prisoners were not tampering with the drain installations. But when they'd been removed from their posts here they hadn't bothered to pass on their knowledge to the new guards who replaced them.

Jonas helped the others lift out the drain cover, then to pry up large chunks of stone which appeared as part of the solid rock floor. This exposed all of the original wide shaft. The smaller pipe had been removed after the prisoners spent days breaking away the stone-filled cement holding it in place, using hammers and chisels, a legacy from the departed guards.

Blumencranz shone the flashlight into the exposed shaft. It was just big enough for a man, and it dropped some ten feet below the prison camp, into the old, original drainage system of the fort. Higgins unwound a length of rope from around his waist and chest. It had been made from unraveled blankets. Holding onto one end, Higgins let the rest dangle into the hole and grinned at Jonas.

"Don't bother sending a Christmas card from London. Expect to be there myself by then."

Higgins and Blumencranz got a good grip on the top end of the rope. The American whispered, "Good luck..." Jonas went into the shaft, climbing down the rope.

Eleven feet down, below the bottom of the shaft, he felt an expanse of dark space around him. A cold, steady draft blew through the darkness, and there were sounds of running water. Jonas lowered himself the rest of the way. His boots sank ankle deep in water and then there was solid ground under him. He looked up at the dim light at the top of the shaft, and gave the rope three short tugs. It was drawn up. Jonas waited, shivering in the cold.

The rope came down again. Tied to the bottom end was the lit flashlight and some other necessary items. Jonas detached the flashlight first, hanging it around his neck by a string loop. Then he removed the other items, acquired from the former guards or the helpful priest: a crowbar, two hacksaw blades, a pair of wire cutters. He stuck the crowbar in his belt, the wire cutters in one pocket, the blades in another which contained a small amount of cash from the escape committee's leader. The money included coins, to be used if he managed to get out and reach a pay phone—to call Nicole.

He was going to need other clothes, and his other set of identity papers, before he headed back to where he'd left the Operation Lila orders. And Nicole had to be warned of the danger posed by the fake RAF pilot who called himself Reggie.

Jonas tugged at the rope again, and it fell through the shaft to him. As he wound it around his body he heard the drain cover sliding back into place in the cookhouse. Jonas removed the string loop from his neck and shone the flashlight around.

He was inside an enclosed cave, high enough in some places for a man to stand. In this region the rock was riddled with similar caves and fissures. The builders of Fort Revère had incorporated them wherever practical into the drainage system. Large pipes led into and out of the cave. Water still leaked out of two of them, running across the cave floor and into a third pipe. Jonas went to that one, crouching as the cave roof lowered.

The outlet pipe was just large enough for a man to get through on hands and knees. Jonas hung the flashlight around his neck and crawled into it, his arms and legs in the running water. Water dripped on his head and back as he crawled under narrow drainpipes descending from the prison area above. The main drain entered a second, smaller cave, and resumed at the other end. Entering this section, Jonas felt the onrush of the water. The drain was inclining gently downward.

He snapped off the flashlight. Soon he would be beyond the area of the prison camp. The runoff shafts out there had not been made smaller. If light was seen filtering through the grille across the shafts, his escape attempt would be ended abruptly.

With one hand extended to keep him from hitting his head where the drain bent, Jonas crawled in pitch darkness, fighting off claustrophobia. Suddenly there was a glimmer of light ahead. Jonas crawled under a wide shaft and looked up at the faint light at the top. He was beyond the prison camp, out under another part of the fort.

Voices drifted down to him, freezing him in position. Two

men, moving near the grille at the top of the shaft, were speaking Italian. Their voices became faint and Jonas moved on.

Several times he came to places where the drain forked. Each time he took the fork which inclined downward, following the flow of the water.

Light appeared directly ahead of him and brightened as he crawled toward it. He had passed under the buildings attached to the inner face of the main wall and was below the base of the wall itself. The light ahead was from the searchlights which swept back and forth over the top of the moat from dusk to dawn. The drain ended in the moat. After that would come the worst part.

Jonas reached the end. There was no need to risk using the flashlight here. The searchlights revealed the water pouring out of the drain and spilling to the bottom of the moat. A drop of fifteen feet, they'd told him. The light also revealed the iron bars blocking the way out, their ends sunk into solid rock, set so closely together that only a cat could slip between them.

But the men from the escape committee who'd tried this route had spent two nights working on the bars with hacksaw blades.

Jonas grasped one of the bars with both hands and tugged carefully. It came away, leaving two iron stubs sticking out of the rock where the cuts had been made. He leaned the bar against the side of the drain and took hold of the next bar. It also came away easily, leaving a space large enough for him to wriggle through. But first he eased his head out, turning to look up.

The searchlights playing back and forth across the top of the moat made it hopeless to attempt crossing the moat and climbing up the other side. With all that light, the sentries on the main wall would spot him before he got to the top. On the other hand, the dazzle would prevent the sentries from detecting any movement in the murky depths of the moat.

Jonas unwound the rope and hung it doubled around one of the stationary bars, letting equal lengths of the rope dangle down the moat's inner side. His heart began to pound; in spite of the murk, if a guard happened to look down at the moment he swung out, he would be spotted. Taking the two cut bars in one hand and clinging to a solid bar with the other, Jonas swung out.

Ignoring fear and the need to hurry, he delicately worked each cut bar back into place. Then he gripped the doubled rope with both hands, put the soles of his boots against the moat wall and climbed down. Above the lights swung back and forth. No one shouted an alert; the sirens remained silent. His legs sank into a mixture of mud and water. He spread his feet, let go of one end of the rope and tugged the other slowly. The freed length snaked up around the bar and came free of it. He had both arms spread to catch it when it fell, but one loop struck the water, with a splash that sounded loud in his ears.

He pressed himself against the moat wall, teeth clenched to control his accelerated breathing. And waited. There was no reaction above the moat; the splash hadn't been heard. Wrapping the rope around him, Jonas moved to his right, sticking close to the inside of the moat, wading slowly through the water and mud.

The moat turned a corner. Around it was what he was seeking: two large sewer pipes emerged from under the fort and crossed the moat at a steep downward angle, their farther ends entering into moat wall on the other side. Jonas stopped when he was directly under the pipes. He stayed under them as he waded across the moat, using them for cover all the way. There, low in the opposite wall, was the large mouth of an outlet for water which collected in the moat.

Knowing what lay ahead, Jonas took several deep breaths, filling his lungs with fresh air. Then he waded inside, the water halfway up to his knees. Thank God it had stopped raining— otherwise the water would have been above his knees. This drain outside the fort had been built to handle the worst rainstorms; it was big enough for him to walk upright. But he had to brace with each step. The downward incline was getting steeper, and there was slippery mud and slime under his boots. The stench ahead was reaching him now.

He snapped on the flashlight when the entrance was far enough behind him. The drain was built square, of old bricks. He continued down the incline, with the muddy water rushing and pulling at his legs. The smell kept getting worse. And then it was much worse.

He stopped and tilted his flashlight. Ten yards ahead the open ends of the sewer pipes stuck out of the drain roof. All the sewers and toilets of the fort finally emptied out there, the wastes falling into a deep cesspool directly under the pipe ends.

The water rushing through the drain from the moat also poured into the cesspool. Most of the time the cesspool was deep enough to absorb it, but not always. During the heaviest rainstorms it filled and overflowed. Jonas waded closer, aiming the flashlight beam across the top of the cesspool.

On the other side was a large runoff tunnel, made of old bricks like the drain section Jonas stood in. The tunnel, as far as he could see, tilted downward to carry away any cesspool overflow. The rains of yesterday and last night hadn't been heavy enough for that. There was no water in the runoff tunnel now. What was in it was drying, decomposing sewer muck, from the overflows of months, sticking to the bricks of the walls and floor. The noxious gases filled his mouth and nostrils, stinging his eyes.

It would be worse once he was inside that tunnel. But hesitating wouldn't help; there was no other way except through there.

There was also no way around the cesspool. Letting the flashlight fall back on his chest, Jonas charged ahead at a driving run, getting up as much momentum as he could with the rushing water pulling at his feet. When he reached the edge of the cesspool, he jumped.

He landed on the other side, well inside the tunnel, but his boots skidded in the slime and he fell forward on one knee and both hands. He jerked his hands up quickly. They were covered with muck. Frantically, he beat them together to shake it off. But some of it continued to stick, even after he frantically wiped his hands on his trousers.

Finally he gave it up and concentrated on fighting off the hysteria, steadying his mind. There was a lot more of the same ahead, but staying put was the most dangerous thing he could do. Already the fumes were beginning to make him dizzy. Every second counted.

He tried to go quickly, but kept slipping as he went down the steep incline. The tunnel grew smaller, lower. Jonas had to bend his head, then move on in a crouch, and finally on his hands and knees. He blanked his mind to what he was crawling through. But he couldn't blank out his physical reactions. The stench of the poisonous fumes was like a claw pinching his throat, twisting his stomach, scratching his eyes. He threw up, and when there was no more bile crawled on. He had to be past the point where the other two prisoners had given up, but there was no way to be sure. No way, even, for him to judge how far he'd come through the tunnel. His brain was so muddled that all he could do was to force his arms and legs to carry him forward.

Shallow breathing didn't help. The poisons were being absorbed through his pores, into his blood and nerves and bones.

There was a time when he found himself sprawled out on the floor of the tunnel. When had he fallen? How long had he lain there? No answers from that distant, deadened brain. Get up. He did. Move. He did. Why? He tried to remember. Thought of Nicole instead; not quite sure who she was. Her image merged with Annick's, with Estelle, with Michael, with the dead face of a young RAF pilot...with the horrible faces of his daughter and son, their eyes and nostrils and mouths filled with dust, their arms and legs dangling as they were lifted out of the rubble of the bombed house...

The image was so intense that he screamed. He had never done that before, not when he'd seen their bodies pulled out of the ruins, not when he'd buried them, not even in his nightmares.

There was fresh air diluting the poisonous gases. He was aware of it first in the heaving of his lungs, sucking at the increased oxygen mixing with the sewer fumes. Then part of his mind was functioning, and he started to push on his hands and knees toward the source of the draft.

He couldn't see anything. His eyes were burning too much. His head struck a barrier. His shaking hands explored it. Metal bars, vertical and horizontal ones, crossing each other. The air came through the openings between them. He gripped the bars, shook them with all his strength, the strength of a baby. He pressed his face into a square opening in the bars, so hard that some of the cuts from the beating opened. He breathed deeply of the sweet air outside, gulped it in through his wide-open mouth.

Gradually, other segments of brain began to function, hesitantly. Partial vision returned. The flashlight, glowing weakly now, showed the rusted iron grille blocking his way out to the open.

It was still dark out there.

The grille was very old, the iron bars eaten by decades of erosion. The grille was anchored in cement.

The cement was crumbling. Heat and cold had expanded and contracted it repeatedly. Rains had permeated the cracks. His fingers dug into a crack, pulled. A piece of cement broke off, disintegrating in his hand.

He remembered, fumbled at his belt, tugged the crowbar free. Driving its pointed end into the widened crack, he levered away a chunk of crumbling cement. Again he drove in the crowbar, breaking off another chunk. He kept at it, hammering, levering, digging. A whole block of cement fell against his knees. He rammed his shoulder against the grille. It gave a little, at the bottom. He did it again. More give, but not enough.

Jonas sat back on his heels, his brain reeling and dark flecks drifting in his burned eyes. He took a deep, ragged breath and was convulsed by a spasm of coughing. Without waiting for it to end he went back to work with the crowbar.

Ten minutes later he lay on his back on a barren slope twenty feet outside the runoff tunnel, breathing deeply. There was new strength to his limbs, his vision was sharper, his mind calculating in the old cool way.

He was outside the old fort, but still inside the double ring of barbed wire surrounding the military complex.

The clouds had great gaps between them, filled with stars. It wasn't going to rain. The man-tracking dogs would have no trouble following his scent, especially with the stench of the sewer on him. No way to get rid of the stink that permeated him.

But the dogs were still in their kennels. Nobody knew he'd gone out yet. If he was clever enough and lucky enough he would be far away before they found out. But he had to get away before dawn.

Rising, he found his legs steady, his mind entirely clear. The poison was out of his system, but God, how he stank...

Jonas turned and looked up at the dark bulk of the old fort, the lights swinging from its walls. He got his bearings from the position of the fort and remembered the directions for avoiding the newer fortifications out here.

The moon shown through a wisp of cloud, illuminating the terrain around him clearly. Much too clearly. There was little cover on these upper slopes. He had to get down to where there was scrub brush, and then below to the densely wooded areas. But even up here there were a few routes which might conceal him. He climbed over the top of the slope and down into a narrow gully.

The tunnel outlet gaped open on one side of the gully, the iron-barred grille forced out from the bottom but the top still stuck in the cement around the hole. Jonas put his back against the opposite side and raised one leg, putting the heel of his boot against the grille and exerting steady pressure. The bottom of the grille creaked back into place. He picked up handfuls of dirt and broken cement and plastered them into the cracks where the bars had torn free. With luck—always so much hung on luck—nobody would discover he'd come out this way, and other prisoners would be able to use it.

Jonas dropped the flashlight into a pocket, then stuck the

crowbar back into his belt. He kept the other items, the hacksaw blades, the wire cutters, the rope wound around his waist and torso. Any of these might be needed for whatever lay ahead, especially the cutters.

He started down, staying inside the gully as long as it took him where he wanted to go, keeping low, only showing his head as he scanned the surrounding terrain.

The escape committee didn't know the routes and timing of the security patrols out here. There was no way to avoid them except by keeping his eyes open. The circumstances gave him one edge: he could spot them before they saw him. He knew they were out here somewhere, and as yet they didn't know about him.

The taut strand of fence wire twanged loudly as it sprang open. The barbed wire looped around the parted segments clattered on the ground. There was no way to do this job without noise. Holding the wire cutters ready for the second strand, Jonas looked swiftly up and down the length of the inner fence: the first of the two he had to get through.

There was dense scrub up the slope behind him, and higher bushes and patches of low forest ahead on the other side, between the two fence rings. But wide paths had been cleared along both sides of this inner ring, to give sentries patrolling it a clear view. It also gave Jonas a clear view. He'd remained hidden in the scrub above until one patrol had come and gone; and there was still no other patrol in sight.

He cut the other strand. A lot of noise again; but now there was a large enough opening between the top and bottom wires. Dropping the cutters back into his pocket, Jonas climbed through to the wide path on the other side. He looked along the fence again—and instantly dropped flat to the ground. A pair of shadowy figures were coming along the inner ring, off to his right.

They were too far away to have heard him cut the wires; and they weren't coming that fast, so they hadn't seen him yet. Staying flat, Jonas snaked across the cleared path and into the bushes. When he was deep enough he got his feet under him and turned, crouched, to look back. The two-man patrol was still approaching at a strolling pace. But within four minutes they'd reach the point where he'd come through the fence, and they couldn't fail to see the gap.

Turning again, Jonas pushed on through the bushes, angling toward a thickly wooded stretch farther down. The outer fence ring was half a mile ahead, if he went directly to it. But with the sentries about to come after him he could no longer take the shortest route. He needed the safest one, with the most cover. When he was among the trees he lengthened his stride, going as fast as he could without breaking into a run. He had to move quietly and avoid blundering into other dangers. There'd be patrols ahead of him, as well as the one behind.

He thought back to a sentry patrol he'd observed when the MP car had brought him here through the fence gates. One of the men had been carrying a walkie-talkie. A lot of what happened next, including how much time he had left, depended on whether the patrol which discovered his break through the inner fence also had a walkie-talkie.

He was crossing the crest of another wooded hill, calculating that the outer fence couldn't be much farther away, when he got the answer. Sirens began going off all over the Fort Revère complex, sounding the escape signals. The patrol behind him had radioed in their discovery of the break in the fence.

Jonas climbed a tree for a swift look at what lay immediately around him. He couldn't spot the patrol coming after him, nor any other patrol, in any direction. What he did see, up on the crests around the area of the old fort, was the headlights of vehicles speeding out in different directions. They'd be carrying troops, to begin cordoning off and searching the surrounding areas. They'd also be bringing the man-tracker hounds.

Looking down in the opposite direction he saw the searchlights on top of the two watchtowers along the outer ring. He couldn't see the fence running between them, or judge the terrain immediately beyond it. Jonas glanced at the sky. A faint tinge of predawn gray showed on the eastern horizon. There wasn't much time left.

He dropped to the ground and hurried down the wooded slope, aiming for a point midway between the two watchtowers. In five minutes he was at the outer fence. It made a sharp curve there, out of sight of the towers and searchlights in either direction. On the other side was a curve of hill road, running north and south. On the other side of the road the ground ended, dropping away abruptly.

Jonas cut one of the fence strands. There was the sound of an approaching vehicle, coming up the road from the south. It stopped, still out of sight. Probably to drop off search patrols. He cut the second strand of wire.

From far behind him, up the slopes, came the baying of excited hounds, at the spot where he'd broken through the inner ring; right now they'd be getting a good smell of his sewer stench. Any second they'd be on his trail, coming fast. Jonas climbed through the gap in the outer fence and crossed the road.

On the other side the ground fell away into a deep, steep-walled ravine. The cliff beneath him was almost sheer but looked climbable, if he wanted to go down there.

There was the sound of another vehicle approaching from the distance, coming from the north. It stopped much farther away than the first one, but now both directions along the road were blocked to him. He could try going into and through the deep ravine. But it would be slow going, with search patrols fanning out to seal him off, the dogs following his scent, and dawn approaching.

Jonas dropped flat to the ground between the road and the ravine drop. A two-man patrol was coming up the road from the south.

They hadn't seen him. Their attention was on the fence, looking for a breakthrough along this stretch. Jonas slid over the edge and lowered himself until he found a small foothold. He could continue down, but didn't want to. There was only one possibility left. Bending his knees until only his eyes were above the road level, he watched the patrol walking along the outside of the fence, coming closer. Both men wore long winter coats against the predawn cold and carried submachine guns.

One had a walkie-talkie hanging from a shoulder strap.

Jonas drew the short crowbar from his belt.

They reached the place where he'd cut through the fence. Quietly, Jonas swung himself up to the other side of the road, getting his feet under him. The one with the radio was slinging his submachine gun over his shoulder before making the call in. The other turned from the fence to look farther up the road. He saw Jonas spring across the road at him, but was too startled to get his weapon up in time.

Jonas swung the crowbar. It thudded into the trooper's throat. His eyes bulged from their sockets and his mouth popped wide open but no sound came out. He went over backwards, his arms and legs dangling like a broken marionette.

The other soldier had dropped his walkie-talkie and was grabbing for his submachine gun. Jonas twisted, gripping the crowbar with both hands, and drove the sharp point deep into the man's midsection. A soft and terrible sound bubbled out of him; he seemed to break in half, doubling up as he fell forward and struck the ground head first, spilling over on his side with his knees folded up against his chest.

Jonas kicked him in the head and turned back to the first one. The man was dead. Jonas sat down on the road beside him, swiftly dragged the boots and long coat from the limp body, then the trousers. Then Jonas stripped off his own boots, uniform jacket and trousers.

He tied the RAF jacket and trousers around the dead man's waist and chest and used his own belt to bind his stinking boots to one of the man's legs. Gripping the man's wrists, Jonas got to his feet and dragged the body across the road, shoved it over the edge and dropped it into the depths of the ravine.

Recrossing the road, he put on the dead man's trousers, boots and greatcoat. The baying of the dogs was getting louder, closer. Jonas picked up the submachine gun and went back inside the fence. He climbed fast, angling away from the nearing hounds, careful not to let his hands touch anything. Entering a dense patch of pine forest covering a low hill between the inner and outer fence rings, he stopped under a tree and slung the sub-

270

machine gun over his shoulder Reaching as high as he could, he seized a branch with both hands and hauled himself up to it.

Climbing, he listened to the baying of the dogs as they continued along his original trail to the hole in the outside fence. The stink they were following was too strong for them to be diverted by other smells. They would follow that stink through the fence, across the road to the top of the ravine. Their handlers wouldn't delay long by the dead soldier. They'd figure the other had followed him into the ravine.

Maybe they'd wait for dawn before working their way down there. Certainly they'd summon reinforcements to enter with them. Eventually they'd find the body and understand they'd been tricked. The search for the escaper would spread out beyond the ravine, into the encircling hills. It wouldn't occur to them that he had gone back *inside* the place he'd escaped from.

If he was right, by nightfall the hunt would have spread thinly into areas miles away, giving him another chance to slip out. *If, chances, hopes...*

Jonas settled into a notch in the pine tree to wait out the coming day.

TWENTY-SEVEN

THE SKY OVER the Toulon region was cloudless, but the wind from the mountains had been growing stronger and colder since sunset. Reggie waited in the shadows of the trees with five other members of the Falcon Resistance group, watching Dithelm Demenus cross the road to a bistro on the other side. They were in the countryside near Toulon. A stolen car, with stolen gasoline, had brought them this far. From here Dithelm would lead them the rest of the way in on foot, to avoid roadblocks around the city outskirts. The stolen car was hidden, to await their return trip to the Maures.

Only there wasn't going to be any return trip. Reggie smiled to himself as Dithelm vanished inside the bistro to make the final check by phone. It had been a long, long wait for Reggie; he had given one of the best sustained performances of his career. But tonight was the payoff.

Dithelm had decided to let the other men wait in a wooded area near his girl friend's house, while he and Reggie reconnoitered to make absolutely sure it was safe. It was strange, Reggie thought with some irritation: the young German trusted him that much, but not with the girl's name, occupation or where she lived.

Reggie had worked for that trust. He had done things to prove his competence and courage; had wormed his way into

273

Dithelm's affections. He had even managed to get him to talk about the girl. Reggie knew a lot about Dithelm's feeling for her, and that she was dark and small and curvy. But nothing more.

The Englishman felt a stirring of a vicious sexual desire. But this time, he knew, he would have to be satisfied with other rewards. By the time Udo Mueller finished with the girl she wouldn't be anything a man would want to look at, let alone touch...

Inside the bistro Dithelm paid the owner for the use of the phone, and turned his back so no one could see him dial. He waited, listening to the ringing at the other end.

In the downstairs study, Nicole picked up the phone on the third ring. "Yes?"

It was Dithelm's voice, quiet and careful: "I'll see you in about two hours. Everything is still fine?"

"Yes."

"Keep checking until I get there."

"You know I will," Nicole told him, more sharply than she had intended. But he'd already hung up.

She put down the phone and went back upstairs, to keep a lookout from the windows there. Her nerves were ragged, and she knew it wasn't just the tension over what Dithelm planned for tonight, and her part in it.

It was having to fight the sickening fear that she was never going to see Jonas again. Never.

Udo Mueller had a pleasant tingle of excitement as he went down the rear stairway of the Gestapo building to make sure everything was in readiness. The two vehicles were in place at the curb just outside the back door, across from the dark parking area behind the prison wall.

One was a radio van. The operator in the back assured Mueller that he was now in radio contact with the Milice and Vichy police squads waiting to spring their traps at both places the Maures Resistance group was scheduled to attack tonight.

The other was a Mercedes sedan with five Gestapo operatives

274

waiting inside it. When Reggie phoned with the address of that elusive young woman, Mueller would join these five and drive there to take her. It would come sometime tonight. Once he had her, the radio van could contact the men he had ready around the Maures, and they would move in to capture or kill the rest of the Resistance group there.

Mueller went back to his office to await Reggie's phone call.

There was a thunderclap so loud and close it felt like hell's own firecracker, exploding inches from the small of his back. Jonas listened to the after rumble rippling away through the mountains, while his hair tingled with electric charges and his spine relaxed from the shock.

The cloud cover was back, low and dark. There was no rain. But the thunderstorm was better than rain, if they had the dogs after him again, trying to follow the new trail he had left after cutting his way out of another section of the outer fence an hour past sunset. He still stank of the sewer, and the dead man's coat and trousers had become permeated with it. Ordinarily the hounds would have had no trouble following that scent. But the dogs would be out of their minds with terror from all the noise and electricity, incapable of following anything.

Jonas was well north of Fort Revère now, making his way along a hillside of olive groves while continuing rolls of thunder shook the ground. There was a better chance of finding a telephone by going in the other direction, south to the towns along the coast and the railroad. But too many hunters would be looking for him around those places: the ones from the fort joined now by Milice, the Wehrmacht and more cops. Even if they missed seeing him they'd be able to smell him.

So Jonas continued down the northern slopes toward Notre Dame de Laghet, half-hidden between foothills. Laghet wasn't even a village. It was a religious sanctuary filled with ex-votos left by people who had been coming there for over two centuries to give thanks to the Madonna for miraculous cures and rescues. There were a few houses and a restaurant—but there might not be a telephone. This area didn't boast many.

If there were none in Laghet he would have to continue north to the village of Peille, which would take another couple of hours of hiking.

A bolt of lightning lashed out of the clouds. As his eyes narrowed against it he saw the dark shape of Laghet below.

Reggie followed Dithelm down out of the woods under Mount Faron, into the walled estate. Each man had a revolver ready. Dithelm pointed and Reggie moved off to circle Nicole's house from the left flank, while Dithelm circled to the right. When the young German was out of sight Reggie stopped under a tree, looking thoughtfully at the house, letting the gun dangle in his hand.

He waited about five minutes, and then a light went on in a downstairs window. Reggie strolled over and looked in. Dithelm stood in the living room with a remarkably pretty girl, dark and curvy, as Reggie had imagined her. It was a shame, really, that he wouldn't have a bit of time with her first. He moved along to a door and knocked quietly.

Dithelm opened it, his gun still in his hand. Reggie smiled at him and stuck his gun back into his belt. "All clear on my side of the house."

"Mine, too." Dithelm slipped his revolver into a shoulder holster. "Come in."

Reggie stepped inside. As he shut the door behind him Nicole appeared.

"This is Reggie," Dithelm told her.

"I've heard good things about you," she said.

Reggie gave her a gallant bow. "And I about you." He took her hand and kissed it. As he straightened, he let his hand rest casually on the butt of his gun.

It would be best to do it soon.

The phone rang in the downstairs study. Nicole got an odd, startled expression on her face. She turned and ran to answer it.

"You can go up now," Dithelm told Reggie, "and bring the others down here."

"Yes. That is a lovely little woman there. Everything you claimed for her."

Dithelm looked automatically in the direction she'd gone. Reggie drew the revolver and slammed it behind Dithelm's ear. The young German's knees buckled and he toppled against a heavy wing chair, fell away from it and sprawled across the rug. Reggie struck him again, just to make sure, but not too hard. Mueller wouldn't like it if Dithelm didn't recover to answer questions.

Taking Dithelm's gun, the Englishman straightened up. Now for the girl, and then the call to Mueller. He'd have these two all wrapped up as a present for the Gestapo man when he got here. The five waiting in the woods were disciplined men. They'd been told to stay there till either Dithelm or Reggie came to fetch them, and they would do that. They'd still be there when Mueller's men closed in and took them by surprise.

Reggie walked through the corridor toward the study, very relaxed now, a gun dangling in each hand, feeling like a cowboy in a Western movie. He stepped into the open door of the study.

Nicole stood beside the desk, the phone off the hook, her father's elegant shotgun in her hands. Reggie blinked and started to bring up the two revolvers, but the shotgun was already leveled at him. Nicole fired it at point-blank range. The explosion was deafening.

The concentrated load of shot smashed Reggie's chest apart and kicked him back out of the doorway and across the corridor, plastering him against the opposite wall for an instant, before letting what remained of him slide down and spill across the floor.

In horror, Nicole threw the shotgun down on the desk. It struck the opened drawer from which she'd gotten the shell and fell to the carpet. She jumped over the Englishman's body and found Dithelm sprawled on the living-room rug. On her knees she turned him over and made sure he was not dead. When she saw his breathing was slow but steady, Nicole hurried back to the corridor.

She stepped over Reggie's body, trying not to look at the

bloody mess of pulp and bones that had been his chest. A voice was shouting through the phone on the study desk.

Nicole snatched it up and said, "It's all right, Jonas. I'm all right...Oh, God. Jonas..."

Udo Mueller paced his office in the Gestapo building. He was beginning to worry. It was almost midnight, and still no phone call from Reggie. Also no radio report from the Milice and police units waiting at the two places the Resistance group was supposed to have attacked that night.

There was a roar of a car engine outside, and a screech of tires. And then one of his men out back yelling something. Mueller got to his office window in time to see a taxicab speed up past the back of the building and vanish from sight going up the side street.

The Mercedes with his five Gestapo men suddenly swung away from the curb, its tires squealing as it executed a tight U-turn and raced off around the corner after the vanished taxi. The radioman came out of the van and began advancing cautiously toward a figure sprawled in the gutter. Mueller spun away from the window and rushed from his office.

Down between cars in the parking area behind the prison wall, Dithelm lowered the hunting rifle when Mueller vanished from the upstairs window. He rested on one knee, waiting.

The radioman was standing over the sprawled figure, staring down at it open-mouthed. Mueller came out of the back door and strode toward him with a snarl. "Get back to your radio!"

As the man hurried back to the van Mueller reached the corner and gazed numbly at the figure which had been flung from the taxi and rolled into the gutter. Reggie's wide-open eyes stared back at him. A startled expression had frozen into permanence on his dead face.

Mueller looked at what had been Reggie's chest. He straightened, taking a deep breath of the cold night air.

In the shadows between the parked cars across from Mueller, Dithelm took careful aim with the hunting rifle and gently squeezed the trigger. The sharp report of the shot echoed be-

278

tween the prison wall and the Gestapo building. Dithelm was up off his knee, turning and running as his target fell.

He sprinted past the end of the prison wall and through an alley, across a street and into another alley. When he reached the other end another stolen taxi appeared, turning a corner and speeding toward him. Two of the men inside were the same pair who had been in the first taxi. They'd left it stalled at a slant across a narrow street, blocking off the Gestapo pursuit car.

The taxi skidded to a halt. Dithelm jumped in back and it raced away.

Back at the corner behind the Gestapo building, Udo Mueller lay sprawled across the body of Reggie. There was a dark hole where his left eye had been.

TWENTY-EIGHT NOVEMBER 25

THE LITTLE FARM was situated in a deep fold of the Tercier Plateau northwest of Notre Dame de Laghet. It belonged to an Italian family, two of whose members had fled Mussolini's Fascist state ten years earlier. Five days after the Axis occupation of southern France the entire family had been arrested and taken to a camp for political prisoners.

The nun who had let Jonas use the phone at the Laghet church had told him about the uninhabited farm. She had also given him food to take with him when he'd set out. Most of it he had wolfed down last night. The rest he finished off as the sun rose. Before falling asleep Jonas had spent an hour in the farmhouse tub, scrubbing the stench from his hair and skin with strong soap and a stiff-bristled brush. But the memory of the sewer crawl made him take another long bath after breakfast.

The farm animals had been removed and the house looted of everything of value, including most of the furniture. But Jonas had found scattered items of male clothing, some too small and others too big for him, all in such bad condition the looters had discarded them. After his bath Jonas put on the oversized items he'd chosen last night: ragged shirt and dungarees, a torn pair of felt slippers, a heavy jacket with holes at the elbows.

He looked at himself in a cracked bathroom mirror. He had a growth of beard by now that concealed most of the signs of his beating, except for a dark bruise across one cheekbone and some swelling around his eyes. That could be explained with a rueful laugh if anyone got curious: the results of a drunken brawl with his brother-in-law. People, he'd discovered long ago, could easily be distracted if you threw in sordid family details.

Jonas had to resist a desire to scratch his face; under the beard the healing cuts itched like hell. He left the house and went back to the small barn where he'd slept. He left the door open so he could watch the approach path, then settled down on a mound of straw to wait for Nicole. The more rest he got now the better. He couldn't see much prospect for more in the immediate future.

There were less than two days left to Operation Lila.

After he left here it was going to take the rest of the day, using buses and one stretch of railroad, to get near the region where he'd left the orders Andreas Keller has passed on to him. He'd have to bypass Bargemon, where the Miliciens had taken him, and go on to the town of Aups. From there it would take all night to hike into the mountains, get to the bowl where the Lysander had crashed and hike back out.

It was going to require all of the next day and much of tomorrow night to get from Aups down to Toulon via buses, local trains and trams. That was if luck was with him all the way. If he ran into bad luck he would reach Toulon too late for it to matter anymore.

For the past week only freight trains had been permitted to run between midnight and dawn. Nicole took the first morning train eastbound out of Toulon. She'd brought her bicycle along. That had become common practice since the occupation, with the drastic cut in fuel supplies, and her bike had plenty of others for company in the baggage car.

She got off the train at Nice and boarded the bus with less than fifteen minutes to spare. It ran only twice a day since the occupation; if she'd missed this one she would have had to wait until late afternoon for the other. The bus carried her north, with her bike on the roof rack with others. At least half the passengers packed into the bus had brought bicycles.

The nearest bus stop to the place where Jonas awaited her was the village of Drap. He couldn't risk waiting in any village or town until he had proper clothes and identity papers. Nicole rode her bike east from Drap over country lanes, passing scattered farms. Jonas had tied a strip of rag to the top of the gate of the abandoned farm. Nicole swung down, unlatched the gate and walked her bike through, along a short path.

Jonas stepped out of the small barn ahead of her.

Until that moment Nicole had kept her emotions under control. But when she saw him it broke. She let the bicycle fall. Abruptly she was running, throwing herself against him, laughing and crying as his arms wrapped around her and she dragged his mouth down to hers. What she experienced in that kiss told her that she no longer had to decide between the two men in her life. Something more qualified than her brain had taken over and made the decision, with startling finality.

They lay on the sweet-smelling hay inside the barn, holding each other and treasuring the final minutes. Their brief time together was almost over. Nicole had memorized the new bus schedule in Drap. The one Jonas had to catch would depart in an hour.

He filled her in on what had happened to him—and to the vital proofs of Operation Lila. Nicole told him about Dithelm killing the Gestapo man.

Jonas grimaced. "Christ! Why did he have to do that *now?*"

"I didn't know he was going to. And Dithelm didn't know about Operation Lila. You told me not to say anything to him about you or it."

"It'll bring ten times more Gestapo into Toulon. The city will be crawling with them and Milice. And the police will arrest people right and left. It's going to make everything that much harder."

"It's already begun," Nicole said. "At the train station this morning they were arresting people at random, to be taken in for questioning. They almost took me. Only my papers proving I'm a good, solid collaborator made them let me go. On top of which the police have the city under a 10 P.M. to 6 A.M. curfew. Even doctors on emergency night calls have been arrested for interrogation. You'll have to be extra careful slipping back into Toulon."

Jonas gave her a crooked smile. "I hope you've saved the good news for last."

"Sorry, Jonas. The worst." She told him about the French navy guards being withdrawn from outside the gates of the base, their posts taken over by the Wehrmacht.

Jonas was silent for a moment. That finished any chance of getting to Lieutenant Martin the way he planned. "With Lila set for Friday morning, the Wehrmacht will arrest anybody trying to get near any gate Thursday night to talk to the French inside."

"I've had more time to think about it than you," Nicole said. "There's one other way we might be able to get through to Martin." She explained it to Jonas in detail.

"I don't like it."

"I'm not looking forward to it myself. But I can't think of anything else. Can you?"

"No," he conceded. And then: "We just might be able to pull it off."

They discussed exactly how, and the preparations Nicole would have to make for it, back in Toulon, before Jonas got there. Then she looked at her watch. The moment couldn't be delayed any longer.

She got up and walked naked to the bicycle he'd brought into the barn and began unstrapping the suitcase fastened to the luggage rack behind the seat. For a moment Jonas remained where he was, luxuriating in the sight of her. Then he stood up, brushed off hay clinging to his body and took the suitcase from her.

The clothes she had brought fitted his new role, complete with an old cloth cap of good quality. According to his second set of identity cards he was Gilbert Dumont, a farmer from the Sospel area farther east.

It was probably the best cover he could use right now. Both Pétain and Hitler were known to be particularly well disposed toward French farmers. The former appreciated the fact that the great majority of them were conservative, averse to political disturbance and strongly pro-Vichy. The latter envisioned the France of the future as one vast farm supplying the food requirements of his New Reich.

When questioned at checkpoints, Jonas decided, he would explain that he was visiting other farms looking for a male calf he could buy for a good price and raise as a stud. For a farmer that was as normal an activity as a real-estate developer looking for land he could buy at bargain rates.

Nicole went to pick up her clothing. Jonas stopped her, taking her shoulder in his hands and gently kissing the tips of her breasts, and then her lips.

She smiled up into his eyes. "No more time for that now, Jonas."

"Here's to later," he told her softly.

She nodded. "We will have later."

"Sure..." Jonas patted her buttocks and let her get dressed. Going back to the suitcase, he took out the compass and flashlight she had brought for the night trek through the mountains below the Verdon Canyon. Putting them in the side pockets of his lumber jacket, he slipped the wallet with his ID into the inside breast pocket and put on the cap.

A few minutes later he was pedaling the bicycle along the lane toward Drap, with Nicole on the luggage rack behind him, her arms tight around his waist, both of them remembering the first time they had ridden a bike together like this, when she was sixteen.

They got to the village bus stop with six minutes to spare and boarded it together for the trip south to Nice. There they took the next train west toward Toulon, sitting very close. Jonas would not be going all the way with her. From St. Raphael there was a bus going northwest to Les Arcs, and there he should just be able to catch the last bus of the day to Aups.

When the train pulled into St. Raphael a five-minute stop was announced. Nicole got off with him and helped bring her bicycle out of the baggage car. They had decided that Jonas should take it with him. It would make for faster going, from Aups partway into the mountains that night and coming back out to Aups tomorrow morning.

Nicole gripped his wrists and whispered, "Come back to me, Jonas.... Don't frighten me so much this time."

The departure whistle sounded. She kissed his bruised cheekbone, the swelling around his eyes. Then she released his wrists and jumped onto the steps of the moving train. Jonas stood there holding the bike, watching the train carry her away from him.

She would reach Toulon in an hour. That would give her this evening and most of tomorrow to investigate any changes in the situation around the waterfront and to buy the things they would need for tomorrow night.

There were thirty-eight hours left to Operation Lila.

In the SS Panzer Korps encampment outside Brignoles, General Hausser strolled along his columns of troops, drawn up for inspection in front of their tanks and trucks, motorcycles and armored cars. He spoke briefly to each officer about the task ahead, nodded to the troopers he passed, paused occasionally to shake the hand of a veteran he remembered from the Russian battles.

He radiated absolute confidence, and it was contagious. Each man, he saw, was as ready and eager as he was.

Hausser was smiling when he finished his inspection and returned to his farmhouse headquarters. Friday morning, between midnight and dawn, the Waffen SS would give a lesson to the old-fashioned military thinkers on how a delicate operation should be carried out.

286

TWENTY-NINE NOVEMBER 26

JONAS BACKED THE bicycle into a shadowed space between the Aups church and a bakery. He eyed the other side of the town square, where passengers were boarding the morning bus south to Les Arcs and St. Raphael. There were two police checking their papers. That wasn't what had made Jonas draw back out of sight. His papers had got him through three checkpoints yesterday, at Nice, St. Raphael and Les Arcs. His trouble now was one of the men near the bus. He was one of the Miliciens who had captured and beaten Jonas.

If the Milicien was just there as an observer, making sure the police did their job properly...and if the man got bored and went away before the bus left...

Jonas clenched his teeth. The Milicien was getting aboard the bus, which meant Jonas couldn't, after having bicycled furiously since before sunrise to get here before the morning bus departed.

He watched it pull out, turning down the route to the south. Now Jonas was left with five hours to wait for the next one. That was cutting it too fine. He couldn't risk taking the train from St. Raphael all the way into Toulon. His papers might not get him through the police, Gestapo and Milice that would be hanging around the station since the killing of Mueller, their tempers hair-trigger and their habitual suspicion multiplied.

He would have to get off outside the city and bike the rest of the way in. What with having to stop continuously to survey the routes ahead and to detour around traps he spotted, it was going to take some doing, starting out so much later than he'd figured, to get to Nicole around midnight.

Jonas pushed the bike across the Aups square. There was no one else around who knew him. The Milicien had been a wild mischance, one he hadn't needed at this point. But the damage was done and couldn't be undone.

Leaving the bike against a big plane tree dominating the square, he went into a café and slumped at a table, ordering coffee with milk and croissants. He was hungry and he was weary. He'd been on the move the entire previous night.

It had been sunset when he'd reached Aups yesterday, and he had ridden the bike from here into the mountains. Leaving it when the going got too rough and steep, he'd walked the rest of the way and reached the bowl just after midnight. The dead pilot had been taken away. But the crashed plane was still there, and so were Keller's two copies of the Operation Lila orders.

There was no need for both anymore. Jonas had burned one copy and secured the other under his shirt and belt against the small of his back before starting the return trip to Aups. The Milicien had made all this furious traveling pointless.

Finishing his breakfast, Jonas wondered if taking the afternoon bus, instead, was going to make the rest of it just as pointless.

He paid the café owner for the breakfast and a half-day's rent of a bedroom upstairs, and asked him to watch the bike. The man promised to wake him in exactly four hours and to have a large hot meal ready for him before he took the second bus south. Jonas trudged up the stairs and contemplated a narrow bed with broken springs and an exceptionally thin mattress. He set his mind for four hours and fell asleep on the bed as though it were soft cotton a mile deep.

Once each day Admiral Laborde exercised his legs with a brisk walk along the docks of the Toulon naval base. This day

288

the prefect of the port and Laborde's general staff officer accompanied him. He had invited Vice-Admiral Marquis and Rear Admiral Dornon to join him to determine if their feelings coincided with his own.

When the Wehrmacht had taken over the guard posts outside the base, Laborde had given orders for the gates to be closed and barred from inside. Marquis had reluctantly agreed to that, and to Laborde's subsequent order that the entire base be put on a twenty-four-hour-alert status.

But the Axis had not voiced a single objection to either of these defensive moves. And since then the Germans had made no further threatening or even unfriendly gesture of their own.

"Personally," Vice-Admiral Marquis said, "I don't believe they have any intention of carrying out anything remotely resembling that warning you received. Hitler has enough other matters on his mind, with Russia and North Africa."

"Our intelligence services," Rear Admiral Dornon added more cautiously, "have not been able to detect any sign the Germans are preparing an attack in this region. They are convinced the warning was an Allied fake, intended to trick us into making a terrible mistake."

Marquis nodded. "Thank God it failed, and we held ourself back from the final madness."

Admiral Laborde had been coming to the same conclusion on his own. The perfidious Allies had managed to panic him into making himself look ridiculous. It was now two weeks since the Wehrmacht had occupied the rest of southern France—but not Toulon. If the warning had been true, Hitler's forces would have made their move against Toulon's naval base by now. If that was their intention there was no reason for them to have waited so long, and to continue to wait.

Laborde was becoming less worried about German intentions than about what Marshal Pétain thought of him. Because of Laborde's proven loyalty to him, the marshal had graciously forgiven him for having ordered the preparations for scuttling without Vichy authorization—excusing it as a result of a "bout of nerves" on Laborde's part.

But a reputation as a nervous admiral would not bode well for him in the future.

"As of six o'clock this evening," Loborde told the two flanking him, "I want that alert order rescinded. Everyone can begin to relax a bit."

"Wise decision." Vice-Admiral Marquis gave a short laugh. "As for myself, I never stopped being relaxed. I never did believe in that warning."

Laborde clamped a rigid control on a flare-up of anger. For some time to come, it would be well to keep his well-known temper in check. "This is Thursday," he resumed. "If by the end of this weekend there have been no further developments, I think we can reopen the gates and restore shore leaves."

And sometime after that, he thought, though he did not say so, it might be wise for him to have the scuttling charges removed, and then quietly inform Marshal Pétain that he had done so.

Laborde did an abrupt about-face and began walking back toward his flagship. The other two turned hastily to catch up with him. But Admiral Laborde was deep in his own thoughts, and in no mood for further discussion.

He only hoped that the new conciliatory moves he had decided on would cause the marshal to revise his opinion about his nerves.

Ten minutes before midnight every vehicle of the SS Panzer Korps coughed to life, the concerted roar of starting motors filling the encampment outside Brignoles. One by one, in precise order, they rolled out and started south along Route 5 to carry out the preliminary stage of Operation Lila.

The SS motorcycle battalion from the Das Reich Division took the lead, gradually drawing farther ahead of the rest. Its objective: to seize each police station and military lookout post along the way, taking the French troopers and gendarmes prisoner, and at the same time to patrol the roads south and insure that no one who had observed the Korps could reach Toulon ahead of it.

Following closely after the lead motorcycle forces were specialized units from the signals section of Hausser's operations communications regiment. Objective: to seize all telephone exchanges and radio transmission stations and cut local phone lines, preventing any warning of the SS Panzer Korps approach from being communicated to the naval base.

When the last of his motorized forces rumbled out of the encampment, General Hausser climbed into his command car and sped alongside the endless column through clouds of churning dust.

Upon reaching the forking of roads farther south, near Meounes-les-Montrieux, Hausser's forces would begin to separate into the three main combat groups. The first to take up a position just north of Toulon, the second circling around to the east of the city, the third to the west. Each was to be established at its designated assembly point near the city by 3 A.M., ready to move in for what General Hausser had called "the closing of the jaws."

Hausser looked up at the sky and grinned. There was hardly a cloud and the moonlight was quite strong. His forces would have little difficulty in finding their way swiftly through the maze of the naval base to the ships, after his tanks broke through the gates.

Even the weather, it seemed, was conspiring to insure that the operation would be a success.

THIRTY

THE CLOCK IN the church tower above him bonged once, loudly. One o'clock in the morning. Jonas had reached the outskirts of Toulon before eleven at night. Getting the rest of the way in, past police patrols and cruising Gestapo and Milice cars, had taken more than two hours. And now he was stuck, just half a block from the place Nicole had set for their rendezvous, waiting as another police patrol came along Rue Jourdan toward him.

He had taken off his shoes, tied the laces together and hung them around his neck. He pressed against one of the three stone pillars on the church porch, keeping it between him and the narrow street. One of the policemen noisily tested the gate to the small churchyard and found it still solidly locked. Another poked a flashlight through the gate bars. The shadows of the three pillars moved across the front of the church with the swing of the light beam.

There was nothing to indicate that Jonas was part of the shadows, and after a moment the patrol moved on. Their footsteps sounded sharply in the silence of the empty street. When they were gone he emerged from behind the pillar and climbed the gate, lowering himself to the sidewalk. His stockinged feet made no sound crossing Rue Jourdan. He entered the Rue de l'Etoile, narrow and only one block long. A building near the

293

other end contained the apartment of the friend who had left Nicole the key.

She had chosen this place because it was only three short blocks from the quays of the Vieille Darse, between the two sections of the naval base. Now that it was impossible to get anything to Lieutenant Martin through the gates of the base, there was only one way left: by water. And not by boat; there were too many lookouts along the quays.

They'd have to try swimming for it; try to make it out beyond the old fishing port and around to the bay front of the Mourillon Arsenal without getting drowned or swept away; try to get inside that section of the base without being seen and stopped; try to find Martin in there before time ran out.

Jonas hadn't attempted to dissuade Nicole from the idea of trying it with him. He didn't intend to now. She had always been the better swimmer. The water was going to be very cold and there were treacherous currents out in the bay. If one got in trouble the other could help. And if they got caught once they were inside the base, a good-looking girl could be more persuasive with French sailors than he.

It was a narrow four-floor building, the ground floor occupied by a rare-book shop with its steel shutters locked for the night. Jonas went up the inside stairway and knocked softly at the apartment door. It swung open before he finished knocking. Nicole dragged him inside and locked her arms around him, pressing her face against his chest.

She didn't waste time asking why he was so late. When she let go of him she said, "There's not much time." And pointed to the couch. There were two waterproofed sacks waiting on it, and a rubber wraparound pouch with a sealing device and straps.

Jonas put the copy of the Operation Lila orders in the pouch, wrapped and sealed it securely so no moisture could get in and strapped it to his left arm, high up near the shoulder. He picked up one of the sacks and looped its strap around the back of his neck, letting it hang against his chest.

Nicole looked at her watch and gestured for him to stay put.

"Four minutes to wait. I've been up on the roof timing the foot patrols between here and the quay."

"What about the car patrols?"

"They don't seem to have a set pattern. But you can hear them coming a long way off."

Jonas nodded. That was one helpful thing about the curfew. Anybody out at night, making any noise at all, had to be police of some kind.

Nicole had pointed out the other helpful thing about the curfew when she'd first told him her idea: All the business places along the Cronstadt Quay would be closed and empty between 10 P.M. and 6 A.M.

"Now," she said softly, and hung the other sack around her neck. They went downstairs and out into the dark streets of the city, deserted except for the hunters and the hunted.

A black Renault sedan cruised slowly along the Rue République. Jonas and Nicole crouched behind a green metal sea monster spitting water into a stone basin and watched the car pass them. The four men inside wore raincoats and porkpie hats: Gestapo. The Renault went on for two blocks and turned into the Rue d'Alger, heading away from the port. Jonas rose with Nicole and they went out from behind the fountain, quickly crossing the wide street and ducking into a short alley.

It wasn't wide enough for them to walk through side by side: a service and garbage alley, cutting behind some of the bars and cafés which faced out onto the Quay Cronstadt. Jonas let Nicole lead the way. She was the one who had worked this out and researched it for them.

Halting at one of the back doors, she whispered: "This one." They were behind the Galleon Café. Nicole took a small flashlight from her sack and shined it on the door. "The things you asked for are in your sack."

It was a heavy wooden door with a solid lock. But that was one of the trades they taught you in the SOE courses: breaking and entering, when it was inadvisable to do it the noisy way.

Jonas fished inside his sack until he found the penknife, the short lengths of stiff wire, the tiny screwdriver. Nicole moved aside to make room and he went to work on the lock. It took him eight minutes.

They stepped inside and he shut the door and relocked it. The flash showed a small storage area, piled with casks of wine and beer, curtained off from the front part of the café. Jonas pointed to the light and Nicole snapped it off. He parted the curtains just enough to peek through, past a little kitchen, toward the front window and the lights of the quay outside it.

At that moment a four-man Milice patrol strolled by. One glanced in the window toward Jonas, but saw nothing and walked on with the others. He let the curtain fall back into place and turned his back to it. "All right, keep the light down around floor level and shield it with your body."

When the light snapped on again he saw her on her knees, the flash braced against her stomach, her back to the curtains. She aimed the beam at some barrels against the rear wall. One by one, Jonas lifted and shifted them. They were heavy and there was little room. He was sweating by the time he'd moved enough of them to reveal a trapdoor set into the floor.

Jonas crouched, got a grip on its ring latch and raised it all the way open. Nicole shone the light down. It gleamed against black, oily water a few feet down, moving sluggishly under the Quay Cronstadt.

"When Prevot showed me this," Nicole said, "he told me in past centuries there were bars and brothels on this quay which used these holes to get rid of sailors they'd robbed and killed."

"They tell that story in every port in the world. And it's probably true in all of them."

They removed their clothes and stuck everything in the sacks with the other items. Dropping the flashlight in her sack and sealing it, she went into the water without a splash, but Jonas heard her gasp. He understood why after he'd swung down, closed the trapdoor above him, and slid into the water beside her.

The first shock of the cold water was intense, like suddenly being gripped in a fist of ice. It penetrated the flesh, squeezing bones and reaching for the heart. The only way to combat it was to get moving immediately, and keep moving.

An ancient seawall was behind them, and ahead they could see the lights of the quay gleaming on the water beyond it. They pushed away from the wall, keeping close to each other as they moved out between the pilings under the quay. Turning sharply to their left, avoiding the open, they headed for the Petit Rang pier.

It was vital to swim as far as possible under cover, until they were out beyond lights and lookouts. They used a breaststroke, not breaking the surface with their arms to prevent splashing. Whenever they heard footsteps across the quay over them they stopped and treaded water, aware of the precious minutes ticking away each time.

The intensity of the cold seemed to ebb, and as long as they kept swimming the threat of numbness was held at bay. It couldn't be held off too long, they both knew that. But before it began to interfere with their ability to move, hopefully, they should be nearing their goal.

They had left the Quay Cronstadt behind now, and were swimming under the length of the Sinse Quay, with the Petit Rang just ahead. When they reached it they swung to their right and began swimming away from the quays, out under the shadowing bulk of the wide, long pier toward the open bay.

Two planes from Luftflotte III left the air base near Hyères and flew west following the coast. Less than four minutes later they were over Mourillon. They carried flares. But these, in accordance with the orders from General Sperrle, were for later, in a little more than an hour and a half from now, when the jaws of Operation Lila snapped shut on Toulon. The flight was confined to the same objective as those preceding it, and those which would follow at fifteen minute intervals until Hausser's zero hour.

They flew very low over the Mourillon Arsenal and winged on to the dock areas of the West Arsenal. They observed no unusual activity in any of the harbors, no vessel in movement or even getting up steam. The naval base slept.

The two planes circled back, dropping even lower as they swung out over the Toulon Bay, almost skimming the moonlit surface. But they were looking for movements larger than two small swimmers fighting their way through the choppy waters of the bay in a final exhausted effort to reach their goal.

With nothing new to report, the planes flew back to their base, where another pair would soon take off for the next reconnaissance flyover.

A powerful cross-current had swept Jonas and Nicole beyond the point where they should have turned in toward the Mourillon submarine entrance, and much too far out across the bay. They had finally broken free of the current and were struggling toward the waterfront of the Mourillon Arsenal. But the wet cold had taken its toll of their strength, biting deep inside them, dragging at them.

It was worse for Jonas than for Nicole. She was much younger, and she hadn't suffered what he had over the past days, with little sleep. All feeling was draining from the numbed nerves of his arms and legs; his movements were sluggish and awkward.

He stopped swimming and tread water, raising his head as high as he could out of the water.

She stopped and turned, and saw how far he'd fallen behind.

Water slopped into his mouth. He spat and shouted: "You take the proof in! You'll get to Martin faster than I can!"

"Come *on!*" Nicole yelled back. "Come *on,* old man! You must have more than that in you!"

He almost laughed at the taunt to provoke him to go on. But he had already swallowed too much salt water. Using hands and feet to stay afloat, he waited for her.

"Come on!" she cried again, but her tone was no longer taunting. She was pleading with him now: "Come on, Jonas! *Please!*"

From somewhere residual reserves stirred themselves. He swam toward her, slowly. When he reached her she turned and swam ahead of him again, but looking back from time to time, making certain he didn't drop back.

The seawall of the Mourillon Arsenal loomed ahead of them. There was an opening in it, not the one to the auxiliary sub base where Lieutenant Martin was stationed—that was somewhere off to their left. But it was a way in, and it drew Jonas like a magnet.

Nicole was inside first, dragging herself wearily onto a dark, disused naval supply pier. She turned and bent and helped Jonas haul himself up beside her. They were both shaking uncontrollably, their teeth chattering and their hearts thudding to force blood to flow in their frozen veins.

They moved around the side of a locked storage shed, out of the wind. Nicole dragged a towel from her sack, large, thick and dry. She scrubbed herself quickly and vigorously, and a moment later Jonas was doing the same. When they were dry and warmer they put on the long woolen underwear. Jonas sat down beside his sack to drag on heavy socks. Nicole already had hers on, and she stood up to button the front of her underwear.

They were jolted by a harsh, nervous voice: "Stay exactly as you are! Don't move or we'll blow your heads off!"

By 3 A.M., the time set by General Hausser, his three SS combat groups were poised at their assigned assembly positions around the city.

Hausser joined the north group. This was the one to which he'd given the task of seizing the military installations on top of Mount Faron. From there he would later be able to look down on all of Toulon when his other two groups took the naval base from the east and west.

He glanced at his watch. Less than an hour to go. In an hour his forces would launch themselves from their assembly points and attack.

Of course he would not be able to see much of it in the dark, even with binoculars from the top of Faron. But he wanted to be up there at dawn. He looked forward to what he would see when the sun rose: the swastika flying above every ship of the Toulon fleet.

The three-man base patrol which had appeared at the corner of the pier shed kept their weapons aimed at Jonas and Nicole. There was no question they were prepared to fire if either of the two made a false movement. They were quite certain they had caught a couple of enemy or Resistance saboteurs.

Jonas stayed as they'd found him, sitting on the rough planks of the pier. Nicole stood beside him holding the unbuttoned front of her winter underwear closed. Their explanations made no impression. Even if the three French navy sentries had believed them, any decision was beyond the scope of their authority.

One held a pistol; the other two had carbines. The man with the pistol was the patrol leader. He sent one of the others off to fetch their superior officer.

That left two. Jonas considered: it would take time for the officer to get here, more time for him to listen to why they had to reach Lieutenant Martin on the submarine *Orion*. He might turn out to be a Vichy man. Even if he was not, he might want to consult his own superiors, he might delay them until...

Jonas rose on one knee and told Nicole in English: "Need a distraction."

She looked down at him and nodded.

The one with the pistol snapped at Jonas: "Don't move again, I warn you. And no more talk between you. Raise your hands."

Jonas, resting on one knee, raised his hands to the level of his shoulders.

Nicole raised both arms high above her head and spread them wide, causing the unbuttoned front of her winter underwear to gape open. There was no way the two sailors could stop their eyes from flickering to what was revealed by that opening.

Jonas launched himself off his knee and rammed head down into the nearest one, driving him against the other and bowling them both off their feet. He fell on top of them and got hold of the pistol with both hands, twisted it free and jumped up, aiming it down at them.

Nicole lowered her arms. "Take us to the *Orion*," she told the two sailors as she began buttoning herself up. "Quickly. If we are lying you'll have plenty of other men there to help you with us. But we're not lying." Her tone became softer, charged with urgency: "Do you want to save your fleet from the Germans or not? Come *on....*"

A pair of Luftflotte planes swung low over the harbors of the Toulon naval base. Their observers saw the situation had not changed at all since the previous reconnaissance flight: the French base still slept. The planes made their turn and flew off, back to the east.

When they were gone Lieutenant Martin maneuvered a small speedboat out of the Mourillon Arsenal. Jonas was with him. Captain Lambert and the other commanders of Mourillon's Reserve Submarine Group had agreed: the proof of Operation Lila would carry more weight if the messenger put his own life on the line to deliver it in person.

The speedboat raced across the bay toward Admiral Laborde's flagship.

It was 4 A.M. North, east and west of Toulon the three motorized combat groups of General Hausser's SS Panzer Korps simultaneously roared away from their starting positions and charged toward their objectives.

THIRTY-ONE OPERATION LILA

THE FIRST OBJECTIVE, the French military installation on top of Mount Faron, had been taken without firing a shot. Caught completely by surprise, with most of its garrison asleep, there wasn't time for the French to radio or phone a warning to the naval base before the SS troops seized the communications center. While the surrendered garrison was disarmed and locked away, General Hausser mounted the south wall of the fortifications and through his binoculars looked down at Toulon spread out in the darkness far below.

If the rest of his forces were on schedule, at this moment part of the East Combat Group would be capturing Fort Lamalgue on the Mourillon promontory. The rest of the group would be advancing on the Mourillon Arsenal, while all of the West Combat Group would be closing in on the West Arsenal containing most of the fleet.

Hausser knew his officers. Each was a commander who had been tested in battle and proven himself utterly reliable. He had no doubts: they *were* on schedule.

Inside Fort Lamalgue, Vice-Admiral Marquis awoke to find four Waffen SS soldiers standing around his bed. He sat up blinking his sleep-blurred eyes, not comprehending what was happening. Through the opened door he saw his officer of the watch, Corvette Captain Le Nabec, standing stiffly in the corridor, disarmed and flanked by two SS troopers carrying submachine guns. Marquis was suddenly fully awake, and now he understood. It was not what was happening; it had already happened.

The vice-admiral was politely ordered out of bed and, while he stood there in his rumpled pajamas, was placed under formal arrest.

In his stateroom aboard the flagship *Strasbourg,* Admiral Laborde sat behind the wide desk wearing the bedroom slippers and robe he'd put on over his pajamas when he'd been awakened. There was nothing sleepy in his expression when his translator finished rendering the Operation Lila orders into quick, clear French. Laborde picked up the two top sheets and read the signature on each. Adolf Hitler and SS General Paul Hausser.

He was having difficulty with his heartbeat and breathing when he put the papers down. But a slight tightening of his lips was the only change of expression which could be detected by his general staff officer, Rear Admiral Dornon, standing in full uniform beside the desk. Laborde looked up at Lieutenant Martin and Jonas Ruyter, flanked by hefty petty officers from the *Strasbourg*'s security section.

"No blame will be attached to you, lieutenant," Laborde said quietly, "nor to your commanding officer, Captain Lambert. Presented with such documents as these it was your duty to bring them to my attention without delay, whatever the hour. However, surely you realize how easily all this could be a forgery."

Jonas looked at the clock on the wall. "If it is, admiral, you'll know it for a fact in about twenty minutes. When the Panzer Korps hits you...or fails to. If they don't, you'll know that's a forgery and that I came here to trick you...instead of to give you your last chance to save your fleet from dishonor. In which case you'll see to it I'm executed as an enemy spy."

Laborde said sharply. "The English wouldn't give a damn

304

about sacrificing one man for a chance to panic me into sinking my fleet."

"*I'd* mind, admiral." Jonas knew Laborde's reputation for hating England. "And I'm not English. I'm Canadian. My mother is French. My father's family was Dutch. And those documents on your desk are *not* forgeries."

Admiral Laborde looked again at the papers spread on his desk. The strain of uncertainty grew. He could not believe that what he had read was true.

He looked to Dornon, but the rear admiral maintained a rigid silence, awaiting orders. In a situation like this the buck didn't stop getting passed up the chain of command until it reached the top. In Toulon, that meant Admiral Laborde.

Laborde considered passing it higher, to Vichy, and knew he could not. To phone and wake Marshal Pétain, at this point and based on this evidence, would be extremely unwise. The marshal would say what Laborde himself had said: that these documents were almost certainly fakes. And if that turned out to be true, the panic call would cause Pétain's suspicion that he was too subject to fits of nerves to become permanent.

Admiral Laborde looked at the clock. It was now exactly 4:12 A.M. According to these orders, false or true, the assault on both arsenals of the base was set for 4:30.

"Dornon," he told the general staff officer, "have communications check with our guards inside the gates. While you're at it contact Mourillon, too—and Marquis—and see if anything's happening over there."

At his palatial home outside Vichy, Pierre Laval sat in his silk pajamas and satin robe, reading a letter from Hitler which the German ambassador had just given him, to be delivered promptly to Pétain. Quickly skipping over paragraphs which merely recounted past history or sugared the bitter pill, Laval concentrated on the few pertinent points:

"Marshal," the Führer had written, "when I was obliged on November 11, 1942, in agreement with our ally, Italy, to occupy the French southern coast in order to ensure the defense of the Reich against the war forced upon us, I did it in the hope of introducing clarification of internal conditions in your country, which is not only in German and Italian interests, but also those of France...

"I have scarcely permitted an occasion to pass since taking over power to convert relations between Germany and France into truly friendly collaboration. It is to be regretted that unscrupulous Anglo-American and Jewish wire pullers succeeded in interpreting every conciliatory gesture of the New Reich as a sign of weakness.

"It is known to me that you yourself, marshal, were always ready to serve European cooperation. But the landing of American and British troops in French North Africa, it now becomes evident, took place in agreement with numerous treacherous French officers. Today I know, and you know it too, that this invasion took place by request of those French elements.

"It is also now known that the Toulon admiral, in spite of past assurances, has issued an order that under no circumstances will the French navy fire against Anglo-American forces in the event of their attempting a landing there.

"I am aware that you, marshal, have no part in these plots and are therefore the chief sufferer.

"After having learned of the proved intention of French officers and admirals to open in the south an invasion gateway to Europe for the Anglo-American-Jewish war criminals, I have now given orders to occupy Toulon immediately and to prevent the ships from leaving.

"It is now in the hands of French authorities to accept German measures which have become a definite necessity in such a way that there is no further bloodshed, and thus create a cooperation which will be mutually profitable.

"Accept, marshal, the expression of my personal devotion to you.—Adolf Hitler."

Laval gave orders for his car and driver to be ready before rushing upstairs to get dressed. It was vital for him to be with Pétain when Admiral Laborde phoned from Toulon, to make sure the old man refused to permit Laborde to scuttle the fleet.

Rear Admiral Dornon returned quickly from the flagship communications center, this time accompanied by the *Strasbourg*'s commander. "None of our guards here or over in the Mourillon Arsenal have seen or heard any sign of trouble," he informed Laborde. Then Dornon added, with pointed lack of emphasis: "But we're unable to get through to Vice-Admiral Marquis, by phone or radio. I had the Mourillon Arsenal try, and they can't raise him either. Something seems to have gone wrong with the communications system up in Fort Lamalgue."

The flagship's commander added quietly: "We haven't been able to get through to our installations on Mount Faron, either."

Laborde looked again at the German orders which might or might not be a forgery. He remembered the part his translator had read about seizing Mount Faron and Fort Lamalgue first...

He looked at the clock. Its hands pointed to 4:19.

"Dornon," Laborde said heavily, "signal the commanders of all vessels. They are to get the men assigned to scuttle details to their emergency stations immediately. They are to stand ready to open sea cocks and detonate the charges—when and if I issue the order. All other members of ships' crews are to assemble on upper decks prepared to evacuate if the order to scuttle is given."

As Rear Admiral Dornon hurried back to the communications center, Laborde satisfied himself that he was hedging as best he could, under the circumstances. If these German orders proved to be a hoax, as they probably would shortly, he would simply have all crews return to their quarters—and explain the emergency stations order as simply a drill, intended to keep everybody in the base on their toes. An old soldier like the marshal would find nothing abnormal about that.

He leaned back in his chair and stared without warmth at Lieutenant Martin and Jonas, waiting stiffly on the other side of his desk for the verdict.

Aboard the six submarines in the reserve docks of the Mourillon Arsenal the emergency standby had been in force well

before Admiral Laborde's order reached them. They had prepared to scuttle immediately after Jonas and Nicole had arrived
with the Operation Lila orders. But they didn't intend to scuttle
until they made the escape attempt first. If that didn't work,
then they could scuttle—in deeper water where the enemy
could never raise the subs from the bottom.

The engines of all six submarines were already idling, warmed
up and ready to go. On each, men stood by to cast off the
hawsers at a second's notice. The senior officer of Mourillon's
reserve submarine group, Captain L'Herminier, was on the
bridge of *Casabianca*, his hand close to the warning klaxon. The
commander of each of the other five subs stood waiting on his
own bridge, looking across the moonlit bay in the direction of
the admiral's flagship.

Nicole climbed part way out of the *Orion*'s conning tower
beside Captain Lambert. He smiled at her; there was no need
to order her to get back down below, just yet. Emergency situation or not, a pretty girl was still a pretty girl, pleasant to
have for company through a jittery period of waiting.

"What is happening?" she asked him anxiously.

"Your friend and Lieutenant Martin seemed to have stirred
the admiral up a bit. That's all we know so far."

Nicole looked across the bay. "Are Jonas and Martin coming
back?"

"Not as yet. Perhaps after..." Captain Lambert cut himself
short in midsentence; the German planes were approaching
low from the east.

Not the customary pair; this time there were six of them.
Lambert and Nicole watched the planes separate as they reached
the bay. Three of them swung out over the waters just outside
the blocked bay entrance and began dropping mines. The other
three flew in over the inner roads, dropping brilliant float flares
which lit up the harbors of the naval base.

When they'd finished dropping their mines and flares the
planes circled away, heading back to base. As the dropped flares
began to lose their brilliance another six-plane flight appeared
in the distance, coming in from the east to repeat the procedure.

Captain Lambert looked at his watch. It was 4:30.

* * *

Sublieutenant Gustin, in charge of the navy guard post inside the West Arsenal's closed and locked Castingneau Gate, listened to the heavy rumbling of approaching vehicles outside the walls. He strode over to a young petty officer peering out through the small peephole. "What the hell is that?"

"Damned if I know, sir. Something is sure coming this way, fast. But in the dark out there I can't make out..."

Gustin pushed him aside and looked through the peephole. Something huge and monstrous rushed out of the deep shadows at him, abruptly blotting out everything else. The sublieutenant leaped backward in terror.

The lead tank of the SS Panzer Korps West Combat Group— a massive Tiger—crashed full tilt against the outside of the gate, buckling it inward, bending the great iron bars locking it shut. But the gate did not go down, though its great hinges were pulled partially loose from the stone walls on either side.

Sublieutenant Gustin darted to the guard post phone and called the flagship.

The lead tank spun away from the exterior of the Castigneau Gate. A second Tiger tank drove forward and rammed the gate. Its treads mounted partway up before the hinges ripped all the way out.

Inside, Gustin dropped the phone in midwarning and scrambled out of the way with other sailors as the gate came crashing down. The tank rumbled in over the fallen gate. It was followed closely by another; SS troopers jumped down with their automatic weapons leveled, ready to fire at anyone trying to draw a gun on them. None of the French sailors tried it. Gustin and the others, under permanent orders from Pétain never to fire on any of Hitler's soldiers, quietly raised their arms in surrender.

Trucks and cars poured through the gateway, disgorging SS squads. They streamed off through the labyrinth of the vast shore installations inside the base, each unit using a map to find its way toward its assigned dock and ship.

Aboard the *Strasbourg*, Admiral Laborde had risen to his feet, with his attention fixed on the control center clock, when the flagship's commander rushed in with the news from the Castingneau Gate. "They've also just broken into the Mourillon Arsenal. Rear Admiral Robin was on the phone to us when the line was cut."

Laborde nodded, looking suddenly calm. "How are our communications here?"

"We still have the phone line to Vichy, admiral."

But Laborde knew it was too late for that. In the time required to reach Marshal Pétain by phone, explain the situation and wait while the marshal considered the pros and cons, the SS assault squads would be not only aboard ship but every other one in Toulon. If anything was to be done, it had to be done now—and by himself. The responsibility could not be shifted elsewhere in the few minutes left.

He was caught in a terrible dilemma. He had given Pétain his pledge not to order the sinking of the fleet without the marshal's agreement. But he had also given his pledge never to let the fleet fall into an enemy's hands intact. For the fleet, there were now only two choices: a dishonorable surrender—or suicide. And only he could make that choice in the time left.

Laborde recalled suddenly that his sixty-fourth birthday was two days away. He had joined the navy just before his seventeenth birthday. If the decision he made now was the wrong one, the reputation he had spent forty-seven years of his life in building would be destroyed. His name would become something to be scorned in the future history books of France.

Suddenly, briefly, Laborde focused on Lieutenant Martin, as though seizing on anything to postpone the decision one more second. "Return to your ship and resume your duties, lieutenant." And then, as an afterthought: "And take this man with you..."

As Jonas strode out after Martin, Admiral Laborde turned to the flagship's commander and gave the order.

* * *

"SCUTTLE! SCUTTLE! SCUTTLE!"

In the Mourillon Arsenal the six submarine commanders saw the signal flashing repeatedly from Admiral Laborde's flagship across the waters of the bay at the Milhaud docks.

On the bridge of the command sub, the *Casabianca,* Captain L' Herminier hit the klaxon button, sounding the starting signal for the escape attempt.

On the *Orion,* Captain Lambert snapped at Nicole: "Get below!" As she swiftly obeyed, Lambert shouted for the hawsers to be cast off and then called down to his engine room.

The other submarines were casting off at the same moment, and then pulling away from the docks in predetermined order. The *Venus,* nearest to the exit from the auxiliary submarine base, led the way. It was followed by the *Casabianca* and then the *Orion,* with the remaining three subs bringing up the rear, steadily increasing speed as the docks were left behind.

The first six-man squad of the SS assault force came into sight running along the side of the barracks near the land end of the docks. As they ran they triggered bursts from their submachine guns at the *Glorieux,* the last submarine in the escape formation. But by then all six subs were too far out for small-arms fire to be more than an angry gesture.

The *Venus* revved up to speed 4 as it charged head on at the light boom which blocked the way out of Mourillon. Its sharp bow crashed into the boom and broke it wide open. But as the rest of its length slipped through, a steel cable trailing from the broken boom got snagged in the submarine's hydroplanes and dragged the *Venus* to a swerving halt.

The *Casabianca* sped through the opening and took the lead. As the *Orion* passed through on its heels Captain Lambert saw crewmen scrambling along the *Venus* to free it from the cable. One by one the other three submarines raced out of the Mourillon Arsenal into the bay. When Lambert looked back he saw the *Venus,* freed from the cable, speeding to catch up.

Then he saw something else: a heavy tank of the SS Panzer Korps lurched past the barracks and came to a halt at the edge of the docks. Its cannon began firing at the escaping submarines. The first shells churned the surface of the bay some twenty yards off the port side of the last subs. Before the tank could correct its angle of fire all six submarines executed a sharp starboard turn and vanished.

But another menace appeared as the *Casabianca* led the way across the bay. A Luftflotte plane began circling low and dropping flares, starkly illuminating the submarines for the bombers that would soon be coming. Their only safety now lay in speed. In loose formation the six subs raced across the surface of the bay to deal with the two barriers across the exit, barriers much too strong to be smashed through.

Behind them, at the Milhaud docks, the *Strasbourg* continued to flash the signal: "*SCUTTLE! SCUTTLE! SCUTTLE!*"

Inside the naval base the SS squads were having unexpected difficulties in reaching their objectives quickly. Sailors dispatched by Rear Admiral Dornon reached the harbor generators and cut the power supply to the main lights in the base. Plunged in darkness, the SS Panzer Korps kept getting lost as they worked their way toward the docks.

When they finally neared their objectives, they ran into another problem which General Hausser hadn't taken into consideration—because he hadn't expected the French to be forewarned.

From every ship of the fleet, all of the crews except those assigned to the scuttling details were pouring down the gangways and swarming across the dock areas. The crowds of French sailors did not attempt to fight the advancing SS troops; but having to push through those milling mobs slowed the German advance considerably.

One of Hausser's boarding squads was almost to the battleship assigned to it when an enormous explosion shook the dock under them, knocking SS troopers and French sailors off their feet. The ship had blown two gaping holes in its hull, on either side of the keel. It leaned sharply over to starboard as it sank swiftly to the bottom of the harbor.

Atop Mount Faron, General Hausser gazed down in shock, watching flames shoot into the air and dark clouds of smoke roll across the Toulon naval base as, one after another, the ships of the French fleet detonated their explosive charges.

Lieutenant Martin had the little speedboat going all out as he steered it across the waters of the bay. The flares dropped by the Luftflotte planes showed clearly where the escaping submarines were now. All six were nearing the exit from the bay—and the first of the two barriers there, a heavy antisubmarine net stretched across the opening between the end of the Grand Jetty and St. Mandrier's Vieille Jetty.

The *Casabianca* reached the barrier first. The antisub net was anchored at both ends almost touching the two jetties. It was impossible to break through, or go around or under. There was, however, a tugboat near the end of the Grand Jetty. It was there to open and close the net when necessary. The *Casabianca*'s commander shouted at the tug's skipper to open it.

On the deck of the tug the skipper spread his arms in a hopeless gesture. "I can't, captain! Not unless you can get me authorization from Vice-Admiral Marquis! Sorry, but those are my orders and I'm not about to get myself in trouble disobeying them!"

Lieutenant Martin maneuvered the speedboat around the lead submarines and drew the pistol from his holster. He handed it to Jonas as he eased the boat alongside the tug, bumping gently against its hull. Jonas swung up onto the deck of the tugboat and raised the gun in both hands, steadying it two inches from the tug skipper's face.

"Open it!"

Minutes later the tug had the anchor up and was dragging the antisubmarine net open, with Martin keeping the speedboat alongside. They couldn't wait for the net to be fully opened. Two Luftwaffe dive bombers were coming in fast, heading for the stalled submarines lit up by floating flares. When there was just enough space, the *Casabianca* slipped through less than two

313

feet from the end of the Grand Jetty on its port side and with only inches between its starboard and the net.

Jonas dropped back down into the speedboat. Martin swung it away from the tug and headed for the *Orion,* which was trailing the lead sub through the opening. The first dive bomber screamed down, releasing its bomb just as it pulled out of the dive.

The bomb plunged into the bay and exploded beneath the surface. The speedboat was rocked violently and then swamped by a rushing wall of water, dumping Jonas and Martin into the bay. They swam for the passing *Orion,* reached it and were pulled up onto deck. The stern of the submarine was clearing the jetty when the second dive bomber screamed down.

The bomb hit the end of the jetty, hurling chunks of broken stone and cement across the *Orion*'s deck. One chunk struck Lieutenant Martin across the back, knocking him off his feet. Jonas managed to grab hold of him before he rolled overboard.

"Get him below!" Captain Lambert yelled. "We're going to dive!"

The last barrier was ahead of them now, the heavy boom, too strong to break through and with no space to get around either end. But the port workmen had revealed to the sub commanders that there was a space between the bottom of the boom and the bottom of the bay. Not much, but perhaps just enough. Up ahead, the *Casabianca* was already submerging to go under first.

Jonas helped Martin down through the hatch as Lambert sounded the dive warning. The lieutenant was groggy but didn't look seriously hurt. Lowering him to a sitting position against the interior bulkhead, Jonas straightened—and saw Nicole.

For a long moment they just looked at each other. Then, without hurry, they came into each other's arms.

They were thrown off balance when the *Orion* nosed down in a steep dive, and fell against the bulkhead still holding each other. They were pinned there by the speed and incline of the dive as the *Orion* went deep and then leveled off—just in time. There was the noise and feel of its scraping across the bottom of the bay. And then it was under the boom and beyond it.

The *Orion* began to rise—but not far. Depth charges, dropped blindly by circling planes, were exploding beneath the surface above, jolting and rolling the vessel, making its seams creak with strain.

There was no more following the leader. As the commanders had agreed beforehand, from here on it was every sub for itself. The *Orion* leveled out and went on submerged, away from the area of the depth-charge explosions.

Nicole rested her head against Jonas's shoulder. "We made it."

He nodded. "And—we *did* it."

The submarine sped south below the Mediterranean, heading for Algiers.

The sun rose over the harbors of Toulon, filled with the wreckage of the French warships sunk in the muddy bottom, their superstructures tilting out of the water at crazy angles. The smoke of the explosions and the fires still burning rolled in the wind, visible for twenty miles.

On Mount Faron, General Hausser gazed upon the scene with a frozen lack of expression. The final tally had just been brought to him: six submarines had escaped, and the rest of the fleet destroyed. They had failed to get a single one of the French warships.

Later that day, in a dark moment of the soul, Hausser scribbled across a page of his diary: "November 27, 1942, is not a day of which the SS Panzer Korps can feel proud..."

The news had already reached the Wolf's Lair—and was added to the rest of the bad news converging on Hitler. He stood in the conference room staring at the two large wall maps: one of Russia, the other of the Mediterranean area. General Jodl and his deputy, Colonel Warlimont, watched their Führer sag under the impact. For the first time since they had known him, he was speechless.

The flag markers on both maps told why. In Russia, Germany's entire Sixth Army had become encircled at Stalingrad and was helplessly trapped within its ruins. In North Africa,

Rommel was being driven back all the way across Libya by Montgomery and had Eisenhower thrusting through Tunisia at his back.

And now Toulon.

The failure of General Hausser's SS Panzer Korps to get hold of the French fleet meant there'd be no way to supply Rommel or cut Allied supply lines; no way to prevent the defeat of the famed Africa Korps; no way to stop the Allies from controlling the Mediterranean and crossing it, to attack Hitler's New Europe itself.

Colonel Warlimont wrote later in his own diary: "The moment at which the strategic initiative really passed out of Hitler's hands...was November 1942, the month of doom in modern German history."

The *Orion* cruised south on the surface, following an American destroyer which had been sent out from Algiers to escort it in. Six American fighters circled overhead, ready to fend off any attacking Axis planes. Jonas and Nicole were out on the deck near Captain Lambert and Lieutenant Martin, who had turned up the loudspeaker carrying General de Gaulle's radio speech from London:

"French sailors with their own hands scuttled the Toulon fleet so the nation might be spared the supreme shame of seeing her ships become ships of the enemy...France heard the explosions...and rage shook the whole nation. On to victory! There is no other road. There never was."

Among the speakers who followed de Gaulle was one with a prediction which would later prove true: "Toulon has taught any loyal Frenchman who didn't realize it before that his enemy is Hitler—and that he *can* be beaten. From this moment on France reunites—to help accomplish the defeat of that enemy."

Nicole leaned against Jonas. "I suddenly feel very, very tired."

"We'll find Michael waiting at the dock when we get to Algiers. He'll get a room for us."

"With a hot bath, please. And a large bed, very soft."

Jonas held her and smiled. "I think even that can be managed, too."